SONG OF THE SHUTTLE

The Lancashire Cotton Saga
Book One

Christine Evans

SAPERE
BOOKS

SONG OF THE SHUTTLE

Published by Sapere Books.

20 Windermere Drive, Leeds, England, LS17 7UZ,
United Kingdom

saperebooks.com

ISBN: 978-1-912786-05-3

PART I

Chapter 1: The Mill

Like rumbling thunder, the clatter and hum of machinery filled the looming expanse of the Invincible Mill. The air was thick with the smell of raw cotton and hot oil. It hung like a pall over the long rows of spinning machines and busy workers. Saturday noon was approaching and the girls were restless as they listened for the welcome blast of the hooter. This was the signal that a whole week of freedom was about to begin, the start of the Wakes holiday. The mill hands were full of plans and excitement, blissfully unaware that, across the wide Atlantic, events were unfolding that would change all their lives before another Wakes week passed.

Oblivious to the noise, Jessie Davenport deftly changed a bobbin on one of her six cotton spinning machines. She gestured to her little piecer, who scurried up with a new bobbin as she tossed the full one into the filling wicker skip.

"Good lad," she praised him.

The scrawny part-timer grinned.

It had been a tiring day. Hands on her hips and arching her back to relieve the pressure of her habitual stance, Jessie turned and noticed her friend Mary at the next set of machines.

"Look who's here!" mouthed Mary with a frown.

In the machine shop, all the cotton hands quickly learnt to lip read. Amid the overwhelming clatter of machinery, it was the only way to communicate and a skill that often came in handy when you weren't working too. Jessie followed the jerk of Mary's thumb. A familiar figure was strolling purposefully towards them along the rows of machines. Jessie bit her lip. Taylor Walmsley, the overlooker had arrived.

"You're working well," he said, checking the skip with a practised eye.

"Aye," said Jessie, blushing despite herself.

She was painfully aware that he was assessing her with his pale eyes, scanning from the top of her glossy, dark hair restrained in a netted chignon to the bottom of her shapely figure. She busied herself with her machine, rattled that he showed no inclination to move on. Jessie wished he wouldn't pay her such obvious attention in front of everyone. Now all her friends would tease her. The startling blare of the factory hooter saved her from further embarrassment. But Taylor was oblivious to the rows of watching eyes.

"You'll be going to the Sunday school outing, then?" he asked.

"Aye, I reckon I will," said Jessie, still refusing to look at him. "That's if Mother's all right," she added to enlighten him that she wasn't readily pursuing him.

All around them, workers brought their machines to a standstill, busily packing up for the week. Jessie began to do the same.

"Perhaps I'll see you there, then," he said, pausing for a reply.

To his evident frustration, he received no sign from Jessie as she silenced her machines and the long metal frames rolled to a halt with a satisfying clang.

Mary handed her her shawl and watched the overlooker reluctantly walk away.

"So you won't encourage your admirer?" she murmured with a wry smile. "I think our Taylor was waiting for a bit of a smile, at least. He looked most put out when he sloped off."

"Don't you start," muttered Jessie. "It'll be bad enough when the others do. Folks round here take too much interest in other people's business."

The rattling belts and pulleys criss-crossing the high ceiling gradually stuttered to a standstill. Immediately, the silence was filled with the happy chatter of doffers swiftly clearing the bobbins from the machines. There would be no wages for the holiday week but sensible people had a little money put by.

Despite the inescapable grime of the busy mill town of Gorbydale, a self-satisfied feeling of industry and plenty coursed through its cobbled veins. Queen Victoria was on the throne and trade boomed in a stable Britain, especially the cotton trade. Everyone knew that cotton clothed the vast Empire, from the wilds of Canada and great swathes of Africa down to the tip of New Zealand. Every child learnt that almost half the atlas was coloured the red of the British Empire.

A noisy, happy crowd spilled out of the Invincible gates in a bustling stream. Hundreds of iron-tipped clogs trampled over the granite cobbles like the rumble of an approaching army.

"What are you doing this week, Jessie?" asked Sarah, one of the factory girls.

"Her brother Jack's getting married on Monday," called Mary.

"So is my cousin Katie. I'll probably see you at the church," Sarah replied.

"And what's all this about a Sunday school outing with Taylor Walmsley?" asked Hetty, another girl, slyly.

Others had been discreetly watching the conversation from across the machine room too, and awaited the reply.

"Everyone from the chapel goes on the annual outing on Wednesday," Jessie told them brightly, ignoring the insinuation. "I'm looking forward to it. It'll be a nice change of scenery."

"Where are you all going?" asked Hetty.

"Hollingworth Lake," said Jessie.

"I'd have come too if it wasn't for all you holy Joes," laughed Sarah.

"So, are you stopping at the pub on the way back, or just taking a crate of beer with you?" someone else joked.

Jessie smiled at their good-natured teasing. Her friends knew her family were strong chapel supporters of temperance and were wary of the evils of demon drink. Across the mill yard, Jessie noticed her brother, Arden, and waved. Some girls giggled and blushed as he waved back, tossing their hair in the hope of catching his eye. Inevitably, their thoughts turned to matters of the heart.

"So, has Taylor Walmsley declared himself yet?" asked Hetty.

"I don't know what you mean," protested a blushing Jessie.

"Come on, Jessie. Everyone knows he's got his eye on you. It's obvious. He's always hanging round your machines."

"Well, he is the overlooker."

"And he 'overlooks' our Jessie very keenly," joked Sarah.

"I wish he didn't hang around so much," grumbled Mary. "He's happiest when he finds fault."

"How can you tell when he's happy?" Sarah replied. "He's got a face like a wet Sunday."

The others laughed.

"Eh, you'd be all right with Taylor. You'd be a fool to refuse him," said Susan, one of the quieter girls. "He's got plenty o' brass. I wouldn't mind living in that nice house on The Terrace…"

"That's his mother's house," said Jessie and immediately regretted it.

"Oooh, she's found out that much," said Hetty.

"My cousin does Old Ma Walmsley's washing," Sarah said. "She's a right fusspot. Thinks herself above us lot. She'd nag you to glory if you got in with her precious son."

They all laughed again. All except Mary.

"Taylor Walmsley is a miserable beggar. He'd order Jessie around like a sergeant major," she said.

"She might manage to sweeten him up — we'd all thank her for that!" said Sarah and some of them jeered.

Jessie grew hot with all the attention. "He's a superintendent at the chapel," she said to stem their teasing. "He was only asking if I'd be at the outing to supervise my Sunday school class."

"Oh aye — and we believe you!"

Her friends winked and nudged each other, but their ribbing ceased anyway. They were all eager to get home. Lots would be going out in their finery that Saturday night. Jessie's father didn't approve of women going out on a Saturday night, even if they were only looking for innocent fun. She wistfully wondered what it would be like to join her friends. Then she remembered her mother would be tired and there was so much to do before her brother's wedding.

Though Taylor hadn't said a single word, it was obvious to everyone that he was interested in Jessie. Her friends reported all the subtle details of his behaviour. His scant praise was reserved for Jessie; he habitually lingered round her machines. Her friends anticipated the moment when he opened his mouth and declared his interest. Yet, Jessie couldn't decide how she felt about him. He was handsome in his own pale way but he was a bit serious. He didn't joke or banter with the girls like some of the other overlookers. They didn't pick overlookers for their popularity, though — only for the order they kept. The girls were continually being reminded that time was money and a silent machine was an unproductive one. Jessie sighed. Did she welcome his attention, flattering though it was? Was he likely to come courting? What would she say? She knew well enough that Mrs Walmsley wouldn't approve of Taylor courting a mill girl. Was that why he'd been reluctant to declare himself? Taylor was a man with prospects. He was meticulously upright, unlike other girls' admirers who tried to steal kisses, flirting and warmly teasing their beloved. She'd tried to imagine him kissing her and blushed warm again.

Weavers Row looked down over the town. Below, her workmates scurried to their houses. Taylor lived with his mother in one of the larger houses. His father, the original manager of the mill, had made enough money to buy it. This distinction gave Mrs Walmsley her superior airs. The wages at the mill gave a girl some independence. If Taylor did offer to marry her, would she really miss the noise and long hours where she was an insignificant cog in a huge relentless machine?

Recently, another opportunity had been presented to her. The previous Sunday after she'd taught her Sunday school class, she'd been approached by Reverend Septimus Carew. There had been rumours that the elders of the chapel hoped to open a small school in a house donated by one of the parishioners.

"Has your father mentioned our hoped-for school, Jessie?" he'd asked.

"Yes, Reverend. Father was talking about it the other night," she told him.

"Mrs Carew would be teaching, of course," he said. "But she'll need an assistant. Would you be interested?"

Jessie was surprised by the unexpected suggestion. The preacher's wife liked to be in control. She hesitated for one moment. She needed a change.

"Yes, I would," she said eagerly.

"Though, I'm bound to say, the remuneration wouldn't be much," he added with apology.

Jessie began thinking about the possibilities. Her father's greatest wish was that she should become a teacher. The schoolmistress at her dame school had suggested that Jessie joined her as a pupil teacher. Jacob had been disappointed that she'd joined her friends at the mill.

"Please do consider me when you've made a firm decision," she said.

"Certainly, my dear. You do wonders with those little ones in Sunday school. I know you'd be a great asset to us."

Full of the innate kindness she showed her little piecer, Jessie was a popular and much loved teacher at the Sunday school. She guessed her work would be to look after the physical needs of the children, something beneath Mrs Carew, but she was looking for change. Her thoughts rumbling with possibilities, she entered the welcoming comfort of her home. They vanished when she saw how much there was to do before her brother's wedding on Monday.

Chapter 2: A Bridal Procession

As Whit Monday dawned, the bright sun gave the soot-grimed town a glow of festivity. The gaiety of wedding parties echoed through the streets and an array of fashions decked them with colour as the first bride stepped out of the church and into the town square. The mill girls had scrutinised any available fashion magazines to discover the latest designs in dresses and bonnets, and tried to imitate them with their limited means. Jessie, in a newly self-made dress of dark rose, and a bonnet trimmed to match, happily followed her brother Jack and his bride-to-be, Elsie, down Weavers Row. Her parents followed behind at a more sedate pace. Jacob was tall but stooped from working a loom since boyhood; his wife Nellie was slight beside him. Jessie was eager to see the parade of brides and their families processing to the church to be wed. As they reached the High Street, pert-nosed Dolly Tate joined them. Elsie's cousin was flamboyant in pink, wearing more ribbons than a maypole. In her colourful clothes, she appeared like an exotic bird amid the drab plumage of the common flock. The other cotton workers wore dull, serviceable colours to work amid the grime of the mill. Despite her colourful dress, Dolly looked grubby, as usual.

"I wonder when I'll be married," giggled Dolly. She winsomely glanced around, clearly hoping to be noticed. "There's that Miss Darwen from Overdale House," she said with a sniff, nodding towards an elegant young woman watching the wedding parades from the doorway of the draper's shop. "Look at that black silk — how dull. Only old women wear black."

"She's in mourning for her mother, I was told," said Jessie. "I like the dress though, it's sort of refined."

"It'll be one of Mrs Overdale's hand-me-downs," sniped Dolly jealously. "I don't know why she puts on her airs and graces when she's only a poor relative of the Overdales. You'd think she was Duchess of Gorbydale."

"I like the dress," said Jessie firmly. "And that Italian straw hat is very elegant."

"Well, I don't know how I'll put up with her when I go to work at Overdale House," said Dolly pettishly.

"Overdale House?" asked Jessie in surprise.

Dolly had worked in the mill since her childhood. It was odd for Dolly to be working for the Master of the Invincible and his family.

"Aye, I'm starting work there after the Wakes."

"You? Working in service? What about the mill?"

"That Taylor Walmsley kept docking my wages for being late. And he warned me to keep up with the other doffers. I'm sick of him and I'm sick of the work. They can keep their old mill," said Dolly, preening herself.

Jessie secretly agreed that Dolly should have arrived for work on time. She knew Dolly was the only one working in her family. Most doffers could clear a machine of bobbins in six minutes, but not the unreliable Dolly. It was a miracle she'd kept her job for as long as she had. Jessie wondered how long Dolly would last at the Overdales with her offhand manner and scant regard for authority. Would she wear a drab uniform and large white apron when ordered to?

"Wait 'til Madam Darwen tries ordering me about," said Dolly defiantly. "I'll give her what for!"

Jessie gave the unsuspecting Miss Darwen a sympathetic smile and silently wished her well. She wondered if Mrs

Overdale realised what she was doing hiring Dolly. With the mill paying good wages, few girls wanted to go into service. Honora Darwen returned a polite nod.

By now, they were approaching the church.

"Come on, Elsie," said Jack Davenport, grasping his bride-to-be's hand, hurrying them all along. "We don't want to lose our place."

A confusion of churchgoers milled at the church door.

"They pop them out of that church like sausages from a machine," complained Jacob, annoyed at being jostled.

"Shush, Father," said Nellie. "It's Elsie and Jack's day. Don't complain and spoil it."

"All the same," said Jacob. "I'd have preferred something more dignified in the chapel. Are you all right, love?"

Nellie was clinging desperately to his arm.

"I'll be better when I'm sat down," she admitted, wheezing with the effort of trying to keep up with Jack and Elsie.

Dolly Tate giggled as she linked Jessie.

"Your Dad's a grumpy old thing, isn't he?" she whispered. "Doesn't he know that chapel's not legal. They'd have to go to a registrar if they didn't come to church."

Jessie smiled at her father. His bristling eyebrows made him look fierce but he was a kindly man. Staunch in his beliefs, only injustice or impropriety made him angry. As an elder of the chapel, her father didn't feel that queueing at the parish church with every other mill hand and his lass was solemn enough for something as important as marriage. He struggled to look dignified in the milling throng, standing his ground amidst the crush. Jacob Davenport, the master weaver, wasn't about to be pushed aside by hordes of revelling wedding guests.

Jessie thought Elsie was the prettiest bride of all. The bride-to-be smiled up at Jack with adoring blue eyes. The blue silk flowers round her wide straw bonnet framed her golden hair like a halo. She seemed ephemeral and delicate beside the handsome and vigorous dark-haired children of the Davenport family.

"I hope they'll make a go of it," said Nellie anxiously, watching Elsie's dainty form.

"So do I," said Jacob fervently.

The night before, Jessie had heard her father complain to her mother that he'd wished Jack had waited to be married. She knew her parents thought that Elsie was a pretty little thing, but she was young. The Davenports didn't think much of her family either. The Tates were always in and out of public houses.

"Young people in love care for nothing but each other. You can't reason with them. It will always be so," Nellie told him. "Our Jack's a sensible lad. They'll be all right."

Jessie watched quietly as, one after another, couples made their solemn promises. Some, like the Davenports and Tates, were dressed in their finest. Poorer couples arrived quietly in their work clothes, clean but shabby, all too often the bride with a protruding bulge beneath her skirts, obvious despite the careful arrangement of a best shawl. Jessie's thoughts wandered. Would she ever be married, and who would take her hand at the altar? Elsie was younger than her and already settled on her life's partner.

Again, Taylor Walmsley protruded into her thoughts. In chapel, on Whit Sunday morning, he'd turned towards her with the ghost of a smile as she'd led her young Sunday school pupils in for the blessing. His mother noticed that look and glared at Jessie. Did she really care enough for Taylor to face his mother's disapproval? Had she any feelings for him at all, or was she just flattered by the attention of a good looking and ambitious man who obviously admired her? Why did she feel so unsettled and hot whenever he stood close to her?

Jack and Elsie were now at the front of the church. Arden, as groomsman, produced the ring. Dolly took her cousin's posy with a flourish for Elsie to make her vows unhindered. Jessie watched her father nodding with approval as the young couple spoke their words solemnly, gazing lovingly at one another. The newlyweds gave each other a chaste kiss and were hurried away for the next couple to take their place. Jessie's mother dabbed a tear from her eye. Beside them, Elsie's mother, Clara, wailed noisily. But the Tates were like that, everything was done with show and a public display of emotion. They bustled out, past more eager couples waiting to be wed.

"Here's some rice to throw for good luck, Eddie," Jessie coaxed as they left the church.

Her brother wriggled in his best clothes. She'd seen a gaggle of his friends hanging at the back of church, hoping to catch the pennies some grooms threw to the onlookers. Jessie knew Eddie would love to join them, but her father had given him a stern warning to behave himself.

Out in the sunshine, Elsie squealed as the newlyweds were pelted with rice. Then the families processed in a happy mood behind the bride and groom back to Weavers Row, greeted by well-wishers all the way. Nellie clung hard to Jacob's arm in her effort to climb the hill. She turned to Jessie.

"Nip ahead and put the kettle on, love, will you," she wheezed.

Jessie hurried ahead to make tea and take the covers off the ample spread prepared for the wedding party. The house was rich with the delicious smell of hams and capons, pastries and cakes, homebaked bread and creamy Lancashire cheese and a splendid bride cake, solid with fruit.

Clara Tate, Elsie's mother, wasn't much of a housewife. Somehow, she'd cajoled Nellie and Jacob to provide the wedding breakfast and, though she'd made numerous promises to help, hadn't made a single appearance at Weavers Row. Nellie had been determined to do her son proud with a good feed.

"It might be the last one he has," she'd joked to Jessie.

But her mother had been feeling well when she'd agreed to cater for everyone. Now Jessie had had to take over as Nellie had developed a worrying pain in her back and started having trouble breathing.

Jessie had been surprised at the number of times Nellie had stopped to catch her breath as they'd walked up the hill. Yet, what else could she expect? She knew that Nellie had been very young when she'd started work among the dusty cotton fibres in a mill carding room. She'd had to work from dawn to dusk before the Ten Hour Bill came into law and reduced the hours for all youngsters. Jessie was spinning with the cleaner American cotton and the manufacturers had begun to install fans in their mills, but only to prevent fires. Her father grumbled that the bosses were untroubled by the lungs of their workers, as all they cared about was profit.

Jessie hadn't had to work in the mill as a child, like many they knew. Her father had insisted she went to the local dame school, dearly hoping she'd become a pupil teacher one day.

Poor father, thought Jessie, *he hadn't reckoned on having such an independent minded daughter.*

Despite her mother's damaged lungs and her tales of hard times, working for a pittance just to help her family stay alive, Jessie had wanted to work in the mill with her friends. For once, she'd defied Jacob. Though she was earning good money at the mill, she sometimes wondered if she'd made the right choice. Money couldn't help you breathe.

"Go and sit down, Mother," she ordered Nellie, who was feebly trying to help. "Arden, pour Mother a cup of tea."

"No, serve the guests first, dear," panted her mother, ever mindful of hospitality.

On Jessie's insistence, Arden settled Nellie in the parlour with a reviving cup of tea. Jessie had been shocked by her mother's struggle to breathe. Lately, she'd only seen Nellie pottering about the kitchen, but her face had been shining with perspiration by the time Jacob had helped her into the house. There was no time to worry just then. Jessie had guests to welcome, her family's reputation to uphold.

The previous evening, Elsie's father, Adam, had arrived with a crate of beer, his one contribution to the party, much to Jacob's disapproval.

"I hope no drunken behaviour will bring shame on the house," he told the family.

"I wonder what beer tastes like," mused Eddie, out of his father's hearing.

"You'll find out what a thick ear tastes like if you try it," said Jessie, laughing.

Though Jessie knew Jacob had rarely smacked her and her brothers, she smiled as she noticed Eddie wisely avoid the beer.

The guests were welcomed and settled in any available corner, lavishly praising the awaiting feast. Now that Nellie had caught her breath, she was back supervising events and making sure everyone was seated with a plate in their hand. Jessie surveyed the scene with tired satisfaction. It was worth all the hard work, cooking, cleaning, trimming bonnets, making nosegays and finishing their outfits. She glanced at Eddie's hair and wished she'd trimmed it better, but he'd squirmed and wriggled until she'd lost her patience. Jessie fervently hoped the young couple would be happy, despite her father's misgivings over how young they were. Her father's contribution had been to move the furniture. She watched him now, deep in conversation with Jack, no doubt giving him some fatherly advice.

With Nellie tired and finally persuaded to relax and chat with her guests, Jessie was relieved when Mary arrived and offered to help. She lived with her widowed mother, where they took in lodgers to make ends meet.

"I thought you'd want an extra hand clearing up," she said.

"You're always welcome," said Jessie smiling. "Especially after your help with the nosegays."

"I might have to do the same for you one day," said Mary.

She was still slyly trying to decipher Jessie's feelings for Taylor Walmsley, precisely what Jessie was trying to do herself. She wondered if he'd call in. Jack had mentioned he'd invited his old friend. Would Taylor say anything? Should she give him any encouragement? Upright and sensible, he was handsome in his way. Her parents liked him. He was a regular chapelgoer alongside her father, and he didn't drink. Women at the mill told such tales about drunken husbands. Some arrived at work with black eyes, hiding behind weak excuses. Even Jack and Arden took a drink now and then, despite their father's views. One Sunday after chapel, Taylor had offered to carry her bible. The chapelgoers watched intently as he paid her this special attention. Her Sunday school pupils waited eagerly for her answer. Embarrassed with so many eyes on her, Jessie had overreacted.

"Mr Walmsley — I'm big enough and strong enough to carry my own bible, thank you," she'd said flippantly.

She knew she'd been rude and regretted it later, but at that moment she couldn't help herself.

Now he was constantly in her mind with all this wedding business, and yet she was still confused. If he'd only show a little ardour — just one word to say that he thought she was the only girl in the world for him; that he didn't care what his mother thought. People would say she'd been left on the shelf soon, especially with Elsie being younger and already married. Jessie smiled to herself as Dolly had made an extraordinary effort to catch the bride's nosegay outside the church and had drawn all the attention to herself.

"She looks like an explosion at a ribbon factory!" Arden murmured as Dolly leapt into the air.

Jessie had giggled at her brother's dry quip. Yet, there he was flirting with Dolly by the dresser. Honestly, there was nowt as contrary as folk!

Despite being busy with the guests, Jessie glanced through the window and, to her confusion, saw Taylor coming up the cobbled street. Immediately she became agitated, her mouth dried and the cup of tea she was carrying rattled in the saucer. Beside him was Reverend Septimus Carew. At least Jessie could greet the preacher and avoid paying all her attention to Taylor. To her dismay, she noticed the Reverend was carrying a newspaper. Her father would be delighted, but what a thing to bring to a wedding!

"Hello, Jessie," said Taylor removing his hat and passing it to her. "You're looking very bonny."

This rare and unexpected compliment momentarily warmed her to him. He was obviously making an effort.

"Thank you, Mr Walmsley," she answered with a mischievous grin.

"She does indeed," said Reverend Carew. "Blithe and bonny. I'd like a quick word with you afterwards, Jessie, if that's all right?"

"Yes, of course. Sit down and I'll fetch you something to eat," she said smiling, aware that Taylor's eyes followed her to the kitchen.

She hurried to fetch more cups and plates. Her mother had subsided into a chair and was presiding over the teapot. Nellie frowned when Reverend Carew handed Jacob the newspaper.

"I thought you might like to see this, Jacob, as the reading room isn't open until tomorrow."

"Not now, Father," pleaded Nellie as he went to open it.

Jacob could hardly contain his curiosity. He beckoned Reverend Carew outside.

"I'm just getting a breath of fresh air, Mother," he said.

"Well, you can leave the newspaper here, dear," said Nellie with a knowing smile. "Not while we've guests," she muttered under her breath.

Reluctantly, Jacob handed her the newspaper. Pushing it firmly in the dresser drawer, Nellie carried on pouring tea.

"We'll have a chat tomorrow, eh, Jacob, when we go on our ramble," said Reverend Carew. "You'll have a chance to read the article in the morning."

Taylor hovered as if he wished a word with Jessie but she slipped past him as she went to take Reverend Carew and her father a plate of food and another of bride cake.

"By the way, about that little matter that I mentioned to you the other day," said Mr Carew. "Mrs Carew is keen to begin the school. One of our parishioners has offered us a small house at a peppercorn rent. The Central Committee will provide funds for the first year. Mrs Carew thinks you're a marvel with the Sunday school children and you're just the kind of pupil teacher she wants. She was trained herself at the Miss Carstairs' School for Young Ladies, you know."

As she never ceased to remind everyone.

"It won't be as much money as the mill…"

"That's not a problem," her father butted in. "There's enough of us working in the house. I've always wanted her to be a teacher — she knows that. But she insisted on being with her friends at the mill."

"Please let me know when the plans are finalised," said Jessie with a smile.

Though the long hours at the mill were monotonous, the good money and the camaraderie made the time fly. She was faced with another decision moments later. Taylor had made his way through the crush and stood beside her.

"I can see from today's wedding breakfast that you're a natural housewife. Your mother said as how you've done most of the cooking and baking yourself. I should like to see you in charge of your own establishment," he said quietly and seriously. "There's a time and a place for everything and I know this is not the time to ask, but I've been seriously thinking about settling down myself and naturally, my thoughts have turned to you."

"Oh really," said Jessie cautiously, aware that if this was a proposal it was a very ambiguous one.

"Perhaps we might have a moment at the chapel outing, when I can outline my plans," he added as he put on his hat and bid her goodbye. "I must go. I've promised Mother."

Why couldn't he have waited until they were alone? Why didn't he call one evening to ask her to go for a stroll, to take her hand as they wandered in the sunshine? His hesitant smile was so fleeting. If only he'd take her in his arms and swear that he'd love her forever with joy. Even a fervent kiss on the hand would have been better than the polite nod and the quick glance over his shoulder as he left. Jessie watched his retreating figure with increasing frustration. His proposal, if indeed it had been one, had sounded like the reading of the Chapel Committee minutes. He could have been interviewing her for a place as a housekeeper. He'd said her 'own establishment'. She wondered how that would work with his mother in residence. Perhaps his intention was to hire her as a housekeeper after all! Jessie sighed. She shook her head and went back to the party. There were too many unanswered questions buzzing in her head.

Someone was singing a sentimental love song in the parlour, accompanied by the violin. A rousing swell of voices joined in the chorus. Adam, Elsie's father, who'd made ample use of the beer he'd provided, began a song with a saucy chorus. The chapelgoers tutted with disapproval and began to sing something more tasteful to drown him out.

Amid the milling bodies, the chatter and the music, Jack and Elsie came down the stairs from his parents' bedroom, Elsie pink with embarrassment. It was time for their departure. They were helped aboard a little gig decorated with ribbons, accompanied by a jig on the violin. The gig was lent as a special favour by Jacob's boss of many years, Mr Eli Gorman of the Endurance Mill. Their honeymoon would be spent at his large cottage up in the hills. Then they would settle in a small railway house in Doveton, where Jack worked as an engineer on the railways. He'd learnt all about boilers as an apprentice at the Endurance Mill.

"I'd rather stay in Gorbydale," Jessie heard Elsie whisper to her new husband as she cuddled beside him. "There's a fair here and I could show off my new ring."

Jack smiled indulgently at his new wife.

"Sweet, sweet Elsie," he murmured. "It'll be lovely at Primrose Cottage, just you and me."

Elsie smiled nervously. She'd confessed to Jessie that she was nervous about taking care of a house and a husband.

"I can't cook like your mam can," she'd sighed.

"You'll be fine," Jessie reassured her. "Our John will love anything that you cook."

"I do hope so," Elsie murmured.

At first she'd been adamant that she wasn't too young, but it looked like she was having misgivings.

Mr Gorman's groom prepared to drive them away in his gig, his whip decorated with ribbons. Everyone cheered the bride and groom as their gig moved off.

"Goodbye, son," called Nellie, her voice choked with emotion. "Goodbye, Elsie."

Jessie put a shawl round her mother's shoulders. They felt surprisingly thin.

"Our Jack's the first to leave the nest." Nellie's eyes filled with tears. "I wonder if I'll be here to see the next one of you leave."

"Hush, Mother — don't think like that," chided Jessie. "Of course you will."

Nellie clutched her hand.

"I'd like to see you settled, love," she whispered. "Taylor Walmsley's a good man — a steady man."

Jessie distracted her mother.

"Come on, Ma, Jack and Elsie are off. Give them a wave."

"Ma indeed! Cheeky young madam!"

Poor though Nellie's family had been, she always insisted on proper speech.

The goodbyes echoed into the cooling evening. The rattle of the wheels on the cobbles faded away and the guests returned into the house and carried on with the party. A silver moon lit the Row as the last of them drifted home. Nellie Davenport looked tired as she surveyed her dishevelled home.

"I wonder why we did all that cleaning, lass," she smiled to Jessie. "We've got to start again tomorrow!"

Despite the busy excitement of the day, Jessie could not sleep, her restless thoughts churning. Was it so wrong to want a little warmth, a little feeling, some hint of passion? She'd never been in love, but she longed to be. She'd certainly felt sentimental for a while towards a couple of chaps who'd courted her. One was too fond of his drink. The other had wayward hands. She'd momentarily felt a frisson of excitement by his inexpert fumblings, but had suddenly drawn back. From birth, she'd been immersed in a strict chapel upbringing and was shaken and repelled by her own weakness. He'd apologised at first then cursed her for being cold, so she'd ignored him and fled. So neither of her tentative romances had lasted long. Yet, a longing to be loved and cared for ran deep within her. Her home was surrounded by the steady affection of her parents. Jack and Elsie were always cuddling and courting at twilight in the garden. If Taylor asked her, if she accepted, would she grow to love him or continually be frustrated by his lack of warmth? He was steady, he had a good position. Didn't Mother say that love soon flew out of the window when poverty came in through the door? She'd seen it a hundred times with her work mates — one minute all starry-eyed, next minute struggling to cope with no money and grubby children clinging to their skirts and wishing they were single. Taylor's offer would be a fair one and she'd be a fool to turn him down. Did she want to be Mrs Taylor Walmsley or the teacher at the Gorbydale Chapel School? Then Jessie's heart sank at the thought of his mother, a looming and disapproving presence.

"Mrs Taylor Walmsley," she murmured to herself. Then, "When I was the teacher of Gorbydale Chapel School…"

Still wondering, she drifted off into a restless sleep.

Chapter 3: Master of the Invincible

Melissa Overdale watched her husband, Matthias, as he surveyed the town from their large bay windows. The dying rays of the sun washed the valley in crimson light. The pervading soot and grime, the fetid hovels by the river and the effluent sluicing down its banks from the Invincible Mill, lay cleansed in the glow. For one rare moment, Gorbydale looked picturesque.

"Red sky at night, another fine day tomorrow, my dear," Matthias Overdale told his wife with a grunt of satisfaction.

"Yes, dear."

Melissa smiled indulgently at her husband. For one week at least, he would not be up at the first peep of dawn to go down to his precious mill. She thought he was looking tired lately.

"It'll be a grand day for the fair tomorrow," he said, looking down over the valley to the sports field where the showmen's cooking fires glowed.

Before the mill made the rural green valley a smoking hive of industry, the field had been the village green, the pleasant gathering place for Gorbydale neighbours. Now it was hemmed in by regimented rows of grey, terraced houses.

"Will you be going with Honora?"

"Do you think she'd like to accompany me, dear?" decided his wife. "It isn't twelve months since her Mamma, my dear sister, passed away. I suppose we could always drive down in the gig and just watch for a while."

"Where is she now, then?" asked Matthias, glancing round the room.

"She's fetching a shawl for me," said Melissa.

Both Melissa and Matthias were fond of the girl they'd taken into their home. She was the daughter of a doctor, before he and his wife had died in a cholera epidemic. Initially, Matthias had complained that she was another mouth to feed but Honora had soon proved her worth, and Melissa enjoyed her company when Matthias was away on business. Melissa thought Honora would be a good match for their son, Robert, but she knew Matthias would not consent to a marriage between a penniless girl and Master Robert Overdale, heir to the Invincible Mill. Matthias was ambitious for his son. He'd raised Robert to be a gentleman, so that the Overdales could take their place among the gentry.

Honora returned carrying the shawl.

"Thank you, dear. Did you enjoy your walk today?"

"Yes, Aunt," Honora answered with a smile.

"Did you see the Whitsun weddings? Were there many this year?"

"The town square was crowded with couples and their families," said Honora. "I saw at least five brides in all their finery."

"There's some girls from the mill getting wed," said Matthias, shaking his head. "I don't know what they're thinking of. These lasses marry too young."

"Like we did, dear," said his wife with a smile.

"We had prospects and something to back us up," Matthias told his wife sternly.

And as junior partner to our Eli in the Endurance Mill, it didn't hurt to keep business in the family, Melissa thought to herself with a secret smile.

The Endurance Mill was old and small, dwarfed by the Invincible up the valley, but it still produced quality goods with the skill of weavers like Jacob Davenport. Cotton damask, being so much cheaper than silk, was in great demand in London and the other great Victorian cities.

The Gormans had been handloom weavers like the Davenports. They'd lived in Primrose Cottage before they'd bought the mill. She and Matthias had begun their married life there until his ambition had grown. Still, they'd been happy enough. She had many loving memories of the wiry young man full of vigour and ideas. Not that his ambitions had faded like his hair. Once thick brown like his son's, his unruly mane was now iron grey, spiking from his head as if at odds with his scalp. Matthias had outgrown Eli and the old Endurance. He'd sold his share in the mill to her brother and embarked on his ambitious founding of the Invincible. Then he'd built their fine house overlooking the town and the mill. He seemed to spend all his waking hours in pursuit of his ambitions.

"Come and sit down, dear," invited Melissa to Matthias.

Matthias turned from the window and surveyed the comfort and grandeur of his home, the plump cushions, the gilded mirrors and the tea set that was only plated silver for the moment, but would one day be replaced with solid silver as he'd promised his wife. His thick gold watch chain hung over his expanding waistline.

"Anyway, where is that son of mine?" he asked Melissa abruptly, changing the subject.

"He's gone to Liverpool to visit his friend, Augustus Kearsley from the Academy," said Melissa. "He said he might stay overnight at Gus's home."

"You'd think he'd want to be at home with his family now Wakes week has begun," complained Matthias.

Melissa sighed. Matthias was continually exasperated with Robert. Sometimes it seemed the boy couldn't do right for doing wrong in her husband's eyes. She wished she could have presented him with more sons but it was not to be. Now, all her husband's hopes and ambitions were centred on Robert. He'd insisted that their son went away to school at the Academy to train to be a gentleman. Both families were only two generations away from handloom weavers and Matthias smarted that, for all his money and status, he was still regarded as socially inferior by the most penniless clergyman. Robert had grown up so quickly and Melissa had missed it all. She knew he was spoiled. If only Matthias would have more patience with the boy. All his minor misdemeanours had been blown out of proportion by her husband.

"Young gentlemen behave as badly too," she'd tried to pacify Matthias when Robert was reported drunk by his headmaster.

"Well, he should behave better than the gentry," fumed her husband. "You'd think he'd appreciate the chances he's been given. He doesn't have to graft like I did. You know what them that consider themselves gentlemen will say, 'He comes from trade, so don't expect anything better'. I know 'em."

'Them' were the arbiter of Matthias Overdale's thinking, an invisible force of the gentry, forever ready to put him down. He resented their condescension, though he could buy and sell most of them.

"Gus Kearsley, eh," Matthias said with a subtle smile, clasping his hands on the comfortable shelf of his stomach. "That's the sort of family Robert should associate with — a shipbuilder's son. The rumour is that old man Kearsley is up for a knighthood after that last navy contract. I hoped our boy would mix with the right sort of people when I sent him to the Academy and it looks as though he's cracked it."

"Let's hope so, dear," Melissa said to reassure him. She wasn't as concerned as Matthias about their social status. When he'd taken a chance and bought a share in the old Endurance Mill down the valley with her brother Eli, she'd backed him with an inheritance from one of her aunts. Once powered by the rushing waters of the river Gorby, Matthias and Eli had worked hard to modernise it. But that was still not enough to quench her husband's ambition. Now, her brother was still pottering about in the old Endurance and Matthias had the great Invincible, seen from every corner of the valley, a monument to his hard work. Cotton was the backbone to Britain's wealth. Her husband's faith in trade was unshakeable. Of late, Matthias had been restless, despite her attempts to distract him. She knew he'd been upset by the unsettling newspaper headline reporting rumours of war in America. He'd mentioned that he'd decided to visit Liverpool to assess the situation for himself.

"That would make a nice trip out, dear," she told him. "We could have a nice lunch at the Adelphi."

"It's not to be a joyride," he chided her. "I just wish I had a bit more money to buy more cotton before the cost goes up further. You know I'm trying to keep costs down. Maybe I could borrow a bit more."

"Is that wise, dear?" asked Melissa.

He was just about to answer when Honora came in holding Melissa's shawl.

"Is my pipe about?" he asked her. "I find a bit of baccy helps me think."

"I'll go an' fetch it," said Honora, with a wry smile.

"I don't like discussing my business in front of strangers," muttered Matthias.

Melissa was about to protest that her niece was no stranger, but through the window she noticed something moving very fast towards the house. Hurrying towards the bay, she saw a smart carriage and pair haring up the drive. Holding the reins was a plump young man in fashionable dress.

"Why it's our Robert!" she called to Matthias. "And he's got someone with him."

"Augustus has driven him home."

She immediately bustled into action. "He must wish to stay, arriving so late. I'll check the guest room. Go and tell Cook we have an extra guest for dinner will you, Honora dear?"

Honora hurried away again.

Melissa watched as her husband welcomed Gus Kearsley with excessive good will. She was glad for this welcome distraction for Matthias, and that Robert was basking in his approval for once.

"Gus has never been to a Wakes week fair before," Robert told his parents. "I told him he'd be welcome."

"Of course, of course!" replied Melissa.

"They have fairs in Liverpool, of course," said Gus, helping himself to a large piece of pie. "I saw a mermaid there myself once when my nurse took me, though it seemed a bit of a bamboozle to me. But with the docks so close, there are plenty of charlatans and pickpockets about. It's best to go with a sturdy groom at your side. Your fair sounds like a jolly affair — pardon the pun!"

He burst into hearty laughter and the others joined in from politeness.

Through the window, Honora gazed down with envy at the free spirits living in the shadows of the fairground. She'd once accompanied her father to the Wakes Fair in Manchester and witnessed a kaleidoscope of humanity, all manner of stallholders, gypsies and mountebanks, rootless people forever on the move. Bound by convention and poverty to be a companion, Honora chafed against the chains of her enforced domesticity.

Chapter 4: The Wakes Fair

Next morning was again filled with hazy sunshine that brightened as the customary smoke from the mill chimneys dispersed altogether. Jessie grew warm as she 'bottomed' the house with her mother, amazed at how bits of food turned up under the sofa and even in a vase. After a restless night, she was glad that her activities allowed little time for thought. Jacob had taken refuge in the garden. All morning he'd been devouring every word of his precious newspaper.

The Davenport's home was the last house before Weavers Row petered out into an overgrown, stony drover's road leading over the hill to the next valley. The largest stone cottage on the Row, it stood three storeys high and overlooked Gorbydale. Jessie's grandfather had been a handloom weaver when he'd bought the house, and his loom was installed on the top floor to catch the very last rays of the dying sun. He'd hewn a garden from the rocky soil and had used the stones for a drystone wall. It kept wandering animals from Jacob's vegetables, a neat square of growing colour amid the wildness of the encroaching moor. Behind it, a rough path rose up to rocky crags, jutting like black teeth into the sky. A crumbling ancient ruin, rumoured to be a Roman Fort, stood guard over the town and both valleys.

At mid-morning, Septimus Carew arrived. Nellie apologised profusely that he could not be welcomed into the parlour but he happily joined Jacob in the garden with the promise of a cup of tea.

"I've been reading all this news from America and it doesn't look good," said Jacob as soon as Septimus was settled. "Is it to be war?"

"It's bound to be," said the preacher. "The rebels have taken Fort Sumpter, even though Lincoln promised not to reinforce it."

"Where's Fort Sumpter?" asked Jessie as she shook the dusters out of doors.

She expected it was some corner of the Empire where uprisings continually erupted.

"America, my dear," said Septimus. "Some of the southern states have renounced the Union."

"Oh right."

Jessie shrugged as she folded her dusters.

"Aye, it's worrying is that," said Jacob looking serious. "If it gets out of hand, the cotton's bound to be affected."

She noticed her father and the preacher looking concerned as they pored over the newspaper. America was a long, long way away and the news meant little to her. In future days, she would recall that moment, a small spark that kindled a fire leaving many helpless in the ashes of their lives. Just then, Jessie was more concerned about her mother and went back inside. Nellie had put the kettle on the range and was slumped on a chair by the kitchen table, exhausted by the morning's efforts.

"Make the tea for the Reverend will you, love? And there's a bit of bride cake in the crock. I was sending some to your aunt but I don't expect she'll miss it."

Jessie cut a couple of thin pieces from the wedge of cake. It was rich and she was sure the offered slivers would suffice.

"Are you coming to the fair this afternoon, Mother?" she asked, pouring tea into her mother's best china cups.

She wondered if Nellie would be fit to go.

"No, lass, you go and enjoy yourself," said her mother with a rueful smile. "You've worked hard these last few days, Jessie. I couldn't have managed without you. Your father's taking a piece and going rambling with the Nature Society this afternoon. I can rest myself without him under my feet. Off you go."

Jessie changed into her second best dress, her new wedding outfit would be reserved for Sundays. Then she called on her friend Mary. As the two girls approached the sports field, the music of fairground organs and the cries of hawkers filled the air, interspersed with the screams of the mill girls. Young men were trying to impress the girls with their prowess at the games of skill. The coconuts on the shy looked so mouldy that Jessie decided they were glued on. They ignored the booth advertising freaks of nature. Mary had been tempted once before and declared them a cheat and a catchpenny.

"I shudder to think of the poor creatures. Shall we go on the swing boats, do you think?" she asked with growing excitement.

"It's a bit unladylike," said Jessie after a moment's thought. "But Father will be out with the Nature Society so he won't be around to scold me." She gave a merry laugh. "I don't see why not."

Much as she loved her father, his restrictions seemed petty at times.

They had to wait their turn as lots of Gorbydale's lassies wanted to go on the swing boats. Young men offered to help and laughed at the piercing screams of the young women soaring high with skirts flying, clutching their hats and ropes with equal determination.

"I don't know if we should," gasped Mary when she saw what was happening.

"We needn't go so high," decided Jessie.

Mary was persuaded and a determined Jessie refused the help of a couple of likely young men.

"No, thank you," she said firmly. "We can manage."

She clambered aboard a boat as decorously as she could and Mary settled down looking terrified. With dismay, she noticed Taylor Walmsley over Mary's shoulder, standing with folded arms, looking stern. No doubt he'd disapprove and even report back to her father, but it was too late. She began to pull gently on the rope and Mary did too with a nervous laugh. A short way from Taylor were two laughing young men in fashionable clothes not often seen at the Gorbydale Wakes Fair. One was plump and flamboyantly dressed with a bright embroidered waistcoat, his florid round face shining with perspiration. Jessie recognised the other as Robert Overdale. He was frequently seen about the mill and the town, accompanying his father. Slightly taller and certainly slimmer than his companion, he was better looking. Jessie decided that his pleasant open face was marred by an annoying air of superiority and condescension. He sometimes strutted through the mill taking an interest in the machinery but ignoring the mill operatives, as if they weren't the ones paying for his lifestyle. Beside him, the plump young man with a supercilious smirk on his face, took a lot of interest in the girls struggling with their skirts and showing their ankles. Then as she began to swing higher, she saw a vision in ribbons over by the hoopla stall. To her surprise, beside Dolly was Arden. Surely her brother had more sense than to mix with such a silly young woman?

Pulling harder on the rope she tried to fly higher and get a glimpse of them. For one enchanting moment she soared upward, tossed as light as a feather in the air. Then, as the boat plunged downward, Mary gave a piercing scream as it shot her into the air.

"Oh, Jessie — don't! Stop it, stop it!"

Jessie herself was surprised at how high they were swinging.

"Time's up ladies," called the operator with a laugh, "before you do any damage to yourself and my boats."

Jessie blushed furiously as she slowed down the boat. She felt hot and foolish when she saw Robert Overdale watching her.

"Got a bit of spirit, eh!" said Gus Kearsley. "Well done, girls!" he said, catching up to Jessie and Mary who were trying to distance themselves from the swing boats. "I say, you showed some of those lads a thing or two. Would you like to have another go and show me how to do it?"

"No, thank you," said Jessie primly.

"Perhaps you ladies would like a drink?" persisted Gus, hurrying to keep pace with them. "A nice lemonade to cool you down perhaps? How about a dandelion and burdock? A sarsaparilla would be very refreshing after all that hard work."

"No, thank you," said Jessie again.

"A sarsaparilla would be nice," said Mary. "My mouth went ever so dry. We were so high, it was quite frightening — but exciting too."

"I know what you mean," said Gus with a sly smile. "Exhilarating, wouldn't you say?"

"Oh definitely!" said Mary with a giggle. "Come on, Jess, don't be a spoil sport."

Jessie instinctively didn't like Gus but she couldn't be rude to her boss's son. Mary had already taken Gus's proffered arm and she needed to keep an eye on her friend.

The young men found the girls a table near the beer tent and then went inside. From where she was sitting, Jessie could see Gus's face and instinctively read his lips.

"A couple of likely lasses, don't you think?" said Gus with a sly smile towards the girls.

Robert looked hesitant but Jessie was incensed.

"What are you thinking about, Mary, accepting drinks from strange men?" she demanded.

"I was only being polite. My mouth is really dry after all that excitement. Anyway, one of them isn't a stranger, he's the boss's son. He might not like it if we snubbed him."

"Well, we'll drink up, thank them and then politely make our excuses," decided Jessie.

Her eyes were shining and her cheeks still pink from the effort of rocking the boat. She wished Taylor Walmsley hadn't been there. He'd disappeared by the time they'd clambered down from the boats. If only she could have had a word with him, perhaps ask him not to mention their escapade to her father.

Jessie stood up as she finished her drink, intent on leaving. She thanked the two men politely. But as she turned to go, Gus took hold of Mary's arm and began leading her towards the back of the tents. He bent and murmured something in her ear. Mary glanced back towards her friend, her eyes wide in alarm. Jessie felt immediately anxious and followed her friend, not trusting Gus one bit. She turned to Robert to protest at his friend's behaviour but as she faced him he suddenly caught her round the waist. She gasped but before she could protest, he kissed her full on the lips. For an instant, Jessie closed her eyes and felt the softness of his lips. Then she snapped out of her trance and quickly pulled away, appalled by her weakness. Furious with herself as well as Robert, she flew at him. The slap that stung his face resounded loud enough to make Mary and Gus turn and stare in surprise.

"How dare you!" growled Robert clutching his stinging cheek in shock. "You're nothing but one of my father's mill girls."

"I may only be a mill girl," snapped Jessie, her eyes ablaze with anger. "But it seems I have to show Master Robert Overdale of the Invincible Mill his manners. Or didn't they teach them at that posh school of yours? Come on, Mary."

As she caught her friend's hand and hurriedly dragged her away from the scene of her shame, Jessie caught the look of amusement on Gus Kearsley's face.

"Well, you won the bet and kissed yours first," he said to Robert with a smirk. "I think that's a fiver I owe you."

Despite the noise and clamour of the fair and her own embarrassment, Jessie could read his lips as clearly as if he'd announced the wager through a megaphone. She would have slapped Robert again if she'd been nearer. Almost blind with shame and anger, she rushed into the fair and fell headlong against Taylor Walmsley.

"Hello, Taylor," she said, breathless in her anxiety to escape.

His eyes narrowed as he saw the two young men emerging from behind the tent.

"Taylor..." began Jessie.

"Miss Davenport," answered Taylor sternly, stepping firmly away from her.

Then he turned his back on her and strode away.

Jessie glared at Robert and Gus. Grabbing Mary's arm she pulled her away.

"What on earth were you thinking of?" she said vehemently. "Just look at the trouble you've got me into."

"I'm sorry," whimpered Mary, glancing from Robert and his smirking friend to the retreating back of Taylor Walmsley. "Oh, Jessie, I hope I've not spoilt your chances with Taylor Walmsley."

"It's a bit late to worry about that now, Mary. Come on, we're going."

With that she linked her friend's arm and hurried her away from the scene of their embarrassment.

Jessie was anxious to leave the fair but, as she rounded one of the stalls with Mary trailing behind, they came across a commotion. Daft Oggy, clinging tightly to one of his placards, was being pelted with rotten fruit by a bunch of schoolboys. Scathingly known as the Gorbydale Seer, Oggy was often in the town with his messages of doom but he was harmless enough.

Passers-by were enjoying the fun but, unchecked, the boys were getting rowdier. Jessie, already seething with anger, had seen enough. She shouted at the boys just as one knocked Oggy to the ground. Checked by an adult the boys ran off and the spectators guiltily turned away.

"Are you all right, Mr Ogden?" asked Jessie, helping him to his feet.

Mary picked up his placard. It read 'War and Pestilence is coming. Repent and be saved.'

"They won't listen," said Oggy, shaking with anxiety. "There's a war coming and I'm trying to warn them. But they won't listen. I've seen it in my dreams. I feel it in my bones."

"Well, your bones are pretty shaken up now, Mr Ogden. I shouldn't take too much notice of them," said Jess kindly.

But the depth of fear and conviction in his eyes unnerved her. His predictions had been right before. He'd once warned that the river Gorby would flood. A mother and three children had drowned. Jacob said it was just inevitable as the banks had eroded and not been reinforced, but ever since then, Oggy had been regarded with a wary acceptance. The girls set him to rights and left him cleaning his placard.

"Would you like to go home?" asked Mary.

"I suppose you'd like to stay?" said Jessie stiffly.

Mary nodded.

"Well, we've not been here long, have we?"

"And already we've been tangled up with trouble," retorted Jessie. "Is there any more mayhem we can find?"

"I'm sorry," said her friend humbly. "I'm truly sorry about Taylor."

"Never mind," Jessie told her with a shrug, unwilling to disappoint her friend. "What's meant for you will never pass you by. Let's go and have a look at some of the stalls, then."

Among the gaily bedecked booths was an army recruiting tent. A smartly dressed trooper in his red coat with gleaming brass buttons was trying to recruit a group of young men.

"You could see plenty of action if this war in America gets going," he was telling them. He smiled broadly when he spotted the two girls. "Afternoon, ladies. Nothing like a uniform to attract the ladies," he told the boys, despite being ignored by Jessie and Mary.

First the conviction of Daft Oggy, now the trooper, all this talk of war sent a dart of ice down Jessie's spine.

Chapter 5: The Sunday School Outing

Early on Wednesday morning, an excited crowd gathered outside the chapel as the two charabancs going to Hollingworth Lake filled with the congregation. The horses were restless with people milling all around them. Everyone was dressed in their Whitsun best, their soap bright faces eager for the journey. Jessie was travelling in the last and most boisterous charabanc with her Sunday school children. She glanced at Eddie sitting with his friends and hoped he'd behave himself and not provoke their father.

In the front carriage were Mother and Father with the Reverend and the older members of the chapel. Despite her day of rest, Mother was tired and wheezing after the walk to the chapel. She'd leant heavily on her husband and daughter's arms, though she seemed to weigh nothing at all. Taylor travelled with the adults. He'd hardly glanced at her. Mary was helping Jessie, though she didn't teach Sunday school. As she settled down, Jessie noticed Dolly at the front of the coach, bedecked with her usual ribbons. Jessie couldn't recall seeing her on a Sunday morning, but beside her was Tommy Dale the son of a chapelgoer. Some people managed to wangle tickets for the outing without ever attending chapel each week.

The children cheered as the convoy moved off. Jessie had a crate of apples and oranges for her charges, and stowed at the back of the front carriage was a huge hamper containing a picnic provided by the congregation. For a while, the children were content to watch the scenery. They rarely travelled beyond the bounds of Gorbydale and everything they witnessed was a novelty. Then they began to fidget and scuffles broke out. Jessie tried to keep the peace. She had little opportunity to admire the passing scenery, a welcome change from everyday sights in the valley. Soon enough, they arrived at their destination and the children clambered off the coach with noisy exuberance. The adults disembarked and stretched their limbs, glad to be off the cramped and jolting carriages. Jessie was surprised to see Taylor ready to help her down.

"Thank you," she said with a shy smile.

"Perhaps if you can spare a minute later?" he asked, his expression frustratingly unreadable.

"Of course," she answered quietly.

She wondered what he wanted to say. He would not propose now — not after that trouble at the fair. He might lecture her. At the fair he'd looked as angry as his impassive features could reveal. Now he seemed stern but calm. It didn't bode well. Jessie momentarily wondered if all her heart-searching was worth the effort. But immediately all her attention was needed by her little charges. As she shepherded the children towards the lake, she spotted Mary talking to Taylor. That was unusual as her friend could barely speak to him. Then she was distracted by a squabble among the children. A great bustle ensued as the hamper was thrown open and pies and pasties and sandwiches were distributed among the waiting crowd. Mary was smiling as she arrived back to help. Despite herself, Jessie glanced round to find Taylor and saw him attending to his mother. All too soon the picnic was devoured and everyone was eager to begin their enjoyments, some to stroll by the lake, those more adventurous and with more money to take a trip aboard the pleasure boat.

When her young charges made a beeline for the small fair, Jessie and Mary hurried anxiously after them. They noticed Dolly loitering by the coconut shy.

"Isn't Arden with you?" she asked with a coyness that belied her knowing eyes.

"He's working at the Invincible," Jessie told her.

"I thought he might be," said Dolly smiling slyly.

With the other engineers and mechanics, he was cleaning and repairing all the machines for the return to work the following week.

Dolly glanced over at Tommy Dale who arrived carrying two toffee apples.

"Here you are — as sweet as you," he said with a grin.

Dolly giggled and tossed her hair coquettishly.

"Are you going to win me a coconut then?" she asked winsomely.

"As hollow as she is!" snorted Mary as they left Dolly with her admirer. "She doesn't waste much time, does she? She was quizzing me about Arden the other day, wanting to know if he had a sweetheart. Now here she is, making sheep's eyes at Tommy. What a wanton."

Remembering the incident at the Wakes Fair Jessie gave a wry smile. Some narrow-minded people would readily have branded the two girls the same.

Despite her previous reluctance to go on the swing boats, Mary offered to take a little girl on them. Left alone but with a wary eye on the children, Jessie gazed over the silver shimmering lake and wondered about her future. She wished she could stop thinking of that kiss. Of course it had been infuriating, but if only Taylor had shown a fraction of that warmth. She knew she was blushing as Reverend Carew approached her. Jessie was ready for a change in her life. The work at the mill was becoming monotonous, though the good wages gave her an independence that would be hard to relinquish.

"So, Jessie, what's your answer?" asked the preacher. "Are you ready to become our new pupil teacher? Mrs Carew's been asking."

She was just about to answer when a stern voice butted in.

"I'm sorry but no wife of mine would have to work, Reverend Carew," came the familiar voice of Taylor Walmsley from behind her.

Jessie hadn't even suspected he was there.

"Why that's marvellous, Jessie! Two of my flock entering into wedded bliss. This is news indeed. Just wait 'til I tell Mrs Carew," said the preacher jovially.

"But I haven't … but you didn't…" stammered Jessie, looking accusingly at Taylor. "And I thought…"

'Bliss' was never a word she'd have imagined for marriage with Taylor. She had been certain he wouldn't ask her to marry him after that incident at the fair.

"Please don't say anything yet, Mr Carew. I haven't given my answer. I'm not even sure if I was asked," she glanced up at Taylor in confusion and could read nothing in his face. "And … and … and nothing's been said to my father."

Jessie took refuge in the lack of her father's permission as she was not yet quite of age.

"Oh!" The preacher looked as confused as Jessie felt. "I'll not say anything then. I'll leave you two young people to sort it out."

He wandered away looking puzzled.

Jessie turned on her would-be suitor. But before she could protest and tell him he had no right to make decisions for her, Taylor raised a hand to silence her. That annoyed her even more. He had no authority over her now they were not at work.

"If you think I am annoyed and shocked by your behaviour at the fair, you are quite right. But your friend Mary has put me right on a few things." Trust Mary to interfere! "I said nothing to your father about your behaviour and I am quite prepared to forgive you, providing you act with proper decorum in future."

"I did nothing wrong," protested Jessie. "Whatever you think you saw, you are quite wrong."

"I said I was prepared to forgive you," repeated Taylor.

"For what?"

"Mary explained all about Overdale and his friend and I exonerate you from that entirely. I know you were acting in the best interests of your friend."

"So what am I to be forgiven for?" demanded Jessie.

"If you don't think you were acting like a … like a … hoyden on those swing boats, I'm afraid I have to disagree…" he began. "And you a Sunday school teacher and in front of everyone from the Invincible."

He had the grace to look uncomfortable under her challenging stare.

"It was only a bit of harmless fun," snapped Jessie.

She hadn't meant to sound so angry defending herself, especially as she knew her father would have disapproved. Taylor was giving her a way out, excusing her behaviour with Robert Overdale. He must think something of her to be persistent despite his doubts. All she had to do was say she was sorry, that she would conform and be submissive. She hesitated and looked into his eyes, not wanting to quarrel, yet feeling that to be docile and submissive was not her nature. What she saw in his eyes was a pleading and a depth of feeling she had not suspected. Why couldn't he love her just as she was?

"What I said to Mr Carew, I meant," said Taylor earnestly.

Jessie trembled with indecision. Could she grow to love him? Her reply dried on her lips as Eddie came running up, panting and anxious.

"Jessie, Jessie, come quick. Mother's not well. Father sent me to fetch you."

She turned to Taylor with a silent plea.

"You'd better go," he said with a frustrated sigh. "Perhaps when we are both of a calmer frame of mind…"

Jessie hurried after Eddie, feeling as confused as ever. Taylor was right. She needed a calmer mind to make a decision that would change her life. Yet, she somehow felt that to accept him would lead her into a life of submission not only to him but to his mother. Could she learn to stifle her very nature? Would she be happy married to Taylor and accept servitude for security?

A crowd of chapelgoers gathered around Nellie who had collapsed onto a bench. Her face was chalk white but beads of sweat trickled down her forehead and gleamed on her upper lip. Someone held a glass of water.

"I'll be all right … honestly … just give me a moment," she whispered, her words as laboured as her breath. "Go and enjoy yourselves. Jacob's here, and Jessie. Please go and…"

She clutched Jessie's hand in desperation, her eyes pleading for the crowd to go away, unhappy to be the centre of all their worried attention. Nellie never liked to cause a fuss.

"We'll just sit here a while until Mother's feeling better," Jessie told their friends, smiling with a confidence she didn't feel. "If we need help, we'll send someone for you, isn't that right, Father?"

Jacob nodded silently, his worried eyes firmly on his wife's face.

"Aye," he muttered. "Aye."

The onlookers wandered off, glancing back now and again. Nellie became calmer as they left, her breathing still laboured but less agitated.

"I don't know what came over me," she whispered. "I just felt so faint and the next minute..."

"Never mind," said Jessie, patting her hand. "We'll sit here and enjoy the sunshine and watch the boats."

Jacob sank onto the bench beside his wife and held her other hand.

"And we'll send for the doctor when we're home. There'll be no excuses this time."

Jessie glanced at her father. He'd wanted to consult the doctor before but a stubborn Nellie had refused, thinking of the expense. Jessie could see her own behaviour mirrored in her mother's stubbornness. But now Nellie had no choice.

It seemed an age until it was time to return home, although they had all decided to leave earlier. Two of the Sunday school children had fallen over in the shallow edge of the lake without Jessie's careful supervision. Their parents were anxious to take them home as they'd been soaked through. The charabanc was driven as near to Nellie's bench as possible and many hands helped her aboard. She sat between Jessie and Jacob, holding their hands. Taylor was somewhere behind them and, although she refused to look round, Jessie could feel his eyes on her. He'd given her a searching glance as he helped Nellie up into the charabanc, but she'd looked away in confusion. There were more important things to concern her.

The charabanc stopped at the foot of Weavers Row and a chair was carried from Mary's house. Fetched by Eddie, an anxious Arden came hurrying down the Row and helped his father and the neighbours carry Nellie home on it. Jessie helped her exhausted mother to bed and so ended a busy and confusing day for her. In her room, staring into the darkness, her restless mind relived everything that had happened. Had Taylor proposed in his ham-fisted way? Could there be any other meaning to that remark about his wife? More importantly, what would be her answer if he did formally propose? Eventually she fell into an exhausted sleep, her dilemmas unresolved. Jessie could not know that any decisions about her future would soon be spirited away from her control.

Chapter 6: The Engineer

In the strangely silent and echoing floors of the Invincible Mill, Arden Davenport had been hard at work cleaning one of the spinning machines. With the workforce away enjoying their Wakes week, Arden and his fellow engineers made sure all the machines were in good working order. He'd served his apprenticeship at the Endurance but his great ambition was to be chief engineer at the Invincible Mill. The great boiler that ran all the machines was cleaned too while the mill was closed.

Stretching to straighten his back after a particularly tricky fitting, he noticed Robert Overdale strolling towards him. Arden envied him his leisure but there was much to be done. Robert stopped by his machine.

"Hello," he said pleasantly. "Are you 'fettling' the machines for the return to work on Monday?"

The dialect word sounded odd coming from him.

"Aye," said Arden, pausing in his work.

"What's that you're doing?" asked Robert.

Arden was unsure how to treat the boss's son. Yet Robert's air of superiority disappeared as he became interested in the machine. Encouraged by Robert's interest, Arden showed him a machine part, pointing to where it fitted. He knew Robert by sight as he was frequently around the mill and the town, usually on his fine chestnut horse.

"Oh, I see where it fits," said Robert with a satisfied grin. "I've come to watch them cleaning the boiler. I used to like watching them at the Endurance Mill when I was a little lad, before we came here that was — and before I was sent away." Arden thought he heard a note of resentment in his voice.

"Uncle Eli let me climb into the boiler once. I got truly filthy and my father was most annoyed. I enjoyed it, though," he added laughing.

"That was one of my jobs when I was an apprentice," said Arden. "Before I got too big to climb in the fire door. I hadn't any choice in the matter though."

He wondered if Robert noticed the irony in his own voice. For the mill owner's son to play about in a boiler was a different matter from having to scrape the insides clean of encrusted clinker in an atmosphere of choking soot. Arden was wary how he treated the master's son but to his exasperation, Robert showed no sign of moving on. He examined the spinning machine, strangely bare without its banks of bobbins and rigging of cotton threads. This was one of Jessie's machines.

"Your name's Davenport isn't it?" asked Robert hesitantly.

"That's right," said Arden.

"And your father's a master weaver at the Endurance?"

Arden nodded.

"Aye, he is."

"I liked Jacob. He was very patient with me when I was a little lad. I'm sure I was a terrible nuisance, always asking questions."

"That'll be my father. 'If you don't ask owt, you don't learn nowt' — that's what he always says," said Arden, his face softening with a smile.

"My Uncle Eli is the same. He let me wander round the mill when Father was his partner. I'd have liked to be an engineer," said Robert sadly. "But when we moved to the Invincible, my father was against me learning a trade. How is your father by the way?"

"He's well — at least I hope he is," said Arden with a sigh. "Mother's not so good, though," he thought aloud to himself. "I was hoping our Eddie would call by with my piece and tell me what the doctor had to say."

"I'm sorry to hear that," said Robert and he did look genuinely sorry.

To the engineer's surprise, Robert took off his jacket and rolled up his sleeves.

"Mind if I help?" he asked.

"If you're sure?" said Arden. "Won't your father object though?"

He could be in trouble for refusing the owner's son but if Robert got hurt he'd get the blame and be in more trouble. But Robert had already armed himself with a wad of raw cotton and looked eager to start.

"I'm just finding out about the business, aren't I?" said Robert with a grin.

Arden had thought him arrogant but, once interested in the machines, Robert chatted naturally with no sense of privilege. He was surprisingly easy to talk to and followed Arden's instructions. They were soon laughing and joking together. The time flew by and, though Arden had to use him as a glorified labourer, Robert was a quick learner. A couple of other engineers came into the spinning room, but quickly disappeared, unwilling to associate with the boss's son. The pair worked on companionably and the allotted tasks were soon finished. The boiler was forgotten. Busy with work, they were surprised to find Honora standing tentatively nearby.

"There you are, Robert," she said. "Your father was looking for you. He said you might be down at the mill."

Honora briefly acknowledged Arden and he bobbed his head to her. She was a striking looking girl with an intelligent face — though not exactly pretty.

"Are you coming now?" she asked.

"I suppose I must go," sighed Robert wiping his hands on a wad of cotton waste. "Thank you for letting me help. It's been most enjoyable. I hope I was a help."

"Most certainly," said Arden.

"I'll see you soon," said his boss's son, leaving with a satisfied grin.

"Are you sure you should be doing that?" asked Honora, quietly.

"Why not?" protested Robert. "I should know how the machinery works. But please don't mention it to Father, will you? You know what he's like."

"I won't," she promised him.

Arden watched them leave with an amused smile. He'd heard Robert ask the girl not to tell his father about his activities. It had been a surprising visit. In different circumstances, they might even have been friends. Despite the heir to the mill's wealth and prospects, Arden felt sorry for Robert.

His thoughts returned to his mother and what the doctor might have found.

Chapter 7: The Doctor Calls

Arden and Jacob had set up a bed in the parlour for Nellie, despite her protests. "You'll be able to keep an eye on things down here and rest up when you want to," Jessie coaxed her mother. "And the doctor won't have to keep going upstairs. You know how steep those stairs are."

"I'll be better soon," said Nellie firmly. "He won't need to come that often."

Watching her mother's frail form struggling for breath, Jessie knew Nellie was only thinking about the doctor's bills.

"Well, then we can move you back upstairs, can't we?" she said briskly.

Deep down they both suspected that Nellie might never again mount those stairs.

"Come on, let's get you ready for the doctor. We'll draw the curtains when he comes. We don't want the neighbours to see your folderols."

The clip clop of hooves on cobbles announced the doctor's arrival on his sturdy old mare. He greeted the family and went into the parlour to examine Nellie. Jessie listened as closely as she could to the low voices but could hear nothing of their murmured conversation. Then the doctor opened the door and asked for Jacob. Jessie's heart sank to see his furrowed brow and grave manner. The doctor went with her father out into the garden but, hovering hopefully, she still heard nothing. At last they reappeared and she eagerly offered them tea.

"Thank you, but I'd best be on my way. I've other folks to see," said the doctor with a tired sigh. "I'll leave you in peace."

Her father accompanied him to his mare, his shoulders slumped.

"Perhaps I'll have that cup of tea, love," he said wearily. "You mother might like one too. She'll be worn out with all the fuss."

Jessie popped her head into the parlour. Nellie seemed asleep but her breathing was terrible. Her chest rattled like dried beans in a tin. Leaving her in peace, Jessie took tea out to her father and found him staring at his vegetable patch, his shoulders hunched in misery. His eyes were red. Father rarely cried. It was serious then. Her stomach turned into a frightened icy knot.

"Well, Jessie love — how is she?"

"She's settled. I think she's asleep," Jessie said quietly. "What did the doctor say?"

"It's not good. They call it byssinosis — a fancy name for a rotten disease."

Jessie knew what that meant — cotton lung some called it. Her father gave a muffled sob and Jessie squeezed his hand. He grasped hers like a lifeline.

"I've suspected it for some time, but you hope it's just a cough — or a touch of bronchitis. But I knew deep down."

Jessie had known too, yet they'd both refused to admit that Nellie was dying.

"Oh, Father," she said, a sob breaking her own voice. "Oh, Father."

What words could comfort anyone when the heart of the family was about to be torn out? She sobbed, with her head on his shoulder. Poor, poor Mother, poor Father — what would become of them all with Mother gone?

"Come now, lass, we must be brave for your mother's sake," said Jacob, patting her shoulder. "It'll be hard. I can hardly face her myself without wanting to howl like a babby." He blew his nose and took a deep breath. "Your mother was nowt but a little lass when she worked in that carding room where all that filthy dust comes off the cotton. Her lungs were ruined then."

"What's to be done?" asked Jessie anxiously. "What will we tell Eddie?"

"Why worry the little chap? He'll know soon enough. Mother will agree with me about that," decided Jacob. "She'll not get better. You know that?" Jessie nodded, desperately holding back the tears, trying to be brave. "We'll make her as comfortable as we can — like she's done for us all her life long. I've a plan to ask Eli Gorman if I might rent his cottage in the hills when the honeymooners get back."

Jack and his new bride Elsie wouldn't even know that Nellie was ill until they returned home. It would be a bitter shock for them after the joy of the wedding.

"The air's cleaner up there at Primrose Cottage. It'll happen to give her a few more months."

"What about your work — and Arden's? And what will Eddie do for school?" she asked, startled by this plan.

Jessie didn't mention herself for she knew what was expected of her. All night she'd slept uneasily. What a reversal had shaken her life in a few short days. As the only daughter, she knew it was her duty to give up work and care for her mother. But she'd thought she'd be looking after Nellie in her own familiar home.

"It's five miles for me to walk to the Endurance. I'd do that for your mother. There's a village school for Eddie. Arden could stay here and look after the house. And then there's you." He took her hand. "Will you stay home and look after your mother, Jessie? I'm sorry, lass, but there's no other way. Your mother can't be left."

58

"I know that, Father," she said, earnestly nodding. "I decided I would last night. You know I'll do anything for Mother."

Her words were brave but Jessie felt very afraid as her life crumbled round her. She'd never nursed an invalid before, let alone looked after a house and family by herself. At Primrose Cottage, she'd be isolated away from all she'd known, from friends and kind neighbours, at the back of beyond with a sick mother to care for and little support. Though she was daunted by Jacob's plan, she'd willingly try her best for her mother. Jessie was determined to be as cheerful and brave as she could to convince Mother she could cope.

"I'll hand in my notice at the Invincible on Monday," she decided. "Have you mentioned Primrose Cottage yet to Mother?"

Jacob shook his head.

"Not yet. I'm trying to compose myself." He looked for a moment as if he would break down again. "Your mother will know it's the sensible thing to do. She's a good wife to me and she'll do as I ask."

Nellie always let Jacob think he was head of the house but Jessie had witnessed plenty of her mother's stratagems! She wondered if Mother would agree with his plans. They seemed sensible, but would they suit Nellie?

They turned to a call of "Jacob!" The Reverend Septimus Carew was coming up Weavers Row.

"How's Mrs Davenport?" he asked anxiously. "I saw the doctor leaving on his mare."

"Not so good," sighed Jacob, shaking his head. "Not good at all."

There was no need to spell it out.

"Oh dear," sighed Septimus. "I hoped I might be wrong. I was just on my way to the station at Doveton to pick up Mrs

Carew's niece, so I thought I'd come and enquire. I was anxious about Mrs Davenport after what happened and everyone from chapel is asking after her. But I'm sorry to hear she's so poorly. Mrs Davenport is a stalwart of our chapel. You know we'll all be praying for her."

"Aye, bless you for that. It'll give her comfort," said Jacob.

"Would you like some tea before you go?" asked Jessie kindly. "I've just brewed and it will still be hot."

Septimus glanced at his watch.

"I've just got time. Thank you, Jessie, that would be kind."

She peeped in at her mother. A pair of weary eyes flickered open.

"Would you like some tea, Mother?" she asked. "Mr Carew's just called to enquire how you're doing. Everyone's asking after you."

"That's kind of him," said her mother with a weak smile. "Make him some fresh tea. I'll have the old mashings — it'll be weaker."

Jessie shook her head. Trust Mother! Ill though she was, she was mindful of the household expenses. Tea was dear and she'd often caught her mother making tea with the old leaves. Then they were spread on the floors before being swept up because Nellie insisted they kept the dust down.

"Then come and have a sit with me, love."

Jessie served her father and Septimus tea out in the garden. Then she did as she was told so Mother would feel she was still mistress in her own home.

"You know I'm not long for this world, don't you, love?" said Nellie in a low and wheezy voice.

She struggled to sit up and Jessie arranged her pillows to make her comfortable.

"Oh, Mother, you mustn't talk like that," she said, avoiding her mother's eyes.

They both knew what was to come, yet Jessie could not speak of it without breaking down. Nellie patted her hand.

"Jessie, love, I hope you've thought about what I said about Taylor Walmsley?" Mother wheezed as she struggled for breath. "I saw him making a beeline for you at the Sunday school outing. Has he asked?"

"I don't know," sighed Jessie. "Mother, that's truly the last thing on my mind at the moment."

"Has he asked?" insisted Nellie.

"He said he was going to ask — I don't know if that's the same thing."

Trust Mother to have been watching her and for her to bring that up. Jessie was confused and agitated with suppressed emotion. She just wanted to rush upstairs to her bedroom and sob into her pillow but somehow she held her emotions together. Her mother chuckled breathlessly.

"Men! They never know their own minds. Take your father when he was courting me. 'So you're asking me to marry you, then,' I said as bold as brass. He'd only mentioned it in passing — but I wasn't going to let him get away!" She drooped back, smiling onto her pillow, wearied with the effort of trying to speak and breathe. "I reckon Taylor will come out with it, if you spell it out for him, our Jessie."

Jessie just knew she couldn't 'spell it out' to Taylor Walmsley. She didn't even know if she wanted to. There was so much turmoil in her thoughts and an urgent need to decide what to pack for their journey. She had to make dinner, wash some bedding while the weather was warm and a thousand other tasks. All without the aid of her mother. Yet, here was Nellie, ill as she was, trying to match make. Despite her worries, Jessie smiled to herself. Small and ailing though Mother was, her indomitable nature shone through. You didn't survive the poverty and grinding hard work of your childhood by giving in. She was very determined when it came to looking out for her little flock.

With a contended smile, Nellie settled back.

"Think on what I've told you. I'll have a nap now," she whispered hoarsely. "You go out and enjoy the sunshine. Don't waste your Wakes week cooped up with an invalid."

"But, Mother…" protested Jessie.

"Off you go," insisted Nellie, her eyes closed firmly to prevent any argument.

Jessie obeyed her.

The Gorbydale Valley looked fresh and green in the warm sunshine. For a week, at least, there was no smoke and soot from the mill. Jacob and Septimus Carew went quiet as she joined them. They had obviously been discussing Nellie's illness and what it meant for the family.

"That was a grand cup of tea," said Mr Carew carefully handing back the best china cup. "I'm so sorry to hear about your mother. Your father told me his plans to move up the valley."

"Yes," said Jessie. "If Mother agrees."

She hoped Father would mention his plan to Mother soon. There were so many things to arrange and she was feeling inadequate, badly needing her mother's advice.

Jessie began making a hearty broth for their midday meal but, when she turned to ask her mother something, she found Nellie dozing. Mother didn't even seem to have the energy to supervise her. Jessie guessed she'd have to manage on her own soon enough anyway.

As she stirred the pot she thought about her mother, the backbone of the family. Nellie Arden had been the only child of a poor widow. She'd nursed Jacob's old father when he was blind and could no longer work his handloom. The Davenports had lived thriftily, building their home and family, but managed to buy little luxuries too. In the parlour, the sun shone through the rose glass of Nellie's best oil lamp, the dangling glass prisms casting little rainbows around the room and twinkling on the glass fronted bookcase holding their precious books. Mother hadn't been able to read until Father had taught her. Nellie loved her home and Jessie felt so proud of her.

She heard Jacob call goodbye to Mr Carew. He came and drew a chair beside her mother. Nellie stirred and opened her eyes. "How's the invalid?" he asked, his eyes searching her face.

"She's been having a little nap," Jessie told him.

"I'm rested, anyhow," said Nellie with a brave smile. "I might get up this afternoon and sit in a chair outside."

Jacob was immediately solicitous. "I'll bring out the armchair and we'll rig up a footstool," he said. "At least the air's clean for once. I've been thinking, Nellie — and I've had a word with Jessie here, and Arden, and they're agreeable…"

"And if Mother agrees," said Jessie quickly, wiping her hands on her apron as she came to the parlour door.

"Plotting behind my back, eh?" said his wife with a wry smile.

"I'll ask Master Eli if I can rent his old home — Primrose Cottage. It'll be for the best, love. The air'll be clean up there. It'll be easier for you to breathe. You'll have more chance of getting better."

"And how will you get to the Endurance?"

"It's only five mile and…"

"Every morning and every night. Oh, Jacob, I know you mean well…" She struggled to breathe deeply as she took his hand and squeezed it. "But you know I'm not going to get better. You know it, don't you, love?"

Biting his lip he nodded dumbly. Jessie turned away, pretending to check on her broth so she could hide her tears. For once in her life, Nellie defied her dear husband.

"Why make yourself ill with all that travel? What will it give me — another week, another month? No, if I'm to die, it'll be in my own home, with my own things about me. You understand that, don't you, love?"

"But…" began Jacob.

"No buts. I'm staying put," Nellie said firmly and closed her eyes again.

She pretended to doze to avoid her husband's arguments.

"Don't worry, Father," Jessie whispered. "Mother always knows best. She'll be happier here and her friends will be able to visit. Come away and have something to eat."

"I expect you're right," said Jacob, defeated for once.

Jessie felt such relief at her mother's refusal to move to the country. At least at home, she would have the help of her friends as she cared for her mother in familiar surroundings.

Eddie charged in and paused to give his mother a scrappy kiss on the cheek.

"Hello, Mam. Are you feeling better? Mrs Connolly says to be remembered to you."

"I'm fine, son," she said.

"Come and get something to eat, Trouble," called Jessie. "Are your hands clean?"

Her brother flopped into his seat and attacked his meal with gusto. Jacob toyed with his food, looking lost in thought.

Later, Jessie fetched a shawl as Jacob carried his armchair into the garden.

"Look what I've done," said Eddie proudly producing his footstool for Nellie, the wooden coal-scuttle from the parlour topped with a cushion.

"What have you done with my best cushion?" she protested, then relented. "Well done, son," she said ruffling his hair. "It's grand."

Eddie grinned proudly and held her hand.

"Aren't your hands thin, Mam?" he said, staring at them.

"Call me Mother, young man — like you always have," said Nellie slumping tiredly against the cushions. "Don't think standards will drop because I'm not well."

"But Bart Kelso calls his…"

"Don't vex Mother so," Jessie scolded him. "Can't you see she's not well?"

Nellie smiled.

"Let him be," she murmured. "He'll understand soon enough."

With a swift kiss, Eddie ran off to his friends with all the careless enthusiasm of youth. Jessie took Nellie's hand. Her brother was right, her mother's fingers lay thin and pale against her own. She squeezed them, as if to urge strength into them. They sat quietly together in the warm sun, each embroiled in their own thoughts.

"Have you seen anything of Taylor Walmsley lately?" asked Nellie.

Jessie avoided the question.

"I don't suppose he'll call as often now our John is married," she said with a shrug.

"We'll see," said her mother with a smile.

Chapter 8: A Visit to Liverpool

Candlelight gleamed in a myriad reflections off the huge and ornate silver centrepiece. Fragrance from the freesias in their tiny vases mingled with the rich aroma of the wine, and crystal glasses twinkled rainbows across the rich damask. The Kearsleys' dining room in their magnificent house in Liverpool was grand and overwhelming. The shipbuilder and his wife knew how to live well. Melissa would have loved a dining table set like this, with fine china and glass and heavy silver cutlery. They didn't entertain much at Overdale House. Their modest dining table easily held the few local guests that Matthias thought fitting. Those invitations didn't include the local vicar or anyone else that her husband thought condescending to those in trade. Melissa caught Matthias's eye and he gave her a faint smile. She knew he too was impressed with all this luxury.

"Isn't it kind of the Kearsleys to invite us," she'd said to him on the journey over.

"There'll be some business deal brewing, or we wouldn't be asked," he'd told her. "Don't think we're invited because they'd love our company."

They'd both been surprised when the invitation had arrived from the shipbuilder and his wife. The Kearsleys and the Overdales had met several times at the Academy. As Gus and Robert were friends, they had naturally been introduced. Glancing round the room, Melissa wished her dress was more stylish. Mrs Maria Kearsley was dressed like a lavishly upholstered sofa. Her husband, in contrast, was tall, grey and elegant. There was little call for ballgowns in Gorbydale and the other ladies had more frills, lace and furbelows than she'd thought possible on dresses. The jewels adorning Mrs Kearsley's ample bosom flashed as she graciously entertained her guests, making Melissa's own rose gold locket seem very modest. Among the other guests, much fuss was being made of a gentleman from America.

"This is Mr Clement Amiens Duplege, our visitor from the southern states," said Maria Kearsley, introducing him to Melissa.

Mr Duplege was a tall and courtly young man. His thick auburn hair, the colour of a summer fox, curled long like a lion's mane. Bowing low over her hand, he'd kissed it as they'd been introduced.

"Charmed, I'm sure," said Melissa with an amused smile as the southerner glanced up with a twinkle in his eye.

She glanced over at Matthias. He was frowning with disapproval. Melissa was tempted to giggle as the young man's curling moustache tickled her hand. She'd never had it kissed so flamboyantly before but she didn't want to appear unsophisticated.

Clement Duplege was immensely proud of his southern home and his French ancestry. Throughout the meal he boasted about the size and beauty of the Amiens plantation and of the magnolia trees in blossom.

"The Dupleges originally come from France, of course," he told the company. "The villa on the plantation is based on our ancestral home near Amiens. The white marble for the pillars at the entrance was imported from Carrera."

"It sounds lovely. I'm sure your wife has made it perfectly comfortable too," said Melissa imagining the graceful classic building among the blushing magnolias, filled with ornate French antiques.

Clement was as gallant as ever.

"I'm sorry to admit, Mrs Overdale, that, unlike your lucky husband, I have not yet found the loving flower that will grace my home and my heart."

Clement was so deliciously chivalrous that Melissa had to smile again. Despite the compliment to himself and his wife, Matthias frowned at this Frenchified dandy making up to her.

"Oh I'm sure you'll find someone just right to be mistress of the Amiens plantation," she said warmly.

"I think I may have misled you, Mrs Overdale," admitted Clement. "The Amiens plantation already has a mistress. My brother's wife is lady of the house. I am regrettably just the younger brother. I am domiciled in Baton Rouge — near my business, you know. I will not inherit my ancestors' estates unless my brother fails to produce a son. He has two fine, healthy daughters at present. But I look upon the estate as my natural home."

"Naturally," said Melissa pleasantly.

At the table, she was seated next to a rather dull cotton importer with little small talk, so had an opportunity to absorb the conversations round the table. The dinner was splendid with dainty morsels that she had never even seen or tasted before. She wished Matthias wouldn't examine the exotic dinner with such a look of outrage. When he wasn't toying with the food, he was discussing the cotton trade right over the bosomy wife of a foundry owner from Manchester. Melissa felt embarrassed for him.

In the place of honour beside his hostess, Clement Duplege continued to sing the praises of his home. Augustus Kearsley seemed, like Matthias, incensed by Clement's boasting. He tried to match the American with tales of the progress and prosperity of his home city.

"There are many fine buildings in Liverpool, Mr Duplege," he interrupted. "We must take you on a tour tomorrow and show you the Cotton Exchange. They say there's as much business done on the Flags outside as in the building itself. And St George's Hall is reckoned to be a masterpiece of design."

"I'd be obliged to you," said Clement with a slow, lazy smile. "Though, I am not sure if I may have the time. I have much work to do."

He didn't seem convinced that anything in Liverpool could surpass his home in Louisiana.

"And there's the new street railway at Birkenhead — the first in the world," continued Gus, still trying to impress.

"Built by an American gentleman," claimed Clement, proudly trumping Gus. "I was invited to the opening by Mr Train himself. A fine occasion."

"Will there be a war, do you think?" asked Matthias. "I called at the Exchange t'other day and the price of cotton's going up by the minute. These rumours are affecting our costs."

"Oh, no talk of war, please," said Mrs Kearsley faintly, with her hand fluttering on her bosom.

But either Clement Duplege hadn't heard her, or ignored her anyway to introduce the purpose for the visit.

"The south are preparing as we speak," he said confidently. "We are a proud people, Mr Overdale, and we are groaning under the arrogance of the north. I have had intelligence today that my own state Louisiana is seceding from the Union. If the north attack, we will be ready for them — with a little help from our friends," he added, smiling and bowing at Mr Kearsley.

With a nod from her husband, Mrs Kearsley hurriedly invited the ladies present to follow her to the drawing room.

"I think we'll leave the gentlemen to their business talk," she announced.

Abandoning them to the port and cigars, and thoughts of war heavy in the air, she led the ladies into another grand and comfortable room. There were a couple of industrialist's wives with their daughters and two women whose husbands worked in the Cotton Exchange. Melissa stared round the drawing room with its massive sparkling chandelier. Though her own home was large and comfortable, she felt a little overwhelmed by the luxury on display. She carefully noted all the details so she could describe them to Honora. She wished her niece had accompanied them but, as she hadn't been specifically invited, Matthias refused to bring her with them.

"Do try one of these violet creams, Mrs Overdale," said Maria, passing round a huge box. "They are quite delicious."

It was clear that the portly Mrs Kearsley was extremely fond of violet creams. Their sweetness melted on Melissa's tongue. Waiting until no one was looking, she deftly folded two into her lace handkerchief for Honora, hoping they wouldn't melt. Then she hoped she didn't need to blow her nose. Smiling to herself, she knew Matthias would be annoyed by what she'd done. He'd protest that they could afford their own violet creams, but she was sure that smuggled violet creams tasted so much nicer.

There were a couple of pale daughters in the company but they were no match for Honora. Melissa would have coaxed her niece to play the piano and sing some sweet song, while these girls just giggled with each other. Clement Duplege had made a great impression on the silly young things. Throughout the dinner, Robert had sat almost silently, seemingly in a world of his own, tongue-tied in the presence of the girls. Matthias was making a big mistake if he thought Honora wasn't worthy of their son. She may not have a dowry but she overcame all that with her sweet temper and common sense — not to mention her accomplishments. Melissa missed Honora.

The gentlemen did not join the ladies until late. The buzz of loud conversation and muted argument rumbled all evening behind the dining room door. The giggling girls had to be content with their own company and the women held polite conversations full of gentle boasting about their families. It was time for bed when the gentlemen entered the drawing room in a cloud of smoke and alcohol fumes. Mr Kearsley apologised sincerely for keeping them from their loved ones. Now most people trailed off to their beds or their homes.

The Overdales had been invited to stay the night, planning to return home early the next day. Over port, Mr Kearsley had persuaded Matthias that a trip to the shipyards the next morning would be in the mill owner's interest.

In an elaborate bedroom, heavy with satin swags, Melissa sat at a large dressing table brushing her hair. It was greying now, but her face still held traces of the pretty girl she had once been. Behind her, Matthias prowled like an agitated lion.

"Old Kearsley wants me to invest in cargoes for his ships," he told his wife, speaking to her reflection in the mirror. "He says there's plenty of money to be made. That Duplege chap is a southern agent. The southern states are arming for war and they want to ship in as many munitions as they can before the Union bears down on them."

"Can't they make their own guns?" asked Melissa. "Mr Duplege seemed to think the south was capable of anything."

"There's very little industry in the south, my dear," said Matthias. "Most of the factories are up north. The south mostly relies on cotton — like us. Our guns and boats are vital to them."

"Do you think that's wise, dear?" asked Melissa. "What if there isn't a war?"

"Duplege says there's bound to be. The south is eager for it. They're determined to shake off the yoke of the north."

"Determined to keep their slaves, more like," said Melissa with a worried frown.

Matthias was ambitious but she didn't want him to come unstuck. He'd sunk a lot of money into the Invincible Mill. It was heavily mortgaged.

"If this war in America blows up, there'll be trouble with the flow of cotton anyway, mark my words. Then where will we all be?" asked her husband. "At least if I invest with Kearsley, we'll have more chance to get cotton supplies."

"Surely it won't happen," said Melissa. "Our government wouldn't countenance such a terrible thing. They'll back the south, of course. The north wouldn't dare start a war with the might of the British Empire behind the southern states. And they've Canada at their back too."

In the mirror she saw Matthias stare at her in surprise, wondering how a woman could know anything about politics. But Melissa and Honora often discussed the news in his abandoned newspapers when he wasn't about. Even *The Times* said Mr Lincoln was nothing but a jumped-up nobody from the back woods. But jumped-up nobodies could start trouble too.

"What do you think of Mr Duplege, dear?" asked Melissa changing the subject. "Isn't he just charming?"

"Hmmph," snorted Matthias. "He's got more curls than those silly girls he was playing up to."

"I should love Honora to see him, though," said Melissa mischievously. "I dare say she'd have more sense than to flirt with such a dandy."

"Well, she'll see him soon enough. I've invited him over to Gorbydale. She could do worse. He's well heeled by all accounts, though he isn't heir — yet — to the plantation."

So that was at the back of her husband's mind. He'd try to prevent her penniless niece from making a match with his son and heir by introducing her to Clement Duplege.

"He's invited Augustus and Robert to visit him over in America," said Matthias. "It might do the lad good to see a bit of the world, and he can keep an eye on my business at the same time. I wouldn't trust that Duplege as far as I could throw him."

"Does Robert want to go?" she asked tentatively.

"Aye. He seems very keen," said her husband, nodding his head in approval.

The once solid ground beneath Melissa's feet began to teeter. Her son, too, was turning his horizons away from home and all she could do was watch.

"So you have decided to invest?" she said with a resigned sigh.

"Aye," said her husband slumping down on the bed. "I've no other choice."

"I suppose not," murmured Melissa.

She supposed men must go out into the world to make their fortune, but America was a wide ocean away. She didn't like the idea of her only child sailing far from home and maybe even into a war. As her husband snored gently, a hundred fears plagued her troubled mind. An inexorable storm of disturbing politics and uncertain times was looming towards the safety of her home and she couldn't do a single thing to stop it.

Chapter 9: A Chance Meeting

Jessie had been at home all day, isolated from all the excitement of the Wakes weeks. She'd been looking forward to a carefree holiday and a chance to be free from the hard and long hours at the mill. Now all her plans had been abandoned to look after her mother and the rest of the family. What a difference a few days had made.

After she'd fed the family and ate a little herself, she made Nellie comfortable in the armchair in the garden. Jacob came to sit beside his wife for a while. Arden was still at the mill and Eddie had been sent off with something to eat for his brother.

To quell her restiveness, Jessie decided to take some exercise.

"I think I'll go out for some fresh air," she said, taking down her summer shawl from the back of the door.

"Aye all right, lass," said Jacob with a dismissive nod. "We're fine, aren't we, Mother?"

Nellie nodded and smiled.

Jessie called first at her friend Mary's house.

"She's gone to the fair with one of our lodgers. You'll catch them up if you hurry," her mother Alice told Jessie.

Jessie didn't want to go on her own, even to meet her friend. She'd had enough of fairs just then. Leaving Weavers Row, she began to climb up the back lane towards the Fort, waving to her parents as she passed. She'd often played in the tumbled ruins as a child. Arden had once found a Roman coin there to confirm its ancient origins. Only a jagged outline of the buildings remained. Many walls in Gorbydale had been built with the pilfered stone. Who would leave good dressed stone go unused?

Resting on one of the larger stones, she felt she could think clearly so high above the town. Far below her were the two mills that had dominated her life. The Invincible, grand but silent. The old Endurance squatted at the end of the valley with a thin stream of smoke puffing from its chimney. The air was fresh and the grass alive with bright flowers. Sometimes, she picked odd exotic blooms from seed brought in with the raw cotton. They flowered for one brief season, never to be seen again. Jessie might live here all her life and never see the far exotic places where these flowers bloomed. She felt so trapped, and after only a short time of looking after her invalid mother. Was married life like this too, a monotonous round of cooking, cleaning and looking after others? Yet, her mother must feel as imprisoned too in her failing body. At least Nellie had refused to move and they didn't have to tell Eddie the awful truth just yet. Jessie and Arden had quietly discussed the situation, meaning to protect the family as much as they could. Father was looking old with the strain of seeing his dear wife suffer. They all had to be strong for Mother's sake. But it wasn't easy. Beneath her brave intentions, a niggling resentment rumbled. Bound by duty, Jessie was no longer free to live her life as she chose.

She enviously watched the birds circling the valley, free and carefree. All her chances were slowly passing her by. Would she become ignored and old, a despised old maid or an unhappy wife, grateful to take the first man that offered? Engrossed in her thoughts, she only noticed the clip clop of hooves when the horse and its rider were nearly upon her.

"Good evening," said Robert Overdale. He stared in surprise as she turned towards him. "Er … Jessie … er … Miss Davenport."

"Mr Overdale," said Jessie stiffly, rising to her feet and bobbing slightly.

"It's a beautiful afternoon, isn't it?" he stammered. "I thought I'd take the air — give my trusty steed a trot out. I was cooped up in a carriage from Liverpool for most of yesterday. So I ... er ... I, er ... thought I'd exercise Surefoot."

As his fine horse nibbled the fresh grass, Robert bent and patted his neck, looking uncertain.

"Liverpool?" said Jessie politely, echoing his words, unsure what to say.

The last time she'd seen him, she'd slapped his face. To her embarrassment, her face burned at the thought of that kiss — that insulting kiss to win a wager. He must have guessed her thoughts. To Jessie's surprise, Robert slid from his horse and stood beside her. She moved markedly away.

"Miss Davenport ... I have to apologise. I'm really truly sorry for what I did. I don't know what came over me. It was a stupid thing to do. My friend ... he sort of ... er ... goaded me." Jessie scowled as he tried to blame his friend for his own behaviour. He glanced up at her lovely but stony face, and tried again.

"Please forgive me, Miss Davenport. Say you'll forgive me."

Jessie looked him boldly in the eyes. He had the grace to look away from her furious gaze and did seem genuinely sorry for the offence he'd caused.

"I suppose I should forgive you," she began, and for a moment hesitated.

Forgiveness was one of the things she weekly drummed into her little charges at the Sunday school over their petty squabbles. But she was determined that she would not bow down to this man — the man who'd insulted her with his casual kiss for a bet — the man who'd said she was 'only one of his father's mill girls' — a man who might even have ruined her chances with Taylor Walmsley. Why should she feel sympathy towards him? Jessie stuck out her chin in defiance.

"But … but you had no right. You were downright insulting. I may be 'just one of your father's mill girls' as you said, Mr Overdale, but I've a right to be respected as much as anyone else. You think you can say a few honeyed words and get away with your foul behaviour — but just think on — it's us mill hands that put fancy clothes on your back — and bought you your fine horse."

Her face felt aflame. She knew she'd gone too far.

"I suppose I deserved that, Miss Davenport," Robert bridled. "And thank you for your gracious acceptance of my humble apology," he added scathingly. "I don't know why I bothered. And as for being a mill hand at my father's…"

"I shan't be one of your father's workers soon, Mr Overdale," she said quickly.

If he thought he could bully her into being repentant with the threat of losing her job, he was quite wrong.

"I'll be leaving the mill to care for my dying mother."

She knew she'd said it to make him feel guilty, especially as she'd stressed the word 'dying'. By the look of distress on his face she knew she'd succeeded.

"Anyway, I've got to go," she said, anxious to escape. "My mother might need me. Good day to you, Mr Overdale."

Jessie was confused as she hurried down the hill. Why had he looked at her like that? Why had she said such things? She'd wanted to crush his arrogance, of course. She was right to be angry about that insulting kiss, about her mother's illness and most of all about her disappearing life chances. All that had been pent up inside her had been furiously released at Robert Overdale. She was annoyed at herself for allowing him to affect her so much. As she hurried down the hill to escape, she suddenly realised the magnitude of what she had done. You didn't talk to a master's son the same way you did to a mill hand who'd taken liberties. What would her father say if he found out? Would Robert complain to his father — or even his uncle? Could he even tell them what she'd said without confessing his own guilt in the matter? Jessie felt suddenly sick. Would he take some subtle revenge on the family for her insubordination? Might Arden be in danger of getting the sack through her rash behaviour? For a moment she hesitated. She'd have to apologise. Jessie spun round on her heel, anxiously gathering her skirts to climb the hill again. But the moment she turned, she saw Robert Overdale staring down at her, an intense look in his eyes. Then he wheeled his horse and rode swiftly away.

So it was with some trepidation that Jessie went to give in her notice at the Invincible Mill. She'd spent those last days of the Wakes week anxiously worrying that her brother would get the sack because of her outburst at Robert. She could not warn her brother of what she'd done. How could she confess about the incident at the fair? To her relief, Arden seemed untroubled by his days working at the Invincible. He'd mentioned that Robert had stopped for a chat and helped clean the machine while the others had been at the lake.

"What did he say?" she'd asked.

"Oh, this and that. I think he'd have liked to be an engineer," said Arden, oblivious to the tremor in his sister's voice.

So Robert hadn't gone straight to complain to Matthias after their argument up at the Fort. But, nervous of seeing him again, she glanced anxiously around as she approached the mill. Her visit was timed for the mill's midday break so she could see all her friends before she left. She waved to them before she went up to the manager's office to tender her resignation. The girls were gathered out in the sunshine to eat their pieces, or to buy hot pies from the pie sellers who congregated round the mill at dinner time.

"I'll be sorry to see you go," said Mr Armitage, the mill manager, as she left his office. "You're one of my best spinners, Jessie. If ever you need another job, you know where to come. I'll have you back anytime after…"

He froze to an awkward silence, knowing the circumstances that would bring her back to work.

"Thank you, Mr Armitage," said Jessie. "I'll remember that."

Who knew how long her mother would last with the crippling disease that had her in its grip? Jessie was needed at home.

She was leaving the office when she noticed Taylor Walmsley at the other end of the spinning floor. Jessie hesitated. She wondered if she should go and speak to him. At the chapel the day before, he'd virtually snubbed her. The preacher's wife, Mrs Carew, was introducing her niece Miss Andrews to the chapel members after the service. Jessie had hovered hopefully for a second, but Taylor had been too busy being introduced to notice her. She'd had to hurry home. Her brother Jack and his new wife Elsie were due back from honeymoon and Jessie had to prepare a meal for them all.

Now Taylor was here on his own. Her heart thumping, she approached him.

"Hello, Mr Walmsley," said Jessie hesitantly. "I suppose you'll know I've had to give in my notice."

He was standing beside a spinning mule, obviously feigning to inspect it. He did not — or would not — glance in her direction.

"Yes. Your brother Arden mentioned it when he passed me your note of absence this morning. I'll be sorry to see you go. You were one of the best in my section."

Was that all? Was there no kind word? Was there no mention of the tentative understanding between them? He'd been about to propose once — even twice. But now, although he'd spent many a time watching her as she worked, he could hardly look her in the face.

"I'll be going then," said Jessie, as if to prompt him.

To her dismay there was no flicker of a response. With a sinking heart she walked slowly away, still hoping he might at least say something more. But he remained stubbornly silent. Jessie felt bewildered by his cold attitude as she hurried out into the sunshine. Perhaps she'd mistaken his feelings all along. Yet he'd spoken out boldly enough when Mr Carew the preacher had offered her a position as teacher in the new chapel school. Taylor had stated quite directly that no wife of his would work. Now he could not even look at her. What was wrong with the man? Mother was right — men could never make up their minds.

Out in the sunshine she was warmed by the greetings of all her friends.

"Oh, Jessie, do you have to leave us?" asked one of them, and then answered her own question. "Aye, I reckon I would too, if my Mam was poorly."

Her young piecer tried to hide his tears and wiped his eyes with a grubby cuff. He threw his arms around her and gave her a hug.

"Don't go, Jessie. It'll be 'orrible if you go. They'll cuff me and kick me and you won't be there to stop 'em. And Mr Walmsley'll shout at me. Please don't go."

"I have to, Nelson," she said stroking his tangled mop of hair. The scrawny child was named after the great navel hero. Wasn't he slight too? "You be a good boy and do as you're told and they won't be able to shout at you."

Poor lad — she was sure he'd been too young to work in the mill when he'd first arrived. But his widowed mother had no choice than to send her son to the mill, other than starve or go to the workhouse. Jessie had taken him under her wing and he was doing well now.

"I gave a penny for the pot," he said proudly through his tears.

Mary frowned at him for spoiling the surprise. She passed an enamel mug over to Jessie. It was very heavy, filled as it was with pennies and halfpennies and farthings.

"We collected this for you," she said. "Happen you'll need it."

"You shouldn't have," protested Jessie.

"Go on lass — you've put plenty o' pennies in the pot for others." So she had — for weddings, for babies, for bereavements. She may never be wed, or have a child of her own but one thing was certain, though. They had little enough themselves but the mill girls were good-hearted in helping others.

"You take it," urged Mary. "You deserve it. You've always been one of the first to help anyone who needed it."

Jessie was so touched at their kindness that tears filled her eyes. She sat on the wall beside them, clutching the pot with her tears splashing onto the copper coins.

"Eh, don't do that, they'll go rusty," joked someone.

She smiled and wiped her eyes. Despite the hard work and the long hours at the mill, she'd miss the camaraderie and laughter. She thanked them all from the bottom of her full heart. Then she insisted that Nelson take back his penny. He refused at first, but then took it with a proud smile when she told him she meant to give him a penny before she left for being the best piecer and the best help on the spinning floor. The other girls nodded their agreement. Nelson's poor mother could ill afford to lose one penny from her son's meagre wages. The factory hooter called the girls to machines for the afternoon shift and they reluctantly went back to work as she waved goodbye. Wiping her eyes with the corner of her shawl, she went home to tell her mother of their kindness.

Mary's mother, Alice, was sitting quietly at her mother's bedside. Nellie was sleeping peacefully.

"How's she been, Mrs Connolly?" asked Jessie.

"Gradely," said her neighbour with a concerned but encouraging smile. "She's resting now. And how are you, lass? Did you have a nice surprise? Our Mary told me what she'd planned."

Jessie smiled.

"Trust Mary! People are so kind."

"Don't forget, Jessie, if you need any help, anytime, I'm just at the end of the Row," said Alice.

Jessie thanked her warmly. Alice hadn't always met with kindness herself, especially when she'd married one of the Irishmen brought over to break a strike. Yet the widow was always kind to others, especially the country girls who lodged with her. She was one of the reasons why Jessie was glad to be staying in her own home.

Jessie was weeping silently over the enamel mug when her mother woke up.

"Did you see Taylor Walmsley this morning when you gave in your notice?" asked Nellie.

"Only in passing," said Jessie, her eyes sad and thoughtful. "Have you seen what the girls collected for me?"

She showed her mother the money.

"Oh, Jessie, that's wonderful," said Nellie. "You must be so well thought of. I wish you hadn't had to give up work because of me."

"Please don't worry about that, Mother," said Jessie.

She wiped a treacherous tear away, knowing Nellie was watching her closely. She tried to calm her thoughts by methodically counting the pennies on the kitchen table and wondered if she should confront Taylor Walmsley about his feelings. At least she'd know then, one way or the other. Why had he turned against her so suddenly? What had she done this time to upset him?

Chapter 10: Honora

Matthias was away in Manchester on business, taking Robert with him. Robert's plans to go to America were taking shape and they had gone to buy lightweight clothing for the journey. Honora envied him, wishing with all her heart that she could travel too.

Dependant on her aunt's generosity for her clothes and keep, she felt little better than a glorified servant. For the present, she must be content with her lot, waiting to seize a moment to fulfil her ambitions to work in medicine. She did what little she could for the family. Her suggestions to improve Matthias's gout had certainly helped, though he wasn't entirely happy to abstain from port and red meat.

Honora's horizons had shrunk to the Gorby Valley, her life limited by her own genteel poverty. Here, amid the warmth and wealth of her aunt's home, there was little to do but read, play the piano and attend to her aunt's needs. She knew many women would be content with such a life, but Honora wished for much more. She was conscious that even the mill girls at the Invincible had more freedom.

Melissa was resting at that moment and Honora chafed at her respectable idleness. She'd suggested some charitable works to her aunt, but Melissa had subtly disapproved of them. Even the cook regarded her as a nuisance when she tried to make simple herbal remedies in the kitchen. The new maid of all work, Dolly Tate, had the most insolent manner and seemed to resent her presence in the house.

Unable to settle, Honora fetched her book and walked up towards the little white temple. It stood at the edge of a small copse, with an unparalleled view of the house and town and, of course, Matthias's great love, the Invincible Mill. He was proud of his monument, a reminder to all the town of his growing status. As Honora followed the rising path, she could see the sports field blotched by yellow patches of dead grass, now that the fair had gone. The townsfolk below her milled like ants about their business. Everyone seemed busy but her. She'd been enquiring how she might train to be a nurse without upsetting her aunt. Those courageous women, Mary Seacole and Florence Nightingale, had made nursing acceptable with their great efforts in the Crimea. Even the good Queen had honoured them. Yet, Melissa relied so much on her for company and Honora hated to seem ungrateful for her aunt's hospitality. She wished with all her heart that she could be a doctor like her father, but nowhere in Britain would train women — and certainly not a penniless one. For the present she must wait, but her busy mind milled over her opportunities. There were possibilities and she might even become housekeeper to a doctor to further her ambitions.

Settling into the cool white walls of the temple, she opened her book but hardly read a word. Thoughts and memories crowded her mind, of her selfless father, of her grieving mother, of all the things she'd witnessed in the slums and was powerless to change. With her father, she'd encountered many respectable people driven by their poverty to live in the squalor and deprivation of Angel Meadow, the notorious Manchester slum. She could easily have been forced to live there too, among the disease and vice.

Honora snapped the book closed and took refuge in exercise. As she skirted the shrubbery, she heard a rustle from an overgrown path leading down to the village. She froze by a bank of delicate mauve rhododendrons, hoping to see some shy woodland creature. The creature that emerged was anything but shy. Dolly Tate's mouth dropped open in shock when she came face to face with Honora.

"And where have you been, Dolly?" demanded Honora. "Does Cook know you've been sneaking down to the town?"

"Er … er…" Dolly stammered, rapidly grasping for some excuse.

Honora noticed her quickly slipping a small basket behind her voluminous skirts and a whiff of the tasty meat pie they'd recently had for luncheon caught her attention. "Have you asked my Aunt's permission to go wandering off?"

"Er … no, Miss — the Mistress was resting. I didn't want to disturb her," said Dolly cautiously. Her eyes lit up with inspiration. "I just had to go and speak to Arden Davenport, Miss. His mother's very ill, you know. My cousin's married to his brother. I was so worried."

Dolly's blue eyes opened pathetically wide and, though she couldn't quite manage a tear, they were quite moist with emotion. Honora didn't believe a word of the excuse. She'd heard through the grapevine that Mrs Davenport was ill and that her daughter had left the mill to look after her. Her aunt had known the Davenports back when Matthias was a partner at the old Endurance, before her uncle had become so grand and mindful of his status. Melissa often enquired about mill workers she knew, though Matthias didn't encourage her. The more ambitious hands from the Endurance had followed him to the Invincible with the promise of more money. Honora knew Arden Davenport was the engineer that her cousin Robert had helped. But she didn't think for one minute that Dolly was likely to fret about his mother. Some impulse prompted her curiosity.

"Is Arden Davenport your sweetheart, Dolly?" she asked.

"Er … sort of, Miss," said Dolly demurely averting her gaze.

Honora sighed in exasperation. She'd never been in love herself, but she could sympathise with Dolly trying to slip away to see her beau — especially someone as good looking as Arden. No doubt Dolly regretted leaving the mill where he worked with so many comely lasses. Stealing food from the kitchen was a different matter altogether, though. As no evidence remained but the tantalising smell of the pie, Honora wasn't incensed enough to pursue the matter. Dolly's behaviour wasn't fair to her aunt, though, and she decided to keep a keener eye on the girl.

"Don't let me catch you sneaking away again," she said as sternly as she could.

Dolly beamed her thanks.

"Oh I won't, Miss, I promise," said Dolly fervently. "I was just so worried, Miss."

"See that you don't do it again," warned Honora. "I won't let it pass next time. It isn't fair to my aunt."

She turned towards the house and Dolly fell into step one pace behind her.

"I'm ever so grateful, Miss," she gushed.

"And how is Mrs Davenport?" asked Honora turning to face her.

Dolly looked uneasy for a second.

"Er … as well as can be expected," she said after a moment's thought.

Honora almost laughed at her ingenuity. She paused for Dolly to catch up. The girl seemed lost in thought, probably thinking about her beau.

"Do you miss working at the mill?" Honora asked.

"Nah. You can keep it," said Dolly.

"Better to work in a nice comfortable house than a noisy, dirty mill, then," suggested Honora, hoping to encourage Dolly to be more enthusiastic. "It would be a shame to lose such a position."

Honora had helped her mother many times and knew that cleaning out fires and black leading the range was no nice, comfortable job. She'd done many more dirty, onerous domestic chores besides in their genteel poverty.

"Yes, Miss Darwen," said Dolly dutifully and added, with a good bit of sycophancy, "and you and the mistress are ever so kind."

Back at the house, Dolly slipped away to the kitchen and Honora wondered if she should mention the incident to her aunt. She decided to stay silent for the moment to see if Dolly shaped herself after the warning. Melissa, now rested, came bustling downstairs.

"I've seen the carriage from the bedroom window. The boys will be home at any moment now and I haven't sorted a thing out with cook. Your uncle will be most annoyed if he isn't fed on time."

It wasn't his dinner that troubled Matthias. His trip to the cotton exchange had angered him. Over dinner, his grumbles tumbled out. Prices for raw cotton were rising sharply with rumours of the war in America. He'd been outbid on several lots by men he knew weren't even buying the cotton to manufacture but to speculate with in the hope of a quick profit.

"Parkinson says it's no better in Liverpool. He was there yesterday," he snapped. "I've had to pay top price and how I'll make a profit is anyone's guess."

To Honora's relief, he eventually fell into exasperated thought. Their meal was finished in uneasy silence

Chapter 11: Clement Comes Calling

Some days later, Melissa Overdale left the draper's shop in the town clutching a neatly tied parcel containing a pair of lilac gloves, a gift for her niece. Hearing a commotion outside the mill, she glanced up and saw a smart chaise flying up the cobbled street at a clatter. It took the corner on two wheels, nearly overturning. A dashing figure in a light coloured suit and a matching slouch hat clutched the reins and some terrified individual was clinging hard to the sides of the swinging carriage. Melissa recognised those luxurious whiskers immediately. The southern gentleman, Clement Amiens Duplege, had arrived with a flourish in Gorbydale. She watched, fascinated, as he slowed down and, with huge grin, doffed his hat to the watching mill girls with one hand while manoeuvring the horses with the other.

The girls cheered and waved at the spectacle. Melissa recognised Augustus Kearsley's alarmed face as he cautiously released his grip and rearranged himself in his seat with affronted dignity. Although they weren't expected, they were heading for Overdale House. Mindful of hospitality, Melissa wondered if there was enough food in the house to feed the extra visitors. She nipped into the butchers to order some more meat. The butcher was surprised to see the mistress of Overdale House in his shop instead of the cook and ordered his assistant to bring her a chair.

"Thank you but I've no time for that now," Melissa told him graciously. "I've just seen some unexpected visitors arriving. Would you deliver the order to the House as soon as you can?"

"Yes, ma'am. No trouble at all, ma'am. Pleasure to serve you, ma'am," said the butcher.

Melissa hurried to the mill yard where her small trap was tethered. She'd felt guilty about driving as Honora was always urging her to walk for her health. Matthias, on the other hand, thought it beneath the dignity of the Overdales to walk about in the town.

"There's plenty of walks in the grounds," he'd protested. "Why, I've even erected my temple for you to rest in."

Now she was glad she'd taken the gig. It took some time to walk the rising drive to Overdale House, especially as her waistline was thickening.

The town had grown from little more than a village and the road that passed through was awkward and narrow until it opened out in front of the mill. The mill girls bobbed a small acknowledgement to her. She listened to their chatter about her visitors as they finished their break and made their way back to their machines.

"Did you see that fancy suit?" said Mary laughing. "Fancy wearing cream linen. He'll be that mucky when he gets home."

"And what about all that red, foxy hair," said someone else. "And them moustaches. He's a bit of dandy, all right."

"Eh, he can take me for a drive anytime," giggled another girl with a saucy grin.

Robert was making Clement and Augustus welcome when Melissa arrived home.

"There is surely an abundance of fine looking young ladies in these parts," commented Clement.

The suffering Gus had barely recovered his dignity after the wild ride.

"I might have been able to judge for myself if you hadn't driven like a madman," he complained, straightening his jacket and smoothing his hair. "I was sure you'd have us out on the road."

"Courage, mon brave," said his driver with a wild laugh. "You're safe now. I do hope you don't mind us arriving unexpectedly, Mrs Overdale?" he added bowing gallantly over Melissa's proffered hand.

"Not at all. I'm delighted to show you our hospitality," said Melissa, twinkling.

She was dying to introduce Clement to Honora.

"Come and have some tea, dear," she told Gus kindly. "That will make you feel better. Those cobbles do rattle a body about so."

She linked Gus's arm and he allowed himself to be led away with a disgruntled glance back at Clement.

If Melissa Overdale was delighted to see Clement arrive, she knew her husband wouldn't be equally pleased. Although he had taken advice on investing with Gus Kearsley's father in supplying the southern states, he never liked to have his decisions rushed. Matthias frowned as Clement declared delight in his home and made his gallantries to the bemused Honora. She blushed prettily and even Gus, who rarely noticed much, gave her an appreciative glance.

"I was telling my young friend as we passed through your fine town, what handsome young ladies you have around these parts. Why, they could even give our southern belles a run for their money."

This was praise indeed from someone for whom the south was the epitome of everything superlative.

"They are bonny, of course, but they're only mill girls," said Gus Kearsley with a sneer. "Miss Honora is a lady and our ladies are the match of anywhere in the whole world."

Honora looked dubious about this compliment and Melissa had the uneasy feeling that Gus was more concerned with besting Clement than praising her niece. She remembered the pasty girls at the Kearsleys' dinner party and secretly thought many mills girls were vastly prettier.

With guests to feed and entertain, Melissa bustled away to arrange the meal with her cook. Even at such short notice, she was determined to put on a spread to match the Kearsleys. In the event, she surpassed herself. Though the food wasn't as fancy, it was certainly hotter and more delicious. She'd even persuaded Honora to change from her usual black into something lilac. The dress she'd given her niece was very becoming.

Dolly, too, looked trim and unobtrusive in black with a dazzling white apron and cap. After her unexpected encounter with Honora she seemed to be more helpful. She'd worked hard arranging all the crystal and china on the dining room table. Though the flower arrangement was not as magnificent as the Kearsleys', the plated silver shone just as brightly as the genuine article. The table looked a picture to Melissa's delight. But to her dismay, the food and the company were not enough to make the dinner go smoothly.

Gus began the decline by asking Clement how soon they could go to America.

"The sooner the better," said the American. "We need to fill and sail as many ships as we can before the northern blockade begins to bite at sea."

"Won't it be dangerous?" asked Melissa in alarm.

"Why no, ma'am," said Clement with an easy, reassuring smile. "Them Yankees ain't prepared for war any more than we are. I'm reliably informed that they've barely one hundred ships, and the south has over three thousand miles of coastline.

What with the Mississippi Delta and bayous and islands — all fine hiding places for a small ship — they don't stand a chance. Sooner we can fill those holds, the better. I've a shipment of arms arriving in Liverpool tomorrow, that's why I've thrown myself on your hospitality today."

"I thought the British Government had declared itself neutral," said Honora boldly.

"Why, Miss Honora, so they have. But if and when they open those cases, they won't be finding guns. When they look inside they might find Paris gowns, or perhaps bottles of your fine Scottish whisky. An acquaintance of mine made a fortune shipping corsages to the south — you'll pardon my indelicacy."

"Corsages?" asked Melissa, wondering why the southern states should import flowers.

"I think you English ladies call them corsets — or stays. Why, he paid for his ship with the profit he made. southern belles are mightily proud of their figures."

"Oh I see," said Melissa with an amused smile. "I suppose the guns would be well hidden."

"If the customs men found out, you could be in terrible trouble," insisted Honora. "You would be breaking the law, and your cargo and ship impounded."

"Miss Honora, don't you fret yourself. There ain't customs men enough to examine all the cargoes leaving Liverpool — that's if they care to look at all. And if they do see something they shouldn't, then maybe their eyesight will dim a little when a few notes are waved in front of them."

Honora was outraged.

"Are you suggesting that our customs men are corrupt?" she challenged him.

"Every man has his price," said Clement smoothly. "It is common knowledge that your Prime Minister himself backs the south. It's only those old women in his cabinet that prevent him declaring for us."

"And the threat that the Union will invade Canada if he does," said Matthias.

"I think it's a disgrace that a government who could honour William Wilberforce, that great destroyer of slavery, could even think of backing a slave-owning nation," said Honora, staunchly. "I've been reading Miss Harriet Beecher Stowe's 'Uncle Tom's Cabin' and I can't believe how cruel and…"

"Miss Harriet Beecher Stowe has spent hardly two whole weeks in the south," said Clement with a steely stare and enforced politeness. "What would she know about slavery? I'll bet she hasn't written a book about those poor creatures slaving away in the sweatshops of the north. Why, if a man pays good money for a slave, he ain't going to treat him like a beast — he'll treat him as kindly as any good horse."

Honora gasped at this remark and Melissa felt uneasy too, though she felt she must, in loyalty, agree with her husband's views.

"After all, we do run the mill with slave picked cotton," Robert said with an apologetic smile at his cousin.

"And if a man's paid good money for a slave, I think it's a rum do to have him stolen from under his nose by some interfering government," added Gus Kearsley arrogantly.

Honora's cheeks turned crimson and she looked as if she was about to explode with anger. Melissa didn't like this heated conversation one bit. Her eyes widened in an urgent appeal to her son.

"How long would a voyage to America take us?" asked Robert, to change the subject.

"Depends on the ship," said their southern guest, settling back and watching Honora warily. "If a ship is purely sail it could take the best part of a month, depending on the wind. Of course, a ship with an engine will halve that. We go first to Nassau in the Bahamas in large ships and then unload our cargo onto smaller ships. That way we will be more invisible to the Union Navy. I'll show you gentlemen a fine time in Nassau. I am acquainted with some of the best families there. They surely love to meet young gentlemen from England."

Gus preened himself and Robert had a shine in his eyes that left his mother uneasy.

"I think we'll leave the gentlemen to their port," said Melissa pleasantly. "Come, my dear, I'd like you to play me that pretty tune you were practising this morning."

Matthias nodded at his wife and gave his niece a grim, wary look. Melissa guessed that Honora had ruined her chances in attracting Clement with her unsettling views and opposition to the south. Yet, Melissa could still coax her to show off her accomplishments. She held out her hand and Honora could not refuse it. The gentlemen stood and bowed as they left.

Melissa paused at the door before she closed it.

"That little lady has a lot of spirit," she heard Clement say. "She may be mistaken in her ideas, but she sure has spirit."

Her husband snorted.

"Though I have to say," Clement added. "You must be sure to keep her out of the way of anyone who might jeopardise our little enterprise. A word in the wrong ear could bring it tumbling down and we wouldn't want that now, would we?"

Matthias and his guests talked long into the evening and made their plans, oblivious to the tinkling of the piano drifting through from the drawing room. Melissa continually encouraged her niece to play on, though Honora did not play well. Her mind churned with distraction by what she had heard. The gentlemen did not join them. Matthias was too wary of what might reoccur. In the end, Melissa admitted defeat and she and Honora went, tired and uneasy to their beds, Honora to restlessly rail at man's injustice to his fellow man, Melissa to stare into the darkness and worry about her son.

Chapter 12: The White Temple

Everyone had gone to their beds and the household grew silent as, one after another, the lamps were extinguished and the windows darkened. Slipping silently through the house, Dolly had been told to lock all the doors. To her annoyance, when she came to the billiard room, she found the French windows open. The evening was warm and she found the American visitor out on the terrace smoking a large cigar, blowing fragrant curls of smoke towards the bright moon. She'd had a busy evening and was tired. Here he was, frustrating her efforts to get to her own bed.

Dolly Tate hovered for a moment, her white apron luminous in the moonlight. She coughed pointedly and he turned towards her.

"Can I get you anything, sir?" she asked.

Clement smiled.

"I'm fine, little lady, just enjoying this fine evening. Folks certainly go to bed early round here. I was hoping for a game of cards to round off the evening. Tell me, what is that white building over there?" Dolly moved beside him and followed his pointing finger.

"Oh, that's Mr Overdale's temple, sir. It's very elegant, don't you think?"

"I certainly do. Is it far to walk?"

"Oh no, sir, and you get a fine view of the town."

Dolly glanced up at the fine southern gentleman beside her, fascinated by his whiskers. He smelt of tobacco and whisky and a subtle hint of some exotic hair oil.

"I can take you if you like."

He looked rich. He might even give her a florin for being helpful.

"That would be kind, though it's very late."

She smiled up at him.

"I don't mind."

Lifting the small oil lamp that she carried to secure the dark house each night, she beckoned and he followed her along the winding path. Dolly frequently turned to smile up at him, her face palely lit by the moon and the dim glow of the lamp. The temple gleamed white and mysterious. Dolly led Clement into its secret shelter and showed him the view over the darkened town, the ribbons of slate shining silver in the moonlight. Beneath them, the houses crouched in darkness, black but for the faint gleam of a candlelit window. Clement smiled down at Dolly and moved beside her. He stroked her cheek, obviously misunderstanding her willingness to accompany him at such a late hour. Like a mesmerised rabbit she stared up at him and, in her confusion, did not protest as he pulled her close to him. His scratchy whiskers brushed her cheek as he kissed the warm depth of her neck. A bewildering cloud of lavender hair oil, stale whisky and cigar smoke engulfed her and a questing hand dragged her apron aside and fumbled in the folds of her skirt. She tried to protest but she was stifled by the folds of his jacket and waistcoat as she was crushed into his chest. She tried to wriggle free but he seemed to take that as a sign of encouragement and pushed her hard against the cold white stone again and again. Dolly winced and gave a little cry when her mouth burst free. But it was too late to protest.

"Why thank you, ma'am," he said finally with a breathless low chuckle. "Much appreciated."

Swiftly he adjusted his clothing and, with a small bow, headed off into the night. Dolly stared after him in horror then slumped down limply onto the cold marble bench, too bewildered to cry. It had all happened so quickly. Her body felt bruised and abused, her most intimate parts chafed and sore. She squeezed her knees together to expel the memory of what had happened. What had she done? Staring out into the darkness in bewilderment and shock, a sudden panic engulfed her. A hundred agitated thoughts assailed her tired mind. No one must ever find out what had happened. Her reputation would surely be in tatters. She would certainly be dismissed from Overdale House. If she was sacked, her family would starve. How could she have been so naive, so stupid? Clement Duplege had taken full advantage of her stupidity.

Chapter 13: A Farewell

Arden despondently walked up the hill back to his home. News had travelled fast that the Master of the Invincible Mill had returned from the Manchester Cotton Exchange with a meagre supply of American cotton. Rumours of war swept the mill like an unsettling wind. To supplement his stock, Mr Overdale had also ordered a delivery of the cheaper Surat cotton from India to mix with it. It was awful stuff and the rubbish, and even stones, left in the cotton to make up the weight, damaged the machinery. Arden had previously repaired some broken carding machines used for Surat. The outlook was not good.

Then the manager had called the overlookers and engineers into his office and told them that on no account was the merest scrap of cotton to be wasted. The spinning mules must be adjusted to accommodate the coarser cotton. All the hands knew that, even with adjustments, the short staple cotton would snap and tangle. The spinners would be frustrated and production delayed. They grumbled amongst themselves but left the mill in impotent despair. Nothing could be done.

"I reckon there's going to be layoffs in the near future," Arden wearily told his father as they sat down for their meal. "We can't work with that poor stuff and there doesn't seem much hope of new supplies."

"Aye," sighed Jacob. "I've been talking with Mr Gorman over the news. He was kind enough to let me have his old newspaper. The southern states say they'll stockpile their raw cotton. They're hoping to blackmail our government into backing the south. And the north are blockading their ships at sea. It's said there's four months of cotton in England, but I don't reckon Matthias Overdale has that much in stock. He's always cut his cloth close. Mr Gorman's been out to some of the spinning mills to see what they had to offer, but some of the suppliers are putting their prices up already."

The old Endurance was a weaving mill and would hopefully be able to keep working for longer.

"Why doesn't he get his yarn from the Invincible?" asked Eddie who'd been labouring over some schoolwork at the table.

Arden grinned at his father and Jacob stared at his son with amazement.

"By heck — the lad's been taking some notice all along! I thought all our mill talk went over his empty head. We'll have him at the grammar school yet," he said laughing. "No, son, the Invincible Mill doesn't spin the fine thread that we need at the Endurance to weave damask. The Invincible spins coarse thread like 40s for weaving cheap cotton. Matthias Overdale reckoned that there was more money to be had in calico — but the world is full of coarse cotton at the moment. The Endurance uses thread as fine as 120. Hopefully, we stand more of a chance in the world selling fine cotton cloth — and damask is always in demand."

He fingered the tablecloth that Jessie had spread, with its shiny design of self-coloured roses and ivy. "Don't worry, lad," Jacob told his older son. "There will always be work for good engineers elsewhere in the country." Arden hoped it wouldn't come to that. "Only, don't mention anything to your mother just yet," added his father quietly, cocking his head in the direction of the parlour, where Nellie was resting.

After their meal, Arden unusually made to help his sister with the pots. Jessie laughed at his offer and told him to leave them for her to see to, but he was determined to ask her about Taylor Walmsley as his mother had urged him.

"You work hard enough," said Jessie, shooing him away. "Go and take the air while you can."

Reluctantly, Arden left to take her advice and a welcome break away from the noise and dust of the factory and the hacking cough and coarse breathing of his mother at home. Nellie struggled to be brave but they all knew her efforts to fill her lungs were becoming harder and harder. Their nerves strained as they willed her to keep breathing.

"Come on, young shaver," Arden told Eddie. "Let's go and see if we can find any Roman coins up at the Fort."

He didn't feel like being alone to dwell on what might happen in the future. Eddie was only too glad to escape from his books.

High on the hill, the air was fresh, with a soft breeze blowing over the valley.

Arden had borrowed Jacob's spade and was digging among the rocks, while his young brother rifled among the rubble with a trowel.

"Eh up, we've got a visitor," said Eddie, stretching his back and glancing down the hill. "It's Master Overdale's son."

Robert Overdale was carefully guiding his fine horse, Surefoot, along the rough path towards the brothers. He stopped to greet them. "Arden," said Robert.

"Master Robert," said Arden with a polite nod.

"What are you doing?" asked Robert dismounting.

"We're digging for coins, Mister," said Eddie eagerly. "Roman ones. Our Arden found one once. It had the head of an emperor and everything."

"That sounds very interesting," Robert told the excited boy. "Perhaps I'll come and help you dig one day. But I'm going to

America in a few days, so it won't be for a while," he added proudly.

"America!" said Arden. "They say that's a dangerous place to be at present, though I don't suppose the north will be affected much by any fighting."

"It's the south I'm going to," said Robert. "I expect you saw our American visitor, Mr Clement Duplege, arriving."

"Aye, I reckon the whole town did," said Arden, chuckling.

"Well, I'm to be a guest at his brother's plantation," Robert told him with a hint of pride.

Arden's eyes narrowed. It was Eddie who echoed aloud his brother's thoughts.

"Are you going to see the black slaves," he asked earnestly. "Will you be able to set some free? Reverend Carew says it's wicked to keep poor men chained like that. He says God made all men free and he says William Wilberforce was a great hero. Our Jessie has been reading *Uncle Tom's Cabin* to me and Mother. I'll bet you'll be able to free some of them at least," he finished.

Robert bridled.

"What other men believe is their own business," he snapped. "Mr Duplege says that men are treated just as badly in the sweat shops of North America. When you're older you'll understand the ways of business."

Arden bit his lip and stayed reluctantly silent. This was the boss's son. He could lose his job for arguing with him. He was saved by the welcome appearance of his sister coming up the hill.

Robert stepped from behind Arden to watch her approaching. She paused and wiped her brow with the effort of climbing the slope in the warm evening sun. Then as she glanced up, she wavered in her stride. Taking a deep breath, she carried on until she reached her brothers.

"Good evening, Mr Overdale," she said with a quick bob, then quickly turned to Arden and Eddie. "Mother sent me to look for you both," she told her brothers. "Have you found any Roman bits, then?"

"No," said Arden shortly. "Master Robert has been telling us he's off to America to be a guest at a slave plantation."

He emphasised the word 'slave'.

"Oh!" said Jessie hesitantly.

"He says that what a man believes is his own business," added Arden with disapproval.

"Oh!"

"My father is doing the best he can to provide supplies for his mill," said Robert tersely. "He has to deal with whoever he can or you lot would be out on the streets without work. If you feel so strongly about the slaves, perhaps you should be fighting for the north."

Arden bristled as Robert said 'you lot' and the mill owner's son blushed red, aware of his blunder.

"If you'll excuse me, I promised to visit my Uncle Eli at the Endurance before I leave for America," he stammered.

Robert leapt onto his horse and with a curious pleading glance at Jessie, hastily rode off towards his uncle's mill.

"You don't think he'll say anything against Father to Mr Eli, do you?" asked Jessie anxiously.

"He can say what he likes," said Arden, jutting his chin out in defiance. "Mr Eli hates slave owners as much as Father does. When I was an apprentice at the Endurance, I often heard him saying how much he regretted that the cotton was produced by slaves."

"Oh good," said Jessie with some relief.

Arden watched his sister curiously. She'd seemed dismayed by Robert's opinions of course, but there was something else in her eyes he couldn't quite fathom. Her very open face showed all her emotions and he knew how hard she struggled to hide her despair and pity in front of their mother.

"I'll leave you to your digging," she said quietly. "I'd better go back and see if Mother is all right."

"Has Taylor Walmsley arrived yet?" asked Arden.

"Taylor? Why?" said Jessie in surprise.

"Mother asked me to give him a message to call on her," said Arden. "I thought you knew."

"No, no. She never mentioned it," said Jessie in confusion. "I'd better go and see what it's all about."

With that she left them and headed down the hill.

Chapter 14: Taylor Walmsley Pays a Visit

Jessie paused for breath as she hurried down the hill. Down below on the valley road, she watched Robert ride out of sight, her feelings bewildered. She'd been half posed to apologise to him for her previous outburst, but now matters had only been made worse. Why did Robert Overdale always affect her in this way? The moment she'd seen him at the Fort, she'd wanted to turn and run but felt she'd look foolish. Yet, deep down something had spurred her on, a compelling wish to speak to him. Once again their meeting had turned awkward. This time he really might speak out against Arden.

To add to her worries, she guessed why Mother had insisted she go in search of her brothers.

"Don't hurry back. You've been cooped up enough all day," Nellie had said, although Father had already left for a meeting at the chapel and she would be left on her own.

Now it was obvious why she'd wanted Jessie out of the way. Nellie had been determined to talk to Taylor alone. Jessie made a dash down the hill, slipping and slithering on the loose stones in her anxiety. Breathless and trembling, she cannoned into Taylor as she rushed through the front door. For a second he held her by the shoulders and looked searchingly deep into her eyes — then he released her and stepped aside.

"Excuse me, Miss Davenport. I've got some business to attend to at the chapel."

She knew it wasn't an excuse as it was the same meeting her father was going to.

"Oh — thank you for coming to see Mother," she stammered.

Taylor nodded abruptly and, his face grave, he left her bewildered and alone.

Jessie rushed in to see her mother. Nellie could not look her daughter in the face.

"I'm sorry, Jessie. I'm so sorry. I shouldn't have interfered."

Nellie was gasping with misery and the effort to talk. Jessie put a comforting arm round her mother's thin shoulders.

"Mother, don't upset yourself. What has Taylor said to you? If he's upset you I'll…"

Nellie limply raised a hand to halt her daughter's anger.

"Oh, Jessie lass," she sobbed and coughed, desperately struggling for breath in her anxiety, tears welling in her eyes. She grasped for a rag nearby and, when she raised her head, her daughter saw it speckled in crimson blood, despite her mother's attempts to conceal it.

Nellie tried to calm herself to catch her breath, her sobbing subsiding slowly.

"Please tell me you're not meeting Robert Overdale on the sly?" she wheezed in no more than a whisper.

"What!" Jessie exploded. "Who on earth told you that?"

"Taylor Walmsley said you'd been seen with Robert Overdale up at the Fort." Nellie gasped on, halting but determined. "He said he'd had his suspicions before. He'd seen you at the fair with young Overdale and you were very flustered, as if you knew you shouldn't be there with him." Her chest heaved with the effort to speak. "Oh, love, you mustn't get tangled up with someone above your station. You know where it can lead and…" She paused again and fought for breath, her eyes pleading for understanding. "There's so many girls go astray and get abandoned by…"

"Mother!" said Jessie sharply, anxious to stop the torrent of unjust accusations. She instantly regretted her sharpness to the ailing Nellie. "Oh, Mother, I've no more been meeting Robert Overdale on the sly than I've been … out drinking grog with Reverend Carew!" She stroked her mother's hot and clammy brow. "If I was out on the sly, I wouldn't be seeing him at the Fort where everyone in Gorbydale can gawp at you — very sly that is!"

Nellie sighed.

"Taylor seemed so certain," she said weakly. "I couldn't believe it myself when he said."

Her mother looked so ill and miserable, Jessie felt guilty that she'd been angry with her. Holding Nellie's trembling hand she tried to comfort her.

"Oh, Mother, it is true that I met Robert Overdale up there but only by accident. I'd gone out for some fresh air — that was all. He's often riding up there on that horse of his. He's just been with Arden and Eddie at the Fort — they'll tell you that."

She didn't explain his presence at the Wakes Fair though. That stolen kiss still made her feel hot and embarrassed whenever she thought about it. It seemed to come unbidden into her thoughts with increasing frequency, though she was sure she didn't welcome it.

"Why don't you explain to Taylor?" whispered Nellie, her voice so tired. "If he thinks anything of you…"

"I just don't know what Taylor Walmsley thinks about me," said Jessie with exasperation. "He blows hot and cold all the time. He called me a hoyden once…"

"Never!" protested Nellie. "Well of all the cheek!"

"All because I went on the swing boats with Mary." Jessie shook her head. "I've a feeling that I can't do right for doing wrong in Taylor Walmsley's eyes. I think he wants a wife that's meek and mild, who'll do as she's told. I don't think that's me, Mother. Best leave it."

"Oh, Jessie, I wish I'd never said anything," fretted Nellie.

"Please don't mither yourself, Mother," said her daughter gently. "Don't you always say 'What's meant for you, won't pass you by'?"

"Aye, lass. Perhaps he'll come to his senses," said the poor ailing woman, comforted a little by her daughter's common sense. "I just wanted to see you settled before…"

She lay back, exhausted by emotion and the effort to speak. She didn't need to elaborate.

That night, alone in her bedroom, Jessie could hear Nellie's hacking cough echoing throughout the house. She wished with all her heart that her mother had not interfered, but the damage was done now. She wondered if she was more upset about Taylor's withdrawal of his tentative offer, or his blackening of her character. He was a good catch, there was no doubt about that. He'd even be easier to love if only he'd bend a little. Yet, he seemed incapable of loving her for herself alone.

Jessie thought long and deeply about Taylor. She admitted she'd been flattered by his attentions. She knew she could make him a good wife. But did she love him? How did love make you feel? Her friends seemed overwhelmed by feelings for their sweethearts and she knew she'd never felt like that. The nearest thing she'd felt was a mixture of unsettling excitement and annoyance whenever she met Robert Overdale — and those were feelings she fervently wished would go away.

Dismissing such thoughts from her mind, she had more distressing news to think about. The news her father had brought home from the chapel meeting had upset her. She'd known something was wrong the moment Father refused a cup of tea and asked to speak to her alone moments after arriving home.

"I'm sorry to tell you, Jessie dear, that the minister's wife has asked that her niece Miss Andrews be considered for the post of assistant teacher at the new school," Jacob told her gravely.

Jessie's heart and hopes fell. Jacob was as disappointed as she was. She hadn't realised the significance of the chapel meeting. Taylor had been there too. Had he mentioned to some of the more petty minded members that a hoyden who chased after the boss's son wasn't fit to teach children. She had never thought him vindictive, but was just sick at heart that her chance to teach had been snatched away. Jessie loved teaching Sunday school. She knew she was good with the children. She'd had enough practise keeping Eddie in order.

"They knew you'd be tied up with Mother," Jacob told her sadly.

"But surely they didn't need to appoint anyone until the school opens in September," Jessie protested.

"Well you know Mrs Carew, she always likes to be in charge. I suspect the novelty of having her niece living with them is wearing off. Personally, I think she prefers the idea of her niece living in the school cottage. She seems the same bossy type as Mrs Carew — and two such women in one household…"

"Me and Mother manage all right," protested Jessie.

"Aye — 'cos only one of you is in charge of the kitchen at one time," Jacob said with a wry smile.

Though they'd joked about Mrs Carew's bossiness, inside, Jessie's heart was sinking. She tried not to let her father know how disappointed she was, though he had probably guessed. His great ambition was for her to be a teacher. Now she must not let Nellie know how her illness had affected her daughter's life and chances. Jessie struggled to be brave but, as Arden had guessed, it was an increasing strain to appear cheerful. In the dark, a feeling of hopelessness overwhelmed her. Below her, she heard her father quietly comforting Nellie. Alone and lonely in her bedroom, Jessie let hot tears flow unchecked. She felt like a discarded empty cotton husk, devoid of hope and slowly filling up with despair and disappointment.

Chapter 15: Melissa Goes Calling

On the docks in Liverpool, the day of Robert's departure to America had arrived. Melissa strained her eyes and waved her tear-soaked handkerchief towards a decreasing spot on the wavering horizon.

"Come along, Mother," said Matthias kindly, putting a comforting arm round his wife's shoulder. "The lad's looking after our business. He's got to learn sometime."

"But it's so far away," Melissa's voice trembled as she stifled a sob.

Deep down she was angry with her husband. He'd wanted Robert to be brought up a gentleman, not to soil his hands with commerce, and now the boy was ill-equipped to conduct business, and in the midst of a war. She felt helpless and afraid for her son. In her heart, she knew he was eager to go to America. He'd been beguiled by Clement Duplege's talk of his new and thrusting country. Robert would surely have resented her for holding him back. His father was right, it was a good opportunity for him to see another side of the business, one that Matthias himself had never witnessed. Yet, Melissa had the uneasy feeling that Robert was glad to go to escape his father's constant complaining. He hadn't been so enthusiastic for a long time, elated at the thought of travelling. At the same time, she knew he wanted to impress and please Matthias for once. It was a frustratingly tangled relationship and she could only stand by helpless, and watch. She hoped this separation would do them both good. Surely they would appreciate one another more on Robert's return, especially if he succeeded in bringing cotton back to the Invincible.

Standing by in quiet support, Honora squeezed Melissa's hand in sympathy.

"Robert will be home in no time at all, Aunt dear," she said. "And he's promised to write. Just think of all the things he'll see — what adventures he'll be able to tell us."

While her son was away from home, Melissa fretted and Honora endeavoured to keep her occupied.

"Perhaps you might visit some of Uncle Matthias's people," she suggested. "The gentry do it all the time and I'm sure my uncle would think it fitting."

"Do you think so, dear?" said her aunt. "Won't they think it an intrusion?"

"I'm sure they'd feel honoured, Aunt dear. What about Mrs Davenport? You knew her at the Endurance, didn't you? She's quite poorly and I'm sure Cook could provide us with some tasty morsels to cheer her up."

"Nellie Davenport," said Melissa, smiling for once as she remembered. "Yes I know Nellie. And my brother Eli is very fond of Jacob, her husband, too. He said Jacob was the backbone of the old Endurance when he and Matthias first started up the business. Jacob's a master weaver, you see, and clever too. He took to those jacquard looms like a duck to water. My father was a master weaver. They understand the cloth. It makes all the difference. Yes, perhaps we should go and see Nellie."

Despite Honora suggesting they walk, Melissa insisted on taking the gig. She could see Weavers Row from the height of Overdale House and her drive and Nellie's street both looked daunting to her. Few vehicles passed up the Row and Jessie promptly opened the door at their knock.

"I do hope we haven't come at an inconvenient time?" said Melissa. "I've come to enquire after your mother."

"Do please come in, Mrs Overdale," said Jessie.

She made a makeshift sort of bob as she removed her apron. "Mother does love company. She'll be pleased to see you."

As Melissa entered into the cottage, her rustling skirts filled the whole doorway. Behind her, Honora offered Jessie a basket with a shy smile.

"There's calves foot jelly and beef tea and some other dainties for the invalid," she said.

"Thank you so much," said Jessie taking the basket. She ushered them in to see Nellie. "Look who's here, Mother," she called gently.

Nellie opened her eyes slowly — then wide with shock.

"Oh, Mrs Overdale. Oh, Jessie … oh what a surprise … oh how kind," stammered Nellie and began to cough and gasp with the effort.

"Please don't distress yourself, Mrs Davenport," said Honora taking her hand gently. "We don't want to tax your strength. We won't stay long. My aunt thought it might be nice to pay a few social calls."

"Please sit down," wheezed Nellie as graciously as she could manage. Jessie flicked the parlour chairs with her apron although there wasn't a speck of dust in the parlour. "Will you take some tea?"

"If it's not too much trouble?" said Melissa as she settled herself down after the bumpy ride up Weavers Row.

"Don't forget to get out the best china," whispered Nellie.

Jessie nodded and disappeared into the kitchen. Moments later they heard some loud whacks as she tried to knock chips from the cone of solid sugar. She appeared with a tray of tea and Melissa took one of the delicate cups with gratitude.

"Just what I need, a nice cup of tea," she said, smiling.

Honora picked up the book next to Nellie's bed.

"Look, Aunt, this is the book I was telling you about, 'Uncle Tom's Cabin'. Have you enjoyed it?" she asked Jessie eagerly.

"We certainly have so far," said Jessie with a smile. "We've been reading it in the evening with our Eddie. Though, I did wonder if it might be a little sad for Mother … er … just at present. But you love it so much we've been reading further on during the day, haven't we, Mother?"

Nellie smiled and nodded.

Honora noticed other books in the glass bookcase.

"I see you love reading just as I do," she said. "Do you like Mr Dickens?"

"We do indeed, don't we, Mother? We've been reading Mr Pickwick again, haven't we? It cheers us up so."

"Have you read *Bleak House* yet?" asked Honora. Jessie shook her head. "Then I'll lend you my copy," decided their guest.

"That would be very kind," said Jessie eagerly.

The girls chatted about books until Nellie showed signs of tiring. She signalled to Jessie to take her teacup before she dropped it. Her visitors politely drank up and made to go.

"I think it's time we went home, Honora dear," decided Melissa. "Your uncle will be wondering where we've got to."

She smiled to herself. Matthias was so wrapped up in his mill that he rarely asked what she'd been doing all day.

Jessie accompanied them to the door.

"I hope we haven't tired your mother too much," said Melissa.

"She does tire easily," Jessie told her, "but she'll be so pleased you've called. And thank you for all the nice treats. Mother will really enjoy them."

She handed Honora the empty basket.

"I'll try and call tomorrow with the book," said Honora. "If that's convenient, of course."

"Oh please do," said Jessie eagerly.

Melissa took the girl's hands in her own.

"I'm so sorry your mother is so poorly, my dear. I remember her so well when we were both young at the Endurance. She was never robust but she was always in good spirits. God bless and keep you both, and your father too."

"Thank you so much, Mrs Overdale," said Jessie. "Your visit will have done her a power of good."

Melissa was quiet as they rode home, remembering the days when she'd been a young bride and Nellie a young mother. They'd often passed the time of day when Nellie called to the Endurance with Jacob's dinner. Without her own mother, Melissa had relied on Nellie's advice and good common sense when she'd had her own baby son. Those were the carefree days, before Matthias had become defensive of his status as Master of the Invincible.

Chapter 16: Aboard Ship

Once aboard ship, Robert felt free and alive with the sea breeze ruffling his hair. A host of opportunities lay before him and he was glad to be out in the Mersey, heading into the Irish Sea and on out to the wide ocean. Beside him, Gus pointed out Liverpool landmarks to a stubbornly unimpressed Clement.

After countless days on the endless open water of the Atlantic, they reached land. Weeks after he'd left home, Robert wrote to his mother from the thriving port of Nassau. He'd told her of the whales and dolphins, flying fish and beautiful birds he'd seen on the journey. He'd written of the hospitality they'd received at the houses that Clement introduced them to in Nassau. He'd said nothing of the cramped conditions aboard ship or the danger he might face. Nor did he mention the hundreds of gun parts he'd seen uncovered from the straw in crates full of Staffordshire pots shipped from Liverpool.

His friend Gus sulked for much of the journey. He'd foolishly lost a lot of money gambling with Clement during their voyage. The kindly captain had taken Robert to one side and quietly warned him that Duplege was well-known as a riverboat gambler and for his friend to be careful. Though Robert tried to warn Gus, his friend stubbornly refused to listen and continued to play cards, though he was an indifferent player. Robert was barely able to keep the peace between the two men as Clement subtly crowed about his winnings and made little jokes about his friend's losses. Gus's simmering resentment poisoned the atmosphere of the journey. Somehow, they managed to reach Nassau without coming to blows.

In the bustling port of Nassau, Clement realised he was playing a dangerous game by alienating the pampered son of a prominent shipbuilder. He made the effort to regain Gus's good graces by introducing him to the family of his shipping agent. The agent's two lovely daughters were more than happy to flirt with the two young gentlemen from England, though their eyes flashed towards Clement whenever he was around.

Surrounded by colour and warmth and the easier manners of the colony, Robert's anxiety soon dissolved along with memories of grey skies and grey places. It was easy to flirt with such delightful girls and his previous gaucheness in speaking to young ladies faded fast in their company.

All too soon, their idyll came to an end. They'd been strolling down to the docks each day to watch the cargoes being unloaded and stowed away into their new vessels. Clement was often away seeking any news of the war from incoming ships.

"We'll have more chance of outrunning the Yankees when we travel in the steamer," Clement explained as they watched the guns loaded into a squat, small ship painted grey to move invisibly in dangerous waters. "The rest of the cargo can go in the sailing ships. If the Yankees board them they won't find anything to trouble them."

Unwilling to trust Duplege, Robert planned to travel with him. Gus decided the sailing ship would offer more comfort and so the company parted for a while.

Relieved of his burden of keeping the peace, Robert was determined to concentrate on business. Somehow, he must prove his worth to his father. His mission was more important now. Matters would be deteriorating back at the Invincible Mill as there was barely three weeks' supply of raw cotton in the basement when he'd left. The bulk was Surat cotton and almost impossible to spin. In Gorbydale, there would already be layoffs among the mill hands. Unbidden, the Davenports came immediately to mind. They weren't the only family who relied on his father for work but they were the ones he had always known, kind Jacob, once friendly Arden and, of course, Jessie; Jessie who angered and intrigued him at the same bewildering time. The Nassau girls were pretty but he could not help comparing their luxurious black hair with the gleam of Jessie's fine dark tresses, the healthy glow of their tanned skin with the delicate porcelain of her cheeks. The Davenports might disapprove when he'd boasted about his visit to the plantation but they depended on him to find raw cotton. Well, he'd see the conditions for himself soon enough. He'd try hard to secure supplies. Robert was determined to show his father, and all of them, that he was not just an idle rich boy. If the mill went bankrupt, he wouldn't even be able to claim that.

Their next voyage began without incident, though the ship was cramped and uncomfortable, the smell of hot oil permeating everywhere. The relentless pounding of the engine seemed to echo loudly over the flat listless water. The air was heavy and oppressive and as they approached the American South, the mood on board became tense, the crew more watchful. Robert stood in the all engulfing blackness on the deck of the throbbing steamer, peering anxiously into the darkness, searching for any sign of a light.

"Seen anything yet?" muttered Clement Duplege beside him.

"Nothing."

He could not even see the three small ships following behind with more precious cargo.

Robert might have been blind for all he could see in the black night. Even the stars seem to have deserted the sky. The only dim light came from the faint glimmering trail of their wake. With nothing to see but blackness, Robert's thoughts wandered back over his journey. He hoped the glowing report of his voyage that he'd sent to Melissa from Nassau would reassure her, and he wondered if he should have accompanied Gus on the sailing ship. Peering ahead, eyes narrowed, he searched for the vital signal to guide them to land.

"Look — a light," he called in surprise, pointing out over the water. Then he hesitated. "How can you be sure that it's a friend and not an enemy?"

Clement looked grim.

"It had better be a friend."

Robert fervently hoped he was right. In the dark he heard a click and recognised it as the safety catch of a gun.

Chapter 17: Honora Keeps Her Promise

Honora was as good as her word and walked up Weavers Row with her book.

She was pleased that she'd suggested that Melissa should visit people. Her aunt had found something to occupy her instead of worrying about Robert.

"I suppose I could visit Mrs Walmsley," Melissa suggested. "Her husband was manager of the Invincible for quite a while before he died. Her son works there now."

Honora didn't relish that call. She'd spoken to the woman a few times and found her cold and haughty. Honora had enjoyed her visit to the Davenports though, and was happy to find a kindred spirit in Jessie.

She was welcomed into the house by a smiling Jessie and offered tea. She hadn't been expected so early and the parlour was unable to be used, but Honora seemed quite at home in the kitchen as Nellie slept. They were polite with each other at first, then they began chatting like old friends about the books they'd read.

"I'll bring Mrs Gaskell's 'Mary Barton' for you to read when you've read Mr Dickens," said Honora with an air of conspiracy. "My aunt doesn't know I have a copy. She's read that it's a bit unsuitable, being about a mill girl and all. I'm sure Uncle Matthias wouldn't have it in the house!" she added with a chuckle. "He might not approve but I'm sure you'll enjoy it as I do. And I have 'North and South', too."

Jessie beamed.

"Would you?" she said. "I've little time to go to the lending library nowadays. And there isn't always much choice. Father recommends books of sermons, but your books are much more to my liking, Miss Darwen," she added with a chuckle. "It's wonderful to be able to read something new to take my mind off…"

She fell silent. Honora nodded in sympathy as she remembered the misery of watching her own dear mother's health failing. "Have you tried putting a drop of eucalyptus oil in boiling water and letting your mother breathe the fumes," she suggested. "It might help. My father often tried it on his patients. It couldn't cure them of course, but it did help them to breathe easier."

"Euca…" Jessie tried to remember.

"Eucalyptus — it's from a tree in Australia. I might have some in Papa's bag," said Honora. "I kept some of his medical stuff — well, you never know. I'll bring some if I can."

Jessie thanked her.

Honora was just about to leave when Arden came up Weavers Row. He bowed to her and smiled. Honora nodded back and thought what a good-looking beau Dolly had found herself. She wasn't surprised the maid sneaked off to visit him.

Satisfied with her visit, she returned to Overdale House, feeling useful for once. She'd enjoyed her chat with Jessie. Her aunt liked nothing but Gothic romances which bored Honora silly. Rummaging in her father's old bag, packed with the smells and memories of better times, she found the oil that might help Nellie's breathing. Feeling happy to be useful once more, an idea grew in her mind. She decided to visit her aunt's doctor and offer her services.

The visit was not a success. Dr Braddock was annoyed that she was not a fee paying patient when she sat down in his surgery. He became more angry when she outlined her ideas.

"So you mean to put me out of business, young woman, selling your quack remedies?"

"No, no," protested Honora. "These are tried and tested remedies used by my father. I only want to help."

"So you think my patients would take the advice of a mere girl instead of a fully qualified doctor," he roared stabbing a finger towards his certificates on the wall. "Out of my surgery, Miss. If your uncle heard of this he would be appalled."

Honora defiantly held her chin up as she left the surgery. The patients in the waiting room eyed her curiously, no doubt having heard the doctor's raised voice. Once Robert was home and safe, she decided she would contact her father's old colleagues for some advice.

Chapter 18: The Barn

As Robert Overdale had predicted, the news from the Invincible was not good. Many mill hands had already been laid off work for lack of cotton. On a sultry day when the weather was as oppressive as the news, Arden Davenport climbed wearily up Weavers Row.

"Well, it's happened," he said, throwing down his tool bag. "I've joined the unemployed."

"At least you've lasted longer than most," said Jessie philosophically, pouring him a cup of tea.

"Only because the machines needed cleaning and repairing after that Surat rubbish had done its worst. They're oiled and ready to go whenever we manage to get more cotton supplies anyway. But me and the other lads are now out of work. I might try and get a job in a woollen mill. They say there are mills in Bradford making cloth for uniforms for the war in America."

"Which side?" asked Jessie.

"Both," said her brother with a bitter laugh. "There's grey for the rebels and blue for the Union — and money for the mill owners. No cotton for us, though. I don't know how men with families will cope."

Arden knew that, now he was out of work, there was only one wage coming into the house. The doctor's bill for Mother was eating into the family savings. The Davenports too must tighten their belts and Jessie was having to economise with their meals as their mother suggested.

"At least Father's still in work," said Jessie with a sigh. "But we don't know for how long. And he's made sure we're stocked up with sacks of dried peas and beans, barley and oatmeal. They're all stacked up in a corner of my bedroom. I put a good helping of them in the stew to bulk it out. I hope we don't attract mice."

"Well, it all tastes very nice," said Arden loyally. "So we won't have to starve just yet. Not like some of the poor folk I saw in town. There were queues outside the pawn shop when I passed."

Young Eddie came into the house chewing manfully on a large sweet. Jessie stared at him.

"Where did you get that?" she demanded.

"Dolly Tate," he gulped.

Jessie shook her head in exasperation.

"I expect she's helped herself to them at Overdale House," she snorted. "That girl!"

Eddie carefully repeated the message he'd been memorising for his brother.

"Dolly wants to see you at Potter's barn, Arden — seven o'clock."

"Dolly? Why? Has she got a message from our Jack?" asked Arden.

"Dunno," said Eddie with a shrug. "She give me the sweetie to tell you."

"I suppose I'd better go and see what she wants," Arden sighed. "Perhaps Jack has some message for me about a job, though why she can't come here and deliver it herself, I've no idea."

Jessie gave her brother a cautious look.

"Just you watch that Dolly Tate," she warned. "She's up to something."

Arden laughed.

"Who — Dolly? She hasn't got the brains to be 'up to something'."

But he was alert, remembering his sister's warning as he approached the barn. Dolly was waiting and waved eagerly.

"Oh, Arden!" she said, gazing soulfully into his eyes. "Is it true you're laid off?"

"It is Dolly — like everyone else at the Invincible," he answered with a resigned smile. "What's all this about? Have you a message from our Jack?"

"No, no — nothing like that. It's just — well, I've not seen you for a while. I was … well, I was sort of … missing you."

She wove subtle fingers round the opened sleeve of his shirt so that he couldn't easily move away. Arden felt an uneasy embarrassment. Of course he'd flirted with her at Jack's wedding, he'd even taken her to the fair, though she'd more or less invited herself. But now she was laying some sort of claim to his affections. He put his hand on hers to extricate himself, but annoyingly found her fingers woven into his.

"Dolly," he began, becoming alarmed as he tried to back away.

"Oh, Arden," she said, peeping up at him with large blue eyes. "I often think about you. Do you think about me?"

She tried to coax him into the barn, her eyes pleading and luminous. Arden felt hot and unable to think.

It was at that moment that a large clap of thunder rent the valley and heavy drops of rain began spattering the dust dry earth. Then the heavens opened in a sudden torrent. Dolly and Arden automatically moved away from the entrance of the barn. They both jumped in surprise as two figures were framed in the bright light of the doorway.

"Well, hello, Arden — Dolly. What are you two doing here? As if we didn't know."

Tommy Dale nudged his friend who gave a knowing laugh. Tommy looked annoyed. Dolly had once flashed her blue eyes at him and now it seemed she'd taken up with Arden Davenport.

The two men watched with interest as Arden subtly tried to extricate himself from Dolly's firm grip.

"Dolly was just giving me a message from our Jack," he excused himself, his eyes signalling a fervent plea for her to back him up.

She did — after a fashion. Smiling winsomely she repeated his words.

"I was giving Arden a message from his brother Jack."

But her knowing eyes told a different story. Her sly smile told a story of an assignation, brought to a hasty close by the appearance of the two men. Arden wanted to escape but the torrential rain prevented it.

"Been catching rabbits?" he asked, though it was obvious from the strings of dangling fur they carried. "There are some fat ones up at the Fort. I'll set more snares there sometime soon."

"Looks like you've already been setting snares," said Tommy with a grim glance at Dolly.

Arden didn't like the way events were going. He wondered who had actually set the snare and if he'd already been caught in it. Jessie had mentioned that Dolly had been with Tommy at the Sunday school outing. Now he was convinced she'd been somehow trying to trap him. All Arden wanted to do was distance himself from the girl and her insinuations. The rain abated a little and gave him his chance.

"I'd better be going," he said. "Thanks for the message, Dolly. I'll make sure my mother gets it. Will you be all right getting home?"

Dolly nodded with a fixed smile.

Arden strode out for home, the sudden storm now exhausted. In the clear evening, the newly washed valley felt clean and fresh. He wondered what Dolly's game was, quite sure he didn't want to play.

"What did Dolly want?" asked Jessie innocently, though she had her suspicions.

"She wanted to tell me she missed me," he said chuckling. "Well, she'll have to miss me some more. I've been thinking on the way home that I'll go to Bradford to look for work. I can't be hanging about idle. Maybe Jack will be able to get me a ride on a train that way."

"You must take some food with you," said his practical sister. "And a spare set of clothes."

They were both confident that an engineer as useful as Arden would soon be in work.

Jacob was of the same opinion when he arrived home that evening. Sitting round the table they discussed Arden's options. He promised he'd write once he'd found a place to stay. With Mother so ill, they hoped he would not be too far from his home. Arden sat by Nellie in the parlour and gently explained why he had to leave. Though she was heart-sore, she reluctantly agreed he must go.

"A good lad like you will surely find work," she said, patting his hand. "And Bradford's not so far away."

Next morning, Jacob and Jessie waved goodbye to him with a heavy heart.

"Take care of yourself," called Jessie. "And don't forget to write."

"I will," said Arden with a confident smile. "Please don't worry."

Chapter 19: Dolly's Dilemma

Dolly had been sick again.

After her ordeal with Clement in the temple, her first thought was that no one must find out. If anyone in the household had suspected what had happened, she'd have been thrown out of the house. She'd felt so ashamed after that bewildering fumble with Clement and was angry with herself for being so naive and stupid. In the past, she'd dallied with a couple of lads around the town and, though she'd been in some dangerously intimate situations, she'd never let them have their way with her.

The next morning as she'd shamefacedly served breakfast at Overdale House, she'd received a brief thanks from Clement and a sovereign pressed into her hand for her trouble. He'd treated her like a common whore and she'd wanted to spit in his food. He and Gus left later that morning and she never thought to see him again.

Dolly tried to forget her humiliation, but now there was another problem for her to worry about. Her courses had not arrived that month. She hadn't been paying much attention, trying to deny what could have happened to her. Her mother had stared at her when she was sick on a visit to her home one morning but she'd hurriedly excused herself that she'd eaten too many of Melissa's sweets. Now she could not ignore her symptoms. Well, she was certainly in trouble now and, after a brief bout of despair, her next thought was to find someone attainable to name as the father of her coming baby.

Her first thoughts were for Arden Davenport. He'd seemed a good prospect; he was respectable and with a trade. As she left the barn, kicking the door with frustration, she wondered if she'd have been better making a play for Tommy as he might have been more naive. Arden had somehow become aware of her machinations. Her plans had collapsed.

She retched in the back alley as she was about to head out to Overdale House. She wiped her mouth and turned to find her mother staring at her.

"Are you in trouble, our Dolly?" asked Maggie, her mother, in an urgent whisper.

Her father Tommo was in bed in a room overlooking the yard and it wasn't wise to wake him up. He had an unpredictable temper as both women knew to their cost.

"No, no," Dolly protested. "It's just something I've eaten at…"

Her mother grabbed her arm and drew her to the crumbling wall, out of sight of prying eyes.

"Listen, love, if you're in trouble you must tell me. I know it happens. Who's the father? Your dad'll make him do right by you."

Dolly was stubbornly silent. What could she say? 'I was stupid enough to let an American visitor to Overdale House have his way with me'. What could her father say to that?

"Don't tell me you don't know?" said her mother in an angry hiss. "Is there more than one of them? Haven't I warned you time and time again? Oh, Dolly, how could you be so stupid?"

She was wondering that herself.

"It isn't like that," she said wearily. "I just can't tell."

"Is it that Robert Overdale? Is that why you can't tell me? Riding round on his fine horse, has he dragged you into a bedroom and…"

"No, no, no!" hissed Dolly urgently.

The last thing she wanted was for her father to go storming up to the Overdales demanding money and getting her thrown out of work.

"We could go and see Ma Randell," said Maggie, dropping her voice in dread.

Everyone knew that a girl in trouble could visit the quiet house at the edge of the river. There were things floating in that river that weren't fish or weeds. But there were girls in the graveyard that had visited Ma Randell and had paid for their trouble. Dolly shook her head vehemently.

"Not after what happened to our Ada," she whispered in a scared voice.

Her cousin was one of the girls in the graveyard, bled white and screaming for death. Dolly didn't want that to happen to her.

"I'll have to get to work," she said, hugging her shawl closely around her like a shield against the memory.

One cold winter evening, as a curious child she'd crept upstairs, drawn by the strange noises. In between the skirts of her milling female relations, she'd seen Ada's writhing body in the nightmare shadows from a guttering candle. Though they'd shooed the little girl away, Dolly was haunted by dreams of her cousin, howling like an animal. She'd been too young to understand then. She was all too aware what had happened now.

"Don't tell Dad," she warned her mother.

"Too right I won't. Oh, Dolly, what will we do? You're the only one what's working in the house. What'll we do?"

"I'll manage somehow," said Dolly, her face set in determination.

Though, in reality, she hadn't a clue what to do.

Chapter 20: Baton Rouge

Clement Duplege had finally reached the east coast of America with his guns. Aboard the blockade runner, Robert had been rigid with fear as they'd approached the coast near Charleston in the all engulfing darkness. He felt as if the beat of his heart echoed as loudly over the water as it throbbed in his ears. Then the tiny distant light had flickered once, twice and once again. Clement remained stiffly vigilant, armed and ready for a fight, but to the relief of them all, the single gleaming lantern that guided them into harbour was in the hand of a friend. In the hazy dawn and, with the boat safe against the wakening activity at the quay, the cargo of guns and machine parts were unloaded onto carts and despatched towards the fighting in Virginia. Now Robert could breathe with relief, although his anxiety about arriving in a strange land remained. He knew no one in the country but Duplege, a man he could not trust despite his bonhomie and showy manners.

Now buoyed by the success of his mission, Clement took Robert up the coast to the house of a friend in Charleston to await the ship carrying Gus. In the early hours, Robert could hear the southerner and his friends gambling and drinking, their voices loud in triumph. He suspected they were laughing at him as he lay upstairs in a cramped room. Though he'd been invited to join them, he pleaded tiredness, anxious to keep a clear head. He'd seen Clement's methods of fleecing his friend Gus by getting him so befuddled he could not think logically. What money he had was for his journey. Robert wasn't so stupid as to get involved in Clement's schemes. With rising confidence, he watched as Gus's ship came sailing into harbour, and greeted his friend with profound relief. Gus was in a happier frame of mind and they were kept busy over the next few days as the cargo was sold under Clement's auspices. Now with money in his pocket, Robert hoped to buy cotton for the mill.

The three of them began the long journey to Clement's home in Baton Rouge. Travelling by train at first, Robert stared out over the new and bewildering country. The wide landscape was ever changing, the views so unfamiliar and fascinating. He hardly listened to Gus's tale of his journey or joined in as Clement socialised with their fellow travellers, ever interested and eager for any news.

"We saw some Yankee ships on the horizon," said Gus. "They looked jolly close I can tell you, but we outran them. It was hair-raising stuff but even if they'd caught us, they wouldn't dare to arrest one of her Majesty's subjects. Still, they could make it jolly damned awkward for a cove."

Gus chatted on as the jolting journey became stuffier and more uncomfortable in the increasingly hot weather. They stayed many places on the way with friends of Clement and everywhere they'd been met with hospitality, especially when he'd mentioned the guns they'd smuggled from England. Robert listened and learnt as Clement demanded more news of the war. At every house they stayed, Clement and his hosts rejoiced again over the south's great victory at Manassas. They'd laughed at how hundreds of Union supporters had arrived in carriages and even brought picnics to watch the battle. The north had been so certain of victory. But the tide of battle had turned and the Union Army had been scattered by Confederate soldiers charging through them, yelling like demons from hell.

"Bull Run they call it — more like a cattle stampede. I'd have love to seen them Union ladies flying in their petticoats," laughed Clement. "The south will soon be victorious."

Robert wondered how soon the Confederacy would win so that the precious cargoes of cotton could flow to Britain once more. The planters were stubbornly refusing to sell their cotton though, in the hope of blackmailing Britain to back them. He'd heard that bales of cotton had even been burned on quaysides.

"But surely the sale of cotton would bring in more money to provision the war," Robert had argued in vain.

"Not one thread!" declared Clement firmly. "Not one thread will be sold until you British have come to your senses and backed the south."

Despite his pleading, nowhere could Robert find cotton to buy on all their long journey. Everywhere he heard the cry, "Not one thread."

They'd eventually arrived in Baton Rouge by riverboat early one morning before the bustling port had come alive. The Mississippi stretched like a silver sheet before them. Gus was dozing in the carriage. Throughout their journey, Robert kept the peace between him and Clement. He felt relieved as they finally reached Clement's fine house on the broad main street. The door was opened by a sleepy black woman in her nightdress.

"Why, Master Clement, we didn't know you was coming," she said rubbing her eyes.

As they entered the hallway, a small pretty woman came down the stairs wrapped in a large shawl to cover her nightwear.

"Mrs Domain," said Clement bowing politely. "I'm sorry to disturb your sleep but I've brought two gentleman visiting. I trust you'll be able to make us comfortable and give us something to eat."

"Mr Duplege," the woman bowed solemnly. "Welcome home. You are of course welcome, gentlemen," she told her two unexpected guests. "Gemima, will you see to it that these gentlemen are fed?"

"Surely will, Mrs Domain," said the black woman, scurrying away.

Robert smiled. The woman was calm and unfazed by the appearance of two strangers in the early hours of the morning. He thought of his mother and the panic and bustle that always ensued when she was presented with unexpected guests.

Mrs Domain showed the two young men upstairs.

"I hope this room suits," she told Robert, showing him a high, airy room.

"Fine," said Robert with a smile. "I can see the river from here."

"Come down when you are ready. I'm sure you are hungry."

After freshening up and changing his shirt, he went downstairs. As he passed Gus's room, he heard loud snores. Downstairs in the dining room he found himself alone.

"Mr Duplege has already eaten and gone out on business," his hostess told him, pouring coffee.

She intrigued Robert.

"Won't you join me?" he asked as she made to leave. "It's so early I'm sure you've had no breakfast yourself yet. I'd hate to eat alone."

Mrs Domain smiled.

"You're very kind," she said and slipped into a chair on the other side of the table. "I usually eat in my room." She must have noticed Robert's look of surprise. "I am Mr Duplege's housekeeper," she said simply, to dispel any other impression he may have had. She gazed round the large and pretty room. "This is … or rather, I should say, was my house. My late husband lost it in a card game to Mr Duplege." She paused for Robert to digest this unexpected piece of information as she poured herself some coffee. "Mr Duplege asked me to stay on and care for his home. He is away a great deal as you must know. I expect he felt somewhat guilty when my husband…" She trailed off and looked immensely sad. "Shot himself," she ended in a whisper.

"Oh, I'm so sorry," stammered Robert, unsure what to say. An embarrassed silence hung between them until he took inspiration from her obvious pride in the house. "This really is a beautiful home — the match of anything I've seen."

"You're very kind," said Mrs Domain with a grateful smile.

She helped him to more steak and eggs. Robert hadn't thought he'd eat so much, but weeks at sea and on the road had made him hungry. Mrs Domain politely asked about his journey and, although he was tired, he chatted happily and told her about his travels.

Now the voyage was fresh in his mind, Robert decided to write to his mother when he returned to his room. He'd already dispatched a long letter from Nassau at the first opportunity, telling her of the wonderful things he'd seen. Now he told of the bustling port at Charleston and the families where he'd stayed. He said nothing of his night of fear as they approached the coast. She'd have enough to worry about with his father and the mill. He hoped that his account of the hospitality he'd received everywhere might put her mind at rest. Somehow the news would get through.

Days later they set out on a riverboat towards the Amiens plantation. Gus had finally learnt his lesson and merely watched as Clement skilfully fleeced some of the other passengers.

"I'm watching carefully to see how he does it," he confided in his friend. "Then I'm going to beat him at his own game."

Robert sincerely hoped Gus never discovered Clement's secret. In the meantime, the simmering atmosphere of resentment slowly dispersed.

Chapter 21: Troubles at Home

Jessie saw Taylor Walmsley out of the corner of her eye as she led her little band of pupils into the chapel. He didn't look round, despite the bustle as the children entered. His mother glanced in her direction though and her mouth tightened. As Jessie had approached the chapel that morning, Mrs Walmsley was loudly inviting Eliza Andrews, Mrs Carew's niece, to tea. She'd smirked in Jessie's direction.

Jessie cautiously glanced at the unmoving head of her erstwhile lover. Not so long ago he'd have cast a sly glance in her direction and she would have demurely pretended not to notice. Her pupils became restless and fidgety and the pin-sharp eyes of Miss Andrews bored into them. Jessie raised a cautionary finger to her lips and the children wriggled into stillness. Miss Andrews turned away with a disapproving sniff. Jessie felt sorry that her pupils would be subjected to the critical eyes of that beak-faced young woman at the new school, but that wasn't her problem anymore. She tried to pray — for her mother, for Arden. Then an unbidden prayer slipped into her head — for Robert Overdale, away over the high seas — but, of course, it was all for Mrs Overdale and Honora's sake. Her new friend had confided how anxious her aunt was about Robert. Then Jessie tried to concentrate on praying for her mother once more.

To add to Jessie's problems, young Eddie was acting strangely. For a few days he'd been very furtive at mealtimes. She discovered why that evening.

"Please may I leave the table?" Eddie gabbled, eager to escape.

Father was a stickler for manners, though Eddie usually managed to mutter his when he was half-way to the door. But this evening he moved in a strange hunched fashion. The moment he cleared the table he stumbled and several pieces of bread fell from under his jacket. He glanced up shamefaced.

"So what's all this, then?" demanded Father.

Eddie shuffled from foot to foot. His open young face contorted as he struggled for an excuse.

"I might be hungry later," he said lamely.

"Then you can come back home for a bite to eat," Jacob told him sternly.

Father was going to insist on the truth. Eddie, knowing Jacob's persistence of old, came clean.

"Bart Kelso's Mam has nothing to eat," he muttered, staring at his boots. "His baby brother was crying. And Bart's hungry too."

"Then why didn't you say so," said Jacob with a sigh. "Here, put a bit of butter on that bread for them. Jessie, put some of that stew in a bowl and Eddie will take it to the Kelsos." He patted his son's head. "We've not so much ourselves, son, but we'll not let folk starve if we can help it."

Jessie spooned a generous helping of the rabbit stew into a bowl and Eddie eagerly went to deliver it. She'd made enough to last for the next day but would have to bulk it out with more barley, carrots and potatoes from Father's vegetable garden. Without Arden at home to catch rabbits for them, she and Eddie were not having much luck. They were improving, though she hated to kill the little creatures. It was either that or starve. The trouble was that more and more people were setting snares at their favourite spot at the Fort and rabbits were becoming scarcer.

"I don't know what the world's coming to, Jessie lass," said Jacob sadly. "Mrs Kelso should be able to get enough for bread for her family from the Poor Relief. They say the workhouse is packed to capacity. I met an old mate with his elderly father the other day on the way there. They were both in tears and I don't blame them. Folks out of work can't afford to keep their old parents at home with them. It's cruel to have to take them up there to that hellhole. They're treated as barely human. It's a crying shame in a Christian country."

By habit he picked up his pipe from the mantelpiece and put it in his mouth, then realised that he'd given up his one small luxury to economise. He left the empty pipe in his mouth anyway. It seemed to help him think.

Arden had been gone some weeks and the family anxiously read his letters. Nellie was fretting but Miss Darwen's visits seemed to cheer her up. Jessie looked forward to her visits too.

"Please call me Honora," she'd said, carefully dropping the pungent smelling eucalyptus oil into a bowl of boiling water and supporting Nellie to help her breathe.

Nellie coughed.

"By 'eck that's good stuff, Miss Honora. It's cleared the wax out of me ears!" said Nellie with a wheezy chuckle. She could not be totally informal with Matthias Overdale's niece. "And it's all the way from Australia, you say?"

"It is," said Honora smiling.

"Eh, the miracles of nature," said the patient as Jessie lowered her back onto her pillows. "And it helps too. Don't they say that God made a herb for every ailment — and fancy that eucalyptus stuff being on the other side of the world. At this rate, I'll live to see Arden come back home."

Honora caught Jessie's anxious look.

"Is there any news of your brother?" she asked casually as Nellie began to doze.

"He wrote last week," admitted Jessie. "But there's no work to be had for love nor money. The mills in Burnley were shut down long before the Invincible, so a lot of their mill hands have been scouring Yorkshire for work. He says he'll give it another week and then head home. It doesn't look promising, though."

"I've seen the queues for the Poor Relief," said Honora in exasperation. "I can't believe the meanness of those Guardians. People have to pawn their blankets before they get a penny. When the winter comes, they'll starve of the cold. I must ask my uncle to intervene."

Jessie had heard tales of hardship from her friends. At least the Davenport family were managing at present. They were being cautious as Father was likely to be put on short time any day. Eli Gorman had been scouring the county for spun cotton to weave at the Endurance, but the fine thread he needed had long been bought up. There were rumours that speculators had bought up tons of cotton and it was rotting in warehouses, waiting for prices to rise.

Arden arrived home many days later, tired and dusty. He had a grey pallor under his skin, despite days of tramping in the sun. He'd had little luck.

"I worked on a steam harvester for a couple of weeks," he said. "But the harvest is over now. I must find something. There's some employers taking advantage of the situation and paying a pittance to people who've no other choice but to starve."

"Can't our Jack put a good word in for you at the locomotive works?" asked Jacob.

"He's trying," Arden told him. "But I'm seriously thinking of going further afield, Father."

"Down south, do you mean?"

"No," Arden shook his head and paused a long silent moment. "I was given a hand bill in Bradford. They're recruiting men to fight in America."

Jessie's hand flew to her mouth in shock.

"America!" gasped her father. "Eh, lad…"

"The bill was recruiting for the Confederate Army. I won't fight for slave owners, you know that. But I reckon the other side need troops too. Jack will find me a ride on the milk train to Liverpool and I'll make enquiries."

Jessie knew then that he'd been stung by Robert Overdale's words that he should fight for the north if he felt so strongly about the slaves. She bit her lip as Jacob laid a heavy hand on his son's shoulder.

"Think hard before you make any decision, son," he pleaded. "The worry would kill your mother."

Arden promised he would but Jessie wondered with a heavy heart if he'd already made his decision. Nellie was fretting. They tried to keep Arden's plans from her, but she'd guessed that something was going on.

"Arden didn't find work, did he, Jessie?" she asked as her daughter gave her a gentle bed bath.

The room was stifling as Jessie tried to keep her mother warm with coal they could hardly afford. A cold wind had swept over Gorby Moor as autumn advanced.

"Something will turn up," said Jessie hopefully.

She helped her mother into a clean nightdress, dismayed at how loose it was on her mother now. Nellie sank weakly against her pillows.

"Don't keep anything from me, Jessie," she pleaded. "He's my son and I've a right to know."

"Nothing's decided yet," said Jessie gently but firmly.

She knew now that Arden would go, despite her father's pleading. What happened later that day would put the matter beyond dispute.

Jessie was pleased to see Honora. Like an old friend now, she opened the latch and called into the house.

"Anyone at home?"

"No, I've just gone down to the shops," joked Nellie, wheezing as she laughed.

Her illness hadn't dimmed her sense of humour.

"I see you're a bit brighter," said Honora with a smile.

"Mother's just had a bath to freshen her up," said Jessie. "Would you like a cup of tea?" They were interrupted by loud knocking at the door.

"Whoever can that be?"

Jessie went to answer. She was upset and embarrassed that Honora witnessed what happened next. On the doorstep was Dolly's father Tommo Tate and his son Seth. Jessie wondered why on earth they'd arrived.

"Where's your Arden?" demanded Tommo rudely.

"He's not here," said Jessie calmly. "Come in the house and…"

"I'll not set foot in your house until I've got satisfaction," growled Tommo.

"I don't understand…" Jessie said, filled with a growing alarm.

"I want to see Arden," said Tommo. "You can stop hiding him and bring him here."

"Mr Tate," said Jessie, staying calm though her heart was thumping, "my brother's not home. You can either come in and wait, or you can leave a message and I'll tell him to get in touch when he comes back."

"You can tell him from me that if he doesn't do right by our Dolly, he'll have me to answer to," said Tommo Tate, folding his thick arms and flexing his muscles as if to show he meant business.

"Dolly?" asked Jessie.

"Aye. He's been, er … I shouldn't be saying this to a young woman. I'll have it out with Arden."

"I'm not a child, Mr Tate," said Jessie hotly.

"Well, he's been … philandering with her," said Tommo angrily. "She's in the family way and we've got witnesses — aye, witnesses, so he can't wriggle out of it."

"You mean our Arden…?"

"Aye."

"Has Dolly accused him of 'philandering' with her?" asked Jessie.

Tommo looked defensive for a moment.

"Not exactly — but we know, don't we, lad?"

"Aye," said Seth with a sneer. "A mate of mine saw them together up at Potter's barn and that Arden was up to no good."

"And has Dolly said that Arden's the father?" insisted Jessie, feeling weak and bewildered.

She desperately needed to talk to her brother.

"Never mind that — we know. I'm not having my daughter ruined and cast aside."

"This isn't getting us anywhere," said Jessie. "Come into the house and…"

"Not while your mother's poorly. I'll be back."

He was just about to leave when Eddie came whistling up the Row with a couple of fresh fish dangling from a string.

"Here a minute, lad. Has your brother Arden been knocking about with our Dolly?"

Eddie shrugged.

"He met her at the barn a few weeks ago," he said nonchalantly.

An awful revelation engulfed Jessie, remembering that meeting and the message from Dolly.

Tommo gave a triumphant laugh.

"There's evidence for you," he sneered at Jessie. "Out of the young un's own mouth."

"It was Dolly who asked Arden to the barn," said Jessie angrily. "I'd like to hear Arden's explanation first."

"So would we," snapped Tommo. "We'll wait and see Arden."

He and his son sat nearby on a stone wall and glared malevolently at the Davenports' home.

"Come in, Eddie," said Jessie dragging her brother into the house. "It's a pity you arrived home when you did."

He had no idea what all the fuss was about. Jessie turned to see Honora behind them looking anxious.

"I had no idea that Dolly Tate…" said Honora and trailed off.

"Jessie — Jessie, what's all the commotion?" came Nellie's weak voice.

Jessie looked anxiously in at her mother.

"A couple of the Tates called looking for Arden. Perhaps they know of a job for him."

She hated lying but didn't want to trouble Nellie. She dragged her brother to the back door.

"Eddie, go the back way to the Fort and see if Arden is there. Tell him not to come home yet," she ordered him.

"I'd better go," said Honora.

Jessie touched her arm.

"Will you do me a great favour?" she pleaded.

"If I can," said Honora cautiously.

"If you see Arden in town, will you tell him not to come home yet? Those two haven't come prepared to listen to reason and I don't want any trouble with Mother so ill."

"Very well," said her guest reluctantly.

Jessie was annoyed by Honora's attitude. Judging by her hesitancy it was obvious she believed that Arden had had his way with Dolly. Jessie didn't care what she believed — she was desperate to warn her brother.

Chapter 22: Arden Calls on a Friend

Strolling home along the Gorbydale high street, Arden was confronted by Honora Darwen. At first he was pleased to see the striking young woman but, with an obvious frown, she beckoned him to one side of the street.

"Is it Mother?" he demanded anxiously.

Honora shook her head.

"No, no. Jessie asked me to give you a message. Dolly Tate's father and brother are waiting for you outside your house"

"For me — whatever for?"

"They look as if they want to make trouble and your sister is anxious about your mother. She says you must not go home yet."

"Why would they want to make trouble?"

"I'm surprised you don't know," said Honora stiffly. "Perhaps Mr Davenport, you should do the honourable thing by Dolly Tate and save your reputation and hers."

With that she turned and marched away leaving Arden staring after her in bewilderment.

Arden watched her leave. He'd felt a glow of admiration when she approached him, yet now he was swamped by her disapproval. What on earth had Dolly been saying? Well, he wouldn't fall into her traps. He'd avoided them before. Undecided for a moment, he wondered if he should confront the Tates, but he knew Seth Tate of old. Arden was not a coward but Seth was not a man to reason with. He had a reputation for clog fighting in the disreputable parts of town. Many a man had a permanent limp because of Seth Tate.

"I'll wait until dark to go home," he decided. "I don't want trouble. Besides, I'm tired."

Unsure what to do next, Arden called in at his friend, John's, terraced house nearby. He was shocked at the transformation in his friend's fortunes. Two wooden crates stood where comfortable chairs had once been. His wife sat on a kitchen chair feeding the baby. One of the chair's legs was broken and it rested on a big square stone cobble.

"I'm sorry to welcome you like this," said his friend, looking embarrassed. "But times are hard for us all. Did you find work?"

Arden shook his head.

"No, though not for want of trying."

John glanced at his wife.

"I'm glad I didn't go travelling then. I couldn't leave Eliza and young Henry. Her Mam's in Wales and their cottage is full. So you say it would have been a wild goose chase, anyway?"

"Aye," said Arden. "But I'm thinking of going farther afield — perhaps to America."

"America, that's a big step right enough," said John.

"Is Dolly going with you?" asked Eliza.

Arden was immediately alert.

"What's all this about Dolly and me?"

"There are rumours that you and Dolly were … well, you know … at the barn. Tommy Dale's been putting it about," said John's young wife, blushing.

"I might have guessed it was something like that," said Arden shaking his head. "The Tates are waiting for me up at the house. You can tell anyone that wants to know that it wasn't me that deflowered Dolly Tate — not that Tommo and Seth will be in any mood to listen."

"But is anyone likely to believe us?" said John sadly. "You know what it's like round here."

"Aye, only too well," said Arden rising stiffly from his uncomfortable seat. "Some folk seem best pleased with other's misfortunes. I'd best get going. I must go and see our Jack."

He found half-a-crown in his pocket and handed it to John with an apologetic smile.

"I'm sorry it's not more," he said.

John shook his head.

"I'll not take charity off a friend. We've a few more things to pawn yet before we go begging."

"It's not for you," said Arden firmly. "It's for young Henry."

"Oh — right," said his friend, glancing at Eliza. She nodded with a smile. "If it's for the babby, then."

"God bless you, Arden," said Eliza, her eyes filling with tears. "And we'll put people right about you and Dolly."

Arden knew now that he would have to go to America. He'd half made his decision already. He didn't want to live pursued by rumours and by Dolly — not to mention the hot-headed Tates. As if he'd known all along what he would do, he'd bought an Army kitbag from the pawnshop. He'd been surprised by the people queuing there and the little luxuries they were pawning after a life of working hard to buy them. They'd avoided his eyes. But you couldn't eat your treasures. The worse sight was the poor families pledging blankets. Surely something should be done for them.

As he walked the five miles to Doveton where his brother lived, he made his plans. He'd return home after dark, then catch the dawn milk train to Manchester and on to Liverpool.

As twilight fell, Jack hugged his brother self-consciously as Arden made to leave. Elsie his young wife stood anxiously at the door. Dolly was her cousin after all.

"Take care," said Jack. "Can I tell him, Elsie — before he goes?" She nodded cautiously. "We're going to have a baby."

Arden shook Jack's hand vigorously.

"That's wonderful news. It'll give Mother a boost when I'm gone." He went to hug Elsie but she folded her arms firmly to forbid such familiarity. He patted her shoulder instead. "I'm right pleased for you," he said.

If it were a boy it certainly wouldn't be named after him!

Returning home in darkness, Arden was surprised when he slipped in the back door to find Jessie and Jacob still up and anxiously waiting for him. They kept their voices low so as not to disturb Nellie.

"The Tates didn't leave until dark," said his sister. "Father went out and tried to reason with them, but they wouldn't have it. That Seth is a nasty piece of work."

"I'm right worried, son. Tommo Tate wants justice done by his daughter. Arden, I have to ask you," said Jacob seriously, "should you be doing the right thing by Dolly Tate?"

"No, Father. I swear it," said Arden looking straight into his father's eyes.

"That's good enough for me," decided Jacob. "What will you do?"

"The Tates wouldn't believe me," Arden began. "Anyway, I getting away from it all. I've bought a kit bag. I'm off to find passage to America — in the morning."

Jacob and Jessie stared at him in silence.

"S…s… so soon," stuttered his sister.

"There's nothing for me here but trouble. At least it's one less mouth to feed."

"We'd starve together if we had to, son," said Jacob. "But what will you tell your Mother?"

"I don't know," said Arden wearily.

He looked in anxiously at Nellie and found her eyes open and questioning.

"Are you going away, son?" she asked in a quiet, sad voice.

"I have to, Mother," said Arden sitting on a low stool by her bed and clutching her hand.

"It's to do with Dolly, isn't it?"

He nodded.

"Part of it is. But I can't find work here. I've tried hard and there's nothing. And honestly, Mother, I haven't done anything to be ashamed of."

"I know, son," she said. "Nobody tells me anything — so as not to worry me, they say. But I'm not deaf and I'm not daft. It's America you're going to, isn't it?"

He nodded again, too full of sadness to speak. He might never see her again, the dear and dauntless woman whose sense of humour and goodness had been the backbone of his life. She squeezed his hand tightly with her small bony one and then laid it on his bowed head and stroked his hair.

"I don't want to leave you, but…" said Arden with a catch in his voice.

"God bless and keep you, son. If you can do anything to release them poor creatures from the whip and the irons, then I'm right proud of you."

"I'll do my best, Mother," he said and brushed away a tear.

"Go and rest now, son," she said, always mindful of his welfare. "You've a long journey ahead of you."

"Let's get some sleep, lad," Jacob said, putting an arm round his son's shoulders. "We've an early start."

"I've wrapped some bread and cheese and stuff to keep you going for a bit," said Jessie tearfully.

Later, Arden would find the last of her meagre savings in a small pouch, hidden under half a loaf of bread in his pack.

As the crimson blush of dawn glowed over the grimy Gorbydale streets, Arden Davenport kissed his mother and the sleeping Eddie. Waving sadly to a weeping Jessie and anxious Jacob, he left his home. He didn't know when, or even if, he would ever see them again.

A couple of days later, Arden wrote to his family from Liverpool. He had found work on the new steamship the *Great Eastern*, in the boiler room. It would be hot and dirty work but he had the experience of working with the great boiler at the Invincible.

Liverpool Quay was loud and crowded with soldiers and their loved ones. Britain was sending troops to Canada to protect its colony should the American war spill over the border. Feeling desolate that he was leaving his home and country, Arden slipped down into the bowels of the ship to lose himself in his duties. He hoped the family would be pleased that he'd found work. They might expect him home when the ship returned to port, but his mother's words echoed in his brain. Despite the roar and thump of the engine, he heard her voice, "*If you can do anything to release them poor creatures from the whip and the irons, then I'm right proud of you.*"

Arden did not intend to return to his home at the end of his journey.

Chapter 23: The Agent

"Is that Taylor Walmsley I see coming up the drive, Honora dear?" said Melissa, pausing from her crocheting as she peered through the window. "I wonder why he's here? I hope that mother of his isn't planning to visit."

Honora went to open the door to their visitor as it was beginning to rain and Dolly was invariably slow.

"What does he want?" asked Melissa.

"He didn't say," said her niece. "Uncle Matthias came to the door of his study and beckoned him in right away."

Melissa was curious but it didn't pay to ask Matthias too many questions. He was very tetchy just then. She'd ventured to ask if it was wise to send Robert overseas. He was her only child and he had no business experience whatsoever.

"Well, he was keen to go America when Duplege invited him. He wouldn't have thanked you for preventing him," growled Matthias.

Melissa acknowledged that was true. Robert had been full of enthusiasm for the adventure.

"Anyway, he'll have to learn sometime," said her husband. "He's got the Kearsley lad with him and Duplege. How hard can it be to buy cotton in a place that grows cotton? And if we don't get cotton, what's going to happen to the mill? We've still got a mortgage to pay."

The meeting with Taylor Walmsley lasted over an hour and a curious Melissa slipped into the hallway when she heard the study door open.

"How do you do, Mr Walmsley?" she said pleasantly. "Is your mother well?"

"Aye," said Taylor bluntly. "She's well enough."

He tucked a folded piece of paper into his pocket and looked distinctly irritated as he headed straight for the door. Just before opening it, he paused and seemed to remember his manners.

"Good day, Mrs Overdale," he said with a quick nod. "Mr Overdale."

Then, closing the door with a loud bang, he marched away home.

Matthias grunted and slunk back into his study and Melissa was left to wonder what had been said. Trying another tactic, she popped her head round the study door. Her husband was sitting at his desk, his head bent over a large leather-bound ledger. When he looked up she was taken aback by his appearance. In the grey light from the window, his face was puffy and mottled, his eyes red-rimmed.

"Would you like a nice cup of tea, dear?" she asked quietly. "You've been chatting to Taylor Walmsley for a long time. I thought you might have rang for some tea."

"Discussing business," he corrected her sharply. "We didn't have time to be messing about with no tea."

"Well, would you like one now, dear?" she tried again. "It's an hour 'til dinner. I'll ask Honora…"

"I don't want her in here," said Matthias firmly.

Melissa was surprised he sounded so adamant. He sat upright in his chair and studied her for a moment.

"Better shut the door while we have a word," he said, with a deep sigh.

With rising anxiety, Melissa slipped into the chair opposite her husband.

"What's the matter, my love?" she asked gently.

"We've no cotton's the matter," he told her wearily. "The mill could go bust. I've studied these figures 'til I'm blue in the face, but I can't make them look any better. I've a mind to invest in this business with the Kearsleys, finding stuff to sell to the south in America."

"Isn't that illegal?" said Melissa in alarm.

"I haven't quite looked into it," Matthias excused himself, though they both suspected it was. "And that's why I don't want Honora poking around. You know what she's like about slavery and the south. That Duplege bloke warned me to keep quiet about this the business.

"But I'm not as young as I was, and I can't go haring round the country looking for goods. That's why I've asked Walmsley to be my agent and do the travelling for me."

"Oh, so that's why he came to visit?" said Melissa.

"Aye, he's agreed to do it for me, but he wasn't too keen. He's another of them chapel lot." Matthias gazed through the window, deep in thought. "But every man has his price. I asked him how he was doing with the mill closed. I know his mother has a bit of brass but she looks a tight old besom and I reckon she keeps him short. Walmsley had said, *'I'm surprised you asked me, Mr Overdale. There's other overlookers with families. Wouldn't they need the money?'*

"But I told him I'd asked Barker and Ormerod and they both turned me down," said Matthias. "Ormerod said he worked with slave picked cotton because he had no choice, but he'd be damned if he'd help slave-owners win the war." Matthias chuckled. "Then he had the cheek to ask if his old job would be there when the war was over. I think when I mentioned that, it focussed Walmsley's mind all right and he accepted my offer."

He sat back and smiled wearily at Melissa, seemingly relieved that he'd unburdened himself. It was the longest conversation they'd ever had about his business since she'd offered him her legacy to invest in the old Endurance.

"I think I'll have that cup of tea now, my dear," he said. "I'm sorry to dump all this on you, but I had to tell someone. And anyway, knowing you, you'd be wondering why Walmsley was always bobbing in and out."

"You know me too well," said Melissa with a chuckle.

She rose from her seat and went to put a comforting arm round his shoulders.

"Don't worry too much, dear. I know it's hard but we'll manage. Our Eli would always help us out."

Matthias bridled at that and Melissa was instantly sorry she'd mentioned it. Yet her husband must learn to swallow his pride if his dealings failed.

"I'll go and get that tea," she said.

Though Melissa was buoyant in front of her husband, a feeling of dread filled her as soon as she left the study; worry for her son; anxiety for the business. She hoped Matthias was not too deep in illegal business and feared the consequences if that should ever be discovered.

Chapter 24: Dolly Makes Her Plans

Dolly was wary when a couple of weeks later she was confronted by Honora.

"Could I have a word with you, Dolly?" asked Honora

"Yes, Miss Darwen. What about?" asked Dolly with a winsome smile. "If it's about the fire in your bedroom, Mrs Overdale say we aren't to light any until it gets really cold because of the er … situation."

"No, it's not that, Dolly," said Honora, unsure how to broach the subject of the rumours.

Dolly felt she'd been watching her for days. She wondered if the rumours snaking round the town had reached Overdale House. She suspected Honora was anxious to see if Dolly showed any hint of pregnancy but she'd been defeated by the large aprons that Dolly had taken to wearing. Honora beckoned the maid into the empty morning room.

"I've heard some rumours about … about you and Arden Davenport," she said finally.

"There's always rumours round here," said Dolly, staring Honora straight in the eyes in defiant challenge. "People have nothing better to do than talk others down now they've got no work. I don't know what it's got to do with me."

"If you were in trouble, you could come and tell me you know," coaxed Honora gently. "You could trust me."

"Well, I'm not and I don't need to," said Dolly abruptly. "But thank you for the offer," she added, softening her tone as she knew she'd been rude.

All the same, she didn't want anyone interfering with her plans, no matter how well intentioned. She'd finally managed to make her father stop shouting his mouth off and broadcasting her shame around the town. The fact that Arden Davenport had left the town was enough to paint him guilty in Tommo's eyes, although Dolly stubbornly refused to name the father of this coming child. Finally, she and her mother had managed to sit Tommo down and make some serious plans.

"If you're willing, Tommo, I can bring up the baby as mine," suggested Maggie timidly. Her eyes pleaded with her unpredictable husband. "Our Dolly's the only one working, and if she loses her job, it'll be the workhouse for us."

Tommo glared at his daughter. She didn't look any different and certainly not as if she was expecting a baby. Not many people dared defy him but Dolly had been a force of nature since she was a tot. At the age of four, he'd raised his hand to strike her and she'd bit his finger hard. To everyone's surprise, especially the fearful Maggie, Tommo had roared with laughter at his daughter and called her a 'chip off the old block'.

Not all the Tates children had survived. A son knocked stupid by Tommo's fist had succumbed to a fever because his father thought a doctor's fee would be wasted on him. Even Seth, who was marginally less feared than his father in the town, was wary of Tommo's temper. Surprisingly, Tommo had always been lenient with Dolly, his only surviving daughter.

"Don't them Overdales suspect anything?" he asked.

"Well, I'm not showing and the Missis is more bothered about old Matthias and his flaming mill," said Dolly. "I don't know about that Honora, though. She was sniffing round the other day but I think I put her off the scent. She's a bit of a soft touch on the quiet, so I don't think she'll say anything. I think I'll get away with it." She gave a deep sigh. "As long as you keep your gob shut."

He looked as if he was about to slap her but she glared at him defiantly.

"The less people know of it, the better. I'll just keep going for as long as I can and if I don't, well…"

"I'll sort out anyone who says anything," growled Tommo. There weren't many people willing to cross the Tates. "It'll be another mouth to feed, though," he added sourly.

"And who's making the money to feed it?" snapped Dolly.

They could not argue with that. Although Dolly's wage was small, it was something to live on and the increasing amount of stuff she smuggled out of Overdale House certainly helped.

Maggie began wearing big aprons like her daughter. If their scheme was to succeed she'd have to appear increasingly pregnant herself. This expected child would not be the first in Gorbydale to call its mother 'sister'.

Chapter 25: The Ball

On a warm evening in Louisiana, Robert Overdale marvelled as a colourful swathe of silks and satins swirled by him in the grand room. How could he fail to be impressed by all this grandeur in a country at war? It was hard to believe. He and Gus had been made very welcome by Clement's brother, Henri, and his wife, Marie. Some men were in uniform, swaggering to impress the ladies, but they were as colourful and pristine as toy soldiers.

Two giggling young women caught him by his arms. He'd presumed that Clement Duplege's nieces were schoolgirls, but Delia and Clementina were young ladies. Clementina was the youngest, a pretty little thing of seventeen.

"Come along, Mr Overdale," she coaxed. "You must show us how they dance in Europe."

"Clemmie, I'm the eldest. Mr Overdale must dance with me first," insisted Delia.

"You only want to make Johnny Bartholomew jealous," said her sister pouting.

Robert was saved from a decision by the arrival of a tall, serious young man.

"Miss Delia," he said with a shy smile, bowing low. "I wonder if you'd do me the honour…"

He hadn't time to finish before Delia linked his arm and dragged him eagerly away.

"Delia should watch herself with Johnny," sniffed Clemmie. "He's a Yankee sympathiser, you know. Papa won't like it one bit."

Henri Duplege frowned as Delia and her beau waltzed by. His wife gave her daughter disapproving glances over the edge of her fan. But Clemmie beamed now she had Robert all to herself.

"Come along, Mr Overdale. I accept no excuses."

"No excuses needed to dance with such a delightful young lady as yourself," said Robert gallantly.

Clemmie preened.

"Oh you Englishmen are just a delight yourself," she exclaimed. "Except for that Gus. Why, he stepped on my toes something awful. I'll never dance with him again as long as I live."

"He's very rich," whispered Robert with a chuckle.

"I still can't forgive the man," declared Clemmie grandly. "He dances like a buffalo."

They swept out onto the floor and, after a couple of hitches, Robert flowed into the dance. His mother had insisted he'd learnt and paid extra for dancing classes at his school, but this was so different from steering awkward schoolgirls round the gymnasium of the Academy. To hold a pretty young woman in his arms and sway round this elegant room was wonderful and he was enjoying himself.

Later that night, unable to sleep for the heat and despite all the dancing, Robert was restless. He lit a lamp and wrote again to his mother. He told her all about the spectacle of the ball and the grandeur of the plantation villa. He carefully reread what he'd written, ensuring there was nothing to alarm her. She would not like to hear about the slaves he'd seen toiling in the stifling sun, men with whips standing over them. Slowly, in the silence of the house, he became aware of the sound of hooves beneath his window. Cautiously, he peeped through the drapes. Below on the drive, Delia was clinging hard to Johnny

Bartholomew. He bent down and their lips met in a long poignant kiss. Then he remounted his horse, and blowing another kiss, galloped off into the trees. Robert wondered if Delia's sweetheart was going to war. He guessed that, with such secrecy involved in his departure, Johnny wouldn't be fighting for the south.

With the image of the young lovers in his thoughts, an unbidden image of Jessie Davenport came into his head. He pictured her in one of those magnificent gowns with her hair swept up in a wreath of flowers. Lovely and dignified despite her lowly status, she'd outshine any of the belles. He wished she wouldn't haunt his thoughts and dreams. She might despise his support of the slave owners but without cotton, they'd all starve. Anyway, why should he care what a mill girl thought of him? There were plenty of girls who admired him; he'd met several on his travels. Robert finished his letter and, still wondering, fell into a fitful sleep.

The sun piercing through the parted drapes roused him the next morning. Despite his head feeling woolly, he heard the shuffling of soft feet nearby. Opening his eyes, he found a young black woman carrying a jug of steaming water to the washstand.

"Good morning," he said pleasantly.

She jumped in surprise to see him awake and nearly spilt the water. Then the girl hastily put the jug down, nodded quickly and was about to leave when he beckoned to her.

"Would you mind if I ask you something?" he asked. She looked alarmed. "What's your name?"

"Kezia, sir," she said quietly, her eyes alert and fearful.

"Do you like living here, Kezia?" he asked, raising himself to his elbow.

She relaxed a little.

"It's very fine, sir," she said with a shrug.

"Do you mind being a slave?" he tried.

She gave him a curious look.

"Ain't got no choice, sir," she said, seeming puzzled by such a stupid question.

"But do your owners treat you well?"

She looked at Robert with as much curiosity as he looked at her. It was obvious no one had ever asked her such a question before.

"House slave is well treated as far as it goes — better than a field hand, anyways. Master Henri never had me beaten. Neither should he, seein' as his Pappy was the same as mine." Robert's eyes opened wide in surprise. Kezia seemed offended that he should be.

"My mammy was a mighty fine woman," she said indignantly. "I ain't surprised Master's Pappy took a fancy to her. Taught herself to read by listening to lessons for Master Henri and Master Clement. Taught me the same — 'a' for an apple, 'b' for a ball, 'c' for a cat. I can read. I ain't stupid — sir."

"You're a remarkable young woman, Kezia," said Robert, surprised by what she had told him.

He hadn't even considered why a slave would want to read. He'd been so ignorant of even the simplest details of their lives. In truth he hadn't wanted to think about them at all.

"Thank you, sir," said Kezia with a huge smile. "'Remarkable' — I like that."

All through the day Robert noticed things that he hadn't suspected. He saw how house slaves crept about like shadows, hoping to go unnoticed. He heard the crack of whips echoing over the cotton fields as he rode out to survey the plantation with Clement. Saw the fear in the slaves' eyes as they toiled in the boiling sun, fighting exhaustion. Gus wasn't happy on a horse, so Robert was relieved when the tour was curtailed. He asked once again if Clement would sell him cotton, but was refused.

"'Not one thread till England have recognised the Confederacy', that is what we intend," said Clement staunchly. "I would be betraying my country if I sold you just one thread. I hear they burnt bales of cotton on the docks in New Orleans to prevent them falling into Yankee hands. The south needs to grow food for its people not cotton for people who won't support us."

Robert could see his point of view but tried to argue his case all the same. He was desperate to buy cotton for the Invincible and go home. As a stranger in a strange land, he did not have the faintest idea how to proceed and Clement refused to help him. To confuse him further, Robert was having severe doubts about slavery.

Strange loud noises had split the silence of the night. Slipping onto the veranda, he'd seen flaming torches over by the slave village. Clement, too, was out on the veranda.

"Go back to your bed," he'd said. "There's nothing to worry about."

Gus slept through the whole episode.

Lying in the dark, Robert had listened to the disturbance, dogs barking and angry voices. Then all fell silent and he'd drifted into a fitful sleep. Next morning, Robert found Kezia weeping silently as she brought his hot water.

"What's the matter, Kezia?" he'd asked gently.

"Nothing the matter, Master Robert," she muttered, desperate to hide her misery.

"You can tell me," he insisted.

Looking up into his sympathetic face she could hold back no longer. All her anguish came tumbling out.

"They done caught Abraham, Master Robert," she whispered. "He was trying to reach the Union Army to be free. They caught him with the dogs. Oh, and they beat him awful, awful bad. He might not live, Master Robert."

The tears rolled unabated down her cheeks.

"You like Abraham?"

Kezia nodded.

"We was gonna marry when we was free. I swear someday I'm gonna be free, Master Robert. I pray and pray to God that Mr Lincoln is gonna win."

Robert didn't know how to comfort her. He wasn't even sure he should but they were two insignificant human beings caught in a curious situation. He took a silver dollar from the wallet on his bedside table.

"Take this, Kezia," he said wrapping her fingers over the coin. "Someday you'll have enough to buy your freedom."

"Can't take this, Master Robert," she said looking horrified. "They'll say I stole it. They might beat me."

"I'll tell them you haven't, that I gave it to you for good service." She looked doubtful at that. "I wish I could give you more but I don't know how I'm fixed until I manage to buy some cotton."

"God bless you, Master Robert," said Kezia, a shy smile emerging through her tears. "I'll pray for you every night."

"I'll probably need it," said Robert with a smile.

He certainly would in the weeks that followed.

Chapter 26: The Dancing Mary

Though Clement Duplege refused to help Robert buy cotton, there were others who saw potential in his intentions. The rumour had spread that an English visitor to the Amiens plantation was looking to buy cotton. Whether it had travelled via a guest to the ball, or the whispering of slaves, was for anyone to guess. Some days later, a tall serious man and his equally serious son rode towards the house. They enquired after the English visitor. Despite their boast of southern hospitality, the Dupleges did not invite the visitors into the house. Robert went out to meet them. Henri watched from one of the windows as the older man dismounted his horse and introduced himself as Nathan Jacques and his son David.

"I hear you want to buy cotton, Mister," he said in a slow drawl. "I've got cotton but I'm not sending it to New Orleans to be burnt. You want to buy it?"

"I do," said Robert eagerly.

Clement, hovering nearby, was not pleased.

"We've got to force the British into supporting us by depriving them of cotton, Jacques," he growled. "Not one…"

"I know all about that 'not one thread' business. It's all very well starving the British of cotton," said Nathan Jacques. "But we're starving too. How am I going to make a living if I don't sell my cotton."

"Your son would get paid if he joined the army," snapped Clement, glancing contemptuously at the young man.

He was well aware that Jacques's son had not joined the Confederacy.

"This is not my war," Nathan defended himself vigorously. "I own no slaves. You fight your own war."

Clement Duplege fumed but Robert was as desperate to buy the cotton as the man was to sell.

"Ride over to my farm tomorrow and we'll talk," Jacques told Robert, unwilling to face the hostility of the Duplege house again.

"I've heard New Orleans is blockaded and likely to surrender any day," Clement told them over dinner. "You won't get your cotton out of the country that way. Besides, I have to get back to Baton Rouge before it falls. There are papers there I need to destroy."

"Are you for England afterwards?" asked Gus.

"Who knows. I may need to contact our friends in Britain to find more supplies. But I can get you on a boat somewhere, maybe at Charleston." He turned to Robert. "Charleston will not allow one thread of cotton to pass through its port Mr Overdale — 'not one thread' as we have sworn. I'm afraid you and your cotton will have to shift for yourself. I haven't the time or the inclination to find you a ship. However, Mr Kearsley, I'm sure I can find you a passenger ship to England. Your father would never forgive me if I let any harm befall you."

And Gus is the son of a shipbuilder, useful to the Confederates, thought Robert wryly. *A mere son of a mill owner like myself must be left to take his own chances.*

Feeling lost and unwelcome, Robert rode over to consult Nathan Jacques the next day. The cotton planter listened to his dilemma and had a solution.

"My boy, David, could take you with the cotton to Galveston, Mr Overdale," he told Robert, "I reckon you'll find a boat. The news is the Union is concentrating all its forces on New Orleans right now. But we must make haste."

Robert galloped back to the Amiens plantation.

"I'm leaving tomorrow," he told Gus. "Nathan Jacques is loading his cotton tonight and we're going to Texas. Are you coming with me?"

"I'm terribly sorry, dear boy, but the sooner I get back to England, the better," said Gus. "I'm tired of this interminable heat. I wish you well, though. Have you enough money?"

Robert nodded, patting the proceeds of the sales in Charleston and the gold sovereigns his father had entrusted to him to buy cotton.

In the cool early morning, Clement's nieces rose to wave Robert goodbye. Delia and Clementina kissed his cheek with pretty tears and told him how they would miss him. Clement watched sombrely.

"I think you're foolhardy, Mr Overdale, but I admire your determination," he said grudgingly.

Gus appeared, yawning on the veranda in his dressing gown.

"See you in England, old boy," he called. "Best of luck."

The Jacques plantation was alive with activity when Robert rode over. There were four long carts piled high with cotton and a smaller wagon filled with supplies for the journey. Four Negroes were ready to drive.

"I'm sending my best men," said Nathan, shaking his hand. "They all volunteered, anyway. You won't have no runaways — all my workers are free. Good workers too."

They set off with a will, Robert riding beside David Jacques on the first wagon. He was a quiet young man and Robert found him hard to talk to at first. But in the hard and uncomfortable days that followed, they became friends. It was easier to become friendly while camping out and eating together. Robert tried to do his share of the work and, though he was unused to living rough, he soon learnt. The country was vast and for many miles they did not meet a soul. Then bands of young men emerged on the road, going to join the Confederate Army. They stared at the cotton but were too eager to be on their way to war to interfere with their journey. Always, there was a thirst for news. They heard the port at Galveston was still free but the Union Navy had been seen patrolling the sea in the distance. Sometimes they met wounded men travelling homeward, their hopes still high that the south would win. On that journey, the six men worked as a team, having to rely on one another. They were cheerful despite their difficulties travelling along the dry, baked road in the heat. Robert compared them to the sullen eyed slaves on the Amiens plantation. At night as the camp fire flickered, they told him their stories. Maurice had been a house slave and saved to earn his freedom. Angel had been granted it by a grateful master. Nathan's father had freed Jonah's grandfather himself and he and his family had stayed loyal to the Jacques family. William had been kidnapped by another plantation owner and claimed as a slave but the Jacques had fought hard to get him back. His fierce loyalty to David and his father was obvious whenever he spoke of them.

Robert Overdale, the pampered son of the Master of the Invincible, with his sleeves rolled up, helped the drivers change a wheel when all their strength was needed. He was hot, dirty and dusty, a hard stubble on his chin. He smiled to think how horrified his mother would be at his appearance, but he felt useful at last.

Finally, they trundled wearily into the port. Robert was elated but his troubles had just begun. He helped David and his men unload the bales of cotton at the quayside.

"I hope to see you again when I come to buy your next crop," he told David.

They were watched with suspicion by men hanging round the docks. Despite the hostility to him and his men, David Jacques loyally stayed with Robert until he could find a ship.

"You expect to find a ship for that?" asked one man. "Ain't no decent captain going to carry cotton for you."

To Robert's frustration, the man proved right. He scoured the quays for a ship to take his cargo, but no one would take the risk.

Finally they were directed to a Captain Ewell in a tavern. The Captain eyed Robert suspiciously.

"I'll take you and your cotton in my ship, the *Dancing Mary*, but it'll cost you," he said and spat on the ground.

Following the shambling man to the quay, Robert's heart fell when he saw the ramshackle vessel. But after his weary and fruitless search, he had no choice.

"Will she cross the Atlantic," asked David Jacques doubtfully.

"She crossed it with a cargo of Irish," shrugged the captain.

"Half of them died of the fever," muttered a man hanging around on the dock.

Captain Ewell scowled at him for interfering.

"The fever wasn't my fault. I didn't bring it aboard. The *Mary* has been in for repairs. I don't doubt she'll make it back but we can take you as far as Cuba, anyhow — or even Nassau if you make it worth my while."

The gold in Robert's purse was dwindling but if he could only reach Nassau, he was hopeful that Gus Kearsley's contacts there would take him home. Anxious to get home and away from America, he accepted Ewell's offer.

Robert shook the hands of his friends with heartfelt thanks. His heart sank as he waved goodbye to David, Maurice, Angel, Jonah and William, and watched the wagons roll back to the plantation, leaving him friendless and alone.

As the sun sank on the leaden water, they set out to avoid any blockading ships in the dark. The *Dancing Mary* should have been named the *Limping Mary*. The ship creaked and wallowed with the cotton bales piled high on her decks and stowed into every corner of the hold. Captain Ewell seemed determined to hug the coast, unwilling to trust his ship out at sea. On the fifth day, they headed out to sea as the Mississippi Delta neared. With darkness approaching over the listless sea, Robert sank wearily into his stuffy cabin. He longed for the green fields of England, the hills that cradled Gorbydale. Drifting to sleep, he became alert on hearing loud shouting. Anxiously he pulled on his clothes and hurried on deck. Everything was in turmoil. He grabbed the first man he saw who was hacking madly at the ropes binding the cotton.

"What the hell are you doing?"

The man pointed frantically at a ship on the horizon.

"It's the Yankees," he yelled. "Captain's orders. We gotta make the ship lighter to outrun them."

Robert stared helpless as his precious bales of cotton were tossed into the sea and bobbed like corks along behind them. They sank as they became sodden. He could have wept with frustration. Hurriedly, he began to help pulling at ropes to haul up the sails with the other sailors, to help in any way he could. The wind was in their favour and filled the sails. Achingly slowly, the *Dancing Mary* began to make headway, though the mast groaned and creaked in protest. There were few bales on deck now. Robert anxiously watched the horizon, his heart frozen in his chest. Then the sail tips of the Union ship finally disappeared into the sea. They'd outrun them.

"Good old *Mary*!" roared the captain.

It had been a close thing. At least there was the remaining cargo in the hold. Weary and disheartened, Robert flung himself on his bunk. Now he noticed his hands stinging and saw the raw scarlet wheals of rope burn. They'd outrun the Union but there were only weeks of cotton supplies for the Invincible Mill, not months as he'd hoped.

Despite their lucky escape, there was more trouble ahead. He was roused from his uneasy sleep by the violent rolling of the ship. The wind was howling through the rigging and grew ever louder as the timbers creaked as if in pain. Everything surrounding him felt as if it would collapse any moment. He tried to reach the door but lunged back as the ship heaved. With superhuman effort he left his cabin.

"Get back to your bunk," yelled a sailor, "or you'll be washed overboard in the storm."

Robert helplessly clung to his bunk as the ship heaved about. Above him, he heard the timber groan and crack followed by terrifying crashes of metal and wood. Heavy items rolled ominously about the deck. The shouts from the men were drowned in the howl of the wind. It wailed interminably like the ghosts of the Irish dead. A dagger of lightening cracked the sky and then the rain came. The thundering downpour sluiced into every imaginable crack and crevice. Robert shivered, the damp cold penetrating to his bones. All through the pitch black night, the ship lurched and strained. Robert prayed fervently, expecting to sink any minute. In the dismal light of dawn, the wind dropped and Robert dragged himself on deck. It was bare of cotton bales. The mast was cracked and fallen, dragging the sails with it. All about him weary men tried to put the stricken *Dancing Mary* to rights. He helped in small ways, needing to be useful. There were still bales in the hold, damp and smelling musty.

"How many days to Nassau," he asked the first mate.

"About a week if we can fix the mast and if the weather holds fair. If not, your guess is as good as mine," he answered with a surly shrug.

Three weeks later the *Dancing Mary* limped into sight of land. They'd been on short rations during the final week and Robert felt weak and hungry.

A hearty cry greeted him on the quay as he listlessly supervised the unloading of his sorry cargo.

"Overdale old chap, I've been waiting ages."

Gus Kearsley looked smart and healthy and had a pretty girl on each arm. Robert was suddenly aware how beggarly he looked.

"Dear me, we are a sorry sight. He's not so frightening when he's spruced up, ladies, believe me," said Gus, reintroducing the daughters of his father's shipping agent. "I'm sure the girls' Pa can put you up as a favour to me."

The girls giggled and agreed.

"I need to find a ship to take this cotton to Liverpool," said Robert wearily. "I didn't expect to find you here. I thought you'd be home by now."

"Just a little diversion, dear boy," said Gus smiling at the tallest girl. "There was some delay on the railway to Charleston. I hoped you'd turn up like the bad penny."

Robert was glad to leave arrangements to the girls' father. He felt more human when he'd bathed and shaved but he was painfully thin and the last of his money was gone now. Gus arranged for his friend's passage home to be paid on his father's account and Robert promised to pay him back. He wondered if that would be possible when they arrived home.

Chapter 27: The Letter

A quiet Christmas passed and still there was no word from Arden. Jessie and her mother lived in perpetual hope that he would come secretly back to Gorbydale one dark night when the *Great Eastern* docked again in Liverpool.

"What's become of him, Jessie?" sobbed Nellie twisting her sheets with her bony hands.

Jessie gently laid her warm hands on her mother's cold agitated fingers in reassurance.

"I don't know, Mother, but Arden is very sensible and capable. He'll be fine, wherever he is."

Though she was anxious herself, Jessie was sure it was the hope of Arden's imminent return that kept her mother's faint heart beating. Honora hadn't visited since the incident with the Tates but Jessie still used her treatments, though with failing success. Nellie dearly wanted to live to see her first grandchild. As Arden had guessed, the news from Jack and Elsie had revived their mother.

Jack called to see his mother one afternoon.

"Elsie feels very queasy these days," he told Nellie and Jessie. "But she sends her love to everyone."

"If I wasn't so useless, I could help her with her confinement," Nellie told him. "But I'm nowt but useless these days."

"Don't fret, Mother," said Jessie. "And anyway, you've been knitting that lovely blanket for the baby. There'll be plenty of people to help Elsie when the time comes."

"You mustn't worry, Mother," Jack reassured Nellie with a smile. "Elsie's Mam and Dad are moving in with us."

Jessie and her mother glanced at each other in dismay. They both knew Elsie's mother was hopeless. 'Shiftless' was what Nellie often called Clara. Jack twisted uneasily in his seat.

"They're behind with the rent and we couldn't see them in the workhouse. So we thought it would be better if they moved in with us. They are family after all, and it'll be company for Elsie while I'm at work. They'll be able to keep an eye on her until the baby arrives."

"Aye," said Nellie with forced enthusiasm. "Aye, it'll be for the best."

"Shall I make us a cup of tea?" said Jessie brightly.

Jack had left for home before Jacob came home, tired and despondent. As Nellie rested, Jessie had a quiet word with him.

"Mother's worried that Elsie's parents are moving in with Jack and Elsie. They were threatened with the workhouse."

"Aye, I reckon our Jack wouldn't let family go in there if he could help it. I wouldn't myself," he said quietly. "Now I don't want to worry your mother, but I must warn you, lass. There's nowt but Surat thread at the Endurance now. It's right rubbish and the very devil to weave. It breaks so often, the lasses are in tears. But it won't hold out long. I might soon be out of work."

Jessie squeezed his arm in sympathy. Was there much more that the Davenports could bear? Yet, when she saw the half-starved faces in the cold, grey town, she knew there were others so much worse off. They might soon be in the same situation but she was trying her best.

"We'll manage," she told Jacob with as much confidence as she could muster. "And we've the veg from your garden."

"Aye," said her father, shaking his head, "But there are a couple of turnips missing when I last looked. I don't suppose you've taken them without mentioning it?"

She shook her head.

"So someone's helped themselves," he said. "If they were that desperate, they could come and knock at the door. How's your mother, anyway?"

Jessie could not look him in the eye as she stirred the pot of pease pudding.

"Not so good," she muttered. "There's a lot more blood on her hankies today."

They were not handkerchiefs but old rags cut from flour bags and Jessie could not keep up with washing them. Her mother's breathing grew shallower and, with growing frequency, a heaving cough racked her frail body. She wasn't eating much either.

The crisis came one cold afternoon. Jessie was beside her mother's bed in the parlour. By lighting the one fire, she was saving coal throughout the day. A small kettle bubbled on the embers, the steam seemed to help Nellie breathe. Jessie watched her mother dozing. She was too mithered to read and was knitting a simple shawl with wool she'd gathered from the hedgerows during the summer. It was obvious it could not be long before her mother passed away and she felt so helpless. Here, alone, she dreaded it, but deep down longed to be free from watching her mother struggle to breathe. Night and day, Nellie's laboured gasps filled the house. Jessie felt trapped. Her only escape was walking on the hill but the wind had been bitter and the rain cold and sleety. Even when she ventured out into the garden, the sound of Nellie's unremitting efforts seemed to echo in her brain. But this longing to be free made her feel guilty too. Nellie was the heart of the family and her dying would rip a large hole in it.

Jessie wondered what would happen to her when it all came to pass. There was no work in the town. Could she leave her father and brother to fend for themselves if she tried to find a place in service somewhere in the country? An unexpected rattle silenced her thoughts and Nellie fell silent. Jessie gasped as she grasped her mother's cold hand.

"Mother, Mother," she pleaded, but Nellie lay still, her struggle to breathe over. Jessie didn't know what to do. Tears pouring down her face she ran, slipping on the icy cobbles, to Mary's house. She pounded on the door and her tears told them all they needed to know.

"Go and fetch Jacob from t'mill," Alice ordered her daughter.

Mary hugged Jessie.

"I'm so very sorry for your loss. Your Mam was a grand woman," she said sincerely before she hurried away on her mission.

Alice grasped the heartbroken girl's hand and they hurried back to the house.

"Sit and I'll make you some tea," said Alice taking charge of the dazed girl and reverently covering Nellie's face with the sheet. "You've had an awful shock but your mother's at peace now. It's been a long time coming but it's a shock all the same."

In a daze, Jessie slumped in a chair. After months of longing for silence, the house felt still and empty now her mother had gone. Before long, Jacob rushed into the house.

"Is she…?" he demanded of his daughter.

Jessie just nodded, her tearstained face revealing everything.

"I'll meet Eddie from school," said Mary, hurrying into the house behind him. "And we'll send a message to John."

"Thank you," whispered Jessie. "I feel so useless."

Jacob rushed into the parlour. His wail of despair wrenched the hearts of all who heard it. Jessie found him kneeling at Nellie's bedside, clutching her icy hand.

Jacob sat with his head in his hands. Jessie didn't know how to comfort him. She needed comforting herself. The day of her mother's funeral had passed like a blur.

Alice paused from drying dishes.

"You gave your Nellie a grand send-off, Mr Davenport," she said kindly. "I've never seen the chapel so packed. And the gentry, too! She would have been right proud."

The gentry in Alice's eyes had consisted of Eli Gorman and his niece Honora. Jessie had been touched and pleased to see her in the chapel. Honora rarely visited since that embarrassing incident with the Tates, obviously convinced that Arden had seduced her Aunt's maid. Jessie firmly believed her brother's denial and wondered what Dolly had been saying. Oddly, Tommo and Seth hadn't returned looking for Arden. No one had said a word to her concerning the rumours, giving her some hope they would fade away. She could not know that, warned by a furious Dolly to 'keep his gob shut', Tommo was now threatening anyone who impugned his daughter's supposed innocence. It was a brave man or woman who crossed Tommo Tate. Still, Jessie was heartened that Honora had paid her respects to Nellie. She missed her friendship.

Eli had sent a huge ham for the funeral tea afterwards, the remains of which sat now on the table.

"Will you take some ham for yourself and Mary," asked Jessie, grateful for all the help that her friend and her mother had given during that afternoon.

A weary Mary had left earlier.

"Oh, I couldn't," said Alice, looking longingly at the ham she'd been slicing all afternoon for mourners.

"You must," insisted Jessie, "as a thank you. We couldn't have managed without you both. Please — we'll have plenty."

Jacob looked up sadly and nodded.

"Aye, please take some. I've no appetite and it'll only go to waste."

"All right, then," agreed Alice and began to slice thinly.

Jessie put her hand on Alice's and made her make thicker slices.

"Take some more for your girls," she said.

"Not so many of my girls left now," she told Jessie sadly. "Ceridwen and her sister have gone home to Wales and Annie left for Shropshire yesterday. But Aggie and Nan are from the workhouse. They have nowhere else to go and I wouldn't send them back to that place. I know they're not paying rent but they're helping round the house."

"You're a good woman, Mrs Connolly," said Jacob. "Here, cut a bit more of that meat."

Alice laid a comforting hand on his shoulder.

"You'll feel as if you want to take to your bed, pull the covers over your head and never come out, as if nothing will ever be the same again. And no matter how many people tell you that life goes on, you won't believe them. That's just how I felt when my Cornelius passed on. But, believe me, Mr Davenport, there is a life to live — not the same life, but life all the same. And you have a lovely daughter and two big strapping sons and a baby on the way. And this young shaver here…" She smiled over at Eddie, who was sitting in a corner, his face pale and dazed. "He needs a father to guide him — and none better than you."

"Aye," said Jacob quietly. "Aye, I expect you're right. My Nellie was ailing for a long time and we knew it had to come to this. But you somehow don't expect it all the same. The house feels hollow."

He coughed and Jessie knew it was to disguise the sob in his voice.

"We all have to go through it — even the dear Queen. All her brass couldn't help Albert," Alice reminded him as she made to leave.

The whole country had been plunged into mourning since Prince Albert, the Queen's husband, had died before Christmas. Young Eddie fingered the black armband that his mother had insisted he wore on the sleeve of his jacket in honour of the Prince Consort. Now it would remain there for Nellie.

"Just you remember what I said, Jacob Davenport," said Alice. "God bless all of you. And thank you so much for this lovely ham. We'll eat well tomorrow at least. And I've some dried peas to make a nice pan of pea and ham soup that'll last us a few days."

"I can't thank you enough," said Jessie, accompanying her to the door. "And for all you've done for Mother and me while she was ailing."

"I'm just at the end of the Row if you need me," said Alice. "Don't forget."

Jacob was damping down the fire when Jessie came back into the house.

"Let's get some sleep," he said, rising wearily from his chair. "We've all had a long day."

Jessie thought he had never looked so old and defeated.

"School in the morning," she said briskly to her little brother.

Although she was sinking inside, she felt she must be positive for the family's sake. To her surprise, Jacob shook his head.

"The lad can have tomorrow off at least." Eddie came out of his reverie and looked gratefully relieved. "But he'll have to pull his weight after that. Grammar schools don't open their doors to slackers."

Eddie's mouth drooped again. Jessie knew her brother was a clever little chap but inclined to be lazy and let things drift. She hoped her father wasn't being too ambitious for him. Still, if it gave Father some hope in the future, how could she dampen his dreams for his youngest son.

Though they were weary, none of them slept well that night. Jessie wondered anxiously if her letter about her mother's death would reach Arden. Apart from a short note telling them he'd reached Canada, they'd heard nothing. They hadn't even had a letter from him at Christmas, much to her mother's dismay. Jessie had addressed her letter to his ship, the *Great Eastern*, but there was no way of knowing if he was still working aboard as an engineer.

Jessie would have cheerfully wrung Dolly Tate's neck. She'd seen little of her since they'd both left the mill. Dolly had often swanned about the town in her colourful outfits but she'd been missing for ages, no doubt trying to stay inconspicuous after the scandal she'd aroused. Would Arden ever be able to come home because of Dolly's lies?

Chapter 28: Arden

Arden knew nothing of his mother's passing. Shrouded in a grave black night, he silently watched over dark water for some glimmer of light, his ears honed for the sound of the rhythmic chug of an approaching engine. Out on the far coast of Carolina, he'd taken a turn on watch away from the stifling heat and engulfing fumes of the ship's boiler room, listening out for the approach of any blockade runners. But all was silent. Here, out in the cool sea air, he had plenty of time to think about his family and home.

He'd worked hard and learnt so much on the huge steamship taking troops to Canada. The chief engineer of the *Great Eastern* had wanted him to stay on and Arden had been very tempted. He'd been well paid and was touched when he'd found Jessie's small purse with her savings in his kitbag.

"Are you sure you won't sail back with us?" asked the engineer. "We'll be going to Australia soon with a shipload of immigrants. Surely you don't want to go to America in the middle of a war."

It was a tempting offer. Arden could have sailed back to Liverpool and slipped into Gorbydale some night to see his family with some money. He'd sent some at Christmas, though there was no way of knowing it had reached them. But echoing in his mind had been his mother's words to him.

"If you can do anything to release them poor creatures from the whip and the irons, then I'm right proud of you."

Arden was determined to join the Union Army and fight to free the slaves. He'd make his mother proud all right.

"I've a promise to keep," he'd told the chief engineer.

Robert Overdale's words at the Fort had stung him, too. Surely it was his duty to fight for the Union if he believed in emancipation so strongly.

With a letter of introduction from the engineer, he set out with renewed vigour into this new and bustling country. Weeks later, he was standing on the strangest ship he'd ever seen. It squatted like a giant iron turtle in the water and at its centre was a low gun turret. Staring into the black, unblinking eye of the barrel, for the first time he had doubts. Could he really blast human beings and ships to bits? Though, now he was committed and must go on.

"How do you like my Pootle Turtle?" asked the engineer in a soft Scottish burr.

Arden had been surprised to find a man from Inverness at the address he'd been given. Calum McKenzie read the letter of introduction.

"You'll do fine," he'd said. "You've had some experience with engines and that's the sort of man we need right now. Most of the Union sailors are used to sailing ships. They could turn on a sixpence in a strong westerly, but they might have trouble steering this beast in and out of the shoals."

Arden had been impressed by the engine room.

"This is the ship of the future man," Calum had told him. "See that turret in the middle, it revolves so we can fire on all sides. Ever since the south brought that murderous iron *Merrimack* to war, all ships with a wooden hull are redundant. I don't know how many of our ships she destroyed. Their returning fire bounced off her steel hull like rubber balls. But we've answered her back with the *Monitor* — and the revolving turret. Once we sent our lass to sort her out, the *Merrimack* scuttled back to port like a black beetle under its stone. There are more of these ironclads ready to go. We've had some setbacks, mind — engines blowing up and turrets jamming and the like, but I think we've overcome them."

Arden fervently hoped so too. Now on the deck of his ironclad, he waited in the darkness for the enemy. When he'd left England, he hadn't expected to fight against slavery in an oily, smelly biscuit tin.

Chapter 29: The Sewing Class

If Jessie had been too dazed to notice anything at her mother's funeral, Honora was not. She'd been shocked to see how gaunt and shabby the mill workers looked.

"Do you think we should do something for the mill girls?" she asked her aunt.

"How do you mean, dear?" asked Melissa.

Though Honora tried to distract her aunt, Melissa was continually thinking about Robert, agitated and unable to settle.

Robert's last letter had been full of joy and tales of the luxury in the southern states, though they hadn't heard from him for an age. Honora knew that Matthias wasn't well, though. He wouldn't admit it, but they knew he was fretting about his mill. Honora had attended Nellie's funeral in her Uncle Eli's gig. She hadn't known him very well, but he was a kind man and was greeted with respect and affection by everyone. There was no evidence of the wary attention she had seen in the eyes of Matthias's workers. Eli deserved his reputation around the town as a good employer. Jessie had often spoken well of her father's boss. Knowing all this, Honora had been planning.

"I don't want to trouble Uncle Matthias when he has so much on his mind," she told her aunt, "but I wonder if Uncle Eli would help us arrange something for the workers."

Melissa roused from her thoughts and began to pay attention.

"Eli has his own workers to worry about, dear. He's nearly out of thread for his own frames, so he tells me. What sort of help could he give our spinners?" she asked. "That's our duty, surely?"

So Melissa hadn't dismissed her suggestion outright.

"I've been thinking," said Honora becoming enthusiastic. "I read in the papers that some towns in Lancashire have started sewing classes for their girls. So I've been making enquiries. I'm sure we'd be able to get some help from the Relief Committee."

A Relief Committee had recently been set up in Gorbydale to help the unemployed. They were already in dispute with the Poor Law Board. The latter saw it as their duty to regulate the destitute, but it was obvious to all that they couldn't cope with the thousands out of work. The workhouse was crammed already. Honora was ready to put her faith in the Relief Committee, who at least were trying to help. Eager to make some contribution, she'd written to the organisers of a sewing class in a nearby town to see how it worked.

"Surely the girls can sew already?" said Melissa.

"Well no, Aunt. Most of them have worked long hours in the mill since they were children. They haven't had the opportunity or the time to learn to make their own clothes and now they certainly don't have the money to buy materials."

"Not be able to sew — I'm surprised at such a thing," said her aunt. "Sewing classes, you say?" Honora nodded vigorously. "If what you say is true, I think it is our Christian duty to teach the lasses to sew."

"Can we start a class, then?" asked Honora clutching her aunt's hand.

"Well I don't see why not," said Melissa with a smile. "Let me see — how about the billiard room. With Robert away…" She looked momentarily downcast. Honora had hoped this new project might distract Melissa, but everything seemed to remind her of her son. She was relieved when Melissa revived. "Matthias isn't a bit interested in billiards. What do you think, dear? Will it be big enough?"

"Oh, I'm sure it will be," said Honora happily. "I'll apply straight away to the Relief Committee for some funds. We could bring some benches from the mill and I'm sure we could purchase some calico cheaply."

"You seem to have given it a lot of thought," said her aunt.

"I'd like to help and I'm sure the girls will be eager to do something useful," said Honora.

She'd been encouraged to hear that the girls in the classes she'd heard about were full of enthusiasm.

"You must have some help, though," said Melissa thoughtfully. "I know you don't mind mixing with the working girls, dear — but I'm… I'm afraid your uncle might not like it for myself. We have a position to uphold. You understand, don't you, dear?"

"Yes, Aunt, of course. I wasn't suggesting you teach the girls to sew. I can do that myself."

Then Honora had an inspiration. She'd momentarily thought of Eliza Andrews but quickly dismissed her.

Mrs Walmsley was a frequent visitor to Overdale House and she often brought her niece, Eliza Andrews, with her. Honora smiled to herself as Mrs Walmsley unsubtly probed for the reason why her son Taylor was calling to see Matthias on a regular basis, especially with the mill closed. Honora had no idea why the overseer called and, if she had known, certainly wouldn't tell Mrs Walmsley. Honora couldn't warm to the woman or her niece with their affected superiority. She wondered if Miss Andrews even liked children, the way she spoke of her pupils. Although their visits gave her aunt some distraction, Honora wanted to engage Melissa in something to help the mill workers.

She thought for a moment and then had an idea.

"How about Jessie Davenport?" she suggested. "She teaches Sunday school at the chapel, you know. I know she sews because I've seen her many a time."

"Oh yes," said her Aunt. "She would be eminently suitable. A nice girl too. I knew her mother for many years. She knitted me a sweet little jacket when Robert was born. Poor Nellie."

Melissa knew nothing of the rumours circulating about Arden and Dolly and Honora hadn't enlightened her. Though she'd watched Dolly and tried to question her, the infuriating girl had been sullen and evasive. Despite Honora watching her closely, there didn't seem to be any sign of a child on the way.

Jacob had just returned home early from the weaving sheds when Honora arrived with her request. The Endurance had been running on short time to preserve their stocks, and at least to give the operatives some wages. Climbing Weavers Row, Honora felt ashamed that she hadn't visited for so long. She missed her chats with Jessie. Her own stupid pride had prevented her from calling after she had been so sharp with Arden. Yet, she'd heard through the ever rumbling grapevine that he'd gone away to sea and wasn't likely to be around. Jacob opened the door to her.

"Hello, Mr Davenport," said Honora shyly.

"Miss Darwen," said Jacob, bowing graciously. "I'm glad to have the opportunity to thank you for attending my late wife's funeral service. It was kind of you to come."

"I was honoured to do so," said Honora with a sympathetic smile. "She was a lovely woman. Even when she was so ill, she had that spark of humour. You must miss her dreadfully."

"Aye, we do that," he said, his eyes straying away in sadness. "Anyway, please come in and take a seat. Jessie will be right glad to see you."

He plumped the cushion on the best chair, although it really didn't need plumping.

"I've come with a request for Jessie. My aunt and I have some plans to help the lasses of Gorbydale and I do hope you approve."

Coming in from the garden shed carrying a bowl of carrots, Jessie was taken aback to see Honora by the fireside.

"Hello, Jessie," she said smiling. "I've really come to ask for your help. My aunt and I are thinking of setting up a sewing class. I was wondering if you'd help teach the local girls to sew. I've seen your beautiful embroidery and I know you have teaching experience from the Sunday school. I wouldn't know where to begin by myself. I'm sure the girls would come if you were there to help them."

Jacob was immediately on his feet.

"Miss Darwen, she'll do it."

"If you're sure, Father?" said Jessie beaming.

"Too right, my girl," commanded Jacob. "You've sacrificed all these months looking after your mother without a word of complaint. Eddie's not a babby and neither am I. We can shift for ourselves. I've heard something of these classes, Miss Darwen. Will they be as long as working days at the mill?"

"Oh no. Oh no," she reassured him. "I've been to see a class in another town and heard how they operate in some others. We were planning to begin at nine, have a bowl of soup and bread at midday and finish at four after tea and bread and jam. I believe there's to be some small payment from the Relief Committee too."

"That's some plan," said Jacob in admiration. "It'll give the girls something to do and a bit in their pockets — as well as something to eat. Our Jessie will certainly help. Won't you, lass?"

Jessie nodded happily as she stood beside her father. She hugged his arm in gratitude.

"I'd love to help. I'll still have time to get home and make our tea," she said smiling.

"We'll all make the tea," decided Jacob grandly. "Eddie and all."

The following week, Jessie went up to Overdale House and between them, she and Honora got to work and made all the arrangements they could. They found some small tables that they could use in the attic, and inspected the benches in the mill. Melissa took an interest but left most of the work to the girls. She listened carefully to their plans, making some suggestions and agreeing to others. Then she and Honora went to explain their plans to Matthias. Honora held her breath as they approached her uncle.

He listened in silence as first Melissa, then Honora told him what they hoped to do.

"So you expect me to have a tribe of grubby mill girls trampling all over my house?" grumbled Matthias.

"The girls will be no trouble, I'm sure," protested his wife. "But if you're not willing, perhaps I could ask our Eli if he will help," said Melissa looking thoughtful, with a sly glance at Honora. "He's very good to his workers. Although, it must be said that most of the girls would be from *our* mill. Some would think it was *our* duty to look out for them. '*Noblesse oblige*', isn't that what our Robert said? But if you think it isn't right, dear…?"

Matthias gave his wife a searching look and she contrived to look completely innocent of her cunning attempt to exploit her husband's rivalry with Eli.

"I run a mill not a charity," he growled.

Noticing the dismay on Melissa's face, he relented.

"Have it your own way then."

Melissa was delighted. She came and kissed the top of his grizzled head.

"Thank you, dear, and don't worry about the girls tramping around the house. They can come into the billiard room through the garden door and Honora is arranging for a privy outside at the back of the shrubbery."

"Honora! Oh, she's paying the bills, is she?" said her husband scathingly and buried himself once more in his newspaper.

"The Relief Committee is giving us some money," Honora assured him. "Thank you so much, Uncle. Aunt Melissa and I will make sure you aren't troubled by the class."

He relaxed back in his chair and glanced up at her.

"Aye, happen it'll keep you ladies out of my hair and keep you busy. It'll maybe stop my wife mithering about Robert and '*Are you feeling all right, dear?*' every few minutes."

With that he went back into his newspaper and dismissed them. The two women went gleefully back to their plans. Matthias wasn't exactly enthusiastic about their ideas, but he wasn't opposing them either. Now the sewing class could get underway. The following week, when Jessie and Mary spread the news around their old workmates, a few girls trailed up to Overdale House, glancing in awe at the billiard room which looked splendid, despite the addition of the benches from the mill. Within weeks, the class had grown when the word spread there was food to be had up at the Master's house and occupation to lift them from their despair and encroaching destitution. Jessie and Honora supervised their pupils with pride. Honora had to admit, though, that the girls were more at ease with Jessie.

Chapter 30: The Homecoming

"Master Robert's home — and he's brought cotton with him."

Everyone looked up in surprise as Dolly Tate burst into the billiard room with her announcement. Two seconds before, a busy class of girls had been sewing and chatting, singing snatches of song and generally making themselves useful.

Melissa leapt to her feet with a joyful cry.

"Robert, Robert! Oh my boy, my dear boy."

She hurried out and Honora and all the girls set down their work and followed. Jessie wished her heart would not pound so hard. Robert Overdale was nothing at all to her. As the girls worked, his mother had been reading out extracts from his letters. Obviously, he'd had a wonderful time with pretty southern belles. Jessie had refused to think about him, even working in the comfort of his home. To her consternation now, she could not control her racing heart. Self-consciously, she patted her hair into place and followed the others.

There was a crowd milling round the gates of the Invincible as the rumour spread. Melissa and Honora were let in at the gates. Matthias was already there, pumping his son's hand eagerly, his chest puffed out in pride. Melissa immediately folded her son in her arms in front of everyone, much to his embarrassment. Behind them was a wagon piled with bales of cotton. The quality didn't seem as good as the cotton they were used to — but it was cotton and cotton meant work.

The crowd pressed towards the gate.

"There doesn't seem enough cotton there to keep us going for long," muttered a familiar voice beside Jessie.

She turned slowly and, to her utter confusion, came face to face with Taylor Walmsley. Interested as he was in the arrival of the cotton, he hadn't spotted her in front of him there in the crowd. He looked shaken to find her so near.

"Miss Davenport," he said in surprise.

Jessie saw him colour, but her own cheeks blushed hot, too. Only the year before she might have been married to him, closer and more intimate than anyone she'd ever known. He might have shied away from asking but his very nearness disturbed her.

"Mr Walmsley," she answered politely, sure he could hear the tremble in her voice.

"I was sorry to hear about your mother," he said quietly. "I'm sorry I couldn't come to the chapel. I was away on business for Mr Overdale."

"Aye, so I heard."

He looked uncomfortable. There was much speculation about Taylor's business. All Jessie knew was that he was well dressed and well fed in a town full of shabby, thin people. There was a rumour he was buying a house on Victoria Terrace and that he was about to marry the schoolteacher. Whenever the girls in the sewing class mentioned his name in their gossip, they'd slyly glance at Jessie. She'd noticed his visits to Overdale House for business with Matthias but he'd been too determinedly set in his purpose to glance at the mill girls around the billiards room.

"Three cheers for Master Robert," called Mr Armitage the mill manager, and the crowd cheered.

Robert took off his hat and bowed to the crowd, smiling broadly. He was tanned but looked thin and his clothes seemed too big for him. The moment he straightened up he caught Jessie's eye in the sea of faces.

In the hubbub of the crowd, few could have heard what he said to Mr Armitage next. But nearly everyone saw. Every one of the mill workers could lip-read. He might as well have stood on the gateposts and shouted.

"Will you give some work to Jessie Davenport?" he asked the manager.

Mr Armitage shook his head firmly.

"Your father's instructions are to give work to married men with families," he said.

The people around Jessie stared at her in surprise and she blushed furiously. She turned away in embarrassment to find Taylor glaring at her. Then, without a word, he strode angrily away. Why on earth had Robert Overdale said such a thing in front of everyone? Jessie was only thankful that his mother and Honora could not lip-read. What would they think when Robert had singled her out from everyone in the crowd? In her confusion, Jessie hurried back towards the sewing class. He had shamed her in front of all of Gorbydale.

The sewing class reluctantly returned to their work. The girls said nothing to her but she could see the curiosity in their sly glances. To her relief, she saw nothing of Robert as his mother claimed him.

A couple of days later, Honora approached Jessie.

"Would you mind waiting for a few minutes after the sewing class?" she asked.

Jessie nodded.

Her heart sank. Why did Honora want to speak to her? Had someone mentioned that Robert had singled Jessie out for special attention? Was she angry?

As the girls filed out from their class, chatting and happy, Jessie lingered anxiously behind. She was tidying up some materials when Dolly Tate wandered into the billiard room.

"Oh, it's you," sniffed Dolly.

"Hello, Dolly," said Jessie icily.

Because of this stupid girl and her false accusations Arden, her brother, had gone to America.

"You needn't look so uppity with me," sneered Dolly. "I'm not the one throwing my cap at the Master's son."

"That's a lie, Dolly Tate," snapped Jessie angrily.

"Oh yeah — and all the town saw it with their own eyes."

Sticking her nose in the air, Dolly strutted out of the room. Jessie seethed with anger despite her worries. What would Honora say? She was quick enough to believe that Arden had seduced Dolly. Would she hear the rumours and believe Jessie was chasing Robert?

Honora hurried into the room.

"I'm so sorry to keep you waiting, Jessie," she said smiling apologetically. "I've just been to consult Aunt Melissa."

"That's all right," said Jessie relieved that Honora didn't seem angry.

"Jessie, I know we're very busy here with the sewing classes and we've achieved a great deal between us, but I wonder if I can count on you for another project."

"Another project?" asked Jessie intrigued. "What is it?"

"It's something my cousin Robert suggested," continued Honora. Jessie's breath froze at the mention of his name. "He wondered if we could teach the girls to read. He met a slave in America and she was so proud of the fact that she could read, he wondered if our girls might learn too."

Jessie felt oddly pleased with Robert, despite the fact she was also annoyed with him.

"That's a very good idea," she said.

"Then you'll help?" asked Honora. "Most of the girls can work unsupervised now and I'm sure we could teach one or two at a time to read and write for a couple of hours each day. Some might just need improvement. I know the young apprentices had some basic instruction."

"I'm sure Mary will help with the sewing," suggested Jessie. "She often helps the girls when they get into difficulties."

Honora smiled.

"That's settled then. I'll see if there are any of Robert's old primers in the nursery. We can ask tomorrow if anyone would like lessons. I wouldn't want to force anyone," she added anxiously.

"I'm sure we'll have lots of volunteers," Jessie told her.

"See you tomorrow then, Jessie," said Honora hurrying away, eager to set up her new project.

Jessie turned to leave but as she did so, a familiar figure blocked her path. Her heart began to pound so hard she was sure Robert Overdale would hear it.

"Miss Davenport," he said smiling, taking the doorknob as if to hold it open for her.

"Mr Overdale," she answered shyly, avoiding his eyes.

"I've been looking out for you," he said quietly. "But I could swear you were avoiding me."

It was true. She had dreaded facing him but she had no choice now. She was surprised how lean his face had become on his travels. He had lost his youthful bloom. She could not know the hardship he'd faced for he'd told no one. Jessie felt an unwelcome wave of compassion, despite the fact that he'd embarrassed her in front of the whole town. She faced him boldly.

"It's not surprising I've avoided you after what you said to Mr Armitage in the Invincible yard."

Robert was taken aback.

"Whatever do you mean?" he asked. "How on earth could you have heard what I said?"

"Surely you've been round the mill long enough to know that everyone can lip-read," she said angrily. "Everyone in Gorbydale knows what you said. I'm so embarrassed. I'm only thankful that your mother and cousin don't know that you asked for work for me before everyone else."

"Oh, Jessie … Miss Davenport … how stupid of me. I should have realised. I'm truly sorry."

"And so am I," said Jessie making to leave hastily.

"Please, Jessie," he said earnestly. "I was only trying to help. When I saw you there … I've been thinking about you a lot."

"Oh, especially when you were waltzing with the southern belles," she answered sarcastically.

"Especially then," said Robert to her surprise. "Despite myself, I can't help myself thinking about you. I thought that none of them compared to you. You might not believe me, Jessie, but honestly it is true."

Jessie stared at him. He seemed so sincere. She hesitated and her hand trembled on the door.

"I have to go, Mr Overdale," she said, hastily coming to her senses.

"Please. I know you think I'm a fool, but when I come back from America, I'm going to prove I'm not."

"You're going to America *again*," she said, surprised at how disappointed she felt.

"I must. Oh, I know I was treated as some sort of hero back at the mill — but we both know there isn't enough cotton there to keep the mill going for a fortnight. I have to find a cargo to take to America and then return with more cotton. But when I come back, will you promise me something?"

"It depends," she said quietly.

"If your heart isn't otherwise engaged when I come back — will you at least let me speak to you?"

Jessie felt rooted to the spot. It wasn't fair that he should affect her like this. How could she tell if he was sincere? Yet, when she looked into his eyes, he seemed so genuine. There was many a poor girl who fell into that trap, only to be abandoned. She was startled by a sound along the hall and hurried to escape. She didn't want to be discovered talking to Robert Overdale by Dolly Tate. Yet, she could not help but glance back into Robert's pleading eyes.

"I'll see," she murmured quickly and ran down the steps of Overdale house.

Her heart was bursting as she hurried home. Why hadn't she said 'no' forcefully? Why did he affect her so? Jessie was panting hard as she climbed the brew to Weavers Row. Her father was peeling potatoes as she burst into the cottage.

"Here, let me do that?" she said.

"No, I've said we'll all muck in and we will," said Jacob smiling.

"You're home early," said Jessie picking another potato and setting to work.

"Aye," said her father. "I've to tell you that your father is no longer a weaver."

"Oh no, Father!" said Jessie in dismay.

So the Endurance had finally run out of yarn for weaving and her father was out of work.

"Nay, lass," said Jacob with a chuckle. "I'm to be a painter and decorator." Jessie gasped in surprise. "Aye, Eli has decided that his old mill needs sprucing up — and who better to do it than his idle weavers."

"At least it's work," said his daughter with some relief.

"That's what I thought too," he told her. "And beggars can't be choosers."

As Jessie scraped the potatoes, she tried to think about Robert. Why had she any feelings for him at all? 'Despite himself' he'd said he thought about her. What a cheek! She wished she'd refused him outright instead of saying 'I'll see' in that pathetic way. Fiercely chopping at the potatoes, she was angry with herself that, despite her deepest instincts, she had not firmly rejected his suggestion.

Chapter 31: An Arrival

Somehow, Jessie managed to avoid Robert for the next few days. She made herself busy with the reading lessons. Then Honora mentioned that he'd gone to Birmingham and Jessie felt relieved that she didn't need to dodge into doorways whenever she sensed his presence.

"I expect Robert's gone looking for arms to ship to America," said Honora tersely, and then checked herself. "Do we need any more pencils sharpening?"

Jessie stared at her and, when Honora rapidly changed the subject, guessed she hadn't meant to criticise her cousin aloud. No one else seemed to have noticed the slip and Jessie wished she hadn't been so anxious about Robert's whereabouts.

Lots of girls wanted to learn or improve their reading and many were making good progress. Jessie felt quietly fulfilled by her friends' progress and Honora felt useful at last. The billiard room was full to capacity. Melissa occasionally wandered in but she spent most of her time pampering her son whenever he was home. Though, he was frequently away finding cargo for America or exercising his horse on the hills. Then Melissa entered the billiard room linking Robert one morning, determined to show him how proud she was of 'her girls' as she called the sewing class. Jessie concentrated hard on teaching one of the girls her alphabet, desperately trying to ignore him. Coming close, he gently teased his old primer from her pupil's hand.

"I'm glad my old book has come in useful. I hope it's helping," he asked her pupil with a smile.

She blushed and smiled back at him.

"Oh yes, Master Robert," she giggled with a sly grin at Jessie. Jessie was aware of a myriad eyes watching her.

"The girls are doing very well," she said evenly, refusing to meet his eyes. "The reading class was a very good idea."

She hated to admit it but felt she should give him credit.

Dolly came in to announce that Gus had called from Liverpool. To Jessie's relief, Melissa hauled Robert away to welcome his friend. Sometime later, their patroness came into the class looking tearful. Melissa sat beside Honora, her face pinched with anxiety.

"Your cousin Robert is insistent that he goes back to America next week. Can't you persuade him not to, dear? He'll listen to you. Surely you can persuade Robert it's time to settle down?"

Jessie, sewing nearby, had a sudden realisation that there might be an understanding between the cousins. Were they promised to one another? If that was so, Robert was wicked to make advances to her and she'd been right to suspect his motives. How could he cynically toy with her feelings like that? She'd been a fool. Before he left, she would tell him never to speak to her again. As it turned out she had no chance to speak to him at all.

That evening Jacob arrived home tired and flecked with paint. But he was content to be doing something useful and the small wage Jessie earned as a supervisor helped too. Just as they prepared to go to bed, there was a frantic knocking on the door. Jacob opened it and found Toby, Elsie's young brother anxiously standing there, his face scarlet with effort.

"Your Jack says Jessie's got to come quick," he panted. "Elsie's having the baby."

"Is your mother Clara with her?" asked Jessie, hastily reaching for her shawl.

"Oh, aye — but she's taken a turn and me Da's thrown a jug of water over her."

Jessie stared in surprise.

"Over Clara, I hope," asked Jacob with a wry smile.

Toby nodded. Jessie smiled with relief — for a moment she'd thought Elsie had been soaked. Obviously, Elsie's family were useless in a crisis.

"I'll get Harry and his cart to take you to Doveton. You can't rush five miles in the dark," said Jacob, disappearing into the night.

A clatter of hooves echoed in Weavers Row some time later and Jessie and a thankful Toby hurried aboard a cart pulled by a sturdy little pony.

"Don't worry, Jacob. I'll get thy lass to Doveton," said Harry.

"I owe you one," said Jacob, stroking the pony's head.

"Nay, lad. I owe you and your dear departed more than you'll ever owe me," said the driver.

Jessie felt very proud of her parents and their reputation among their neighbours. They hadn't had much, but what they'd given was time and commitment to those around them.

"You'll let them know at Overdale house, won't you?" she asked Jacob.

"Don't you worry, lass. I'll send Eddie up in the morning before he goes to school. You get going before there's more water flung about."

The drive in the dark seemed to take an age but soon the lights of Doveton appeared. The cart jogging over the cobbles increased Jessie's anxiety. She had never delivered a baby before, only made herself useful as Nellie helped her neighbours. She fervently prayed that there would be no complications.

Chaos prevailed in the little railway house when they arrived, with Clara flapping and Elsie's father trying to clear up. The house looked as if it hadn't been tidied in days. Jack rushed downstairs to greet his sister.

"Thank goodness you've arrived," he said, glaring in exasperation at his in-laws.

"How is she?" asked Jessie.

"She's better now I've thrown the midwife out," said Jack. Clara glared back at him as he led Jessie upstairs. "She was some cousin of Clara's," he whispered, "an awful woman. I could smell drink on her. Poor Elsie was terrified of her and she's in such pain. Oh, Jessie, please help her."

His sister promised to do what she could.

Elsie looked very young and very frightened as she lay on the bed waiting for the next wave of labour pains to engulf her. Jessie ordered a basin of cold water and bathed the poor girl's temples.

"You'll be fine now, Elsie," she told the anxious girl with a confidence she did not feel.

Elsie became calmer now Jessie was present. "When you feel the urge to push take some deep breaths and pant — you know, like a dog when it's hot," she advised.

Jessie smiled as she remembered Nellie instructions to girls in labour.

"Are you sure?" asked Elsie, looking bewildered.

"It was what Mother used to say and she helped to bring lots of babies into the world. Just do it and I'm sure it'll ease things."

Jessie had no idea why, but her wise mother knew a thing or two — so it must be right.

It was a long anxious night and Elsie was weeping with exhaustion. Ada, the wife of one of Jack's older colleagues arrived to help and Jessie felt relieved she had some support.

"I can see the head," said Jessie in awe.

But it took a worrying age before the little face completely emerged. Then finally, Elsie gave a loud cry and a couple of convulsive heaves and her baby slithered to the world.

Finally, the family had a new member to celebrate.

"What is it?" asked the new mother tearfully.

"Elsie, you have a lovely daughter," said Jessie crying with relief.

The baby roared in surprise at its bumpy entrance into the world. With Ada's help, Jessie remembered what Nellie had done and tied off the umbilical cord. Then she scooped the baby into a clean white towel and cleaned her nose and mouth. Seconds later, there were heavy footsteps on the stairs and an urgent tapping at the bedroom door.

"Wait a moment," ordered Jessie.

Once the afterbirth had come away, Jessie bundled up the soiled sheets and towels from under her sister-in-law. Ada propped an exhausted Elsie up on pillows and bathed her face. Then Jessie handed her her new daughter.

"You can come in now," had hardly left her lips before Jack rushed in to his wife.

"Oh, Elsie, Elsie. Are you all right, love? I could hardly bear it."

"*You* could hardly bear it!" said Jessie laughing. "Congratulations, Jack. You have a lovely daughter. You can be really proud of Elsie. She was so brave."

"I couldn't have been brave without you," said Elsie sobbing. "Oh, Jessie. Oh, Jessie, thank you, thank you."

She hugged her daughter to her.

"What will you call her?" asked Jessie.

"We thought Eleanor," said the happy parents together and began to laugh in relief.

"Mother would have been so proud," said Jessie. "It's a beautiful name and it's a shame she was only ever called Nellie."

Drawing the curtains, she was surprised to see a dawn blush in the sky. She crept away to let the new parents greet their daughter together. She began to wonder why any woman would want to marry and bring children into the world when it was so dangerous, but that was just life and all life was a risk. Although she hadn't slept all night, she found herself making breakfast for the rest of the family. Clara looked on helplessly, complaining how badly she'd slept on the chair.

Later that day, Father and Eddie arrived to see Eleanor, sensibly bringing with them the layette that Jessie had prepared. Clara had been superstitious about having it in the house before the baby arrived.

"Are you sure you want to stay here?" asked Jacob quietly when Jessie told him her plans.

"I should stay close by for a few days, just until Elsie can cope," she told him. "Clara's a waste of space and Ada has offered me a bed at her house."

So Jessie missed her chance to tell Robert what she thought of him. By the time she arrived home, he was on the high seas, determined to buy cotton for the Invincible. Though, he was about to sail into problems.

Chapter 32: Overboard

"The enemy ship on the starboard."

Aboard the squat blockade runner, Robert Overdale knew instantly that they had been spotted. In the darkness, the intense, silent and anxious wait was shattered and there was frantic action everywhere. He heard the first shell whiz overhead and automatically ducked. The second shell shot across their bow.

"Get below if you don't want to lose your head," hissed Clement Duplege.

Robert had been dismayed to see him board the ironclad at Nassau. Clement continually mocked Robert's last voyage to find cotton. The southerner seemed angry that he had actually managed to do it. He had not expected Robert to be successful, though not surprisingly for a spy, he'd known what little cargo Robert had managed to cart into Gorbydale. It had been rapidly used up, but for a brief couple of weeks the silent Invincible had been a busy humming shadow of itself. Robert desperately needed more cotton.

He was climbing down the iron ladder when a shell hit the side with a loud 'crump'. With arms flailing, he fell sideways and plunged down the steps. Dazed and unable to move for a paralysing moment, he heard the immediate call for a damage report. A sailor barged past him down the steps to find out.

"She's hit below the water line," he gasped to the captain. "The water's pouring in. And it's the side where the ammo is stashed. We could blow up at any minute."

Robert hadn't suspected there were armaments on board, although it should have been obvious with Clement around.

His own cargo of blankets and bearings would be lost too if the boat went down. There was a hasty exchange of fire in the darkness and another shell crunched into the gunnery turret. A couple of sailors staggered out, dazed and bloodied.

"Get the guns out," barked Clement and rushed down to the hold.

The ironclad lurched drunkenly to one side and Robert had to grip hard to stay upright. Bruised by the fall, his leg was painful. Then the boat shuddered and the steady beat of the engine died. As Clement staggered back dragging a crate of guns, the captain told the men to abandon ship.

"Every man for himself," he barked.

"We've got a valuable cargo down there," snapped Duplege. "The south needs guns."

"If the ship goes, the cargo goes. I ain't risking my men for a pile of guns," growled the captain. "If we're caught with guns, we're dead men. You'll be shot as a spy, anyways."

Robert dragged himself some way up the ladder and turned back to give Clement a hand with his crate. Somehow they reached the deck.

Robert wavered. The men around him were scrambling onto a small wooden boat that they'd been towing behind. Clement did not hesitate. He abandoned the guns and climbed over the side. The small boat was now full of men and low in the water. There was no room for Robert. Silently, but for the small splash of the oars, it moved away into the darkness. The Union boat was so near now he could hear the steady beat of its engine and the loud call for surrender. Robert came to his senses. As a British citizen they could not touch him. But if they suspected he was a spy, he could be shot. Quickly alert to his plight, he was glad he could swim thanks to his Uncle Eli's lessons in the shallows of the Gorby river. Lurching down the heaving stairs into the mess, he grabbed a small table and struggled to the deck. Hurriedly pulling off his boots, Robert threw it overboard and dived into the water after it. He grabbed for the table and paddled frantically with his feet, leaving the ship and his cargo as far behind him as he could. In the darkness he could hear the splash of men jumping overboard as the Union ship loomed ever nearer.

As the sun rose on the sunburnt face of Robert Overdale, he awoke and wearily tried to crawl along the sand to find shelter. His clothes were ragged, his feet bare and his mouth was chokingly dry. The gold sovereigns sewn into his jacket were at the bottom of the Gulf of Mexico and he had no idea where he was. But the small hard lump in his waistcoat pocket reminded him all his gold was not lost and his signet ring was firmly on his finger. It was a relief to know he was not entirely destitute. Struggling to his knees, he noticed the battered table that had saved him some way along the beach. Propping it up against some rocks, he made a makeshift shelter against the beating sun. Then he waited, exhausted, until twilight, before setting out to find where on earth he had landed in the vast continent. As the sun sank down he strained his eyes to find some sort of habitation to find something to eat. Cooling his parched throat with some tepid water from a small stream, Robert headed into the unknown.

Chapter 33: The Patient

Melissa had been anxious ever since her son had left. There had been no word from him since his arrival in Nassau weeks before. She could think of nothing else and paid little attention to Matthias. Honora was ever vigilant though, and asked her uncle how he was feeling.

"I'm fine," he grunted. "Don't fuss."

"Perhaps we could call Dr. Hughes to take a look at you," she tried.

His eyes were bloodshot, his face ruddier than his normal high colour, but still he refused to see the doctor. On Friday evening once the sewing class had finished, Melissa screamed for Honora. She rushed in to find Matthias slumped at his desk.

"We must get Dr Braddock — at once," said Honora, urgently trying Matthias's pulse.

Dolly was hovering by the door alerted by the commotion.

"Dolly," cried Honora. "Go and fetch the doctor. The Master's very ill. Tell him to hurry."

Eventually the doctor arrived to examine Matthias, lying in bed looking old and ill, his face distorted.

"He's had a stroke," said the doctor, feeling his patient's pulse. "He needs rest and quiet. I've brought some leeches."

Melissa glanced at Honora, looking appalled. "I'm not having those awful old fashioned things in my house," Melissa protested. "My husband must have the best treatment there is."

Dr Braddock sighed.

"Explain to your aunt that leeches will relieve the pressure on the haemorrhage," he told Honora. "Some of the old cures are still the best. We'll know better in a day or two what the damage has been."

Honora gently explained what the doctor had said, but her aunt still shuddered when the black sucking creatures were put on her husband's temples. Honora was relieved when later, Matthias looked to be resting quietly. "Whatever will we do?" sobbed Melissa.

"We must wait to see how much Uncle Matthias is affected," Honora gently told her aunt. "But you mustn't worry. Mr Armitage will manage the mill," said Honora. "And we can ask..." She thought for a moment. "Taylor Walmsley to continue as his agent. I'm sure that's what Uncle would do. We must let Uncle Eli know too. Perhaps he'll be able to help with the business end of things."

"Oh, Honora, you're such a comfort," sobbed Melissa, clutching her niece's hand tightly. "But Robert should be here to look after his father's business — not gadding about in America."

By Monday, Matthias was sitting up in bed and fretting about his business once more, but Honora insisted he stayed there. She gave him some laudanum to help him rest.

The sewing class was already busily working with Jessie and Mary when Honora arrived looking worried.

"What's the matter?" Jessie asked her quietly. "Our Eddie said Dolly promised him a penny to run for the doctor. Is someone in the house ill?"

"My uncle has had a mild stroke. He's improving but we don't want it generally known because of his business. If anyone asks, we're to say he has a bad cold," Honora told her confidentially. She knew to trust Jessie. "My aunt is very fretful this morning. I doubt she'll be visiting the class. I do wish we would hear from Robert. He's needed at home and we have no way of getting in touch with him."

"I know how you feel," said Jessie sadly. "We've given up waiting for a letter from Arden. Every day my mother…"

She took a deep breath as tears came to her eyes.

Melissa did call into the class later. The girls lifted their heads from their work and greeted her politely.

"Matthias is a little better," she told Honora. "He's resting so I thought I'd join you."

"It might take your mind off things, Aunt dear," Honora sympathised.

But Melissa sat by the window staring into the distance. The girls didn't stay quiet for long. As usual someone began humming as she busied herself with her sewing. Then another took up the tune and began to sing. Honora loved to listen to their sweet voices. Perhaps the music would cheer her aunt. Mary began singing 'Sweet Polly Oliver', about a girl who followed her true love to war.

"When sweet Polly Oliver lay musing in bed, a sudden strange fancy came into her head," sang Mary. "Nor father nor mother will make me false prove. I'll list for a soldier and follow my love."

The other girls were about to take up the tune when, to their surprise, Melissa began to sob loudly. Mary's voice trailed off.

"I wish I could go and find Robert," sobbed Melissa bitterly. "If I were a man, I'd go and bring him back home. He has no business in America while his father is ill. Oh, when will he come home?"

Honora hurried to put a comforting arm round her aunt.

"Come along, Aunt dear," she coaxed. "I'll make you a nice cup of tea. You've had a disturbed night with Uncle and all. Come and rest."

"You mustn't worry, Mrs Overdale," said Jessie. "I'm sure Master Robert will be home soon."

"I wish I could believe you," wept Melissa.

She allowed herself to be led away by Honora.

The girls glanced uneasily at one another. You didn't have to be poor to be visited by troubles. Although the billiard room was in a different wing from the bedrooms of Overdale House, the girls stayed quiet in sympathy with their hosts.

"Perhaps we should find a different place to hold the classes," suggested Jessie to Honora when she came back.

"She'll be fine when she's had a proper sleep," said Honora. "But I do wish Robert would write."

Chapter 34: A Meeting on the Bridge

Jessie walked home alone. As she passed the bridge over the Gorby river, she noticed Tommy Dale and a few of his friends idly throwing stones into the water. The town was full of jobless young men hanging about. Although she was nervous of approaching them, she decided to say a civil 'hello' to Tommy if he spoke to her. Although he had started the rumours about her brother and Dolly Tate, it wasn't wise to make enemies of anyone in the small town. She froze as a stone bounced very close to her feet. Another hit the side of her shoe.

"Well, well," sneered Tommy. "Here's young Master Overdale's fancy piece."

Jessie had never felt so afraid in her own home town. Taking a deep breath she steeled herself to ignore him and walk on. But her fear turned to anger.

"How dare you, Tommy Dale!" she hissed fiercely. "You're a worse gossip than any old woman." His friends sniggered. "It's you and your evil tongue that blackened our Arden's name — and all because you were jealous that Dolly Tate was chasing after him instead of you."

"He didn't run very fast then, did he? Except he ran away fast enough to America when he heard the Tates were after him," snapped Tommy.

"They might be after you an' all if they hear you talking about their Dolly," she challenged him. "You're nothing but a coward, throwing stones at women."

He hesitated but stung back.

"And you ain't running so fast yourself if what they say about you and young Master Overdale is true."

"Well, it's a lie. You've an evil mind and an evil tongue, Tommy Dale. Robert Overdale asked for work for me because he knows our family and he was just being kind — no other reason."

Jessie turned away knowing she had made things worse by retaliating. She'd tried to clear her name, though knew it was useless. The lads began to jeer at her. She heard them call 'scrubber' and 'whore' and making lewd suggestions. Then suddenly they went silent, shuffling uneasily on their worn clogs.

"Are you having trouble with these idlers, Miss Davenport?" demanded a familiar voice. Jessie turned to find Taylor Walmsley beside the bridge. "Haven't you anything better to do?" he demanded of Tommy and his cronies.

"No, Mr Walmsley," they muttered.

Taylor strode past them and fell into step beside Jessie.

"I'll walk with you as far as Weavers Row," he said quietly. "You'll have no more trouble from them. They'll be afraid to cross me in case they'll not get work when the mill reopens."

"Thank you," said Jessie humbly. "Thank you, Mr Walmsley."

Yet still they were not left in peace. A bitter aside from the humiliated Tommy followed them.

"He's a hypocrite an' all dealing with the south. Them chapel lot are all the same — a big bunch of hypocrites."

Jessie and Taylor ignored them and walked silently on. Jessie did not know what to say. She'd heard the rumours too.

"I expect you heard Dale," said Taylor wearily as they stopped at the end of the Row. Jessie nodded silently. "He's right, though. I could have turned Matthias Overdale's offer down but I didn't. A man's got to live, Jessie."

"Your mother wouldn't let you starve, Taylor," she said.

Unconsciously, they were calling each other by their old familiar names now — no formal 'Miss' and 'Mr'.

"A man has to have some pride in himself too," he said, looking down at her thoughtfully. "There's no saying if Matthias Overdale would have employed me again if I'd refused to become his agent. Anyway, it's done now. There's no going back."

She wondered if he was thinking of their tentative relationship.

"Our Arden might be fighting for the Union," said Jessie earnestly. "You could be buying bullets to kill him."

"And if we didn't weave and wear cotton, they wouldn't have slaves to grow it. There's no answer to it all, Jessie. Commerce can be a dirty business and war is a dirty business too, but a man's got to live. But one thing I don't buy is armaments — not for myself, anyway," he added as if that excused him from buying them for his employer.

She had never seen him so dejected. He was usually so full of self-righteous pride but now they both knew that his conscience troubled him. She preferred this new, humbler Taylor and would have gladly accepted his marriage proposal if he'd actually asked. Could he have been more tender, less controlling? Could he have loved her with kindness and affection and … and … passion? Jessie blushed at her own thoughts.

"Goodbye, Taylor," she said quietly as she turned to go.

There was no going back he'd said.

"And thank you."

"Take no notice of them, Jessie. They're not worth it. Goodbye."

She knew he was watching her as she walked to her door. His concern for her bothered her. She wondered what her life might have been married to Taylor and what would happen to her in the future. She'd been shaken by that encounter with Tommy Dale. One thing was certain, her reputation in the town was tainted by that stupid request by Robert Overdale and some folk would never forget the rumours, however false. She wished she could escape and leave it all behind her.

Next morning, Honora met her as soon as she arrived at Overdale House.

"How is your Uncle?" asked Jessie anxiously.

"He's much better. But he must rest. My Aunt is getting anxious, though. We've arranged for people to look after his business interests but…" Honora paused and looked thoughtfully at Jessie. "My aunt is insistent that Robert comes home. What's more, she's asked me to go and find him."

"To find him — in America — in the middle of a war?" asked Jessie, astounded.

It was such a great risk. Honora must be very fond of her cousin to want to take that risk. *The understanding between them was obviously very strong*, thought Jessie. She did not suspect that Honora was eager to go and spread her wings in the world.

"My Aunt's sure that Robert's friends will help. She says that the men of the south are gentlemen and a lady will be safe. But she doesn't want me to travel alone. We were talking long into the night. She's asked if you would be willing to accompany me as a companion."

Jessie stared in amazement. Then the strangest thought came into her head. She remembered standing up by the Fort admiring the exotic blooms transported as seeds on the cotton bales. Now, by some miracle, she might see them bloom in their native land after all.

"I'd be willing to go but I'll have to ask Father first," she said, though already her thoughts were flying far from Gorbydale.

PART II

Chapter 35: The Big City

Jessie Davenport closed her eyes but couldn't sleep. The sounds of the city echoed in the darkness. Did New Yorkers never sleep? Her head was filled with her long journey from Gorbydale. New York was impressive but daunting, the buildings much grander than even those in Liverpool. The noise was as bad as the mill at its busiest.

Luckily, she and Honora had met Mrs Susannah Daly during their long sea voyage. Honora had already introduced herself to the ship's surgeon.

"Dr Maitland has invited me to visit his surgery," she told Jessie. "You can come if you like."

Jessie preferred the bracing air on deck than the fetid air of a sick bay. She'd been cooped up with illness for too long. Now she was free, she was fascinated by life on the ship. Her life had changed dramatically, the air so fresh out on the undulating endless sea, far away from the smoky dales and black chimneys of home. On deck, she'd chatted with Mrs Daly, a motherly Yorkshire woman who was travelling alone and glad of company. She'd travelled to Sheffield to nurse her dying mother and that was an immediate bond between them. Now, returning home to her husband in America, Susannah told Jessie that she was a nurse at the army hospital in Washington.

"I'll be glad to get home to George," said Susannah. "He works for the War Office. Though, he's so busy at the moment, he'll surely help you find your brother."

For months, the Davenports hadn't heard from Arden, then suddenly a letter arrived days before the girls were due to embark from Liverpool.

By the state of the envelope it had been redirected from several places. Jessie and Eddie watched impatiently as her father opened its crumpled folds with shaking hands.

"He's alive! He's in New York — by heck, our Arden in New York! And he's joined the Union Navy. He's due to embark on an ironclad — a what? Oh, he says it's one of these new-fangled iron ships. He's the engineer. He'll write again when he reaches a safe port. Look, he's sent some money. And he sends his love to…" Jacob faltered, then took a deep breath. "To Mother. Oh, Jessie, he didn't get your letter."

"I wonder where he is now?" said Jessie, anxiously scrutinising the many postmarks on the battered envelope. It had been travelling for weeks. "And if he's safe. I do hope he's safe."

They'd stared at the money. Arden explained in his letter that the English notes were from his wages aboard the *Great Eastern*. Her father had insisted she take it with her for emergencies.

Jessie had told Susannah that Arden had joined the Union Navy, though she did not elaborate on Honora's search for her cousin. Who knew if Robert was in the north or south? Now here in New York with blue uniforms everywhere in the teeming streets, Jessie searched in vain among the sea of faces, hoping desperately to catch a glimpse of Arden. She wondered if she would ever find him. At least Susannah had given her hope and maybe her husband would prove helpful.

Jessie had shared a cabin with Honora aboard ship, but slept in the tiny adjoining dressing room. They'd become friends, though Jessie was conscious she must not be over-familiar with

Honora as the Overdales were paying her passage as a travelling companion. Though, somehow, Honora had subtly changed from the correct and respectable young woman from Gorbydale. Jessie wondered if Melissa would approve of all the time her niece spent with the ship's surgeon, although he was a steady, older man.

"Should you spend so much time with Dr Maitland?" she asked tentatively, aware that Melissa might ask the same question.

"But I'm learning so much from him," said Honora smiling. "He's such an interesting man. He reminds me of my dear father."

"Best be careful though, dear," cautioned Susannah. "You must think of your reputation."

Honora just smiled and continued what she was doing. Thrown in each other's company, Susannah and Jessie were becoming firm friends and she was now taking her meals with the two girls. They discussed what the girls should do on arrival.

"You must stay with me at my sister, Ella's, home in New York," Susannah told them. "I'll be there for a few days before going south. She has plenty of room and sometimes takes in lodgers. I'm sure she'll gladly welcome my friends, especially as your brother is fighting for our country. I'm sure you won't mind sharing a bed."

Honora was quiet. Jessie wondered what she was thinking. Was it beneath her dignity to share a bed with Jessie? They had little enough funds and no plans. Honora must still believe that Arden had run away to avoid Dolly Tate and there was nothing noble in his joining the Union Navy.

"Please don't mention that Robert has travelled to the south, Jessie," Honora murmured when they were alone. "I'm not sure how welcome I'd be."

"Of course I won't," Jessie reassured her.

It suited them to stay with Ella, not only to save money but to avoid the search for a suitable hotel. They arrived, exhausted, outside a tall brownstone building on a busy street. Ella flew out of the door to hug her sister. The two women clung to each other, full of tears for their mother.

"It was a blessing in the end," whispered Susannah and her sister nodded.

Then Ella turned to the girls and once Susannah had explained their presence, she ushered them in and made them very welcome. The sisters treated Jessie and Honora the same, ignoring any class distinction, a marked difference from Gorbydale.

Thoughts churning, Jessie could not sleep. She worried how her father and Eddie would manage without her and if her mother would have approved her leaving Jacob to fend for himself. She thought back to happier times when Nellie was well and Jessie was the treasured daughter of the house, the darling of her father; her two older brothers protecting her and how she in turn protected Eddie. She had been safe and, despite her ailing mother and lost opportunities, she had felt secure. Though she had longed to escape, now she felt responsible for Honora. Though her friend was nominally in charge of their expedition, she relied on Jessie and her natural friendliness to ease their way in America. Jessie suddenly felt very alone. Among friendly strangers in an alien city, she thought about Gorbydale and felt homesick.

"Are you awake?" asked Honora quietly in the dark.

"Yes. I'm really tired after the journey but my mind's so full, I can't sleep," whispered Jessie.

"Me neither. Perhaps we should travel to Washington too. It's further south and we may have more chance to hear about Robert."

Jessie hesitated. Arden had been in New York but who knew where he and his 'ironclad' were now. In Washington, she could discover his whereabouts herself with the aid of Susannah's husband in the War Office. Waiting for letters to pass backwards and forwards would mean delays.

"Yes, I think that's a good idea," she said.

"Good," said Honora. "We'll make arrangements to travel with Susannah in the morning."

She rolled over and was soon sleeping soundly. Jessie wondered about Honora's feelings for Robert. She must care for him to come so far, yet she was sleeping as if she hadn't a worry in the world. Still, sleep deserted Jessie. The approaching journey didn't trouble her. She was resigned to casting her fate into the prevailing wind of fortune. Another exasperating problem rumbled through her mind, robbing her of sleep.

Just before she'd left, Taylor Walmsley had called at Weavers Row.

"I hear you're off to America," he said.

"Aye. Mrs Overdale is desperate for her son to come home, what with Mr Matthias ailing. Miss Honora is being sent to fetch him and she needs a travelling companion," she'd told him.

She'd been disconcerted by his steady gaze.

"You could always stay and marry me," Taylor had said so quietly that, at first, she wasn't quite sure she'd heard him correctly.

Jessie gaped at him open mouthed. There had been no hint he'd say such a thing; no smile, no tender glance.

"But I've given my word," she stammered, bewildered by his proposal.

"And that's your answer. Well, I hope you have a very pleasant journey, Miss Davenport," he'd said brusquely.

"But…"

He hadn't even given her a chance to explain, just turned and left abruptly without saying goodbye. Why hadn't he waited a moment or even suggested that he called again when she came home? She hadn't been given a chance to consider his proposal. Hadn't he said 'there's no going back'? Now Jessie was more confused than ever about his feelings for her. Marriage was such a big and important thing, and yet, all he could think about was his hurt pride. Jessie was exasperated by how he blew hot and cold. He could never accept her as she was.

Yet, Taylor was a small problem compared to what faced her in America. It was vast and teaming with people from all over the world. Melissa had massively underestimated their task. How on earth would she find Arden in this huge sprawling country split by war? Somewhere out there was Robert too, and she must help Honora find him. Jessie tried to forget their last meeting. The enormity of the task before them was daunting.

Chapter 36: Limey Bob

Robert Overdale, the pampered heir to the Invincible Mill, walked barefoot down a dusty road like a country boy. His only possessions were a grey blanket and a pair of boots. He'd hung the boots round his neck as he had no stockings and they chafed his feet without them. Carrying them also saved them from wear. To his shame and horror, he'd taken the boots and blanket from a body he'd found by the road. The man had worn a grey uniform and had obviously died of his war wounds trying to get back home. In gratitude for the boots, Robert buried him and muttered what scant prayers he could remember. He had very little money left to pay for any cotton. Using the money from selling his signet ring, he'd bought train tickets to Louisiana and travelled on hard wooden seats for miles. His back hurt, his feet were painful and his leg was badly bruised from the fall in the ironclad. All he had left was a little money. He slipped it into his ragged waistcoat pocket. Hoping to find help, he was heading for the Jacques plantation. His only hope was to find work there to pay his way home.

Robert had been walking some time when the sun became a furnace. He sank into the shade of a tree, exhausted. His eyes closed. He dreamt of cool water, of the green hills of Gorbydale, of his last meeting with Jessie. He was dozing fitfully when he was woken sharply by someone dragging the boots from his shoulder.

"Hey — stop that!" he shouted.

Men in grey uniforms gathered round looking shocked.

"We thought you was dead," said one.

"Couldn't let a good pair of boots go wasted," said another, clutching Robert's blanket.

"Well, I'm not dead," protested Robert, struggling painfully to his feet.

"You a Limey?" asked one.

"I'm English, yes."

"What they call you?"

"Robert Overdale," he told them.

"For the south?"

"Er … yes."

"Well, Limey Bob, take this rifle. Ain't no use to the man we took it off. We're goin' to find us some action."

It was easier to go with them than argue. Robert planned to sneak away at the first opportunity, but it hadn't proved so easy. They hadn't been walking long when gunfire echoed in the distance.

"Come on, boys — action," said their leader.

What little strength they had left was forged into a headlong charge towards a stand of trees. Robert charged with them, until he heard bullets whizzing past his ear. They threw themselves into a ditch.

"How many?" barked their leader to a boy who'd scrambled up a tree.

"'Bout twenty I reckon," called the boy.

"Hell. I ain't got no more 'n five bullets."

Robert had two. But their meagre ration of bullets was no match for a field gun. There was an explosion in the earth behind them. They were covered in soil and the boy was thrown from the tree by the blast. Robert held his breath. But the bluecoats were just finding their range. The next ball hit the ditch. For a moment, Robert felt as though he was flying and then he hit the ground with a jarring thud. The second he regained his breath, he instinctively wriggled on his belly into the undergrowth and lay still. Another explosion sprayed him with soil and roots. The explosion had badly affected his hearing, though there was just enough left to distinguish a loud cry of pain. Then all fell silent. Straining to hear, Robert thought he heard voices approaching. Through barely opened eyelids, he noticed boots and blue trousers through the vegetation. He hardly dared to breathe, afraid the pounding in his chest would betray him. But gradually, the voices receded and as his hearing returned, he heard the rumble of the gun carriage and the thud of horses' hooves fading into the distance. Only the buzz of mosquitoes and the echo of a bird cry broke the silence. Frozen in fear, he lay for ages, then raised his stiffened body and shook away the dirt. The bloody, broken bodies of his companions lay scattered around like stringless puppets. He wondered if he should bury them, but his leg hurt and a sharp splinter of wood stuck out from the crimson stain on his ragged trousers. He must find help. With gritted teeth he pulled out the splinter and staunched the flow of blood from the jagged wound with the sweat soaked handkerchief he'd had tied round his neck. Nathan Jacques was too distant. His only hope of help was the Amiens plantation. Though he had initially decided to avoid the Duplege family and, in particular, Clement after his betrayal, Robert hoped they might give him shelter overnight on his way. Perhaps they might even loan him a horse.

After some miles and hardly daring to rest again, he finally came to his destination. It was growing dark as he dragged his leg and weary body up the beaten path towards the slave quarters. A child playing on the path screamed and ran towards the shacks. Robert fell to his knees with exhaustion. Moments later he was surrounded by people.

"Master Robert!" said Kezia staring at him. "What in heaven's name are you doin' back here?"

The tall Negro behind her glared suspiciously at him.

"Abraham — Master Robert is back. We'd better get him into the house."

"No."

"He's not our enemy," said Kezia, softly touching the big man's arm in supplication. "Jonah from Massa Jacques's says he's all right."

Abraham didn't seem totally convinced but, urged by Kezia, her neighbours carried Robert into her shack. He sank gratefully onto a rough sack stuffed with cotton.

"What you doin' here?" demanded Abraham.

"I got mixed up in some trouble," said Robert humbly. "This was the only place I knew."

"We heard the guns," said Abraham gruffly.

"My leg's been hurt."

Robert flinched as Kezia removed the blood soaked neckerchief. Gently, she washed it and dressed the wound while Abraham glared at him.

"Ain't you the one that gave my Kezia the silver dollar?" he asked suspiciously.

"I'm sorry but I've nothing left to help buy your freedom," said Robert humbly.

"We'll be free soon, Master Robert. Old Abe Lincoln, he promised it — look here."

Kezia passed him a crumpled piece of paper.

"'*On the first day of January, in the year of our Lord one thousand eight hundred and sixty-three...*' You'll be free in the New Year! That is truly good news," he said warmly after he'd finished reading.

It was dated September.

"Would you like your silver dollar back?" asked Kezia. "Won't cost me a penny to be free now."

"Please keep it," said Robert smiling wanly. "I'm very glad for you."

Abraham seemed surprised by his views.

"It's gettin' dangerous here," said Kezia. "Soldiers comin' and raidin' the big house to see what they can find. The family's gone to Vicksburg. They left the overseer in charge, but he's gone too. Ain't nothin' to plant and nothin' to pick and nothin' to sell. We livin' on our little plot of corn. Tomorrow night, we're plannin' to go north so as Abraham can help the Union Army. There are people that will help us."

"Don't tell him nothin'," said Abraham gruffly.

"He's our friend," said Kezia, her brown eyes pleading. "He believes in our freedom. Anyways, he could be arrested himself for desertion," she added.

Abraham looked doubtful.

"Very well, Kezia," he said eventually. "I don't trust him — but I trust you. But this is a dangerous business, Master."

"I'm not your master," said Robert sincerely. "I mean to be a friend."

He held out his hand. After a moment's hesitation, Abraham took it and nodded his head.

Next morning, they made plans.

"We leave after dark, then walk many miles to a chapel," Abraham told Robert. "The Reverend there is our friend. He'll get us on a boat down the river. But it ain't easy. His house is watched. There are bounty hunters everywhere. I was headin' for that boat when their dogs tracked me down. But I never told — no, sir, I never told."

They all remembered the awful night when the runaway Abraham had been returned to the plantation.

"Folks call it the underground railway," said Kezia. "There's people everywhere that'll help us, secret and brave. We'll get to freedom, Master Robert. Just see if we don't."

As Kezia dressed his leg, he told them how he had travelled across the country, avoiding the fighting. Sparingly using his little money, he'd revisited the places where Clement had taken him until he could take the train to Louisiana. The houses were deserted, or those who'd stayed had little food. The occupiers could spare little hospitality for a solitary Englishman in rags without Clement's backing. He'd had a better welcome in the slave village, though many of them eyed him suspiciously.

"We'll leave just as soon as your leg is fixed," Kezia told him.

"Don't worry about that," said Robert. "It will soon heal. We'll go as soon as you're ready."

It was a decision he might come to regret.

Next day, he limped towards the plantation house and witnessed the desolation and destruction. The windows, with their cracked and broken glass, stared out over the plantation like lifeless eyes. Inside was a pervading smell of human waste and damp where passing vagrants had spent the night. There was nothing of use left by the looters, not even a handkerchief to use as a bandage.

By midnight the following night, they hauled their packs onto their backs. With tearful goodbyes to their neighbours, they followed the dark moonless road a long anxious way, melting like ghosts into the shadows at any noise. Eventually, after a long and footsore journey, they came to a small chapel far from the outskirts of a town. Robert, having nothing but his blanket and the clothes he was wearing, helped to carry what few provisions they had. His leg ached painfully but he tried to hide his limp, unwilling to be a burden. In the shadows behind the building, they gave a tentative tap at an obscure door. It opened in darkness and they were quickly ushered inside and told to lie quietly among the pews. Despite his overwhelming weariness, Robert could not sleep. Next day, they hid in a musty cellar, anxiously silent until darkness had fallen again. It was damp and cold despite the heat outside and reeked with the scent of stale bodies, urine and worse. Who knew how many had hidden there before them? Robert's leg throbbed and Kezia tried to dress it as best she could by the light of a guttering candle. She tried to scrub the blood from the dirt floor, but with little success.

Robert was shaken awake from a miserable doze on the gritty floor. From the gentle and rhythmic snoring of Kezia and Abraham throughout the night, he'd assumed they'd slept better than he had. Maybe the hope of approaching freedom calmed their sleep, though the brutality of what had happened to Abraham on his previous attempt made Robert uneasy. He'd heard tales that there was little pity shown to white men who helped slaves and, knowing Clement Duplege, did not doubt them.

"Get up, Master Robert," whispered Kezia. "The conductor is here. We got to get moving before the sun comes up."

They said goodbye to the elderly pastor who had given them shelter and food, and who'd provided them with some for the journey, and began to follow a grizzled black man away from the distant town and out into the rough country. Sneaking along worn paths through high vegetation, they avoided any signs of habitation. Trailing behind the group, Robert had no idea where he was. The man refused to give them his true name when Kezia asked.

"Best you don't know," he said with a gap-toothed smile. "Then they can't beat it out of you. Call me Sunny."

When the sun became too hot, they lay exhausted in a small patch of brushwood and ate what little food they had. Flies buzzed about them and explored the bloody bandage round Robert's wound. He felt dirty and stale, his leg stiff and hot. They managed to bathe it in a little stream of brackish water and rinse out the makeshift bandage. Then as the light began to dim, they began their journey again.

"Trying to get to the Mississippi river," said Sunny. "People there will get us on a raft and take us upstream."

Days later, they were still trudging along, avoiding civilisation, sleeping in the homes of sympathisers. The black helpers were wary of harbouring a white man among them and eyed Robert with curiosity and suspicion.

"A deserter, you say?" he heard one woman whisper to Kezia. "And he was fighting with the Confederate Army? You sure you can trust him?"

"He's English," Kezia defended him. "He don't hold with slavery."

All the same, he suspected some folks would have liked to have got rid of him quietly. He slept warily, especially as his leg throbbed continually and refused to heal.

Then the scenery changed and the ground beneath them seemed unstable and marshy, the vegetation reedy.

"Be at the river soon," said Sunny.

Though there seemed no features to mark their way, he had unerringly brought them towards their destination. By now, Robert was leaning on a broken branch to help him walk. As dusk fell, they arrived at the gleaming expanse of the wide Mississippi. By following the marshy shore, they reached a small dilapidated hut. At the river's edge, a long boat was tied to a rotting stump. The boatman clutching a long oar stared at Robert. Robert watched warily as he and Sunny exchanged a few angry words. Then their guide beckoned them over and they were hastily stowed under a pile of damp sacks stinking of river mud. The swirl of the river swung them effortlessly out into the flow and they were away. For days they travelled upstream, stiff with the effort to keep still during daylight so as not to cause any suspicion. They travelled by any habitation during the night and fear travelled with them all the way. In the moonlight, Robert saw the high bluff of Vicksburg soaring above the river. This was a rocky stronghold of the Confederate Army. He knew the Duplege family had taken refuge there and, looming in forbidding majesty above them, it looked impenetrable. With sacks draped around them, they stayed as still as they could until they'd drifted away from any watchful eyes high above.

Chapter 37: News of the Wanderer

The train journey from New York was long and uncomfortable, and increasingly hot, as Jessie and Honora travelled south with Susannah. There were frequent hold ups as the train pulled into sidings for troop trains to pass. As they finally pulled into the busy Washington station, Jessie and Honora tactfully held back as Susannah greeted her husband, a dapper man with a clipped moustache. She had already telegraphed to him about their visitors and he welcomed them politely, if not enthusiastically. When they reached the substantial house on Pennsylvania Avenue not far from the War Office, they were shown to a comfortable bedroom near the top of the house. As in the rest of the house, the furnishings were plush and expensive. Jessie had never slept in such a sumptuous room, the thick curtains decorated with heavy swags. She smiled and knew her mother would have loved the large ornate bowl and pitcher decorated with roses on the marble wash stand for their ablutions. Early next morning, a little maid tiptoed into the room with a jug of hot water as they lay in bed. It all felt very luxurious to Jessie, although Susannah's sister Ella had plumbing in her house in New York. Although in the capital city, Washington houses didn't seem to have developed the same amenities. Jessie automatically let Honora use the bowl first.

After breakfast they started for the War Office, filled with hope.

"Oh, I'm sorry," said Jessie.

She had automatically linked Honora as they accompanied Susannah's husband George Daly down the bustling street to the War Office.

"I'm so used to linking my friend Mary going way home from the mill that I just did it automatically."

She was about to withdraw her hand when Honora took it and held it firmly in place.

"Now you can link your friend Honora," she said smiling. "Surely we've been through enough together to be friends."
Jessie left her arm in place. They were filled with hope that morning.

In the bustling War Office, George introduced them to a busy clerk.

"Look after these ladies for me will you, Davis," he commanded. "I must go to my desk."

The young man smiled at the girls and went to find a large battered ledger after Jessie had explained her mission to find her brother.

"This is the Navy list," said the clerk, opening it along his desk. "It isn't always up to date. But news at the Navy Yard may be more recent and you can try there if we have no luck."

Honora stayed silent. She'd told Jessie that the only plan she could think of was to write to the Amiens plantation and await a reply.

With dismay, the girls noticed that many entries ending in the word 'deceased'.

"Davenport, you say," he said. "Here's one — Davenport Anthony Walker."

"His name is Arden," said Jessie anxiously staring at the ledger with its myriad crossings out.

"Davenport, Arden Eli, Lieutenant on the USS *Irene*," read the man.

"That's my brother — and a lieutenant?" said Jessie in surprise.

"Arden Eli?" asked Honora.

Jessie nodded.

"He was named for your Uncle Eli. Is he…?" asked Jessie hesitantly.

"Alive and well and about to join his new ship. The *Irene* is being fitted out in New York," said the man smiling, "She's to be commissioned in a week or two."

Jessie clutched Honora's hand in happiness.

"Oh that's wonderful," she said, tears of relief welling in her eyes. "New York, though. Oh, Honora, we were there only a week ago. We should have enquired while we were there. We might even have passed him in the street and not noticed him."

"Oh, I think he would have noticed us," said Honora smiling at her friend. "All the men in uniform seemed to turn their heads when you passed by."

"Oh, but if only we'd known," Jessie shook her head in exasperation. "It's just wonderful. Arden is still alive. Oh, thank you, thank you, sir."

"It's a pleasure, Miss. Would you like me to send a message up the line?"

"Oh, could you really do that? I'd be so very grateful. Please just say that his sister Jessie has come all the way to Washington and has been looking for him."

Leaving their address, the girls left the office delighted with their news. Despite her own elation, Jessie noticed Honora's silence. She'd said little enough when George Daly was with them. Jessie knew why her friend was so anxious.

"I do hope we can find some news of Master Robert soon, Miss Honora," she said, tempering her happiness for her friend's sake.

They passed women searching anxiously among the long lists of casualties and fatalities posted on the wall of the building. They witnessed wild sobbing and despair when the news was bad. Honora trembled.

"Surely Robert will have gone to the Amiens plantation," she said. "He would be safe there. But what if he's been arrested for smuggling? Or got caught up in the fighting…?"

She sighed with frustration at the task ahead of them. Jessie squeezed her hand to comfort her.

"We must live in hope," she said.

"I don't know where to begin. All my hopes are pinned on this letter," said Honora, staring at the thick cream envelope.

Making their way to the post office, Jessie wrote a joyful note to her father saying that Arden was alive and well. She included it with a letter from Honora to Melissa. The clerk looked doubtfully at Honora's letter to the south.

"There may be some problems with this, here," he said, giving her a searching look.

"Try and send it all the same," she told him. "I'll call and see if there are any replies."

It would be embarrassing for a letter from the south to arrive at the Dalys' house. They would not be welcome if their hosts knew Robert associated with a southern agent. Honora was vague whenever they'd asked about him, mentioning business.

"I find your friend is quite shy," Susannah mentioned to Jessie when they were alone.

"She's led a sheltered life with her aunt," Jessie excused Honora. "Not like me at t'mill with loads of folks around me."

She deliberately lapsed into broad a northern accent to describe her life and Susannah smiled. For the moment, Honora's secret was safe.

Chapter 38: A Familiar Face

Over the following days, Honora called in vain for a reply to her letter. But the Amiens house was empty. Kezia, the one person left on the plantation who could read, had disappeared with Robert into the night.

As Honora left the building after yet another disappointment, she glanced about her. Then she stopped and stared. The man by the post office casually reading a newspaper had an oddly familiar face. His hair was no longer curled and flowing but cropped close to his head. It seemed darker than she remembered, his moustache clipped and neat and his white linen suit replaced by a sober dark business suit. But the man was undoubtedly Clement Duplege. All the same, Honora stared hard again to make sure.

He looked up in surprise as she approached him.

"Mr Duplege? Clement Duplege?"

"I'm afraid you are mistaken madam," he said tipping his hat.

He'd disguised his accent too. He was about to leave when she grabbed his arm.

"Madam, I assure you…"

"I know it's you," said Honora fiercely. "Where's my cousin Robert?"

Glancing into her determined face, he sensed she was about to make a scene and cause trouble.

"Don't draw attention to yourself," he hissed urgently. "Just come with me."

He offered his arm and she took it. They walked down busy streets, Clement with his head down as if speaking intimately to her until they reached a quiet place by the river. Anyone watching would think they were a normal couple, attractive and sedate, strolling by the water. Honora was trembling, glancing anxiously about her, determined that Clement would not lead her into a dark place and dispose of her. No one could guess he was a southern spy.

They reached a point where they could not be overheard, their only witnesses on the miscellany of boats out on the wide Potomac.

"Where is my cousin Robert?" she demanded, facing him.

"I am very surprised to see you in Washington, Miss Overdale," he said smoothly.

"My name is Darwen and I'm surprised to see you in a Union city full of soldiers," she retorted. "I've come to find Robert. Where is he and why hasn't he written to his mother?"

Clement faltered.

"We are at war. A man must take risks to make greater gains. Your cousin was determined to go to the south to buy cotton despite my advice. A war is not an English tea party, Miss Darwen."

"Where is my cousin?"

"The Union blockades are becoming tighter..." Clement avoided her eyes. "We were nearing the coast. It was dark. They were upon us before we realised."

"And my cousin...?" Honora's voice faltered.

"I honestly do not know, Miss Darwen. He was not in the escape boat with us. He may have swam ashore — or even been taken prisoner by the Yankees. He's British, they'd soon let him free. The Yankees don't like to annoy your government."

"Or he could have … could have…"

The word 'drowned' froze on her lips. Her whole body felt frozen with shock.

"Robert may be alive, Miss Darwen, for all we know. The Yankees would take him ashore. They'd have deported him…"

"Then why didn't you come and tell my aunt all this? Or write to her, to let her know?" asked Honora coldly. "You were eager enough to visit us when you wanted to extract money from my uncle."

"I have not been to England recently," Clement defended himself. "I have been in France. Their government has the courtesy to recognise my own in the south. I'm sorry, Miss Darwen, but while there is life, there is hope. Many strange things happen in war. For all we know, your cousin may be in England as we speak."

Honora turned away as a sob escaped her.

"I will make enquires for you, Miss Darwen," said Clement. "I can do no more. Now I must leave. Where are you staying?"

"You must not send a letter there," said Honora anxiously.

She did not want to tell him that she was staying in the home of a War Office official or he might conveniently forget to enquire after Robert.

"Leave a letter at the post office if you have news."

"Very well. I trust you will say nothing of my visit to the authorities. If I am arrested, I will not be able to help you in your search."

"I'll say nothing," sobbed Honora.

"Goodbye, Miss Darwen," said Clement, touching the brim of his hat. "Do you know your way home?"

She nodded, though unsure, determined he should not accompany her to the Daly house. He left her staring across the wide river, her body wracked with sobs. What could she tell Aunt Melissa? All her aunt's hopes were pinned on Robert, her only son. Honora wandered, blinded by tears for some time until she came to a place she recognised. She trembled as she went into Susannah's house, hoping that Jessie had returned.

Chapter 39: A Reunion

After Jessie had left her friend at the Post Office, she found her way to the Naval Yard, hoping for news. The river was busy with traffic, including the extraordinary ironclads. Many men smiled at the pretty girl hurrying anxiously towards the office. Many offered to help, but she went resolutely on, shaking her head gently in refusal. She was all the more annoyed when a tall man stood in her way. She moved to avoid him and glanced up. The naval uniform was unfamiliar — but the face was not. It was leaner, the face of a man who had seen many things since he had left Gorbydale.

"Arden!" she gasped. "Oh, Arden!"

"Jessie, I was just coming to find you."

"What are you doing in Washington?"

Tightly enclosed in his sister's arms, Arden was helpless to salute a passing officer.

"I was in New York helping to provision our ship but my captain gave me permission to come to Washington when I got your message. I sailed south with a friend. I have a few days leave and then I must return."

"It's so, so good to see you. I wrote to Father immediately I knew you were alive. Oh, Arden, you look so handsome in your uniform," said Jessie. "And a lieutenant too."

"How are the folks back home?" he asked. "Did you get my letters?"

"We got one," Jessie told him. "It had been diverted all over the place before it reached us. Did you get mine?"

He shook his head.

"How is Mother?" asked Arden anxiously.

Jessie fell silent and tears welled in her eyes as she shook her head.

"So she didn't know I'd joined the Union Navy?"

Jessie shook her head again, dumb with emotion.

"She was expecting you back in Liverpool with the *Great Eastern*," she said eventually through her tears. "But she'd have been so very proud to see you now."

They linked arms and walked silently together in their grief, each one with memories of their mother.

"Come and see where I'm staying. I know the Dalys will be happy to meet you. I've told Susannah all about you. I came with Miss Honora to look for Robert Overdale. Matthias has been ill and Mrs Overdale wants Robert to come home to look after the business. But we don't know where to start looking. America is so vast."

Arden looked at his sister thoughtfully.

"Did he go south?"

She nodded.

"But all routes to the south are blocked. Honora's afraid to say anything to the Dalys in case they throw us out. George Daly works at the War Office. But they're good folk. They make a great fuss of me because you're in the Union Navy."

"You must deserve it," said Arden smiling.

It was true that Jessie was a great favourite in the house, being her usual helpful self. But then, Honora had been unusually quiet, anxious about letting her secret slip out aloud.

Their happiness at being reunited received a setback, though, when they reached the house. In the drawing room, Honora sat weeping into her hands as Susannah tried to give her a sip of brandy to revive her.

"She came home moments ago in a terrible state. She's had a terrible shock," said Susannah, anxious with sympathy. "She's heard her cousin might be dead."

"Oh no, Honora," said Jessie, hurrying to her side and putting a comforting arm around her.

Honora stared up at Arden in bewilderment.

"Can you be sure, Miss Darwen?" he asked gently. "War is such a confusion."

She shook her head.

"I c… c… can't be sure," she stammered. "Someone said they thought…"

She dropped her head and sobbed bitterly.

"Whatever will I say to his mother? Robert is her life."

"But you don't know for certain? While there's life, there's hope," urged Jessie. She'd been shaken by the news but she knew she must stay strong for Honora's sake. "We'll keep on searching until we do know for sure."

Susannah shook Arden's hand warmly.

"You must be Jessie's brother. You're most welcome, Lieutenant. It's a shame you've arrived at such a moment. And you've come all this way to fight for our cause. I'll make us all some tea," she said and left the room.

"How did you find out?" asked Jessie.

"I … I … met someone," sobbed Honora through her tears. "I didn't dare tell Susannah."

"Someone from the south?" Arden asked quietly, his face grave and unreadable. "Your uncle was visited by a southern gentleman once. I remember him arriving in Gorbydale, driving his carriage like a lunatic."

Honora looked anxiously at Jessie but said nothing. Comforting her friend, Jessie felt her tremble.

"Honora's had a terrible shock, Arden. We don't know if Robert is alive or…" she hesitated over the dreadful word. "But we do need to find out. Please don't ask any more questions for the moment?"

Her brother nodded and agreed.

"Of course. But if you think of anything that might help, Miss Darwen?"

Honora sobbed but stayed silent. Jessie didn't know what the repercussions would be if her friend was caught associating with a southern spy, but it was no doubt serious.

Chapter 40: The Riot

Unaware of the disheartening news in Washington, Melissa had ridden in her gig to the old Endurance Mill with Jessie's letter to Jacob in her bag. She knew he would be eager to see it. She was hopeful that her son would soon be found when she had read Honora's letter, little suspecting the awful news that her niece had heard barely an hour after posting it. Eli was always glad to see his sister. Everyone seemed busy, painting and fettling the machinery, tidying the grounds.

Melissa had felt uneasy driving through Gorbydale, seeing the people with their pinched faces and shabby clothes. The once bustling town looked grey and derelict, many of the shops boarded up. Blank and broken windows stared over the miserable streets and the only sign of despondent activity was around the pawn shop. There were surly groups of men hanging about the street corners. Some glared at her in her gig. Melissa wished Matthias could do something for his workers like Eli.

She was justifiably proud of her girls in their sewing class. But there was little for the workless men of the Invincible to do, unlike at the Endurance, where all was busy and useful industry. Melissa felt guilty too, that she'd neglected her work on the Relief Committee. All her time was spent with her girls and in looking after her husband. That wasn't easy as Matthias wasn't a patient man. His speech had recovered, though he walked with a stick and refused to rest as the doctor had ordered. She wondered if she'd been too hasty sending her niece overseas, and at the wisdom of sending two girls into a country at war. Perhaps one of the trusted workmen could have gone instead. Taylor Walmsley was busy about the business on Matthias's behalf — and on his own too, if the rumours were to be believed.

Jacob paused from painting as Melissa and his boss came into the office. He bowed in slight deference towards her.

"Mrs Overdale."

"Hello, Mr Davenport. I have something here for you," she said, rummaging in her bag. "It's here somewhere."

They were interrupted as one of the apprentices dashed in.

"Mr Eli, Mr Eli," he panted. "You must come quick. There's riots in the town."

Eli looked startled.

"Oh heck. I'd better go. I've been expecting something like this."

Growing unrest and rumours had rumbled round the town when news of other riots across Lancashire had reached them.

"I'll come too," said Jacob. "You can't face a mob on your own. This has been brewing for days."

"My gig is ready in the yard. We'll go in that," decided Melissa.

"Nay, you stay here, lass," ordered her brother. "The mob might be dangerous."

"I'm coming," said his sister, with a stubborn look that he knew of old.

They clambered aboard her gig and drove briskly into town, though Melissa's groom was very nervous.

"Some of the chapel people might listen to me and return to their homes," said Jacob, hanging on to the side as they swerved round a corner.

Despite her previous courage, Melissa felt her anxiety rise when they saw the belligerent crowd of people milling round the workhouse. An ominous crash of tinkling glass echoed over them as they approached and the crowd surged forward.

The mob went quiet and parted when they saw Eli arriving. He was a Justice of the Peace for Gorbydale and, despite their simmering anger, they all knew him for a fair man. He stood up in the gig and addressed them.

"I've to warn you that I must read the Riot Act," he said loudly. "We cannot have riots on our streets. If you've a grievance…"

"Aye, we've grievances a plenty," called one of the ringleaders. "It's not our fault we're out of work, Mr Gorman. We've made good brass for the masters — and now we're treated like dogs."

"Winter's coming on and we've no blankets and no coal to keep warm," shouted another. "Our childer will starve."

"Now calm down, lads. Go back to your homes and I'll talk with your leaders. We don't want the troopers called, do we?" said Eli. A restless silence fell over the crowd, the dreadful massacre of Peterloo heavy in their minds. "Give us a list of your complaints and I promise you — promise you, mind — that we'll look into them."

The leaders talked among themselves as the crowd milled in silent menace. Then one spoke up.

"We know you're a fair man, Mr Gorman." The crowd muttered in assent. "But our wives and childer are starving and winter's coming on. How can we feed them on the slops they dole out?"

Though her knees were trembling, Melissa stood up.

"We'll see what we can do," she promised. "I'm on the Relief Committee."

"The Relief Committee, that bunch of useless…" shouted one man until he was quietened by his neighbours.

None of them wanted to cross the Relief Committee and face the consequences. Everyone knew there were some who bore grudges among the gentry.

"Perhaps your leaders can stay behind and talk. The rest of you, please go to your homes before someone gets hurt," Eli tried to persuade them.

"Aye, lads, no one wants an accident," said Jacob, appealing to members of his chapel. "You know Mr Eli will try and sort things out."

The crowd reluctantly shuffled away, glancing back with surly threat.

"What's your name?" Eli asked the most prominent of the ringleaders.

"John Bridger," replied the man.

Jacob recognised him as one of Arden's friends.

"He must be at the end of his tether to come out rioting. He's usually a quiet law-abiding lad with a wife and babby," he told Melissa.

"Something must be done," she said quietly. "I'm ashamed that I've neglected my duties. The people in the town needed me and I'm afraid I've let them down."

She'd heard her girls in the class talking about the meanness of some Committee members, but she'd chosen to ignore it. They said they'd made people sell everything they owned before they could get a ticket for some broth. She'd paid little attention, wrapped up with worries about Matthias and Robert, and her work with the girls.

The workhouse girls who cooked the soup were gathered together in a pathetic gaggle in the kitchen. They looked frightened. The hard-faced cook stood by, arms crossed and ready to defend herself with a ladle. Melissa dipped an enamel mug into the steaming cauldron of broth. The smell was cabbagy and unappetising. She took a sip and wrinkled her nose in disgust.

"Taste that, Eli," she said.

Eli sipped.

"That's disgusting," he said. "It's nowt but cabbage water."

"There's nowt wrong with my soup," the cook complained loudly.

The girls glanced fearfully at one another. Melissa beckoned to one.

"Come and show me your provisions," she asked gently.

The cook blustered forward.

"Not you," Eli commanded. "Come on, lass. You show us."

There was no meat on the bones she showed them, they smelt rancid and old. The greens were mouldering, the carrots shrivelled. Melissa clasped a dainty handkerchief to her nose to try to mask the stench.

"This is appalling," she said in disgust. "You wouldn't feed it to a dog."

"She gets it cheap," whispered the girl. "They get money for the beef and veg from the Relief Fund, but she buys cheap muck and pockets the difference. She threatened us with starvation if we told on her. I won't get into trouble, will I?" she asked pathetically.

"No, dear," said Melissa kindly. "You won't."

"I'd be surprised if the poor starving souls of Gorbydale don't erect a statue to you!" joked Eli.

The girl giggled with relief.

"Come on, then. We've work to do."

The cook was dismissed instantly.

"Unless you fancy jail, I suggest you cough up the money you've extorted from the authorities," ordered Eli.

She tried to protest but there was no appeal against a determined Eli. Jacob and John Bridger escorted the trembling cook home where a crock pot full of money was discovered on her kitchen shelf.

"We'll need someone who can cook," said Melissa, "someone reliable to make proper nourishing broth for the people."

Jacob immediately suggested his neighbour Alice Connolly.

"I'll have to ask her first, though," Jacob told Melissa.

"Of course. I have met Mrs Connolly at your house. She seems eminently suitable. Oh, here, Mr Davenport," she said handing him Jessie's letter. "I almost forgot this with all the excitement."

Jacob opened it carefully.

"Thank the Lord," he said joyfully, tears springing to his eyes. "Our Arden's alive. I must go and tell our Eddie and let Jack and Elsie know too. They'll be over the moon."

"I'm so pleased for you. I wish I'd had better news myself. But at least the girls are well. They're staying with a friend in Washington. You won't forget to ask Mrs Connolly about the cooking, will you?" Melissa reminded him.

Alice was delighted when Jacob arrived with his news and the offer of work.

"That's grand," she said. "My girls bring in a bit from the sewing, but this'll help."

Leaving Mary in charge of her girls, Melissa attended the next meeting of the Relief Committee instead of giving her usual excuses. The vicar's wife had heard of her presence at the riot.

"You must have been terrified of those fiends," she said.

"I was a little afraid," admitted Melissa. "But when I saw those poor starving folk, I felt truly sorry for them. I'm determined to help now."

The first poor creature who came begging for a bread token from the Committee was surprised when Mrs Overdale told her to bring in her pawn tickets.

The vicar's wife looked outraged.

"How many children do you have?" Melissa asked the woman, ignoring the noises of protest beside her.

"Three — no two," said the woman, her thin face wretched with sadness. "We lost little Jenny — they said it was pneumonia but it were…"

The woman fell silent, ashamed and in dread of the word 'starvation'.

"Then we'll see you don't lose any more," said Melissa firmly.

She awarded the woman some money to buy extra blankets, along with more tokens for bread and soup.

"God bless you, Mrs Overdale," said the woman, her eyes filled with tears of gratitude. "I were that afeared we'd all die of cold this winter."

"Not if I can help it," said Melissa kindly.

The vicar's wife was affronted by Melissa's generosity.

"We can't give way to these people's demands," she sniffed. "It will give them no incentive to work."

"There is no work," said Melissa abruptly. "There's just a lot of hardship. Surely it's our Christian duty to try and alleviate it?"

She stared the woman straight in the eye.

"Well, I suppose so," muttered the woman, unable to deny the challenge.

By the end of the day, Melissa was touched and humbled by the gratitude of the struggling townsfolk. With their labour, they'd contributed to her home comforts and her husband's business. Now she could do a little in return. An uneasy peace returned to Gorbydale.

Chapter 41: Confessions

Honora's restless night had left her with an aching head. That morning, she was faced with the dreadful task of writing to her Aunt Melissa about Robert's disappearance. Her mind struggled with the right words to tell her aunt. A gentle tap on the door announced Jessie.

"Are you awake?" she whispered.

Honora raised her head and nodded.

"Would you like a drop of tea and a bite to eat?" asked Jessie kindly.

Honora shook her head.

"You should, you know. You'll feel better for it. Our Arden called this morning. He said he'd like a word with you." Honora's heart sank. "I told him you were upset about Robert. I said you'd been weeping most of the night and that I couldn't disturb you."

"Has he gone?" asked Honora anxiously.

Jessie hesitated.

"He said he'd wait a little longer, though I insisted you weren't in a fit state to see him."

Her friend looked surprised as Honora made to rise.

"You needn't…" began Jessie.

"Tell Lieutenant Davenport I'll be down shortly," said Honora quietly but firmly.

She wanted to get the conversation over with, whatever the outcome.

"But…" protested Jessie.

"Please, Jessie."

They awaited her in the drawing room, Jessie anxious and sympathetic, Arden standing tall and serious in his uniform. Honora momentarily thought how handsome he looked. It was a great shame his mother hadn't lived to see him. Nellie would have been so proud.

"Would you mind leaving us for a moment please, Jessie?" asked Arden.

Jessie looked bewildered, especially as Honora nodded her consent.

"Miss Darwen, you must have realised the consequences of meeting a southern spy," he began once Jessie had left.

"We met by accident," said Honora and then a traitorous sob escaped her.

Arden looked concerned, started forward, then stopped himself.

"I truly never expected him to be here in Washington. He is my only hope to find my cousin. My aunt is desperate that we should find Robert. He's needed back home at the mill."

"I do understand. But you must understand my position too."

"Yes," she admitted in a whisper, looking down to avoid his searching eyes.

"Just tell me his name and I'll mention it to the authorities. I'll try to keep your name out of it. I'll say I've noticed someone from the south that I'd seen back in Gorbydale."

Honora looked into Arden's troubled face. Could she trust him? Yet, if she revealed Duplege's name, she might never find Robert.

"If the worst happens, Miss Darwen, you could be deported. But being deported is little hardship when you consider the plight of the widows and orphans left behind when a ship is sunk through the work of these spies."

"I know." Honora began to sob. "It's Duplege."

"Pardon?" Arden had barely heard her desperate whisper.

"Clement Duplege."

"Thank you. Please trust me, Miss Darwen. I'll do my best to shield you from trouble. He's probably working under a different name, anyway. Perhaps when I sail south, I can discover news of your cousin."

Honora looked up into his earnest face. She had no choice but to trust him.

"You're to sail south?"

"When my ship is ready, yes. I'll do what I can if you tell me where he might be."

"Oh, could you? Thank you, Lieutenant Davenport," said she faintly. "Duplege said that Robert was on board a ship off the coast of Carolina when the Union Navy spotted them. He obviously escaped himself, but just doesn't know what happened to Robert."

Her tears flowed freely once again and sobs wracked her body. Could Robert have survived? He was a good swimmer, taught by Uncle Eli in a safe pool in the Gorby river. But could he manage in the pounding waves of the Atlantic? Arden made a move as if to comfort her but stopped himself once again.

"There may yet be hope, Miss Davenport. War is confusing and unpredictable. I've witnessed so many improbable things over the last months. Let's hope for your aunt's sake he will turn up."

Arden bowed as he left her, his admiration plainly visible in his face, despite her tear-stained face and red eyes. Honora heard Jessie talking to her brother as he left and next moment her friend burst in, full of concern. She evaded Jessie's questions and changed the subject.

"I have some enquiries to make and some letters to write but I can do little until I hear from the Amiens plantation. I'm going to ask Susannah if there's work for me at the hospital. I need something to occupy my mind," said Honora purposefully. "I'll go mad otherwise."

"I could help too," said Jessie. "But I must spend more time with Arden before he rejoins his ship."

"Yes, you really must," said Honora.

"Would you like something to eat now?" asked Jessie.

Honora nodded. She clutched Jessie's hand.

"Thank you, Jessie. You always look after me so well."

True to her word, Honora went to the hospital that afternoon to see Susannah. Her friend introduced her to the tall grey-haired orderly Elmer Casey.

"Mrs Daly tells me you'd like to help us here at Harewood Army Hospital."

Although Susannah had tried to persuade her to rest after her bad news, Honora was determined. Arden's words about widows and orphans had touched her. At least she could try and prevent more women from becoming widows by trying to save their husbands.

"Yes, I have some nursing experience," she said. "My father was a doctor and I sometimes helped him."

"We need all the help we can get," said Elmer, scrutinising her carefully. "You're a bit younger — and prettier — than Mrs Dix likes. She's in charge of recruiting army nurses. I'd welcome you with open arms but some doctors might object. Some of 'em don't like women on their wards. But we've a couple who worked in the Crimea who appreciate the efforts of you ladies. You just arrive and we'll find you something to do."

Next day, she reported to Elmer and followed him about the wards. The wounded lay in every available corner on makeshift beds and pallets. Honora had seen many pitiful sights on her visits with her father, a doctor, but she was hardly prepared for the sea of broken humanity stretched across the floors of the hospital. The nauseating smell of blood and sickness, and worse, hung like a pall over the wards. She'd faced such conditions in the hovels of Manchester, but here was misery on an unparalleled scale. She was appalled that so many men were suffering from fevers and diseases caught in the chaos of the field hospitals. To Elmer's surprise, she began working at once, trying to ease what suffering she could. He'd suspected she'd be daunted by the sight of so many wounded, but Honora was stubbornly resolved to help without flinching. She had found a cause and, with a chance to be useful, seized it with determination. Even Susannah was anxious at the relentless passion with which the young woman threw herself into the work. But Honora's knowledge and experience were invaluable. As she needed little training and had mercifully little squeamishness, she was a welcome addition to the nursing staff.

That evening, bone weary but feeling fulfilled, Honora found Arden at home with Jessie.

"We saw Mr Lincoln walking to the War Department this afternoon," said Jessie, full of excitement. "Then we had our photograph taken to send home to Father. And I've been aboard an 'ironclad'. It was truly fascinating but very stuffy in the engine room. And I met some of Arden's old shipmates. They told me how brave he'd been and how he deserved his promotion."

Arden muttered modestly and Honora gave him a tentative smile. Her opinion of him was confused. He'd abandoned

Dolly back in Gorbydale; he could easily betray her to the authorities, yet he'd seemed concerned to protect her reputation. His friends saw him as a hero and it was obvious that Susannah thought so too, and insisted he stayed to dinner.

Honora had planned to retire early to her bed with exhaustion but she was anxious that Arden might have some news. She answered their questions about her work at the hospital very briefly, turning the conversation instead to Jessie and her brother. It wasn't until later in the evening that Arden managed a private word with her.

"Your man is known to the authorities," he murmured. "They already have him in their sights. Please have no assignations with him whatsoever."

Reluctantly, she promised she would avoid Duplege if possible.

Days later, Honora accompanied Jessie to the Naval Yard, much to Jessie's surprise. As Jessie waved goodbye to Arden, Honora raised a hand and Arden bowed slightly to her.

"I'll write," he called as the steam ship pulled away into the river. "And give my love to all at home when you write."

"I will," called Jessie. "And I'll send them our photograph. Do please take care."

Honora was grateful to Arden. Once he had joined his ship, the *Irene*, he was bound for Baton Rouge. Honora had told him that Robert had written to his mother about Duplege's house there. Perhaps there was some hope after all.

They trailed back home, chatting about very little, avoiding the words that they both dreaded.

"You mustn't worry. Your brother will be safe, I'm sure," said Honora.

"I do hope and pray so. And hopefully we'll soon discover something about Master Robert," suggested Jessie. She added, "I'll join you in the hospital tomorrow. I'm sure they can find something for me to do."

They must hope. It was all they had.

Though, when they arrived back at the Daly house, there was an unwelcome surprise waiting for them. George Daly opened the door to them, his face like thunder.

"Please come in," he said, his voice clipped and unusually stern.

Susannah waited anxiously in the drawing room beside a serious looking man.

"Miss Darwen?" he asked in a soft Scottish burr.

They stared in surprise.

"Yes," said Honora.

"I am from the War Department."

"Aren't you Alan Pinkerton — the detective?" asked Jessie. "I saw you when our Arden and me were walking around Washington, and he told me who you were." The man looked annoyed at the interruption.

"I believe you know a man called Clarence Delahay?" he asked, ignoring her and turning his attention to Honora.

"No," she said shaking her head in confusion.

"How about Clay Davies — or Clement Duplege?"

Honora gasped.

"Wasn't that the chap that came to the Invincible Mill?" asked Jessie innocently. "Proper toff he was in his linen suit."

She snapped her mouth shut, realising in horror that she'd said too much. Arden and Honora's secret revealed.

"How did…?" began Honora.

"The clerk at the post office brought your letter to the attention of the authorities Miss Darwen," said the man sternly. "You were observed meeting Duplege. He is a known enemy of the Union, Miss Darwen, and we were about to discover his accomplices when you showed up."

"I met him by accident," said Honora, full of distress. "I promise you, I… My sympathies are with the Union. I'm just desperate to find my cousin Robert. I thought that…"

She was interrupted by George Daly.

"You were associating with a southern spy and you dare to use this house," he said angrily. "You will pack your bags, young woman, and leave this house immediately. I had no idea…"

Mr Pinkerton interrupted.

"You may rest assured, Mr Daly, we have no reason to suspect this woman is lying. Her letter to a property known to be associated with this man proves she is telling the truth."

He showed Honora a familiar thick cream envelope. It had been opened.

"But that's your letter to Master Robert isn't it?" said Jessie. "You mean we've been waiting all this time and they haven't even sent it?"

Honora held out a hand for it, but the man shook his head.

"We may need this as evidence, Miss Darwen."

"But Honora isn't a spy," cried Jessie. "We're looking for her cousin Robert — that's all. His father is ill and he's needed at home in England. We support the Union. Why, my brother is fighting for the north and Honora has been working at the hospital, helping the wounded soldiers."

"It's true," said Susannah in Honora's defence. "She works very hard too. We are desperate for help."

Her husband frowned at her.

"Very well," said Pinkerton. "But I think you have been very foolish, Miss Darwen, and a little naive. We will leave this matter for the moment. But if you have any contact with this man — or any of his associates — you must report to me immediately at the War Department."

"Yes, sir," said Honora. "I promise I will."

But once he had left there was no placating George.

"You have abused my hospitality," he told them. "I will not tolerate you in my house."

Susannah finally persuaded him to let them to stay for that night at least. The girls stayed in their room, sitting miserably on their beds, their possessions packed for the morning. They had no idea what they would do next.

Chapter 42: Gold

Melissa stood anxiously by her husband's side. She'd heard that Taylor had arrived back in Gorbydale and was desperate for news of her son. Jacob had been proudly showing her the photograph of Jessie and Arden that had arrived that morning. Leaving the Relief Committee in his capable hands, she'd hurried back to Overdale House on news that Taylor had returned from Liverpool.

"I'm afraid I've no news of Master Robert for you," Taylor told her. "Clement Duplege was in Liverpool but he'd heard nothing. He said he'd keep an eye open. I'm sorry, Mrs Overdale."

"I just pray and hope that Honora and Jessie can find him," said Melissa sadly.

She'd had a letter from Honora putting the best possible light on Robert's disappearance. There was still hope but with no glimmer of news from her son, that hope was slowly ebbing away. Bitterly disappointed, she fought back her tears. Taylor bit his lip at Jessie's name.

"What's all this?" demanded Matthias staring at the unfamiliar money on his desk.

"Confederate dollars," said Taylor. "I had no choice. The south are running short of gold. Did you want me to bring back the cargo?"

"Well, I've laid out money for it, but my bank won't accept this stuff," said Matthias angrily.

"Duplege tells me that there are banks in Liverpool that take them," said Taylor.

But Matthias slumped in his chair and sighed. Melissa knew he couldn't pay the mortgage on the Invincible with illegal money.

"You mustn't worry, dear," said Melissa, trying to sooth him. "I'll go to Liverpool and see Mr Kearsley. I should like a word with Augustus. Mrs Kearsley invited me to call anytime."

She knew the invitation was made from automatic politeness but she'd go anyway. They'd both heard the rumours about the uselessness of Confederate money, though neither would admit it to the other. There was little hope of having the bills cashed.

"I'll trade no more with the south if it's this rubbish I'm paid with," said Matthias with a groan. "I've been sold a pup and they've got my goods for nowt."

Melissa nervously played with her wedding ring. If she was unsuccessful at the Kearsleys, she might yet pawn her jewels. She would never enter the pawnshops in Gorbydale and shame her husband, but perhaps a discreet jeweller in Liverpool might be able to help. She would do anything to save the Invincible. Her wedding ring was the only jewellery she needed. Surely the bank would never foreclose on their mortgage. Who would buy a mill at that time of cotton famine?

Chapter 43: A New Arrival

Dolly was summoned by the bell for tea. Her figure beneath the copious apron was growing but still small for a first child. Without a vigilant Honora on hand, she felt safe from discovery. Her back was aching unbearably and she placed a bracing hand on the edge of the sideboard awaiting orders.

"Would you like to stay for tea, Mr Walmsley?" asked Melissa.

Taylor gave Dolly a curious glance. She guessed he'd heard the odd rumours rumbling about her about the town but she strived to looked as unperturbed and insolent as ever.

"I won't if you don't mind, Mrs Overdale," said Taylor. "My mother was expecting me to show my face when I came back from Liverpool. She's overcautious about trains."

"I expect they can be dangerous things," conceded Melissa.

Dolly had encountered Mrs Walmsley many times on her visits to Overdale House and knew her for an interfering old fusspot.

Dolly bit her lip as he passed as a shooting pain ripped through her body. Her grip on the sideboard rattled a pair of ornate vases. She had to get home.

After giving the cook the instructions to serve tea she took a deep breath.

"I'll have to go home. I've had a message that Mam is near her time. I'm sorry, but I'll have to go," she said.

"What message? I didn't hear anyone call," said the cook, outraged by the suggestion that she should serve the tea as well as make it.

People had noticed that Dolly's mother Maggie had been swelling round the waist lately and congratulated Tommo as a 'sly old dog'. Dolly had almost laughed aloud as he'd acknowledged the compliment to his supposed manhood. Luckily, no one was around when the pillow came from under Maggie's apron at night.

"I spotted, er … Eddie Davenport coming up the drive and he told me," said Dolly, grabbing her shawl and turning her back to ignore the cook.

"Dolly Tate, just you wait a minute," the cook protested.

"I've got to go," yelled Dolly as she fled out of the door.

She was halfway down the drive when she felt a rush of water trickling down her legs. With a sob, Dolly clutched her belly and hurried home as best she could, pausing now and again when the pains became too intense to move. With enormous relief she burst into her home.

"It's time, Mam," she gasped and slumped onto a kitchen chair.

"What do I do?" wailed Maggie. "I can't go out to fetch your Dad. I'm supposed to be having this dratted baby."

Pain pumped through Dolly once again and she gritted her teeth. No one must hear her cry out when it was her mother who should be making all the noise.

"Right," said Dolly, urging herself from the chair. "Out of my way."

She staggered to the front door and grabbed the nearest urchin.

"Get to the Feathers and tell Tommo Tate that his wife's time has come and to get back here right away. Have you got that? Right away, mind," she commanded fiercely with an urgency brought about by another shooting pain.

"What will you give me?" demanded the urchin.

"I'll set Seth on you if you don't," she threatened.

The boy turned pale and scurried away in the direction of the Feathers. Dolly took a deep breath.

"I'm going upstairs," she said wearily and, gritting her teeth, crawled up on her hands and knees, exhausted and damp and with the pains coming ever more urgently.

She had begun by hating this small growing niggle inside her, a reminder of her own stupidity. Then, gradually, as the emerging life began to move and kick, it had become something she was curious to see. Though it was so obviously part of herself, she was perversely beginning to think of it as her little sister or brother, and to feel very protective towards it. Now it was about to come into the world, and with much pain and effort, she would fight for it to survive.

Her mother hovered about ineffectively as Dolly suppressed every urge to scream against the world. She vaguely heard her father return, his boots heavy on the bare wooden stairs.

"Has the little bastard arrived yet," she heard him say. "I'll smother it at birth."

"You'll do no such thing — yer bastard yerself," snarled Dolly savagely, clutching desperately at the iron bars of the bed head. "I'm the one paying for its keep. If you want your bloody beer money, you'll shut your bloody gob."

"Oh, Dolly, don't use such language," chided her mother. Dolly sobbed in her pain and exhaustion.

"I can't help it, Mam. It's just sort of bursting out of me."

She heard voices downstairs and her father galloped down to prevent the helpful neighbours from entering the house. Nobody argued with Tommo.

Whether it was due to the desperate dash back home or the small size of the baby, Dolly's labour went quicker than they'd anticipated. Well before midnight, amid stifled curses and clenched teeth, another young Tate came into the world. Drenched in sweat, Dolly demanded to see her child. It was a baby boy, his hair a soft fuzz of red.

"What'll you call it?" asked Tommo, surprisingly with his eyes shining. "Will it be Arden then?"

"I've told you, I'm not saying who the father is," snapped Dolly, gently touching the soft cheek of her son. "He's Albert, after the Queen's fella."

"One Albert gone and another come into the world," said her mother smiling in pride at her first grandchild.

Though their names were the same, their situations in life could not have been more different.

Two days later, Dolly put in an appearance at Overdale House. She had sent a message to say she was needed at home but now reluctantly decided that she must go back to her work as if nothing had happened. She was sore and her breasts were bound tightly to stem the flow of milk, though they continually leaked to her embarrassment. If Honora had been home, she would have made note of these things, but Melissa had problems of her own to see to and noticed nothing. The cook gave Dolly many a sly glance but said nothing.

Dolly and her mother had found a wet nurse for little Albert, a woman whose own child had been stillborn and was glad to earn a few pennies to feed the living babe. So, despite his unwelcome entrance into the world, the baby thrived, skinny but determined to hang on to life.

Chapter 44: The Hospital

Once they had been evicted from the Dalys' home, Jessie and Honora finally found a cramped boarding house in the packed city behind the main thoroughfares. They were given a small, stuffy room at the top of the house. It was awful, the bed linen soiled, bugs in their bed and the smell of filth was atrocious. They were used to such smells at the hospital but hadn't expected to have to live with them. They refused the food as it was meagre and tasteless and made do with what they could buy elsewhere. Some of the male lodgers tried to take liberties and the girls carried sharp hatpins to deter any unwanted advances. All the decent hotels were full and there was nowhere else to go. It was bad enough that the weather had turned the Washington streets to a quagmire, and mud and worse trailed everywhere. There was a daily struggle to keep the hospital clean with so many people coming in and out. The smell of horse manure mingled with that of the ever present blood and wounded flesh.

"You wouldn't think I'd miss cobbled streets," Jessie told Honora with a smile.

A wave of homesickness welled up in Jessie. She wondered when they would go home, but her friend was determined to wait until she had some news about Robert. Jessie had a strong suspicion that their vigil was hopeless but kept her thoughts to herself. Honora somehow clung on to her fragile hope and, in the meantime, immersed herself in nursing. She wasn't as despondent as Jessie in their futile attempts to stem the endless flow of sickness around them. Honora saw everything as an opportunity to learn.

"I'm surprised that a place as important as Washington doesn't have decent roads. And they haven't even finished the dome on the Capitol building yet," said Honora.

"I suppose all the builders have gone to war," said Jessie, picking up her skirts against the mud.

The girls were now working at the Judiciary Square Hospital. Once they had left her house, Susannah had arrived to warn them that George would not allow them to go near soldiers in the military hospital.

"He said you might overhear military secrets and inadvertently pass them on," she told the girls apologetically.

It was nonsense, as soldiers inhabited every nook and cranny of the capital, especially after a skirmish. Carts of wounded trailed down the roads, able-bodied men marched in columns, convalescent soldiers trailed in groups to rejoin their units and sailors hung about the river near the naval yard. Everywhere, uniforms of every shape and hue thronged the city. They were impossible to avoid. Despite her protests, Honora was still under suspicion.

"I have a friend at the Judiciary and they are crying out for help. Go there and mention my name," suggested Susannah.

They approached the hospital with trepidation. As most of the hospitals in the capital were run by the military, the girls had limited choice. George Daly would no doubt protest if they applied to the new hospital set up in the Patent Office. Their funds were running low and they needed to work. Judiciary Square was modern by most standards, and a civilian hospital, but its regime was reputed to be harsh. Churches, hotels, anywhere where a shakedown could be squeezed in, were being used to tend the broken men.

Honora and Jessie were welcomed as women with some experience, especially as they mentioned Susannah's name to Dr Jacob as she had suggested.

"We can only do our best," said Honora, tying on her apron with purpose. "Though, I should like to be a doctor in a modern hospital that was well run."

"A doctor? You know, it's ridiculous that they won't train women in England," said Jessie, shaking her head in disbelief.

"That's true," said Honora thoughtfully. "But England isn't the only place…"

Jessie glanced at her friend's serious face with growing realisation. She wondered if her friend's determination to stay in Washington had another purpose than to find her cousin. Honora had mentioned that women could train as doctors in America a number of times. But there was no time for speculation at that moment; they had much work to do among the wounded and dying.

Then they had a stroke of luck. Susannah had not abandoned them entirely. She arrived one day with good news for the girls. One of her friends had decided to go north to stay with her daughter as the fighting crept nearer to Washington. At times, the inhabitants held their breath and glanced to the horizon when distant gunfire echoed over the city. Susannah took them to the outskirts of the city and stopped outside a little old clapperboard house. Outside it was shabby but they went inside to find it neat and clean, despite the primitive amenities.

"The house originally belonged to my friend's in-laws," explained Susannah. "After her husband died, she didn't want to move into a newer house."

"It's perfect," said Honora. "Please tell your friend we will look after it."

"I shouldn't have suggested you lived here otherwise," said Susannah smiling.

It felt like a palace after the grimy boarding house. They even had the luxury of a bath in a zinc tub in front of the fire to wash away the filth of the boarding house and hospital. Jessie used the water last, of course, but she didn't care. She felt so refreshed afterwards, and clean for the first time in days as she put on a crisp white apron. There was a longer walk to the hospital, but the luxury of cleanliness and privacy made up for that.

"I'm so glad we don't have to go back to that filthy boarding house," said Honora. "It was kind of Susannah to suggest her friend's house for us."

That night, Jessie slept in a bed on her own for the first time in an age. The room was small, the furniture old and plain and looked homemade, but a quilt on the bed was sewn with such colourful intricacy that Jessie admired it for a long time. She wondered about those who had made it. Perhaps they were simple folk like her own family. Although, both Susannah's home and that of her sister in New York were more luxurious, she felt more settled in this little house. It was painted white throughout but it had a homeliness that reminded her of Weavers Row. There was even an overgrown vegetable patch in the little garden behind the house. With no news yet of Robert, it seemed they might be there for some time. Jessie tried to remember her father's gardening methods so they could grow some fresh food. She hoped Jacob and Eddie were coping without her. She would write to them the next day with her new address. Pondering all the unexpected changes in her life, she fell into a deep and dreamless sleep and woke refreshed next morning for the first time in weeks.

"There was a rush of arrivals during the night," said the matron as Jessie and Honora reported for work one morning. "There's been a skirmish up river at Fredericksburg. There are lots of casualties."

Broken military men were lying everywhere. Every spare corner where a makeshift bed could be placed, was full. They were too crowded together, but it was impossible to do otherwise in the middle of a war.

The girls hurriedly made their way to their ward, carefully stepping their way along crowded corridors. Jessie had taken some time to get used to attending to men's bodies. She wasn't afraid of nursing, having tended to her mother's most intimate needs, but to do the same for a man had daunted her. She'd tried to nurse the wounded soldiers by averting her eyes, strictly reared as she'd been. It hadn't worked. Now she ignored her qualms and found many men were more embarrassed at being tended by a woman. She soon put them at ease with her brisk kindness.

Honora was checking the patients' progress with the night nurse when Jessie heard the faint call.

"Nurse, nurse, can I have some water?"

As she fetched a mug of water, Jessie noticed a black girl standing by the adjoining bed.

"I could have gotten it for him but he didn't ask," said the girl shyly.

Despite fighting for black emancipation, many soldiers were still reluctant to even associate with black people.

"Not to worry. I'm here now," said Jessie kindly.

Jessie was helping the man to sip when she suddenly felt she was being watched.

She glanced towards the next bed. Jessie stared in confusion at the thin, bearded figure staring at her.

"Jessie, Jessie? Is that you or am I dreaming? It sounds like you. It is! Jessie, it is you," said a weak but familiar voice.

The man struggled to pull himself up. Putting down the mug of water she automatically went to him. Before she could say anything, he held her face in his hands, pulled her toward him and kissed her with a passion that surprised her. She felt the raging heat pulsing from his face and hands.

"Oh, Jessie, I can hardly believe it. You've come to take me home," said Robert Overdale weakly, his voice subsiding into sobs.

Jessie felt confused and weak with emotion. Gently, she untangled the arm he had curled round her waist. It felt so hot, so thin.

"Robert, Robert what on earth are you doing here?" she said softly. "We've been looking for you. Honora and I have been looking for you. I can't believe it's you."

As she straightened up, she saw Honora staring at them both in stunned amazement.

Jessie didn't know what to do or say, her feelings in a tremendous turmoil at the astonishing discovery of Robert. He was in a bad way and her whole instinct was to gather him up in her arms to comfort him. Yet, she knew she must be professional and above all, hide her overwhelming feelings and instincts from Honora.

"Oh, Robert, I'm so, so relieved to see you," said Honora gently taking her cousin's bony, hot hand. "Robert, tell me where have you been wounded?"

"My leg," he said. "I was hit in the leg. Kezia has been helping me. We've come all the way from Louisiana. It won't heal. It got worse as we came to Washington. Kezia and Abraham brought me straight to the hospital."

The black girl gave a worried smile.

"Don't like the look of that leg, Miss," she said quietly. "I did the best I could."

"We'll try and be as gentle as possible," Honora told her cousin. "Oh, Robert, your mother will be so happy you're alive. She sent us to find you." She gave Jessie an unfathomable look. "Could you give me a hand?" she asked.

Robert winced as they pulled back the sheet. The leg looked horrible and smelt worse. Even Honora, who was used to such things, winced. The wound was sewn up neatly with what appeared to be purple embroidery silk, but it looked swollen and an unhealthy colour of purple and red. The wound seemed to go deep.

Honora worked in silence, hardly looking at Jessie. The wound seemed to swell and looked about to burst as his cousin gently cut the stitches. Jessie blushed to see Robert's poor bruised body, his ribs so prominent.

"Can it be saved?" whispered Jessie.

Honora hesitated. She turned to Jessie so Robert could not see her speak.

"I don't know. I'll ask Dr Jacob. He must have seen lots of these injuries," she murmured.

"I'll go and get him," said Jessie, eager to be useful.

She arrived back minutes later.

"So, you say this man is your kin," the doctor said, smiling at Robert. He glanced up at Kezia. "I noticed you last night. This little lady refused to leave him."

Honora nodded and pulled back the blanket silently, revealing Robert's leg. The doctor took a sharp intake of breath.

"Can it be saved?" mouthed Honora.

He shrugged.

"It'll take a lot of work — a lot of nursing, and even then I still couldn't tell you," he told the two girls when they had moved a little way from the bed. "You know the score. It's in God's hands. I'll see what I can do by way of laudanum. You know we ain't got much, though."

"Oh, thank you, Doctor," said Jessie warmly, then fell silent as Honora gave her another sharp and searching look.

They went back to Robert and made him as comfortable as they could. He desperately grasped Jessie's hand.

"Will you look after Kezia for me?" he asked. "And Abraham, too. They've saved my life. And you must take these and keep them safe."

He gave Jessie a battered leather satchel. She opened it tentatively. Inside there were two bills of sale. One for a slave named Kezia Amiens and the other for Abraham Amiens. They had been sold to one Robert Overdale of Gorbydale, Lancashire. She stared at Robert in amazement and horror. He was a slave owner!

He saw the abhorrence and shame in her face.

"I can explain," he stammered. "Jessie, I can explain. But not here — not with everyone…"

He was interrupted as his cousin came back to his bedside. Jessie glanced at her and let her eyes fall to the papers. Honora's eyes automatically followed. She was silently shocked.

"Robert," she hissed. "How could you?"

"It's not what you think. We were travelling through the south," he muttered urgently. "Kezia will explain."

Kezia nodded solemnly.

There were other patients to attend to. Now that Robert was at least comfortable, the girls left him under Kezia's watchful eye and went about their duties, always glancing over to where Robert lay. Honora seemed away in a world of her own as she automatically tended to her patients.

Chapter 45: Explanations

Kezia watched Robert faithfully during that day, never leaving his side unless to fetch something to make him more comfortable. She fed him with soup and was persuaded to have some herself, which she drank greedily and gratefully. At the end of a gruelling day, the girls took her back to the little house with them. Moments later, there was a knock on the door and a tall black man stood hesitantly outside.

"This is my husband, Abraham," said Kezia shyly as they invited him in. "We got married like normal folks," she said eagerly as if to assure the girls. "Master Robert, he arranged for us to get married by a minister that sheltered us on our way here. He stood as our witness. Master Robert ain't our master, rightly. We only called him 'Master' 'cos it was safer that way. Those papers was forged so as we wouldn't be sent back if we was caught. We needed them to travel on the train with Master Robert lookin' like he owned us. That train was so frightenin'." She paused and took a deep breath, her eyes wide in fear as she remembered. "It was full of soldiers, Miss Jessie. When they asked him, Master Robert said was travellin' to Richmond to stay with his sister and his slaves, that's me an' Abraham, had come to look after him with his bad leg an' all. They asked if he'd been wounded in the fightin' and he just nodded. They looked at them papers and didn't say a word, but their eyes seemed to look right into your head. I was feared for our lives. He took a big, big risk to save us. Some of them bounty hunters, they tear up a legal paper, no messin', and God help those that cross 'em, white or black."

"So, Robert is no slave owner," said Honora, the tension in her face visibly relaxing. "At least that is a relief."

Kezia shook her head smiling. Jessie smiled too. It was deeply abhorrent to them both to think that Robert should own another human being.

"Your cousin is a brave, brave man," said Kezia. "He took a big risk bringing us here. And we helped save Master Robert likewise. Abraham here carried him over from the river when he was too sick to walk."

"Thank you," said Honora warmly. "My aunt and uncle will be forever grateful for what you've done."

They sat down at the large, scrubbed table to a simple meal which Jessie prepared. They were both earning the same wage at the hospital, yet Jessie still felt obliged to look after Honora. Her friend, though, had been very cool with her since she'd witnessed Robert's kiss. Abraham ate as if he had had nothing to eat for a long time. They seemed shy and uneasy at first, their eyes downcast. Gradually, Abraham relaxed as Jessie and Honora coaxed the new arrivals to tell of how they had arrived in Washington. He told them of some of the places they'd stayed on their perilous journey, sometimes hidden, too frightened to breathe as they were surrounded by Confederate soldiers. Contrabands were continually hunted down by bounty hunters with dogs and clubs eager for the reward for escaped slaves. They'd continually lived in fear of being sent back to the plantation at any time.

"We didn't know if Master Robert was a deserter or not," said Kezia. "He got his wound in some skirmish, but he said he'd somehow got dragged along with some soldiers. He said he tried to evade them but then it was too late and the Union was on to them."

"I mean to join the Union Army now I'm here in Washington," said Abraham. "I've been talking to some of the other contrabands like us, and they say Negroes are helping out in the army camps. Rumour is, we can join soon. They say someone said will the slave fight? If any man asks, you tell him 'No'. But if anyone asks you will a Negro fight, tell him 'Yes!' So I say, 'Amen to that'. I'll surely fight if I's given the chance."

"We must talk some more tomorrow," said Honora, getting up stiffly from her chair. "But it's very late now and we all need our rest. You and Abraham can have the bedroom under the eaves. Jessie, do you mind sharing with me when Robert arrives home?"

Jessie shook her head, wondering if he would indeed come home. With such thoughts heavy in their minds they all went wearily to bed.

Unable to sleep, she came down in the middle of the night to find Honora with her head in her hands at the kitchen table by the light of a flickering candle.

"I'm writing to Aunt Melissa," decided Honora. "I can tell her Robert is safe at least. I think — that is if you're willing — and I think you are — that we should work on separate shifts for a few days. Then we can both keep an eye on my cousin round the clock."

"Yes, that would be best," said Jessie, lowering her eyes.

She knew Honora was as surprised as she was by that kiss. Yet, how could Jessie have prevented Robert when he was obviously so relieved to see her in his weak, confused and emotional state? Now they both had to work together to help him.

"I'll take the evening and night shift," said Honora. "It wouldn't be fair to you to lose sleep over my cousin."

If only you knew how much sleep I've already lost over Robert! Jessie thought to herself.

Faced with her friend's coolness and obvious disapproval, she wanted to clear the air.

"Honora, I think we should talk about Robert. I know you must have been shocked when he kissed me like that. It was a shock to me, to say the least. But I'm sure he wouldn't have kissed me like that if he hadn't been wounded and so far away from home. He must have been delirious. He didn't know what he was doing. He's so feverish and, and … confused. He must have been so relieved to hear someone from home. He's obviously been through hell to arrive in the hospital in that state and…"

She knew she was waffling but faltered on with weak excuses until Honora raised her hand to stop her.

"Jessie, I don't know what to think," said Honora with a huge sigh. "I heard all the rumours in Gorbydale, but I chose not to believe them at the time. Now I don't know."

"I suppose Dolly Tate had a hand in that," said Jessie quietly.

Honora's silence told her what she already suspected.

"So, was there truth in the rumours?" asked Honora, looking straight at Jessie.

Jessie felt her face redden and wondered how she could best say what she had to. She took a deep breath.

"Your cousin has caused me a lot of upset," she said eventually. "He once stole a kiss from me at the Wakes Fair to win a wager with his friend — that stout man that comes to visit him. Taylor Walmsley was about to ask me to marry him — but he witnessed what happened and misunderstood the whole thing. He backed away from asking me then. Yes, your cousin has caused me a lot of upset and trouble."

"Taylor Walmsley?" asked Honora in surprise. "The overseer from the Invincible?"

Jessie nodded.

"I swear I didn't encourage Robert," she continued. "And I wouldn't do such a thing, and certainly not if I'd known you were betokened to your cousin — honestly, I wouldn't."

She felt a twinge of guilt when she remembered those two little words of betrayal 'I'll see' as she left Overdale House, but that had been before she'd known about the understanding.

Honora looked astonished.

"I'm not 'betokened' to Robert as you so quaintly put it — or anything like that," she protested. "I expect you've been listening to my Aunt Melissa. I know she had hopes … I do love my cousin — but only as a brother."

Jessie stared at her.

"So there isn't an understanding between you?"

"No," said Honora firmly. "I've come to appreciate him more after what Kezia has just told us but, to be honest, I always thought him a bit of a spoilt brat. Honestly, Jessie, I've come to know and rely on you over these past weeks. I couldn't have managed to find Robert without you. I think you'd make him an excellent wife. But it doesn't make any difference what I think. But, do you think Uncle Matthias would allow his precious only son to marry a mill girl? You know very well he wouldn't. You do realise that, don't you?"

"Of course I do, and that's why I would never encourage Robert," Jessie defended herself.

And yet she remembered so much in those moments. How she'd tried to smother her feelings for him, only for them to surface again and again. Robert's bravery at saving Kezia and Abraham had revealed his deeper, finer qualities to her. She was sure that, like Honora, she had never suspected him of such courage. Ultimately, she must face reality. After a moment's thoughtful silence she began to talk, slowly and sadly.

"Robert can seem so sincere, but I'm not a fool, Honora. I know full well what happens to girls who fall for men above their station."

"Uncle Matthias could cut Robert off without a penny," added Honora. "And that would break Aunt Melissa's heart. Robert is her only son, her world — and she has been so good to me."

"I mean no offence — but your cousin was a spoilt young man who'd always had his own way," said Jessie thoughtfully. "I'm sure he saw me as a challenge when I rebuffed him and that's why he's been pursuing … I mean…"

She finished lamely. He had pursued her and she had to admit to herself she'd been flattered. She wished she wasn't so attracted to Robert. But she had known all along the situation was impossible. If she'd had any doubts, Honora had just spelt them out for her in stark truth.

"He is spoilt and very headstrong, it's true," admitted Honora, then her eyes filled with tears. "But I'm so very glad we found him."

"I am too. Let's go back to bed," said Jessie. "I'm bone weary. We'll need our strength in the morning."

Chapter 46: The Operation

Next morning, Kezia rose early and made them breakfast.

"You didn't have to," said Honora, but she was eating heartily for the first time in ages.

"I like to help," said Kezia shyly. "If I may, I want to call at a local church and see the Reverend. I have a letter to give him from an old friend. I'll come to see Master Robert at the hospital later. I feel I can leave him for a while now he is in good hands."

"Please feel free to do as you wish, Kezia," said Honora smiling.

Filled with hope, Jessie and Honora headed for the hospital. But an anxious Dr Jacob was waiting outside the ward.

"Your kinsman will have to lose his leg," he said abruptly. "If it doesn't come off soon, the infection will spread. He might lose his life."

"Could you — would you…?" began Honora, her eyes pleading with the doctor.

He gave her a doubtful look.

"I could try to cut out the infected flesh," he said thoughtfully. "But he is weak and it will take a lot of nursing if he is to pull through. Even then, he still might lose the leg. The inflammation is deep. He will be disfigured. Are you sure you would want me to try? It is a risk. You might lose him with delaying the inevitable."

"Please try," begged Honora. "Jessie and I will look after him."

She glanced at her friend, who nodded in anxious agreement. They had seen such operations work in the military hospital and wished to save Robert's leg if at all possible.

"I'll do it straight away, then," decided Dr Jacob.

Robert smiled wanly as his cousin and Jessie arrived with the doctor. Dr Jacob carefully explained what the operation would mean and the consequences of any delay.

"I can still take the leg off," said the doctor. "The other is a risk. Do you want to take such a risk?"

Robert looked at Honora, willing to trust her judgement. She nodded tentatively.

"Do what you have to," said Robert bravely. "But if you think the leg is worse when you cut into it, then take it off."

The orderlies carried him to the operating table. Despite the efforts of the hospital staff, the room smelt of stale blood and the floor was stained deep brown. The surgeon's apron was cleaner but covered with the ominous shadow of stains that refused to budge.

"I have a drop of ether that will help," said the surgeon. "But I don't have much. There are other patients I have to deal with today."

Honora nodded then watched fascinated as he poured a few precious drops onto a mask over her cousin's face. Once Robert became unconscious, Dr Jacob began to peel away the dressing and revealed rotting flesh beneath. Even Honora was appalled at the smell and the sight of it. She wondered for a moment if she had made the wrong decision. She might even be the cause of Robert's death with the delay in chopping the leg straight off. What would she say to her aunt? Jessie gave her an anxious glance as the surgeon began to cut away the putrid flesh. It seemed to go on forever, the hole in the skin, the fat and then the muscle growing deeper. Finally, some healthy flesh appeared and they visibly relaxed.

Then they stared in horror as Robert's eyes opened in terror. The effect of the ether had worn off and his body went rigid with pain and fear. Jessie grabbed his hand and his eyes turned to her, pleading for her to stop his nightmare.

"It will soon be over," she whispered, trying not to flinch as he clutched even harder to her hand.

Another drop of ether saw him collapse in a stupor. He roused as the final stitches closed the wound over a much distorted leg. Honora stared at her cousin's deformed limb. She hadn't realised how bad the infection had been, and wondered if she would have pleaded to save the leg had she known. Still, there was a chance that Robert could walk again without the aid of an artificial limb. She was acutely aware that the infection might take hold again and spread through his body to kill him, and it would all be her fault. He smiled weakly at her and then his eyes searched out Jessie. Reassured of her presence, he closed them in exhaustion and relief, his body was bathed in sweat.

Honora stared at the leg before it was covered in a makeshift dressing. Jessie instinctively put a comforting arm around her friend's shoulder, but Honora felt her hesitate. A certain reserve had arisen between them but raising her own hand, Honora patted Jessie's in mutual support.

"Go and take a break now," the surgeon ordered the girls as the orderlies carried an exhausted Robert back to his bed. "He is young but weak. He needs building up but I'm sure you can do that. The rest is in the lap of the gods."

Kezia hovered round Robert's bed and looked relieved when they brought him back. Honora nodded to her and she and Jessie went out into the air. The heat was rising and there was little relief from the stifling surgery but at least the overwhelming smell of blood and putrid sickness was just a taint on the air. Jessie thought she would never escape that clinging stench.

"Why don't you go home and take a rest," she said to Honora. "Kezia and I can keep watch. If you want to come back during the night you'll need some rest. Let's go and ask Matron."

"I'm not running a private hospital for your kin, young woman," the matron told Honora angrily. "My nurses have to abide by the rules. Our fighting men are more important than some English…" She struggled for some word of insult and then just snorted in disgust.

The English were not popular with many folk, especially those steeped in stories of the War of Independence passed down through their families.

"You'll work as you should. If you want to come and pamper your brother during the night, that's your own business," added the matron glaring at Honora.

Honora nodded and walked away without bothering to correct her relationship with Robert. Deep down, she knew the woman was right.

Honora had anticipated the matron's response. The woman had never disguised her animosity towards the British. At the end of her shift, she quietly asked another nurse who usually worked during the night if she would swap duties with her. "She's agreed but I'll have to work for two days more," Honora told Jessie.

"But don't worry, Kezia and I will share the nights with you until then," said her friend loyally.

They were not the only people caring for their families as many army wives arrived at the hospital to nurse their loved ones. Many found themselves overwhelmed and unable to help. Often, they hindered the professional nurses or made demands that were impossible to fulfil. Between them, Jessie and Honora anxiously watched over Robert. Helped by Kezia, they tended his wound with extra vigilance, scrutinising it for tell-tale signs to make sure the infection had not returned. They put as much effort into their other duties to prevent any criticism. Though tired beyond exhaustion, their anxiety made them alert. Finally, they fell into a routine. Honora by night and Jessie by day watched over Robert. They brought him extra food from home and gradually his gaunt features softened. The wound slowly began to heal.

Chapter 47: A Bargain

Back in Gorbydale, Melissa ticked the columns in a ledger and handed it back to Jacob.

"All correct, Mr Davenport," she said with a smile. "We can report to the Relief Committee that the Gorbydale branch is solvent and getting value for money. Perhaps now they'll look kindly on Eli's request for more money. We're desperate that the men should have some project to work on. He's hoping that derelict patch by the river might be turned into a municipal gardens. It would at least give work to the men. The town looks so sad and neglected these days."

The grey rain cast a dismal pall on every building, the shuttered shops, the peeling paintwork and broken windows. Many houses stood neglected and derelict as extended families huddled together in small terraces to save on rent. There was no room, no privacy and no escape from the poverty grinding them even lower. Huddles of jobless, despondent men hung about in doorways or lolled round public houses clutching a drink they could ill afford. At least the girls in the sewing class were bringing in a few shillings to their benighted families. The Relief Committee, now under the competent management of Jacob, Melissa and Eli, made sure that no one went hungry whether they had a ticket for the breadline or not. The vicar's wife had resigned in disgust, telling anyone who was interested of the shocking waste of resources on the undeserving poor.

"Have you heard anything from Jessie recently?" Melissa asked Jacob.

"I have that. I was going to mention it. I received a letter yesterday," he said with a beaming smile. "She says that when

Master Robert is well enough to travel, they are hoping to head home. Miss Darwen says that the journey on the ship, with the rocking waves and all, might open up the wound, so they're making sure it's well healed before they attempt the journey. God willing, she could soon be coming home. All of them could and Master Robert too. I'm right pleased for you, Mrs Overdale. To have lost and found your son, why it's quite biblical somehow. God be praised."

Melissa smiled at him and his happy enthusiasm. But her happiness was tempered with sadness.

"Poor Robert is very lame," she told him. "Honora wrote that he's had an awful operation on his leg. He almost lost it. Poor Robert."

"Aye, our Jessie did mention summat about it," admitted Jacob. "But he's alive, Mrs Overdale, and that's what counts."

Of course it did, but Melissa wondered what her precious son would find at home. The mill was silent and still the mortgage must be paid. His father's health wasn't as stable as she wished. Matthias continually fretted about his business and refused to rest. How could Robert, lame and uneducated for the needs of the trade, be able to help? Matthias had had such ambition. Their mill dominated the valley, their house had every convenience, their son had had every advantage of education. Yet, it might all be lost. Her brother Eli, with the old Endurance Mill, had managed to help his workers and a good many of the townsfolk during the cotton famine. Matthias, for all his display of wealth, had not.

Melissa wondered if she should ask Eli for help. She knew in her heart that Matthias would be too proud to accept it. Searching for some other way to raise the mortgage money, she thought of her son riding proudly about the valley on his fine chestnut horse Surefoot, and an idea came to her.

Melissa stood with her hand resting on his shoulder for support as Matthias counted the money on his desk once more.

"I'm still a bit short," he sighed. "Perhaps they'll let me have a month or two grace."

"They should — nobody wants to buy a mill in these times," said his wife sensibly.

"You did well to get so much for those Confederate dollars, Lissy," he said with a fond smile.

"The Kearsleys were very helpful," she told him, avoiding his eyes.

She did not mention that her son's friends had given her very little for the illegal money, and even that meagre amount perhaps through pity. Nor had she told him that her jewellery was in the vault of a pawnbroker in Liverpool. Sending money to bring her son home had dented the proceeds, but there was something else she might sell.

Melissa saw Taylor Walmsley approaching as she came from the stables. Behind her, the groom was leading out Robert's fine chestnut horse.

"That's a handsome animal, Mrs Overdale," he said, pausing to admire the beast.

Melissa nodded in agreement. Everyone in Gorbydale recognised Robert riding round the town and country on his chestnut.

"Have you called to see my husband, Mr Walmsley?" she asked.

"He asked me to call," said Taylor.

"Perhaps we can walk to the house together," suggested Melissa. "I'd like a word with you. Thank you," she told the groom as he slipped into the saddle to exercise Surefoot.

Walking in silence, Melissa paused before they entered the house.

"Would you be interested in the horse if I were to sell it?" she asked.

Taylor looked at her thoughtfully.

"It's a bit flash for me, Mrs Overdale. I've a quiet mare that pulls my trap. Your chestnut would be an extravagance."

"Yes," said Melissa quietly. "I understand."

Because of that extravagance, it must be sold. Surefoot's sale would bring in much needed money for the mortgage, though she hated the idea of selling Robert's beloved horse. There was no other way.

Melissa tried hard to curb the tears welling in her eyes. Taylor noticed.

"Are you strapped for cash, Mrs Overdale?" he asked boldly.

Her eyes widened with distress at his impertinence.

"I do apologise — I didn't mean to be so blunt — only I might be able to help."

With a long penetrating look, Melissa assessed Taylor. He had helped her husband during the aftermath of his stroke but for a fee. He was a prominent chapel member, but could he be trusted? Matthias had told her he suspected that Taylor Walmsley was dealing with the south on his own behalf. Though he wasn't working at the mill, he'd bought a fine house in the town, as his mother continually boasted. There was a reserve about him Melissa could not fathom. She remembered that he rarely gave more than a laboured smile. Even Matthias at his grumpiest could laugh and chuckle. Faced with the reality of impending bankruptcy, she had no choice.

"Would you come into the parlour for a moment," she asked. "And if your ideas are helpful, we could go to my husband and discuss them."

Taylor gave her a rare smile.

An hour later, Matthias shook hands with his former overseer. Taylor Walmsley was to be a shareholder in the Invincible Mill.

"Well done, lass," Matthias praised his wife. "We'll meet our commitments this time. This war in America will not last forever, and then maybe we can buy back Walmsley's share. Britain has clothed our country, our colonies and the world in cotton before and we'll do it again. I wish our Robert had as much business instinct as Walmsley."

"Our Robert will learn, dear — when he's given the chance," said Melissa in pointed criticism of her husband.

As usual Matthias ignored her as he gleefully counted his cash once again, despite the fact that she had just saved him from certain bankruptcy.

Chapter 48: The New Recruits

Along Pennsylvania Avenue in Washington, the crowds were gathering in excited anticipation. As the new recruits approached, they began cheering. The volunteers had no uniforms and were unarmed, but badges of red, white and blue were proudly displayed on their chests.

"Look, look, there he is," Jessie cried in excitement, pointing to a familiar face in the parade.

Abraham turned his head smartly and smiled at Kezia as he drew near. Then a stone whizzed past them and thumped with a swirl of dust at his feet. It was followed swiftly by another and an angry buzz of jeers. A belligerent element were protesting, angry that Negroes would be armed and allowed to fight for the Union. So far, they had only been allowed to do menial tasks around the army camps. From the front of the crowd, Jessie whirled angrily towards the people behind her. She was confronted by a small knot of invalided soldiers from the convalescent home. One of them froze, his arm raised with another stone. They recognised her at once and guiltily avoided her eyes. He dropped the stone, shamed by her angry glare.

"Nathan Cox, I'm ashamed of you. Have we saved your life so you can insult a fellow soldier — a man who's prepared to lay down his life for his country," she shouted at him.

The man shuffled uneasily and looked ashamed. People about them turned with scathing glances in his direction at Jessie's angry words.

"Nurse Davenport, I didn't see you there," he muttered.

"Obviously not," said Jessie angrily.

The group shuffled away muttering to themselves, not without a glance at Robert who, like some of them, was leaning on crutches.

"Please let's go home," said Honora, anxiously glancing around. "I don't like the feel of this crowd."

Abraham and his company had passed into the distance, followed by a crowd of children joyfully mimicking their march. Echoing down the Avenue, they could hear boos and jeers at the soldiers. Kezia began to weep openly. They had all been shocked and upset by the hostility shown towards the newly recruited black soldiers.

"I don't even know where they're sending him. I's just scared I ain't goin' to see Abraham ever again," she sobbed.

"Of course you will," said Honora, putting a comforting arm round her shoulder. "He'll let you know as soon as they reach camp. They say it's kept secret so there won't be any trouble. You've seen what some of these stupid people are like."

"I expect you're right, Miss Honora," whispered Kezia. "But I's so frightened for him."

"He's a very brave man," said Jessie. "You must be very proud of him."

Kezia nodded.

As the sound of marching boots faded into the distance, they set off toward their little house, Honora with her arm still protecting Kezia. Many of the dispersing spectators sneered and murmured at her intimacy with a black girl. Vigilant against the jostling crowd, Jessie stayed beside Robert hobbling on his crutches. They fell behind because of the crush, though she strained to see Honora and Kezia some way in front of them. Her friend was anxious to get away from the crowds and hurried ahead. Robert's steps were hesitant along the rough sidewalk and Jessie could see the pain in his eyes as he tried to keep pace beside her.

"You did a very brave thing there," he told her. "I wouldn't have the guts to confront a mob like that."

"It's lucky I spotted Nathan Cox," she admitted with relief. "He knows full well what we did for him in the hospital — one or two of the other men too. I hope they are all thoroughly ashamed of themselves — though I don't expect they will be." Exasperated that she could do nothing about the men's ignorance, she changed the subject. "You're doing so much better on your crutches now. Hopefully, we should be able to go home soon."

"Yes," said Robert thoughtfully. "But I doubt I'll ever be able to walk without the aid of a stick. The doctor has suggested I wear a leather brace on my leg."

"That's a good idea. After what you've been through, you're lucky to have a leg at all," said Jessie smiling with encouragement.

She met his eyes and blushed. They'd grown close over the weeks following the operation. She remembered the fear in his eyes and the hard grasp of his hand during the operation. Her hand had been bruised for days afterwards. As soon as Robert's fever had dropped and his leg began to heal, Honora had insisted he came home to their little house to ensure he avoided the infections and fevers so prevalent in the filth and confusion of the overcrowded hospital. At least at home, Kezia could care for him while the girls worked at the hospital.

Yet, Jessie felt she must hold him at arm's length, ever conscious of their divided social status. It was hard in the confines of the small house. They were forever thrown together, accidentally touching. There was no avoiding the added intimacy of changing the dressing on his leg. Sensing Jessie's reluctance, Honora endeavoured to do the task herself.

Yet, the old arrogant Robert was a pale shadow of the broken man Jessie saw daily. She saw in his defeated eyes and broken body that his failure haunted him. He had secured no cotton for the mill. He would return home crippled and other horrors lurked behind his eyes. Robert seldom spoke about his journey from the south, though Kezia quietly told them of the things they'd witnessed. She'd spoken quite naturally as though such things were not new to her, but witnessing rotting corpses beaten to death and lying in unspeakable filth had never been part of Robert's experience before. Sometimes, his eyes looked red from shedding secret unmanly tears. Jessie longed to comfort him but kept as much physical distance between them as was possible. Of their former fleeting intimacy, he said not one word.

As soon as they reached their home, Jessie made tea as Kezia sank into quiet desolation.

"Abraham always wanted to join the army," she said, lifting her sad eyes to Jessie. "He was determined to do it. Didn't take no notice of me when I begged him not to. We could have gone to Canada. Most of the Underground Railway goes that way. We had a time of it makin' our way to Washington with all them rebels making for Richmond. We was nearly stopped on the train. If it wasn't for those sale papers Master Robert had, we could have been in deep, deep trouble. Don't know what I'll do if anything happens to Abraham," she said and burst into uncontrollable tears. She gasped under her breath. "We've come so far together."

"We've all come a long way," said Robert thoughtfully, patting her shoulder to comfort her.

Jessie caught his eye and he smiled sadly. She knew he was remembering Gorbydale. The once proud heir to the Invincible Mill would return home lame and, if this war continued, his inheritance might crumble to nothing without cotton.

As Robert's health improved, Kezia left him to fend for himself. She went frequently to the little black church to help where she could. With a smile, she told them that she had begun a class to teach some of the children to read and write. In what little spare time she had, Robert helped her with her own literacy at the kitchen table. That table seemed to be the centre of their lives at the little house.

Meanwhile, Jessie and Honora battled daily with a growing tide of wounded, struggling to make some inroad into the sick and battle maimed amid the chaos. The hospital was almost overwhelmed. Each evening the girls returned exhausted, but convinced they were doing some good.

Ever mindful of Honora's words of warning, Jessie treated Robert with affectionate teasing as she nursed him, just like she treated her brothers. But every time she touched him, the longing in his eyes matched the longing in her heart. It was impossible. She wanted to go home to Gorbydale where their social status would safely divide them. Yet there was a delay.

"Robert's leg might not heal properly on a pitching ship," Honora insisted.

Jessie had a well-founded suspicion that her friend was reluctant to leave America. They could not go home without Honora who was holding the money for the tickets. Jessie had some savings from her work in the hospital but it was not enough to pay her own way. Then a chance remark from Susannah Daly enlightened Jessie as to Honora's plans.

"Have you received a letter from that medical school in New York, yet?" asked Susannah when she visited.

"Not yet," said Honora blushing and avoiding Jessie's surprised stare.

Later, when Robert had gone to bed, tired after his efforts to walk, Honora could not avoid an explanation.

"I've written to the Geneva Medical School in New York to ask for a place," Honora said resolutely. "Dr Jacobs and Susannah Daly both wrote testimonials for me. I hope to receive a reply soon."

"You mean to become a doctor?" asked her friend in surprise. "In America?"

"I can't do it in England, can I?" said Honora, biting her lip. "I'm sorry I couldn't tell you before, but you might have mentioned it to your father in a letter. I didn't want Aunt Melissa to know just yet. She will think me ungrateful and I don't even know if the school will accept me."

"I hope they do," said Jessie warmly. "You'd make a fine doctor. You know so much already. I'd rather you treated me than a man. Though, I suppose our doctor did what he could for Mother. But your remedies helped as much too."

Yet, there was a problem. How could Jessie and Robert travel alone all the way back to Liverpool? They might travel in different sections of the ship, of course, but that would still be thought unacceptable.

Chapter 49: A Letter for Honora

Honora anxiously called at the post office each day. Then to her joy, the clerk handed her an envelope. Nervously she scanned it, but the stamp was unmistakeable, the letter was from England and not from New York as she'd hoped. She hurried home to open it and, to her surprise, several bank notes fell out.

"It's from your mother," she told Robert as he hobbled towards the table and sat down heavily.

She skimmed the words quickly. It contained a page of news from home. There was also a note from Jacob for Jessie and her friend opened it eagerly.

"Young Eleanor is thriving," said Jessie with a smile. "Oh, and Maggie Tate has had a baby!" She paused for a moment and looked puzzled. "That can't be right. Surely Maggie is too old to have a baby. Oh, I see... It's a little boy — with red hair. Well that's odd for a start. Tommo certainly hasn't got red hair. There certainly isn't anyone in the Davenport clan with red hair," she said raising her eyebrow.

"Do you suspect Dolly is the mother?" asked Honora. "Perhaps Maggie is going to rear it as her own. He wouldn't be the first child in Gorbydale to call his mother 'sister'."

"And to think she was trying to pin it on our Arden — the madam. I must write to him and tell him. Red hair, though. I can think of a few people round the town. Do you remember that American fella that arrived in style at the mill with all the red flowing locks?" said Jessie, laughing as she threw on her shawl to leave for the hospital.

"Yes," said Honora thoughtfully. "Yes, I do."

She began silently calculating the months from when she first suspected Dolly of carrying a child only to be met with vehement denials from the girl. If her timings were right, then it did indeed coincide with the arrival of a certain Clement Duplege. At the time she had been too full of her own concerns to bother much about Dolly's affairs. No doubt the minor scandal would all be forgotten with time, though it had had a momentous effect on Arden Davenport and all his family. Dolly certainly had a talent for causing trouble.

Honora read her own letter and was pleased to find that her aunt was working with the Relief Committee with Jacob and helped by her Uncle Eli. Then came the reason for the money. She read the letter aloud to Robert.

"This is the money for our fare home. Your mother wants you home as soon as possible. Your father isn't well and she needs me to nurse him and you to take the business from his shoulders."

Robert nodded.

"What else does she say?"

"Duplege paid them for their last cargo in Confederate dollars — which are virtually worthless — but she's sent enough for second class fares. She wonders if Jessie might travel steerage."

"Over my dead body," said Robert angrily.

Honora glanced up at him.

"Are you serious about Jessie?" she asked quietly. "I can't help noticing how you feel about her. But she's my dear friend and if for one moment you're thinking of dallying with her feelings…"

"I would never do that," said Robert fiercely. "I admire her too much." Then his face fell. "But, anyway, what would she want with a pathetic wretch like me? I'm a useless cripple with a deformed leg. My family could well be penniless by the time I arrive home. Exactly what do I have to offer her?"

Honora chuckled and glanced towards the door.

"Love, affection, your unwavering devotion, a true heart — something like that might just suffice. I don't think our Jessie is the kind of girl who's after your money. Anyway, you can ask her yourself — she's standing right behind you!"

Robert twisted round to see Jessie standing in the doorway with a thoughtful smile.

"I'd better get back to the hospital myself," said Honora, reaching for her shawl. She gave Robert a wry smile. "I think my cousin has something to tell you, Jessie. I'll see you both later."

Jessie came into the room, her face pink with wonder at his words. He reached out a hand and sat her down beside him. He was suddenly shy, playing with her fingers.

"I don't know if you heard all that…"

"I heard the bit about you being a pathetic wretch," she teased him.

"Well, that's true," he said humbly. "But I've loved you for ages, Jessie — though I haven't always recognised it. I know my behaviour has been inexcusable at times. And I know that's why you didn't always trust me. But I do love you and I do want to marry you, Jessie. I've been thinking about it — sometimes I can't think of anything else. I don't know if I have the right to ask. I'd understand if you turned me down… what with my leg and…"

He stared at his feet. She touched his cheek and their eyes met.

"Your leg doesn't bother me — I've seen it often enough. I just want to know that your heart is true."

"Oh, it's that all right," he said eagerly, clutching her hands. "You will marry me, won't you?"

She nodded.

"Yes, Robert, I will."

In a moment they were in each other's arms and their lips met in a tender kiss. It had been a long time since their first kiss, rushed and passionate, at Gorbydale Wakes Fair. The kiss at the hospital had been fevered and confused. To Jessie, this kiss was by far the sweetest and held so much promise. All her uncertainties and longings melted away in the passion of their embrace. Sweet release flooded through her as she finally tore herself away from his arms to witness the love in his eyes.

Though, Robert was still as impetuous.

"Good, we can get a licence and marry as soon as..." he started eagerly.

She put a gentle finger to his lips.

"I will marry you, Robert — but not without my father's blessing — and not without your parents' consent."

"But..." he protested.

"I'm not going to be married in some underhand way. I want my father to take me down the aisle as he would want — and as my mother would have wanted."

"But..." he began again eagerly.

"Robert, I've told you how I feel. I hope you'll respect my wishes."

"Gladly," he said. "Oh, Jessie, I'd do anything for you."

"We'll talk some more when I get back from the hospital," she told him, dropping a kiss on his cheek. "I'll have to hurry as it is."

She hurried away as the joy and hope of her newly declared love gave her feet the lightness of wings. They had waited so long for this moment, what did a few more months matter. In the euphoria of their newly proclaimed love, the thought of Matthias and his consent slipped far from their minds.

Chapter 50: A Loss

Kezia was slumped at the table. Her pitiable cries wrenched the hearts of her friends. The soldier who had called with the awful news shuffled on his dusty boots.

"He fought bravely, Mrs Amiens — but they was overwhelmed. So many of my comrades — so many…"

He looked so young in his dusty makeshift uniform, his cap clutched respectfully to his chest as he fought to stem back his tears.

Jessie knelt by Kezia, trying to comfort her. But there was no comfort to be had at the terrible news that Abraham had been killed in battle. Honora wanted to ease the boy's distress.

"Would you like a drink? Or something to eat?"

He stared at her in surprise.

"I'd sure like a drink, Miss — if an' that's all right. Water would be nice."

"I've tea or coffee," she said kindly.

"C… coffee would be nice — if an' that's all right."

Kezia roused herself a little as the boy sat uneasily on a chair and sipped his drink.

"Was you there?" she asked.

"I was runnin' with a message for reinforcements when they fell on us," he said, his young face a mass of misery. "I saw it all happen but I had to run for help. There was so many of them and … and…" The boy looked sick as he remembered, "They was so savage. Our boys were fighting like tigers, Mrs Amiens — like ferocious tigers they were. They was so brave — but we was outnumbered."

Kezia nodded through her tears.

"You're a brave boy yourself, son. I remember you from the chapel. God protect you in this world. When it's all over, you remember to tell your sons and daughters how bravely our boys fought — like tigers."

"I surely will, Mrs Amiens. I's so sorry you lost your man."

Kezia began weeping again, her head falling into her arms on the table.

"I'll look after you, Kezia," promised Robert, touching her heaving shoulder. "I promised Abraham I would."

Over the next few days, there were many Negroes who came shyly to the door of the little house to offer their condolences to Kezia. They were all welcomed in. The Reverend called too, and tried to persuade her to come back to teaching the children.

"Abraham would have wanted you to look to the future," he told her gently.

Kezia was too miserable to even consider it.

It was Honora who gave them both a way forward. She had been quiet for some time, perfecting a plan for her future.

"Why don't you go to England in my place?" she suggested, unexpectedly.

She could not bear to leave America if there was the slightest chance she might train to be a doctor. Her letter to the medical school had not yet received an answer. With the girls' wages from the hospital, there was no question of any of them travelling steerage as Melissa had suggested.

Kezia looked surprised at the suggestion, then thoughtful for a moment.

"Don't you want to go home, Miss Honora?" she asked in amazement. "Ain't you sick of all this war and killin' and misery?"

"I can be of more use here," Honora told her. "But I know you're sick and weary of all those things. Why don't you go to England in my place and find some peace? Robert and Jessie will take care of you. And my aunt will welcome you most warmly, especially as she knows you saved her only son."

Kezia stared at her in surprise and her tears filled her eyes.

"I don't rightly know, Miss Honora. I just feel so tired and weary when I think about my poor Abraham fightin' so hard for our freedom. Can't seem to do anything but cry. They say we no longer slaves, but we treated just as bad as ever. I just fill up with despair when I think about all those poor boys being killed in cold blood. White boys was taken prisoner but not our boys. Why, I just can't seem to stop cryin'."

"You've been through so much, Kezia. You've just lost your dear husband," said Honora gently. "You should give yourself time to grieve."

Kezia bowed her head and covered her face with her hands, her body wracked with sobs. Then slowly, her sobbing subsided. She took a deep breath and gazed up at Honora.

"I'll go, Miss Honora," she decided with a deep sigh. "What is there to keep me here now? I've an old aunt back at the plantation but I can't go back there 'til this war is over. Maybe I'll never see her again. I'll go."

For the first time in days, there was a glimmer of hope in her eyes.

Honora told Jessie and Robert of her plans that evening. Jessie had been at the hospital and Robert was sleeping when Honora had made her suggestion to Kezia.

"I've decided I won't be going back to England just yet," she said quietly. "Kezia has agreed to go in my place. I want to stay and train to be a doctor here in America."

"A doctor!" said Robert in astonishment. "You want to train to be a doctor? Is it possible?"

"It is in America," she told him.

"Honora's always wanted to be a doctor like her father," said Jessie loyally. "She's near enough doing a doctor's work now. She'll make a fine doctor."

"I'm sure she will. Though, I don't know what Mother will say," Robert said. "She's expecting you to take care of my father."

"She'll probably say I'm a very ungrateful young woman," said Honora with a wry smile. "But it's something I've always dreamed of, Robert, ever since I helped my father. This is my one great chance. I must take it or forever regret it."

"Yes," agreed her cousin, smiling at Jessie. "We must take our chances when we know we are right, despite what others may think."

Now that Honora was free to stay and Robert was needed at home, they began to make plans to leave. Susannah came to make her farewells. She'd been very helpful in providing them with second hand clothes for the journey. Although her husband's old suit had been drastically altered to fit Robert, it still hung loosely on him. Her black dress for Kezia had had its furbelows subtly removed.

"I'll surely miss you, Jessie," she said hugging her friend tightly. "Now be sure and stay with my sister Ella when you reach New York. I've written to her and she says you're most welcome. And when you write, remind that handsome brother of yours to call if ever he's in Washington."

Jessie promised she would.

Honora gave Jessie a tentative hug and then abandoned her usual decorum for a heartfelt farewell embrace.

"I shall miss you so much. I could never have done any of this without you. What will I do when you've gone?" she said tearfully.

Jessie clutched her friend's hands.

"You'll become a fine doctor, that's what you'll do. And the minute you can come back to England to practice, you'll come and show them what fools they were to prevent women from becoming doctors."

"Here's hoping," said Honora smiling through her tears.

Kezia's friends carried their baggage to the station and cheered as the train pulled away. Honora waved until she could see nothing but a wisp of smoke. She stood gazing along the tracks, feeling very empty and alone.

Chapter 51: A Grand Reception

So, some days later when Honora collected a letter from the post office, she had no one to share her excitement when she received her reply from the Geneva Medical School. Her dearest wish was about to come true. There were another few hours before her shift at the hospital started. She wondered if she should go and tell Susannah her news and thank her for her help. She was tired though, having worked extra hours to bolster her savings. Reluctantly, she returned to an empty house. It was so quiet without her cousin and her friends. She read the letter again, devouring every word as if it might vanish from the page, so engrossed that she hardly heard the knock on the door.

"Miss Darwen, what a pleasant surprise," said Arden Davenport, smiling and removing his cap.

He was carrying a large parcel.

"Is Jessie at home?"

"Oh, you mustn't have received her letter," said Honora in dismay. "They left Washington a week ago. They are on the sea as we speak, sailing for Liverpool."

Arden looked disappointed.

"That's a pity. We're sailing down south and stopped for supplies. The naval officers in port have been invited to a reception at the White House," he said. "Jessie would have loved it. She was so excited when she saw Mr Lincoln. I've even taken the liberty of buying her a dress — with Mrs Daly's help. I knew Jessie would have qualms at the extravagance." He paused and looked at her thoughtfully. "But why are you here on your own? Why haven't you travelled with them?"

"I've had a wonderful opportunity presented to me, Mr Davenport," said Honora happily. "I wish to stay in America a while longer."

"I don't suppose… Would you do me the honour of accompanying me to the reception? It would be a pleasure for me to escort a lady like yourself. And it would be a pity for you to miss an experience of visiting the White House."

Honora hesitated.

"Please?" he begged.

She smiled.

"Why not! An evening of frivolity is just what I need at the moment. I truly miss Jessie. She's always so optimistic. And I have something incredible to celebrate. Come and look."

Leading him into the house, she seated him at the table and showed him her letter. Bubbling with excitement she explained her plans. He was quiet for a moment.

"Are you sure this is what you want to do?" he asked seriously. "Is it really the calling of a gentlewoman?"

She had not expected someone with Arden's background to query her choice of career. After all, his sister was a working woman as his mother had been. Honora was too euphoric to bother with decorum.

"I could limit my practice to Washington ladies and senators' wives with the vapours," she said with a mischievous smile.

Arden studied her thoughtfully.

"But, of course, you won't, Miss Darwen," he said, smiling slowly.

She shook her head.

"I wasn't put on this earth to advise ladies to loosen their stays, Lieutenant Davenport."

"No, of course not. You have more substance than that. I know how hard you and Jessie worked at the hospital. You are already very skilled. I truly wish you every success, Miss Darwen. And will we go to the White House to celebrate?"

"We will!"

Arden was amazed when Honora opened the door that evening in the lilac silk dress he'd bought for his sister.

"Miss Darwen, you look lovely," he said as he offered her his arm.

The bodice was a little big, but she'd disguised it by tightening the sash. The satin slippers had paper stuffed in the toes to make them fit.

"You look very fine yourself," she said shyly.

The sight of Arden, tall and manly in a dress uniform, affected her more than she'd thought.

"The trousers are a little short," he whispered with a grin. "I borrowed the dress uniform from a smaller man. I may have to bend my knees to disguise it."

He had hired a cab and Honora blushed as their knees touched in its confines. She wondered if her aunt would approve of such intimacy. There was a long line of cabs going into the president's residence but soon they joined the throng waiting to be introduced to the President and Mrs Lincoln.

"I hadn't expected so many people to be here," said Honora.

"He certainly likes to pack them in," Arden answered with a grin.

It seemed an age before Honora had time to bob a curtsy and Arden bow briefly before they were swiftly moved on.

"The President is not a very handsome man," decided Honora, disappointed at being hurried through. At least she would have liked a few words with him. "But he is a very striking one."

"Certainly, the anxiety of the war has given him more wrinkles since Jessie and I saw him last," admitted Arden smiling.

They filtered under the newly constructed Rotunda and through into the magnificent state rooms.

"There are my shipmates."

They waved and, once they had pressed their way through the crush, Honora was introduced to them all. She was the only woman among the group and Arden's fellow naval officers made a great fuss of her.

"And how is our acting Commander?" someone asked Arden with a grin.

He smiled modestly.

"I only took the captain's command when he was wounded," he explained to Honora. "But he has hinted…"

"Your mother would have been so proud of you," she told him, and he bathed in her obvious admiration.

As more people arrived, the room became stifling. Honora stared as she saw seemingly respectable ladies snip tassels off cushions with discreet scissors.

"I can't believe they're stealing souvenirs," she gasped.

"Perhaps you'd like me to appropriate a cushion as a souvenir of your visit, Miss Darwen," suggested one of Arden's friends. "I'm sure the Lieutenant will smuggle it out for you under his jacket."

Arden laughed.

"There's barely enough room in this jacket for me," he said.

There was a rush for the buffet and Arden and Honora became separated from his friends. Arden kept a protective arm a fraction from her shoulders.

"I should not be disappointed to go home," she told him. "It was wonderful to meet the President and your friends too. It has been a great pleasure to see the impressive rooms, but this crush is becoming unbearable."

They struggled out of the room against the tide of guests searching for food and were surprised to see yet more people arriving fashionably late. Out in the cool evening they could breathe easier.

"I'll hire a cab," decided Arden.

"We could walk," suggested Honora. "It's a lovely evening."

He held out his arm and she took it gratefully, wondering at her folly of walking in satin slippers.

"So, what did you think of the mansion?"

"Magnificent, but I should love to see it empty and wander through at my leisure," she told him. "I'm truly grateful you invited me and I was very pleased to meet your comrades."

"That was my pleasure," said Arden smiling. "They certainly made a fuss of you. I'm only disappointed that it was so crowded."

"Aunt Melissa will be truly impressed when I write."

"What does she think of your plans?" he asked.

Honora hesitated. She had not yet written to tell her aunt. It might be some time before Melissa discovered what Honora was going to do.

"She doesn't know yet. Of course, Robert and Jessie know why I stayed behind in America. She'll find out when I'm not with them. I will write and explain but the mail takes so long. But I am of age. She will be angry with me at first, I think, probably call me ungrateful. I should in conscience be going home to help care for my uncle but, to be honest, he takes no notice of my advice. But this opportunity is too good for me to miss. It's something I've always dreamed of since I was a little girl. I feel it is my destiny. Someday I'll go home and explain."

"And how will you manage in New York?"

"I really don't know," she admitted. "The work will be hard and I must do some nursing to pay for the training. But there will be other women studying too, and I hope to make friends."

"I hope you know you have a friend in me, Miss Darwen," said Arden deliberately.

She turned and smiled up at him.

"Yes, Lieutenant, I know."

They walked down Pennsylvania Avenue arm in arm as people passed by and wondered at the handsome couple in formal dress strolling among the crowds.

"Shall I hire a cab, Miss Darwen," asked Arden, as she paused to examine her shoes.

Honora smiled up at him. "It's such a lovely night and we did leave the reception early," she said, reluctant to end the evening with a rushed cab drive back to the little house.

She was enjoying the bustle of the city on the arm of a handsome man, despite her toes pinching.

"I plan to join a shipping line as a marine engineer when this war is over, Miss Darwen. I'll be in New York each time the ship crosses the Atlantic. I should be safe enough to call home nowadays. My father has written to say that Dolly Tate's mother Maggie has supposedly had a baby. I suspect it's really Dolly's child. She was obviously looking for a father for the child when she came looking for me. It has red hair so the Tates can't possibly blame me for that anymore. None of our family have such hair."

"Yes, Jessie heard from your father too."

"There are a few boys around in Gorbydale with red hair but to be honest, I couldn't think of a candidate," said Arden. "Except… Do you remember that red-haired dandy that came driving into town to see your uncle?"

"Clement Duplege," said Honora. "It is odd that Jessie mentioned him too. Although, of course, we could be totally wrong. It would be interesting to find out, though."

"It wasn't me, anyway, I can assure you," said Arden with a chuckle. "Though, she tried hard enough."

Honora recalled the incident with the Tates. Dolly had much to answer for, but at least Maggie was bring up the child and it wasn't in the depths of the Gorby river.

They strolled along thoughtfully amid the rushing cabs hurrying to and from the White House reception.

"Miss Darwen, perhaps I might call and see you when I'm in port?" asked Arden tentatively.

"I would like that," she said sincerely.

She felt guilty she'd suspected him of abandoning Dolly Tate, though he wouldn't have been the first man to have run at the news of a pregnancy.

They finally reached the little house and paused by the gate. Arden took her hand. She did not take hers away.

"I must leave with my ship in the morning, Miss Darwen. Do you know the story of Walter Raleigh and Queen Elizabeth?"

"You mean when he threw his cloak over a puddle for her?" she asked.

He shook his head.

"No — a different one. The Queen presented Raleigh with a diamond. In a bold move, he took it and scribed on a window pane. He wrote 'Fain I would climb, yet fear I to fall'. He had seen so many of her favourites perish, you see. Yet, he still wished to gain her favour. She took the jewel from him and wrote underneath, 'If thy heart fails thee, climb not at all'." Honora gazed up into his serious face. "What would you write underneath to me, Miss Darwen?" he asked.

She thought for a long moment. He had proved himself her friend. Although she hardly knew him, she liked and trusted him but she had a burning ambition to fulfil.

"I should write that I cherish your friendship, Lieutenant," said Honora shyly. "But I have so much to do. It would not be fair to ask anyone to wait until I had finished my studies."

"And what if that person was willing to wait?" asked Arden. "I do understand, though. Who knows what our future holds? I might not even survive this war."

"Oh, I'm sure you will," she said anxiously. "You must. Will you write to me in New York?"

He smiled at her.

"Yes, Miss Darwen — and I will await your replies with anticipation."

Arden kissed her gloved hand as he left. She glanced at the very spot and wondered what the future would hold for them both before she drifted to sleep.

Chapter 52: The Journey Home

Jessie clutched Robert's hand as the ship slowly moored against the Liverpool Quay.

"It will be all right," he whispered. "I promise."

"I hope so," she said, her confidence shrinking as the skyline loomed towards them.

Beside them, Kezia looked out across the city.

"Such fine buildings," she said. "I will be so glad to have my feet on dry land."

The crossing had been rough at times and Kezia had been very seasick. But in calmer days, she worked hard to improve her English, and Jessie and Robert helped her with her reading and writing. Some of the other passengers, though, were indignant that a black woman was travelling freely with them. Some just assumed that Kezia was their servant and treated her accordingly.

"Please do not take any notice of them," she murmured whenever Jessie was about to leap to her defence. "Ignore them or it will only make things worse."

"If you're sure?" said Jessie, simmering to correct to the offenders. "I expect you're right."

Jessie inwardly seethed and sometimes was angry enough to shoot a barbed word at the offenders.

Even in New York, Susannah's sister had been unsettled by the arrival of a black woman in her home. She had given Kezia a bed upstairs with her little servant.

Robert's bad leg had been knocked in one violent swell and he'd had to rest it in his cabin. He also had nightmares about his shipwreck. The girls had heard him crying out in his sleep from the cabin next door. But there was calm and sunny cruising too, and warm nights when a myriad stars lit their way and the wake of the ship glittered in the moonlight. Robert began to look healthier and had put on some weight. The gaunt and haunted look that sometimes suffused his face was gradually fading. It was a journey of discovery for Jessie and Robert. They tenderly held hands, Jessie restraining Robert's more passionate and impulsive nature while holding herself in check. It was hard for her not to abandon all her principles when faced with such passion and longing. Yet, she remembered her mother and her warnings, and longed for the day when their passion would be fulfilled. They spoke of their hopes and dreams for the future, though, to Jessie, they sometimes seemed destined to remain as insubstantial as dreams. She was glad to be going home, where reality would show them what their future really held.

Jessie stared over the endless shimmering sea and remembered all she had seen. She had witnessed so much hardship, such useless destruction of fine young men and so many lives ruined and changed. Yet, she had also seen kindness and bravery, nobility and skill as her colleagues, the doctors and nurses struggled to piece those lives together again. And in the middle of all the struggle and confusion, she had found love.

Jessie knew now how love felt, how her feelings for Robert overwhelmed her. Deep down though, she was glad she had held firm and hadn't abandoned herself to her passion for Robert. What if she had done so and then Robert rejected her when their lives slipped back into the roles allotted to them by society? Jessie knew her heart would shatter. As they neared land, she watched the Liverpool skyline approach with trepidation.

Chapter 53: Home At Last

Though Robert had improved immensely since his days in the hospital, Melissa was shocked when she saw her son, tentatively negotiating the gangplank.

"Overdale! Over here!" shouted the enthusiastic Gus Kearsley beside her.

Robert glanced up and stumbled, clutching a rope to steady himself. An anxious Jessie beside him took his arm to help him. The look of love and gratitude he gave her did not escape Melissa's notice.

She knew by now that Honora was not coming home. For days she had tried to pacify Matthias as he raved about the girl's ingratitude. How she would reconcile her husband to this new development, she did not know. Melissa liked Jessie, had relied on her to help set up and run her sewing school, but to have her as a wife for her son was a very different matter. Matthias had spoken of a brilliant marriage for Robert to bring more money and status into the family. In his eyes, Jessie was just another mill girl, and penniless with it.

Melissa sighed. She must face that problem if and when it arose. For now, she was just relieved and happy to see her son alive, though he looked thinner and older since she had last seen him. With them was the black girl she supposed must be Kezia Amiens.

"Mother," said Robert, handing Jessie his crutch and enveloping Melissa in a heartfelt hug.

"Oh, my boy," murmured Melissa into his shoulder. "My dear, dear boy. Thank God you are home." She could not help but wet his coat with grateful tears. "You look so thin — your poor leg — oh, my dear."

He hugged her again.

"You have no idea how glad I am to be home. And here's Jessie and Kezia too," he said, warm with pride and enthusiasm as he brought the two girls forward.

"Jessie, welcome home. Mrs Amiens, welcome to our country. And thank you for looking after and saving my son. Your father will be so happy to see you," she told Jessie. "I'm to send a telegram directly and they will all be waiting to meet you at Overdale House. But first, Mrs Kearsley has kindly offered to give us lunch."

Gus shook Robert's hand vigorously.

"Glad to see you, old man," he said.

Jessie and Kezia were taken to the shipbuilder's mansion in Melissa's little gig while the others rode ahead in the Kearsleys' carriage. When the girls arrived, they were directed towards the kitchens to eat. Robert was about to protest but Jessie subtly shook her head as Kezia looked on anxiously. Melissa noticed all this and wondered what would happen when they arrived home.

"I say, striking looking girl that," said Gus enthusiastically. "Her face looks familiar, though. Wasn't she the one who…?"

Melissa noticed Robert's warning glance to his friend and was immediately alert. Now she became suspicious that something had been going on before her son and Jessie had ever been to America.

Over lunch at the Kearsleys, she relaxed slightly as Robert and Gus chatted and laughed like old times. But Melissa could not help noticing that Robert's glance frequently wandered in the direction of the kitchen where Jessie and Kezia were eating.

The conversation strayed towards the war. Melissa was anxious to hear news from the conflict first-hand so she could relate it back to Matthias. Peace was so important to their business. Mrs Kearsley immediately tried to change the subject, obviously uneasy about her husband's involvement in supplying armaments. She was even more agitated when Robert began to praise Honora, Jessie and Kezia lavishly. He was even bold enough to mention that Kezia was a half-sister to Clement Duplege. Gus coughed in embarrassment and Mrs Kearsley looked affronted.

"I think we should be going soon," said Melissa, rising from her chair. "Your father will be getting anxious. Thank you so much for your hospitality, Mrs Kearsley."

With that they all rose, to their host's relief.

The girls were summoned from the kitchen and the Gorbydale party all climbed aboard Melissa's gig. She could not help but notice the delicate intimacy between Robert and Jessie, though they tried to conceal it. Matthias would not be pleased.

"Your father has been very ill," Melissa told Robert, though gazing intently at Jessie. "Any shock or vexation might induce another stroke. Perhaps you'll allow him a little joy in your homecoming before you make any announcements about your future."

She spoke very deliberately, her comments obviously aimed at Jessie. She hadn't mentioned or even acknowledged the girl's attachment to Robert, but they were left in no doubt that she'd noticed and disapproved. Robert hesitated and gave Jessie a pleading glance. She looked into his eyes and gave a barely discernible nod.

"Very well, Mother," he said slowly. "I'll do as you ask."

The journey was awkward with restrained emotion. Robert chatted quietly to Kezia, pointing out landmarks on a journey he had made many times on visits to his friend Gus. Jessie was quiet for the rest of the journey, though Robert frequently smiled her way. Melissa just clutched at her son's hand and prayed fervently that all would be well. It was a relief when the journey ended.

If Melissa had been dismayed by her son's altered appearance, it was nothing to Robert's shock when he saw his father standing on the steps of Overdale House. The once vigorous Matthias looked old, his steps shaky as he leant on his stick to approach the carriage. With a rare display of emotion, he grasped his son.

"Welcome home, son. I'm so glad you're back with us."

The smiling group of Davenports hovered politely on the steps and waited for Matthias to greet his son. Uncle Eli was there too, to greet his nephew. Then the family rushed forward and claimed Jessie as their own. Her father hugged her; Eddie clung to her hand.

"How big you've grown!" she exclaimed ruffling his unruly hair.

Jack and Elsie came forward and kissed her, her sister-in-law obviously plump with pregnancy. A little girl with fair curls clung tightly to her father.

"This must be our Eleanor?" said Jessie, tickling the tot under her chin. "Aren't you pretty?"

Eleanor clung to her father, until her big Uncle Eddie teased her away.

"Say hello to your Auntie Jessie," he coaxed. "She's come all the way from America to see you."

Jessie was rewarded with a shy smile.

"Oh, Father, here's Mrs Amiens too," said Jessie, holding her hand out to her friend.

Kezia came forward shyly and was welcomed by the family.

"You're most welcome, Mrs Amiens," said Jacob grasping her hand warmly.

"Please call me Kezia," she said, "I'm so pleased to meet you. Jessie has told me so much about you all."

At that moment, Dolly Tate came out of the house with a careless curtsey.

"Tea's up. 'Lo Jessie. Glad to see you're home."

Melissa ushered them all into the dining room, Matthias leaning on Robert's arm, unwilling to release him.

Back at Overdale House, once they were alone, Melissa spoke seriously to Robert.

"I've noticed your feelings for Jessie Davenport," she murmured. "I'm not blind."

"We're going to be married," said Robert excitedly.
His mother sighed.

"We'll see. At any rate, please give your Father time to get used to idea. He's been beside himself about Honora's decision to stay in America. Please give him time? I don't want him to have another stroke or we'll be sunk."

"Very well," said her son reluctantly. "I'm sure Jessie won't mind waiting a little longer."

Chapter 54 Full Circle

In the following days, Jessie gazed out of the window of her old home over the familiar hills. It was almost as if she had never been away. After all the excitement of her journey home and all the euphoria of her love for Robert, she had come full circle. Robert hadn't contacted her for days and she was feeling uneasy, without a plan in the world. Despite all Jessie's travels and experiences, it felt so good to be home, but she wished she knew what her future held. Would Robert decide the social gulf between them was too great now they were back in Gorbydale? All her old doubts about his reliability came rushing back. Yet they had been so close, so tender since his declaration of love.

  She wondered what would have happened if she'd married Robert at once in Washington as he had suggested. Yet, Jessie had insisted on waiting until she had her father's blessing. She knew Jacob would have been so disappointed if she had married behind his back. There was no doubt Matthias would have been furious with his son for marrying a mill girl. If that had caused a further stroke as Melissa hinted, there would be so many more problems. For now, the Davenports must remain unaware of Jessie's secret engagement. She would mention it to her father only when Robert gave her the word. It was too much of a risk if Eddie spoke of it and Matthias found out by default. But Robert's word seemed an unbearable time in coming.

  Jessie had also expected Melissa to send a message with Mary for her to return to the sewing class once more. No such message arrived. She was certain that Melissa knew and disapproved of her involvement with Robert, and so would not have her at Overdale House. She could not know that Robert had been confined to Matthias's study while his father explained the extent of their financial problems. He'd learnt of Taylor Walmsley's share in the business and regretted that Surefoot must be sold.

Needing some action to take her mind off her predicament, Jessie offered to help her father at the Relief Committee, but he insisted she rested after her travels. There was certainly plenty to do in the house. It was tidy enough but not to her late mother Nellie's standards. So, Reverend Septimus Carew provided a welcome interruption from her cleaning when he walked home with Jacob that afternoon. He shook her hand warmly.

"Jessie, I'm so pleased you're home. I hope you'll come back to the Sunday school. Miss Andrews has complained about too many commitments alongside her school work."

Jessie readily agreed. After all her busy hours working in the hospital, she felt unused.

"There was another favour I wished to ask," said Septimus. "Do you think Mrs Amiens would be willing to speak to the chapel folk? It would be a great privilege if an ex-slave like herself could tell us something of her life. I've seen her with Mrs Overdale in town and she seems a nice, friendly young woman."

"I'll ask her if you like," said Jessie eagerly.

"I hope she will. I had the privilege to hear Frederick Douglas, the escaped slave, speak at the Free Trade Hall in Manchester many years ago. What a great orator and such a gift to us abolitionists. And only last year I saw 'The Mirror of Slavery' with Mr Smith and Henry Box Brown. Most entertaining. Mr Brown re-enacted his daring escape. He was posted to Philadelphia in a box on a train, you know. That's how he got his name."

"In a box you say?" said Jacob laughing. "Well, that's a novelty!"

"I'm not sure that Mrs Amiens could be so eloquent, but she could simply tell the chapel folk about her harsh life as a slave," said Jessie. "She's told me a little of it and I could have cried for her. I'll go and ask her."

Now she had an excuse to go to Overdale House. She'd been meaning to visit her friends in the sewing class but didn't know how welcome she would be. Hopefully she would see Robert too.

Chapter 55: A Familiar Face

The little house in Washington felt lonely without Jessie and Kezia around. Now Honora began to realise how much Jessie had done for her with cooking and cleaning and she had to shift more for herself. Then Susannah called with the wife of a wounded officer and asked Honora if she could offer her a room to sleep in while her husband was in the hospital. Honora readily agreed, only too pleased to have company, though the woman was quiet and spent most of the day at the hospital tending her husband. There were lots of war weary soldiers around the town, many trying to forget their experiences through drink. A lone woman, even in a nurse's uniform was not always safe. Jessie had had a way of diffusing awkward situations with humour and confidence. She'd joked that she was used to dealing with saucy mill hands. It was a skill which Honora had not mastered and she was often fearful on her journeys home. She was relieved that soon she would be leaving for New York to work and study. Kezia had been right. Deep down, Honora did want to escape from all this war and misery. The boom of guns was heard over the capital and she no longer felt safe on her own as the tide of war ebbed and flowed around them.

Clutching a welcome letter from Arden, Honora was leaving the post office when a man bumped into her. Like herself, he had received a letter but was engrossed in reading it.

"My pardon, Ma'am," said the man raising his hat.

She was surprised to recognise a vastly changed Clement Duplege. Now he was wearing a beard and spectacles. His once russet hair was oddly coloured black. He stared at her for a moment then, taking her arm, led her into the nearby street.

"Miss Overdale, I have just arrived back from Baton Rouge and I'm afraid I have had no good news for you."

She didn't bother to remind him that her name was Darwen and it took Honora a moment to realise that he didn't know that Robert had been found. By some instinct, she stopped herself from telling him. He would still consider Kezia a slave of the family plantation and she might not yet have left the country.

"I don't think we should be seen together," said Honora stiffly.

"Miss Overdale, you could be of considerable help to me," he said smoothly. "I am, of course, actively seeking your brother."

"Cousin," Honora corrected him.

"Pardon my mistake. In the meantime, you might be of help to me. I need an opportunity to dine at Willards. Having a young lady accompanying me would be most helpful. My usual dining companion is — shall we say — otherwise detained."

Honora wondered if that companion had been the notorious spy Belle Boyd who had recently been arrested, to the annoyance of many southern sympathisers.

Willards was the best hotel in town. Many senators and generals dined there. She was unsure what to say. Then an idea occurred to her.

"Very well," she said simply.

He took her address and left with a jaunty raise of his hat.

"Until tonight, dear Miss Overdale."

He was insufferable. He had swindled her uncle out of many dollars, he had deserted Robert at sea and here he was up to his spying tricks — tricks that might mean danger to Arden and his comrades. He thought she was indebted to him because he was the only link with her cousin. Well, he was quite wrong and Honora made her plans.

That evening, she dressed carefully in the lavender gown she had worn to the White House, and wrapped her dark cloak around her. Duplege arrived on time in a cab, he was gracious and it was easy to see how people were taken in by his charms. Honora had seen the grand carriages drawn up outside Willards. The cream of Washington society dined there, with many senators and governors visiting the city. Now in this time of war, generals and other officers of high rank thronged through its doors. She was curious to see inside and now, as they disembarked from the cab, Clement led her into its grand lobby. Grey drifts of smoke curled up to the elaborate ceiling from a myriad candles and fragrant cigars. They were led to a small discreet table near a group of prosperous looking gentlemen. The waiter took Honora's cloak, and Duplege stared at her.

"Miss Darwen, you do look lovely, but I hardly expected you to draw attention to yourself in such a manner," he murmured stiffly.

Honora smiled sweetly.

"But I couldn't possibly appear shabby in Willards."

Duplege looked distinctly uneasy as the striking Honora drew attention to their table. It was inevitable that the curious would surely take notice of her companion too. While she had his attention, Honora needed to discover something from him, something that would put her mind at ease.

"I have had some very interesting news from Gorbydale," she began, once they had ordered their food.

"Really," said Duplege politely, though paying her little attention.

She noticed he was trying surreptitiously to eavesdrop on the conversations of a group of men at an adjoining table. Their neighbours were becoming louder as the alcohol flowed and their conversations more indiscrete.

"I wonder, Mr Duplege, if you remember a maid at my aunt's house," Honora tried again.

Something in her tone made Duplege take notice.

"Yeah, sure. A little woman. Lots of ribbons." Then he gave a wolfish grin. "Very obliging as I remember."

"She gave birth to a son a little while ago," continued Honora, holding his gaze. "His hair is red they say and we can't for the life of us think who the father might be."

"A son — she had a son?" Duplege stared at her. "Surely you aren't suggesting that I have anything to do with this child? Has she claimed I was to blame?"

"I didn't say who was to blame," said Honora pleasantly. "In fact, her mother has claimed that the child is hers — although that would be a miracle of nature as she is somewhat too old."

"I mean, I hardly touched the girl," he blustered, then stared in thought. "A son with red hair, you say. Well, I'll be damned!" He seemed amused by this, then felt uneasy under Honora's gaze. "A son — though, of course, I don't know what that has to do with me."

"Apparently not," said Honora with a wry smile.

"Has she asked for money?" he tried.

"No — as I say, her mother has claimed the baby as her own."

Clement looked relieved at this but stroked his chin, a wistful look on his face.

"Well, I'll be damned," he murmured to himself.

Honora had her answer. Dolly was 'most obliging' according to Clement Duplege. Arden was not to blame.

Now she had dropped that piece of news into the conversation to her own satisfaction, Honora was becoming uneasy. She glanced around and nervously toyed with her food. They had almost reached the second course when several large men entered the dining room and approached their table. She recognised the detective, Alan Pinkerton, immediately. It was such a relief that he had received her hastily sent note. He appeared to deliberately ignore her.

"Mr Clement Amiens Duplege?" he asked sternly, standing beside Clement's chair.

Everyone in the room stopped to watch.

Clement struggled to his feet and one of the men grabbed his arm. He shook Clement's sleeve and a small pistol clattered onto the plate. Clement was prevented from grabbing it as his arms were rapidly pinioned to his side.

"I would be obliged if you should accompany us, sir," said Pinkerton, neatly slipping the pistol into his pocket.

As Clement was led away, he gave Honora a searching glance. She contrived to look confused. Now her hastily thought out scheme had come to fruition, her legs began to shake and she was about to sink into her chair when Pinkerton slipped her cloak around her shoulders and led her out.

"I would advise you to leave Washington as soon as possible, Miss Darwen," he murmured in the lobby. "Duplege has friends who may not take this lightly."

Once outside, he found her a cab and paid the fare. Then he slipped an envelope into her hand.

"Your reward," he muttered.

"But…" began Honora.

"It is quite legal," said the detective with a brief smile. "You have done the country a great service."

As the cab led her away, Honora's fingers trembled as she opened the envelope. There was enough money inside to fund her studies and, with her savings, it would give her time to establish herself in New York before she began them. She did not take pleasure in her betrayal, but knew deep down it was so necessary. She hoped Arden and his comrades would be safer with Duplege behind bars.

Next day, Honora called on Susannah when she knew her husband had left for the War Office. She told her friend she must leave Washington as soon as possible. Her old friend had learnt of the arrest through George at the War Office.

"Oh, Honora, I'm so pleased for you. My husband knows now that he misjudged you. What can I do to help you?"

Honora sat on the train, amazed at the speed with which everything had been accomplished. In her bag, she had testimonies from Dr Jacob and Susannah, and the names of their colleagues in New York who might find her work and shelter. Her letter from Arden was in her pocket. She drew it again from its envelope and read of his devotion and hopes for the future. Holding it to her heart, she gave a fervent prayer that he would come back safely from the war to share it with her. Life held so much promise for her and she was relieved to be leaving the turmoil of Washington behind. As the train pulled away, the boom of guns echoed once more over the city.

Chapter 56: A Visit to the Chapel

Jessie dressed carefully to visit Overdale House. The French windows leading to the sewing class were open and, avoiding the front door, she slipped in. Her old friends were pleased to see her. Abandoning their work they crowded round her. Melissa glanced up from inspecting a girl's embroidery and looked anxious at the unexpected visit. Kezia hurried forward, her face alight with a smile.

"Oh, Jessie, it's so good to see you," she said, hugging her. "I wanted to come and see you, but I was afraid I would get lost in the town. Robert has been very busy. He is away with Mr Overdale on business today."

So Robert wasn't at home after all her anxious hopes. A chill of disappointment touched Jessie's heart.

"It's you I've come to see, Kezia," she said smiling bravely. "I met the Reverend Septimus Carew the other day and he has asked if you'd address the people at the chapel. They'd be so interested to hear your story."

Kezia hesitated.

"Me?" she asked, looking surprised. "To speak in a chapel?"

"Oh, please say you will," said Jessie. "He heard Frederick Douglas speak as a young man and he was very impressed."

Kezia's eyes widened in apprehension.

"Mr Douglas is a great man. Mr Lincoln thinks highly of him. I don't know if…"

At that moment, Melissa came up.

"Perhaps you would ask Dolly to make some tea, Kezia dear?" she said.

Kezia gave a nod and disappeared. She seemed to have taken Honora's place as an unpaid help in the family.

"Do come and have some tea, Jessica," said Melissa kindly. "I would love to hear your news of America. Robert tells me so little. I'm sure you ladies will manage without me."

"Certainly, Mrs Overdale," said Mary as she gave Jessie a sly, knowing wink.

They both knew that the girls worked just as well whether Melissa was present or not.

Jessie followed Robert's mother into the drawing room.

"What would I say to your chapel folks?" asked Kezia humbly, as they sat down to tea.

"Just tell them your story," suggested Jessie. "I've seen you entertain a class of children. Just pretend our chapel folks are big children!" Kezia smiled at this idea. "Perhaps you'd come and talk to Mr Carew tomorrow. He's very keen to meet you."

"Very well," said Kezia, looking doubtful. "If you're sure?"

"I'll call for you. You must come to supper and I'll invite him too," said Jessie eagerly.

Perhaps Robert might be home when she called.

Next day, though, Jessie was destined for disappointment once again. Robert was nowhere to be seen. She could not know that Melissa had sent him on an errand to Eli, making sure he was out of the house when Jessie called. She took Kezia to her home with a heavy heart, and wondered if perhaps the brief kiss that she and Robert shared before they embarked from the ship had been their very last.

Jacob and Eddie warmly welcomed Kezia to Weavers Row and made her feel at home.

"I'm so happy to see your home," she told Jessie. "I don't know how you could have borne to leave it."

She seemed very sad and Jessie wondered if she missed the plantation and her friends. The meeting was productive, though. Septimus was so enthusiastic that Kezia agreed to address the chapel on Sunday and they wrote down some notes for what she might say.

Once again, Jessie glanced around her as she approached Overdale House, hoping for Robert to appear. Kezia guessed her anxiety.

"Robert has been away a lot with his father on business," she said. "I overheard Mrs Overdale mention something about a mortgage, but she didn't say anything to me about it."

"Oh," said Jessie sadly. "I just wondered."

Kezia squeezed her arm.

"You mustn't worry. It will be all right," she said. "I know they mustn't worry Mr Matthias because of his illness, but Mr Robert's heart is true. I know it."

"I hope so, Kezia," said Jessie. "I truly hope so."

Though, as she walked home with a heavy and disappointed heart, Jessie wondered if the differences in their status had once again become too overwhelming. Robert had once mentioned that his father expected him to marry into money and if the Overdales had trouble with the mortgage on the mill, that would be even more important. He might have sent her a note. Surely he must have known that Kezia was going to supper at Weavers Row.

Her heart sank lower and her feet dragged with the weight of her disappointment as she rose up the hill. Jessie glanced around the town of her birth, shabby and neglected. She had witnessed so many things in her travels, yet she had come full circle. Now, though, she had no work and her promise of love lay broken and as empty as the gloomy derelict buildings.

Days later, to her surprise, a familiar figure drove Kezia to the chapel in Melissa's gig on a bright Sunday morning. Robert grinned at her and Jessie's heart rose once more.

"So, the Overdales' carriage is sold," said Jacob thoughtfully. "Things are getting worse at the mill."

Jessie heard his words with dismay as, once again, a small niggle of doubt spoilt her happiness. Matthias Overdale would be more opposed to their liaison than ever if he needed Robert to make a good match. To remind her of her modest place in society, she had noticed Taylor Walmsley standing apart as everyone welcomed Kezia and their unexpected guest. Acutely aware of his eyes on her, she turned away from his stony gaze. Everyone was surprised to see Robert, as they knew the Overdales patronised the parish church in town. The chapel was full and even Dolly Tate had made the effort to attend. As Mr Carew escorted them into the little chapel, Jessie saw Robert glance longingly over at her, a faint smile on his lips. Her spirits rose with this little crumb of recognition. Surely it would be impossible for him to show his feelings openly in front of so many witnesses. The congregation settled down on the plain pine benches. As Kezia began to speak slowly and nervously before the attentive audience, Robert's eyes wandered until they found a home in Jessie's. Perhaps there was hope for their love after all, though, deep down, Jessie was still afraid to hope too much.

Kezia spoke simply to the parishioners. She told them of her life on the plantation, how she worked all hours for no pay. She spoke of the slaves toiling in the hot blistering sun all day, beaten if they slackened under the heat. There were gasps of sympathy when she spoke of how families would be split up and sold, husbands parted from wives, children torn from their mothers, brothers and sisters separated, never to see each other again. There were tears in many eyes when she spoke of the cruel and inhuman punishments of those who tried to escape. She told them of Abraham's cruel beating at the hands of the bounty hunters. If mothers held their children closer, and if husbands thoughtfully handed handkerchiefs to their wives, it was only to be expected. They all agreed that she had spoken well and touchingly, and she was surprised at the amount they collected for her school in Washington, despite their own privations.

"It's lovely to see you again, Miss Davenport," said Robert, grasping Jessie's hand as he left.

"You too, Mr Overdale," said Jessie very formally.

Their eyes met hungrily as they parted. She watched the gig until all that was left was its trail on the dusty road.

She turned to find Taylor Walmsley standing behind her.

"I wonder if I might walk a little way home with you, Miss Davenport?" he asked with a frown.

"Aye, a nice walk in the fresh air will do you good," said Jacob amiably.

Jessie remembered her mother's hopes for a match with Taylor, and no doubt Nellie had shared them with Jacob. Unaware of Jessie's feelings for Robert, her father had annoyingly taken this opportunity to further her mother's wishes to encourage Taylor now that Jessie was back home.

"Come on, Eddie, let's get home and put the spuds on," he said, smiling at his daughter. "There's no need for you to rush, love. Taylor's been asking me how you got on in America." Jessie wished to hurry home too and escape, but Taylor walked slowly and deliberately until the rest of the chapelgoers had disappeared along the lane. They spoke of the weather; of how well Kezia had spoken; of anything that was neutral and impersonal.

"I, er … noticed, Miss Davenport, that your feelings towards the Overdale whelp have not changed?" said Taylor eventually.

"That's none of your business," said Jessie, furiously blushing.

"Oh, but I think it might be."

He stopped in the lane and faced her.

"Do you think, Jessie, that I've waited all this time to be told you've still not rid yourself of your absurd notions? Do you honestly think Matthias Overdale will let you marry his only son? The lad's dallying with you and still you cannot see it."

Jessie felt anxious. He was only saying what she'd felt herself in a jumble of uneasy emotions. Yet, she was sure she'd recognised the love in Robert's eyes only moments before. Now all her anxieties came flooding back.

"I'm warning you, Jessie. I hold a substantial part of the Invincible business now. If you persist in these foolish notions and refuse me, I'll make sure the Overdales don't prosper."

An overwhelming anger took hold of Jessie. Furious, she faced him.

"You mean to tell me that you'd ruin Matthias Overdale — a man who has given you every opportunity, who has encouraged you in your career, who has done nothing but help you…? You'd ruin him — because of me? Just so you can get your own way? You see, that's why I won't marry you, Taylor Walmsley. I'll not be blackmailed and intimidated into love by a vindictive man like you. It's a strange version of love you seem to feel. Say I did marry you and then I didn't do as I was told, you'd no doubt turn on me an' all. Call that love — well, I don't. No, Taylor Walmsley, I wouldn't have you. I'd rather stay single."

Leaving him stunned with rejection, she marched away, head held high.

Chapter 57: A Confession

Seeing Jessie so pretty in her best clothes at the chapel had put new heart into Robert. He could not settle. With his promise to his mother niggling his conscience, he still longed to see Jessie again. He'd noticed Taylor Walmsley hanging around as they'd left the chapel, and remembered that Honora had mentioned a proposal from the overseer. His father had explained to him that Taylor now had a share in the Invincible. The man was doing well for himself. Robert hoped Jessie would keep faith with him. He was anxious to do something towards their reconciliation.

"Perhaps we could go and sell my horse tomorrow," he told Matthias. "I know Surefoot has to go. Perhaps we could approach the stables where we bought him. He'll surely fetch a good price."

"Now, I'm glad to see you're taking your responsibilities seriously," said Matthias, patting his son's arm. "I know Surefoot means a lot to you, lad."

"Yes, Father. I mean to help where I can. Uncle Eli has suggested I help him with his project to build the municipal gardens now he has some money from the Central Relief Committee. I'm to help with requisitioning the materials and the wages, and suchlike. I can't do much physically just yet, but I can use my head."

"But what about the mill, son? Surely the mill is your business. Why, Taylor Walmsley mentioned investigating the possibilities of cotton in India."

"The mill isn't running yet, Father. When we're back in business, then…"

But his father had other plans for Robert's future brewing in his thoughts.

"Maybe you might think of taking a wife — settling down. Those girls we met at your friend Augustus Kearsley's house are fine girls. Their father is likely to stump up some brass as a dowry."

Robert bit his lip.

"Anyway, I don't think those girls would look twice at me now — what with my leg."

"Not look twice...! Why your leg's getting better all the time. And you're not so bad to look at. Even that Davenport girl has a smile for you. Don't think I haven't noticed her giving you sly looks."

So, even his father had noticed the signs of their love, although Robert had tried hard to disguise them. Robert suddenly felt the time was right for his confession. He took a deep breath.

"That's because she loves me, Father. Jessie loves me." He looked his father straight in the eye. "And I love her too."

"But she's a ..." stuttered Matthias, dumbfounded.

"I loved her even before we went to America — but she wouldn't look at me twice then. She thought I was an idler, a time-waster — and she was right. But I'm going to prove myself worthy of her."

Matthias looked at his son's earnest face in surprise.

"Prove yourself worthy of a mill girl!"

Matthias sat down abruptly, his face growing red. He took a deep breath. Robert noticed his father's distress but could not hold back now he had begun his confession. His love was out in the open now and he longed to be with Jessie.

"She's a grand girl — brave and beautiful. I wouldn't have survived to come back to you and Mother without her love and care," he said vehemently.

"But have you thought about…?" started Matthias, as if to dissuade his son.

"I've thought about nothing else but marrying Jessie," said Robert flatly.

Matthias stared at his son.

"I know it's not what you want — that you might disinherit me. But I can provide for us both. I'm not stupid. I can become a schoolmaster. Jessie's clever too, and we could even start a school together."

"There's no need for that, son," said Matthias quietly. "Your Mother would never see you starve. Neither would your Uncle Eli for that matter."

"Thank you so much, Father," said Robert in profound relief.

His confession had not been as fraught as he thought. His father's illness seemed to have mellowed the old man.

"I have to say, I'm a mite surprised, but I can see you've made up your mind," admitted Matthias. "Well, I reckon she's not so bad. She looks healthy enough, anyways. I expect she'd have no trouble providing you with children. And I'll… Well, I'll welcome your lass into the family for your sake."

Robert awkwardly hugged his father.

"Thank you. Thank you, Father, so much," he said.

They had rarely been so close.

"Have you told your mother?" asked Matthias.

"Mother knows," admitted Robert, "but she said I was to wait until I told you. She didn't want to upset you."

"It seems everybody knows but me," said Matthias shaking his head in disbelief. "I'm not made of china, our Robert. I've survived this far and I mean to survive to see my grandchildren. Mind you have a few, like. It's a worrying life when you've just got the one." He paused for a moment. "But don't tell your mother I said that. She's a mite touchy on that subject."

"I won't, Father," promised Robert.

He shook his father's hand and held it fast.

"You'll not regret it, Father. Jessie's a grand girl. You'll soon love her as I do."

"Aye, happen I will, happen I will. But we've not the brass for a fancy wedding, you understand — not nowadays."

"Jessie won't expect one," said Robert. "All the same, she wouldn't get married quietly in America like I asked her to. She wants her father to give her away right and proper."

"That's just as it should be," said Matthias. "Jacob Davenport wouldn't expect anything else. She sounds a sensible lass. You'd best go and fetch her and introduce us properly."

"I'll have to go and ask her father's permission first," said Robert. "He might not be keen to see his daughter married to a cripple with uncertain prospects."

Matthias looked outraged at the thought of the heir to the Invincible to be despised as a bridegroom but stayed silent.

"Perhaps you could ask Kezia to bring me a tot of brandy," he said eventually. "And ask your mother to come and have a word. I want to find out what else she's been planning behind my back."

Robert had a word with Kezia about the brandy and whispered that his father now knew about his romance.

"I am so delighted for you, Master Robert," she said. "Jessie will be so relieved. I have prayed for you both to be happy."

Then he went to inform Melissa. She rushed to see her husband, with Robert trailing behind her.

"Are you all right, Matthias?" she asked. "You look a bit flushed."

"I'll be right enough in a minute," said her husband, sipping his brandy. "This news is a bit of a shock all the same. Happen it'll turn out all right, though. The Davenport girl seems sensible enough. And our lad here seems pretty much taken with her."

"I'm so glad you're reconciled to the match," said Melissa, hugging him. "And I know Jessie's a good girl. She'll look after Robert — and you."

"Aye, happen you're right," admitted Matthias.

"Matthias, love, I don't care who our Robert marries. I'm just so pleased to have him back home alive and well. And Jessie is no flibbertigibbet who'll want to spend lots of money on fripperies."

"Aye. I expect you'll be off to see your lass with the news?" said Matthias. "Don't wear that horse out before we sell him."

"I won't, Father. Yes, I'm going to see Jessie right away," said Robert laughing with joy.

A euphoric Robert saddled Surefoot and rode him out for one last time. He headed for the old Roman Fort and stopped a small scruffy boy on the way.

"Do you know Miss Jessie Davenport from Weavers Row?" he asked.

"Her as went to Amerikay?" asked the boy with a grin.

"That's right. Here's a penny. Will you tell her Robert is at the Fort — can you remember that?"

"Aye, Robert the toff is at the Fort," said the urchin with a cheeky grin.

Deftly catching the coin he scurried off towards Weavers Row.

Robert waited anxiously at the ruin until he saw a dear familiar figure hurrying up towards him. She looked anxious until she saw his smiling face as he hurled himself towards her. They clung to each other as if they would never be parted.

"We can marry," he gasped. "Jessie my father says we can be married. Oh, Jessie, I can't believe it."

Their kiss held so much passion, so much promise, the release of all their yearning. They could not bear to let each other go. Eventually, Jessie took a deep breath.

"We'd better go and see Father," she said, smoothing her hair as she smiled at her beloved. "He's in for a bit of a shock!"

Chapter 58: The Wedding

If Matthias was expecting a quiet wedding, he was to be disappointed. The plans took on a life of their own. Mary was to be bridesmaid and Kezia maid of honour. Little Eleanor was very young but she must have a pretty dress and hold Mary's hand.

"I'm glad to be doing you this service before I go home," said Kezia warmly.

"You're leaving Gorbydale?" asked Jessie in surprise.

Kezia nodded.

"I'm nothing but a housemaid here, same as in the plantation. Ain't paid either!" she added with a grin. "I should be back with my own folks, helping to prepare them for the future — reading and writing. Here, I'm a black woman in a white town. People look at me strange. Some folks want to feel my hair as if I'm an animal or something."

"Whoever did that?" asked Jessie angrily.

"It don't matter," said her friend, unwilling to say.

"You must tell me," insisted Jessie. "I'll bet it was that Dolly Tate. I'll have words with that madam. Why, I'll…" said Jessie, incensed by the insult to her friend.

"Please don't say anything," said Kezia. "I don't expect any better from her. But you must know I don't fit in here, Jessie. I want to go home — back to the school at first. Maybe one day, I'll go back to Louisiana — when this old war is over."

They had been eagerly following the news from America, anxious about Arden. They'd all been worried when the south had had a brief revival. Robert E. Lee had even driven to the outskirts of Washington, but they knew that Honora was safely away in New York by that time. The Confederate Army was now in retreat. Vicksburg, the high bluff on the Mississippi river, the last stronghold had at last fallen into Union hands after years under siege. The Davenports had taken a great interest in that campaign as they knew Arden's ironclad was involved. The end of the war was sure to follow.

Jacob read out his son's letter with great relief.

"I'd best write and tell him about this wedding of yours," he said, smiling fondly at his daughter.

"I hope you're not upset with me, Father," said Jessie. "I've been away so long and now I'm leaving you again."

"Bless you, child, it's only natural. I know Robert will look after you."

The marriage was to be at the Anglican church in town, like Jack and Elsie's. It was the law, but Septimus was to bless the couple afterwards at the chapel and there was to be a feast at the Sunday school, organised by Alice and Mary.

"Don't you think we should have the wedding breakfast at Overdale House?" urged Melissa.

She'd arrived at the Davenports for tea to discuss matters.

"Only if you want the Gorbydale hordes trampling on your precious things," said Jacob with a grin. "It seems like all the Sunday school are coming, and the lasses from the sewing class."

"But what will the Kearsleys think?" insisted Melissa.

"Only Gus will be coming," her son reassured her. "After life aboard ship, the Sunday school will be a palace."

Jessie went out on to Weavers Row to wave to Robert and his mother as they left in their gig. He told her that his horse had been sold but that the money had gone to pay debts at the mill.

"I promise you, things will get better after this war is over," he said anxiously. "I don't want you to think you'll be marrying a bankrupt or anything."

"I can work to keep us," she'd said lightly but was sorry when she saw a shadow of pain cross his face.

He had been such an arrogant young man, and through his trials, the war had changed him for the better. But she hated to see the defeated look that sometimes haunted his eyes. She wondered as she watched them leave. How would she fit into life at Overdale House? How would she cope with Dolly Tate?

Then she spotted the unsuspecting Dolly at the bottom of the Row. Quickly, Jessie slipped down the cobbles and stepped smartly in front of her.

"Hello, Jessie," said Dolly with a smirk. "Ready to become Lady of Overdale House?"

To her surprise, Jessie grabbed a piece of her hair and pulled it. Dolly squealed.

"What did you do that for?" she asked in outraged surprise.

"I just wanted you to know what it felt like," said Jessie fiercely. "And if you touch my friend Kezia's hair again I'll leave you bald. Do you understand?"

Dolly preened herself and patted her hair into place.

"I only wanted to know what it felt like. I've never met a blacky before and…"

Jessie felt like slapping the ignorant girl.

"Mrs Amiens may have dark skin but she's a better woman than you'll ever be."

"You can't say that," protested Dolly.

"Oh, can't I? Don't think anybody round here believes little Albert is your brother."

"Of course he is." Dolly's eyes widened with alarm. "Nobody dare say he isn't."

"No, because people are afraid that your father and brother would batter them," said Jessie. "But it's funny that they came demanding to see our Arden that one time. And I know of a certain American gentleman with red hair…"

She was only guessing but Dolly's face was frozen in alarm. It confirmed Jessie's suspicions. Then she had another odd thought.

"It's none of my business who little Albert's father is but if you want to know, Mrs Amiens might actually be his aunt. You see, Clement Duplege's father is the same as hers. His father took advantage of her mother because she was a slave. That might give you something to think about."

Dolly bit her lip. She stayed silent for a moment then took a deep breath.

"Albert is my brother," she said firmly. "Ask my mother."

Jessie let her go, satisfied that she had given the silly girl something to think about. She hoped she would have no trouble at Overdale House from a truculent Dolly Tate. At least the unspoken confession in Dolly's face had given her some ammunition if Dolly decided to be awkward with her.

The day of the wedding was warm and a few threatening clouds drifted away.

Jessie stepped carefully onto the stairs of her home, anxious not to tread on her wedding dress. At the foot of them stood her father, his eyes bright with emotion.

"Well, lass, you're a proper picture."

Mary echoed his sentiments.

"You do look lovely, Jessie. Doesn't she, Kezia?"

Her friend nodded.

"Surely does. Just beautiful."

Laughing and merry, Jessie's friends went before her as she stepped into Weavers Row on her father's arm. A gaggle of neighbours gathered to see the bride and wish her well, and her family assembled to accompany her to the church.

"I'm only sorry your mother didn't live to see this day," said Jacob. "She'd have been right proud of you."

Jessie squeezed his arm as she remembered Nellie and all her mother's hopes and fears for her. She hoped her mother would have been happy for her, though Nellie's own plans had not come to fruition. She was nervous as she clung tightly to her father's arm. This longed for moment had, at times, seemed like a mirage, fading before her. Now it had arrived, she wondered if she was prepared for whatever the future held for her.

All of Jessie's anxieties disappeared the second she saw Robert waiting at the church. It was with a firm conviction that she said those sacred and affirming words, "I do."

A crowd of laughing seamstresses, dressed in their finest, threw petals as the young couple emerged from the church. Rice was too precious.

Robert smiled at his new bride.

"Happy?" he asked.

Jessie nodded, too full of happiness to speak.

He helped his new wife into his Uncle Eli's gig, gaily decorated with ribbons and a hoop of flowers to arch over the happy couple. The whole procession headed for the chapel.

As the bride and groom drove past the work progressing on the municipal gardens, Robert pointed out the work he was helping with. Jessie smiled and squeezed his hand. She felt she knew every wall, path and flowerbed, and had been proudly told about them a dozen times.

"We'll be starting a new drainage system for the houses by the river when we come home from honeymoon," he told her proudly. "You wouldn't believe the state of the privies…"

"Not on our wedding day, Robert!" Jessie said laughing.

But she was pleased he had found something useful to do to help the town. Eli had told her how enthusiastic his nephew had been, and how helpful with the work.

Elsie, because of her advanced state of pregnancy, had been given a place in Melissa's gig with little Eleanor. Jessie's brothers, John and Eddie, walked behind, leading the rest of the guests.

The Master and his wife with his son and his new bride were grandly welcomed to the chapel. Reverend Carew and his wife made sure that they were treated with all the deference due to them. If the urchins who followed the gig had to be content with coppers instead of silver, the marriage of the heir to the Invincible to one of Gorbydale's daughters was something to be proud of and to celebrate. Everyone was determined to do it with gusto.

The war might be still continuing in America, the future of cotton far from certain, but in a shabby Lancashire town that afternoon, there was a glimmer of hope for the future.

Once the blessing had been solemnly made, the party burst out of the chapel to the Sunday school rooms. But the rooms weren't large and most of the party spilled out into the sunshine. Melissa and Eli had provided some provisions for the feast, and cakes and fancies had appeared from many corners. Jessie, too, had been busy, helped by Mary and Alice. If dancing was forbidden in the confines of the buildings, it wasn't prohibited outside. The fiddler that mysteriously arrived after the ceremony, soon had the mill girls dancing in the road in front of the chapel.

For a moment, the gentry hesitated and watched the happy display. Then Robert began clapping to the music and held out his arms to Jessie.

"Shall we, Mrs Overdale?" he asked laughing. "We must dance on our wedding day."

He was awkward, and he and Jessie had never danced together. Yet, they made a valiant effort to the delight of the crowd. Then Matthias and Melissa joined them and made a sedate turn around the makeshift dance floor. John, unable to dance with his heavily pregnant wife, did a lively dance with Kezia. Jacob's offer to dance with Miss Andrews, the Carews' niece, was politely declined. Her face seemed to have become more disapproving since Taylor Walmsley's disappearance to India to find a new source for cotton.

As her brother before her, Jessie boarded Eli's gig with her new spouse and headed for Eli's cottage in the country to begin her new life. The crowd cheered and she gave her husband a shy smile. He squeezed her hand and they rode into a future uncertain except for the strength of their love.

Weeks later, Jessie and Kezia had a tearful parting. Her friend's baggage had grown considerably with all the donations to the school that she would be taking home with her. She had made herself a favourite at the sewing class and the chapel.

"I'll miss you so much," said Jessie.

"I will miss you too, Jessie. You must take care of yourself."

"Oh, I'm only teaching girls to sew and read in the luxury of a billiard room," said Jessie smiling. "You'll be going home to a country at war."

"It's where I'm needed," said Kezia. "Home is where your heart feels right and easy, Jessie."

"Thank you for everything — and give Honora our love when you see her in New York," said Robert.

He slipped his arm round his wife's waist as they watched Kezia board the ship. The band began to play as the ship slipped out into the Mersey and their friend's waving form faded as it sailed into the distance.

"She certainly is a remarkable woman — remarkable," said Robert, echoing the words he had said what seemed a lifetime before.

Jessie brushed a tear from her eye. She had once dreamed of escaping the mundane confines of her life, sailing over an ocean away from her cares. Now she treasured Kezia's words. 'Home is where your heart feels right and easy' felt so true. Squeezing her husband's hand, she knew just where her own heart lay.

A NOTE TO THE READER

Dear Reader,

Thank you for reading *Song of the Shuttle* and I hope you enjoyed it. The story began life as a serial in a magazine a few years ago and friends said it could make a good novel, so I set to work to expand the story of Jessie and her family and friends and to give a glimpse into the challenging times some of our ancestors lived through. The Lancashire Cotton Famine, brought about by the American Civil War, is a little known part of our history, but the famine saw so many people out of work and starving and was the trigger for thousands of Lancashire people leaving our shores and emigrating all over the world. Some even went to fight in the Civil War for both sides. The story has fascinated me since I was a little girl and noticed a statue of Abraham Lincoln in one of our Manchester parks. My Dad explained to me that the American people had sent it to the mill workers of Lancashire in thanks for writing to support that great president in his fight against slavery. That statue now stands in Lincoln Square in the centre of Manchester, so now more people know its history.

This is my first full length novel, though I've written many short stories for magazines, and I'd really appreciate some feedback. You can find me on **Facebook/ChristineEvansStoryteller**. If you've enjoyed it maybe you might have a moment to post a review on **Amazon** or **Goodreads**. It would be really helpful to have your thoughts.

Naturally once I'd finished writing the book, I wondered what might become of Jessie and the other characters.

Somehow they seemed to take on a life of their own and one book has expanded into a trilogy. The second book in the series is called *Twist of the Thread* and has a surprising heroine. At the moment I'm working on the third book.

Christine Evans

Sapere Books is an exciting new publisher of brilliant fiction and popular history.

To find out more about our latest releases and our monthly bargain books visit our website:
saperebooks.com

Printed in Great Britain
by Amazon

41825355R00213